Advance praise for *Brand New Memory*

"Bravo for Elías Miguel Muñoz's *Brand New Memory*. This original and wonderfully written tale is laced with vivid symbolism and plenty of Cuban/Caribbean humor."
–Nicholasa Mohr, winner of the
Hispanic Heritage Award for Literature

"An engaging and many-layered story about the burdens of exile and the redemptive power of imagination. Elías Miguel Muñoz's best and most ambitious novel to date."
–Gustavo Pérez Firmat, author of *Next Year in Cuba*

"Elías Miguel Muñoz is one of the most exciting American writers to spring out of the U.S. Latino/a experience . . . *Brand New Memory* brings it all together: the American dreams, the Cuban exile diaspora, and the mall pop-culture mentality. And it does so with such heartaching force, you can't help but be swept into his world. This novel will be remembered for a long time to come."
–Helena María Viramontes, author of
Under the Feet of Jesus and *The Moths and Other Stories*

~~~~

Praise for Elías Miguel Muñoz's previous novel, *The Greatest Performance*

"The snapshot-like reminiscences of the alternating narrators are sometimes comic, frequently poignant, and almost always strongly sensuous."
<div align="right">–*Library Journal*</div>

"A sensitive, lyrical novel about how it feels to be an exile, even in one's own country."
<div align="right">–*Publishers Weekly*</div>

By Elías Miguel Muñoz

Novels

Los viajes de Orlando Cachumbambé
Crazy Love
The Greatest Performance
Brand New Memory

Plays

L.A. Scene

Poetry

En estas tierras/In This Land
No fue posible el sol

Brand New Memory

Elías Miguel Muñoz

Arte Público Press
Houston, Texas
1998

This volume is made possible through grants from the National Endowment for the Arts (a federal agency), Andrew W. Mellon Foundation, the Lila Wallace-Reader's Digest Fund and the City of Houston through The Cultural Arts Council of Houston, Harris County.

Recovering the past, creating the future

Arte Público Press
University of Houston
Houston, Texas 77204-2090

Cover design by Giovanni Mora

Muñoz, Elías Miguel.
    Brand New Memory / by Elías Miguel Muñoz.
    p.   cm.
    ISBN 1-55885-227-1 (trade pbk. : alk. paper)

    1. Cuban Americans—California, Southern—Fiction. I. Title.
PS3563.U494B7   1998
813'.54—dc21   98-12855
                                                                CIP

8 9 0 1 2 3 4 5 6 7   10 9 8 7 6 5 4 3 2 1

To my brother Jorge,
because I owed him this one.
And to the memory of our grandparents,
Josefina and Tomás,
who still visit.

Acknowledgments

Gracias to the friends who helped me keep this story alive during the past seven years: Monica Enriquez, Miguel Gallegos, Lillian Manzor, Luis Pérez, Rob Frost, Nick Bach, Mercedes Limón, Antonio Prieto, John Miller, Teresa Marrero, Carlos Medina, Tarik Benbrahim, Frederic Courteau, Polly Hodge, Vicki Chen, Paco and Gabi Feito, Teresa Rozo, Erika Gary, Ruth Behar, Larry Goldstein, Lázaro Lima, and Carlos Carrazana.

Gracias to my sister Virginia, without whose memories this book wouldn't have been written. To Mary Nelle Rogers and Lydia Vélez, who were brutally yet lovingly critical of the first draft. To Karen Christian, faithful companion, first—reader and editor of everything I write. And to. Virgil Suárez, whose insightful comments brought me closer to the ideal text.

I am indebted to Linda Allen, my agent, for her encouragement and support. To Robert Redford, for the Sundance experience. And to my Sundance soulmates, who heard and reacted to an early version of this story in 1989: Mariano Barroso, Enrique Berumen, Piedad Palacios, Fernando Palacios, José Rivera, Ela Troyano, Helena Viramontes, Tizuka Yamasaki.

And I am deeply grateful to Gabriel García Márquez. Because one summer day in Provo, Utah, Gabo's magic turned Bernarda Alba into Celia Cruz.

Contents

PART ONE

PART TWO

"Whatever isn't image isn't memory."
Alan West-Durán, *Finding Voices in the Rain*

"But the memory, like the mind,
has the capacity to dream . . ."
Alice Walker, *The Temple of My Familiar*

- PART ONE -

Chapter 1

-I-

The truth that looms over their home is that Gina's parents went through hell in Cuba. But what does that mean? The girl is supposed to accept their alleged suffering and yet she hasn't seen any of it, not really. By the time she was born fourteen years ago, her father had a flower shop and would soon be buying a Pinos Verdes mansion. Life was good then and better, much better than it ever was on the island. The truth.

One must always go forward in life. That's Daddy's motto. Big empty words for a Pinos Verdes adolescent: *Salir adelante.* "It hurts to remember," claims her mother, and Gina doesn't get that, either. She has a few memories of her own but none is horribly painful. What is it like to hurt because of something you remember? How does one "go forward in life"?

Some fading photographs hold her only clues. Telling depictions of early exile, circa 1966: Benito with a head of curly black hair, slim and youthful, behind the wheel of his secondhand Rambler. Elisa in a waxy blonde wig and a polyester dress. The Domingos seated in the living room of their first apartment in suburban Los Angeles. Uneasy smiles, awkward poses, plastic-covered furniture and barren walls. The beginning.

Once upon a time, her parents had been "refugees," that much Gina has learned. And like most refugees, they endured their share of hard times and costly dreams: factory work, frugal meals, Bargain-Mart shopping. Sacrifices that were needed to achieve success, so that their daughter would never go through hell like they did. So she could live like a princess.

Among the pictures, there's the classic shot of Mother with Baby. Elisa Rochart de Domingo at the hospital, worn-out from a long labor. A Francophile mother who is descended from monarchs (or so she says), and who would ask her daughter, one day, to call her "Maman." She would coach the girl, help her acquire the proper nasality, pronounce the word gracefully, *Maman*, just like a true Parisian.

There are snapshots taken with the first Polaroid, like the family's first visit to Ramosa Beach: Daddy and Maman by the shore, building a sand castle with their plump little girl. And too many shots of Gina's different stages: her triumph with potty training, baths, birthdays, the first communion. A toddler playing by the den's picture window. Preteen Gina watching TV with Daddy, dancing in her rose-colored bedroom. The straight-A student in her school uniform. The stoked teenager hanging at the mall, totally groovy. Gina Domingo everywhere.

But her parents don't take photos anymore; they haven't in a long time. Now they own a video camera which is solely Gina's responsibility. It has also been the girl's job (her folks don't have the time) to put all the pictures into albums. Those yellowing images are helpful. As primitive as they seem to Gina, compared to video, they fill in some of the gaps.

~~~~

The Princess smiles, assesses her look in front of the mirror. Is she for real? She has a deep velvety voice, full lips, dimples. Her style is a tad retro, early Eighties perhaps, just like her room. She's wearing a black tie-dyed sundress, with a white leather belt riding low on her hips, ballet slippers (she's not into ballet, but the slippers are cool), and a pink ribbon in her messy-on-purpose auburn hair. Ms. Domingo wants to learn all about "moving forward." Ms. Domingo wants to solve mind-boggling mysteries and yet there she stands, working on her image. But why can't a person be curious and hip at the same time? Yeah, she's for real, exactly who she's supposed to be! Got a problem with that?

Bedroom. Night. Soft waves coming from the radio, New Age music that she listens to on occasion, when she's tense. If Gina were shooting this scene, the camera would zoom in on her own face: a grinning child with no worries, carefree, cared for and spoiled. The lens traces her moves as she turns off the light and fixes her pillow. She's all tucked in, ready for some shut-eye, but wide awake. The music is helping, though; mellow strings, a distant flute, chimes, sounds that always rock her to sleep.

Yeah, she's finally dozing off . . .

Her recent dreams are rife with meanings she can't comprehend. What do her dreams mean exactly? Gina longs to find the puzzle's missing pieces, the gaps in her family's history. Answers.

And her subconscious life could be traced like a map leading to some of the answers, like a blueprint of the character's self. A sort of fiction.

She knows, somehow, that a journey awaits her. The first phase of her voyage: imagining a time when Gina didn't exist. Quite a job, conjuring up a make-believe past through her oneiric mind, then giving that text the appearance of truth. But her biggest challenge is surviving. She hopes to live a full life because that's probably how long her journey will take her. Will she make it? The girl often wonders if she'll live long enough to unearth just a handful of facts. Long enough to have both good and bad memories.

Gina is only fourteen and in great shape; she was given a clean bill of health at her last physical. When she looks out her window, she doesn't see guns and urban squalor. When she goes to bed at night, no one—and especially not the police—will break into the house and kidnap her, torture her and disappear her. Gina is lucky and privileged. Daddy's princess. Why would she wonder, then, if she'll live a full life?

The girl simply believes she might die young. In her enchanted castle all her needs are met and most of her wishes fulfilled. Yet her safe haven exists in the midst of a nightmare. Crime, danger, death. Gina is very much aware (afraid, at times) of the world beyond her rosy walls, and tries to keep it out. Blink like a sitcom genie. Twitch your nose like a benevolent witch and then, suddenly, magically, there's peace, safety for all.

But it's no use. The world filters through and reaches her fantasies, pouring over her like a dark cloud. Like a knife that never quite touches you, but which stays there at a short distance, ever present, eager to cut out your heart.

Sometimes, when the Domingos leave their mansion, the road leading to town becomes a river and the girl is swept away, dragged down to its depths. Her mind is then flooded with visions of dying, with facts and descriptions and very real depictions of the way people get killed. News on TV, on the radio. Images in movies, magazines, newspapers. Words about wars and drive-by shootings and bombings, child abuse and child molestation, rape, wife beatings, domestic violence. Violence for the sake of violence. For the fun of it. Reality.

You have to escape that reality or go crazy. You need movies, pizza, malls, a pretty bedroom, a computer, cute guys, dances. You need designer clothes and CDs, cable, frozen yogurt. You need all this to forget that you could cease to exist at any minute, for the stupidest reason.

Prayers come in handy, too, but not the ones you learn in catechism class: Hail Marys, Our Fathers. No, Gina merely talks to "someone up there," sure that this invisible someone listens and helps. The Catholic rituals bore her. If Ms. Domingo had her way, she'd skip Mass altogether on Sundays and stay in bed, watching music videos. She hates the fact that Maman *expects* her to go to church. "You want people to see that you're a devout Catholic girl, don't you? *Alors,* you have to frequent God's Home."

There are hundreds of dictates in Catholicism, but Gina thinks she's grasped the religion's key premise: God is a powerful, bearded old man with a bad temper. She can't accept this image, can't trust it. Is there any chance at all that *He* might be a *She*? If He has no gender, then why does one have to call him Father, Lord, Padre, Señor, Papá Dios? Why is He always portrayed as a grumpy old dude? And there's that other biblical bit that's so hard for her to swallow: Woman was made of man's rib to satisfy the needs of Man, and then she was accused of causing his fall. Unfair! How can you help feeling inferior if you were created as an afterthought?

Gina has tried to envision her Creator. He (She, ideally) is gentle and kind, not a deity you fear. He or She isn't very powerful, but strong enough to help Gina Domingo through the rough times. Those times when the teenager falls asleep dreaming about running, when she closes her eyes (like she's doing now), hoping to hear and feel nothing. Those times when she grabs her tummy and rocks herself (like now), wishing to forget the latest news flash about the latest war, or the story of a five-year-old Santana girl who was shot during a gang fight.

He or She is mighty enough to help Gina hold on to her earliest memory: a picture window overlooking the bay, the den where the Princess used to spend her mornings when she was just a baby. She'd sit there and pretend she could touch the houses and the ocean down below, that she could play in the rain.

~~~~

Last night's dream wasn't one of her usual movie dreams. There were no clowns under the bed, no monsters in the closet. The tree didn't push its branches through the door, grabbing her and eating her up in one gulp. Gina didn't tremble, sweat, or cover her face with her hands, afraid of a doll full of needles or an evil alien. She just moved through the vision in slow motion, transfixed, watching . . .

A young woman who strolls along a winding trail, singing, *Zun zun zun* . . .The woman's hands are deep in the ground, making holes to plant a sacred root. She takes off her breezy blue dress, walks into a stream. The woman needs to heal her raw and wounded fingers.

Time is slow and dense in the stream. She will use it, seize this moment and blend into it, be time itself soothing her skin. Be water. Pour.

The dreamer looks away from the bathing woman and sees the sky bursting with birds and moistened leaves. Rain falls on her eyes, quenches her thirst, revives her. And then the rain is gone. Could I fly up—she wonders, suddenly—over the great arch of light, beyond the colors and the birds, to the beginning? Could I?

Clouds are never whiter than after the big storms, she says to herself. Like the sand at dawn, white and luminous just like *casabe*. But how does the dreaming girl know this? She knows it because she's the person bathing in the stream. Dreamer and Dreamed are now one and the same: a beautiful woman named Taina.

The stones by the riverbed are calling out to her. She carves them during the time of light. The stones are warm, thriving with spirits. Taina will work them until her fingers burn. The beginning, this is the way it must have felt. When the First Ones made the water, the fire, and the people. Carving.

If only her brothers and sisters could move, like she does, into bright space, see the river creatures escaping their fate of silence and flying. Taina sits by the shore and gives herself over to them. *Zun zun zun* . . . Bodies of animals whose names only she knows. She's not the one who creates them; they are the ones who give her strength. Sustenance. Air.

But it always happens that the stones want to sleep. So Taina listens for other voices down the shore, up in the hills, through the thickets, until she finds the guayacán forest. Loud, tall, demanding trees. She carves their solid flesh till it feels like her own skin. Then she seeks the smallest shells and presses them into the softened surface. Taina bathes wood and shells in the stream, lets them all sleep under the white light and grow together. She turns them into a powerful Guayo, her most precious tool, for the Yuca.

Taina can almost see the root crumbling over the Guayo's face, the long strands falling on her lap, becoming her food. The son of the guayacán will be one with the Yuca, daughter of the Earth. Inside her.

Her brothers and sisters believe that the spirits inhabit the other island. But they don't know what she knows. They've never freed the stone-beings. The dead are supposed to live in that other land, yet Taina has seen souls right here. And not during darkness, but in the brightest of hours. Souls that dance and sing without touching the ground. All free and all around her, extending their misty arms to her, beckoning her to join them.

Her people sing and pray only during the Areito, when time means the past, long ago. The eternal Areito. Not this moment of carving, of bathing, of eating sacred roots. Not this song and this laughter, the soft rain in her eyes, not the present.

They all look behind, living backwards. And so they can't hear the voices she hears, since those voices are born now, this instant. Because, like her, those souls know nothing of what came before.

-II-

Family conversations. In the old days, her parents' youth, one had to use a tape recorder. Sound but no image. Nothing to grab onto but empty, scratchy voices. *Boring.* Better to be a child of the Nineties (or the Eighties, which were fab). In this era you can get a much more accurate copy of reality. High resolution, digitally-mastered duplicates. And it can all be yours instantly.

Weird to see yourself on the screen. You look bigger than you are, your outfit doesn't seem as rad, the voice is much too high. You act and sound like a syndicated geek. That's what you get for putting yourself in front of the camera instead of behind it, where you belong. Suffer!

Weird to see your parents on the screen. Once in a blue moon they lounge by the picture window and chat. It's usually on weekends and in the morning, too early for Camerawoman to be up and ready. But she's managed to get some candid footage on Sundays, before Mass. Her folks sit with their coffee and stare at the hills and the Pacific shore. What do they see out there? Do they pretend they're seeing the Island? A peaceful oasis of coconut groves and sugarcane fields. Pristine beaches. Paradise.

~~~~

Daddy used to whine a lot about his business problems. "What am I going to do? I wake up in the middle of the night and can't go back to sleep, tossing and turning and looking for a way to pay off my debts, to solve my problems!" One of Daddy's key words: *problema.*

Growing old has done him good; he's mellowed out. Or maybe it's just that his finances are in better shape. Whatever. The thing is, now he laughs and doesn't get all worked up about work. He drinks his coffee slowly, savors each drop, as he looks out at the ocean. Soon he'll have a new reason to complain, though, and Gina sees this other type of problem coming: old age.

Maman seems to be doing fine health-wise; she hardly ever gets sick and when she does, she tries to hide it. But not Benito. He's such a baby when it comes to illnesses! The last time he had blood drawn, he fainted. Daddy hates doctors, hospitals, nurses. He can't bear the thought of having surgery: "Your body all cut up, at the mercy of strangers!" The family physician has told him repeatedly that he needs to have his hemorrhoids removed. The only solution, no more suffering. But he'd rather put up with the pain and the burning. "*De eso nada!*" says Daddy. What a baby!

~~~~

Her parents in front of the Pinos Verdes shop, holding hands, looking nervously at the camera, at each other, trying to strike a pose. You can tell Daddy feels proud as he points to the name of the store, his own name in lights. Yeah, his smile is for real.

The flower business was Maman's idea, supposedly. "Aren't they lovely, Benito?" she'd asked him, holding up a bouquet of red roses. "Wouldn't you like to make a living selling these beauties?"

"If I start selling flowers," he'd reacted, "our relatives in Cuba will think I'm a faggot. It's not a manly job to have!"

His reaction inflamed Elisa, who stated, for the hundredth time, that the Domingos had nothing to do with their relatives in Cuba. No one here, in the North, would think he was a homosexual. Who cared what those prejudiced and backward island people thought of him, anyway? If he could make money selling flowers, the hell with their opinion!

Maman's idea worked, obviously. Daddy used his savings to open a shop in Santana, right smack in the heart of the Mexican community. He'd done some research (his main source being the magazine *Bloom Boom*) and found out that Mexicans loved flowers. The rent in Santana was affordable, so that town would be ideal for his enterprise. He would have to spend extra money on a guard, but it was still a good deal. A sure thing.

Benito's wildest dream was to own a flower shop in Pinos Verdes. He knew that dream required big money, yet he could do magic with numbers. The glorious day when the P.V. shop finally opened, Daddy had flyers announcing the event showered over the city. He hired a pilot to draw the words DOMINGO'S FLOW-ERS in the sky, and he bought commercial time on a local radio station so his slogan would become a household item: DOMIN-GO FLOWERS CONQUER HEARTS!

The store's facade was festooned with roses on opening day, and the florist greeted each of his customers with a steaming cup of coffee. He hired a chauffeur to drive his wife and daughter to the shop. And when they got there, Benito flung open the store's door, acting gallant. He hugged them and declared, "What a great country we live in!"

~~~~

Her lens captures the florist and his wife having a heated discussion about voting. "You should vote," Daddy says to Maman. "It's your duty and your privilege as an American citizen. I wish I could." He can't because he hasn't gone through the naturalization process; it's too involved and time-consuming for a busy Cuban man. But the truth is, according to Elisa, that he's afraid he won't pass the test or the interview.

Maman admits she doesn't understand what those "two elderly gentlemen" are all about. Both candidates sound the same to her. To which Daddy says, "Just vote for the one who'll give us the biggest tax break!"

Benito Domingo is a devout admirer of the United States and its people. He loves this country passionately, and makes no secret of his feelings. Yet, if you talked to him during the months of March and April of any year, you'd have serious doubts about his star-spangled-banner patriotism. Those two months comprise a tormenting period for Benito: TAX TIME. He does nothing but swear *coño* and *carajo* at his adoptive "great country."

"The North," he philosophizes, "has its own way of making you pay for living here. A fair price for the freedom it gives you!" But fairness doesn't necessarily make him feel better about the process. Daddy complains about his burden and his dog's life. He hires two accountants, one to do the initial paperwork, and one to review the first accountant's calculations and offer a second opinion. "*Coño, chico!*" he bellows when they tell him the sum he'll have to fork over. "A Mexican family could live on that for two whole years!"

Benito's financial struggles are the price he pays for living in America. But his daughter doesn't want to pay the price of putting up with him. The Princess can't stand him during IRS time. She tries to avoid him whenever she can, hiding in her room or hanging at the mall (her two favorite places).

Gina can tell Daddy is getting scared, although he'd never admit it. His Santana store was robbed once. The masked criminals held him and his guard at gunpoint and took all the money. He reported the crime to the police, but the thieves were never found. So he started carrying a gun. This violent scenario, the gun and the risk, too, are all demands this country makes in exchange for his success and his freedom. *A fair price.* Poor Daddy.

Fortunately, the Cuban florist has found a way to assuage his business angst, and that's listening to his Optimistic Mood tapes while he soaks in the Jacuzzi. Benito loves those recordings; he can tell the music is especially orchestrated for him, for the tastes and the needs of a businessman from Cuba. Mambos and boleros mixed with ocean sounds and the mellow voice of a lady who says, among other things, *Relax, my love, relax.*

~~~~

Camerawoman doesn't have much footage of her mother; she's not all that interested in her. Gina feels guilty about this, but her guilt hasn't yet moved her to action. If you were to ask her, "Do you love your mom?", Gina would hem and haw. Then she'd try to be honest and say, "You bet. But not always. You can't love your mom *all* the time! Definitely not when Maman speaks French, when she pretends she wasn't born in Cuba, and when she forces me to act and talk and think like a Pinos Verdes lady. Like a damn *jeune fille!*"

Yet her video movie wouldn't be complete without Maman. Elisa is part of Gina's story, a full-fledged character. The Supporting Actress? So the girl has forced herself to get some shots: Madame tanning by the pool. Madame in her room, reading and writing poetry in a journal she shares with no one, not even her husband. (Gina knows about this book because she's a resourceful filmmaker, nosey and curious and sneaky.)

Maman places her private notebook in a safe, where she also keeps her passport and her citizenship diploma. She puts lotion on her skin, combs her long black hair, and looks at herself, facing the mirror . . .

~~~~

Benito deep in thought as he drives. He was just remembering his first impression of the interstate freeway. In this huge town, he recalls, you were always far from your destination. Places were miles away from where you lived, and yet, in minutes you'd get there by "taking the freeway." This action entailed more than just getting in the car and driving down a road; you flew over it! Unless there was a traffic jam; an accident or a patrol car that suddenly appeared could slow the flight and turn it into a turtle-paced procession. But if you took the interstate when it was truly *free*, it became a roller coaster. Vertigo. Perfect motion. Like flying!

Back in Cuba, he couldn't have imagined that one day he'd own two Mercedes Benz and have a phone in his car, that he'd be making business calls while stuck in traffic. Or that he'd keep himself amused by trying to decipher license plates and bumper stickers. Those words say a lot about Americans, and understanding Americans is one of his goals. Mr. Domingo reads the messages intently, with the same care as when he reads his florists' magazines. Those phrases define his new culture more clearly than any book or movie . . .

DADSGIFT . . . I LOVE HERBAL TEA . . . I'D RATHER BE FISHING . . . GOD GUNS AND GUTS MADE OUR COUNTRY AND DON'T YOU FORGET IT . . . AMERICA: LOVE IT OR LEAVE IT . . . SUPPORT THE WAR: BE REAL! . . . RAMOSEANS DO IT IN THE DEEP . . . ANGELENOS ARE A REAL RIOT . . . ABORTION IS MURDER . . . A CHILD IS A PERSON NOT A CHOICE . . . PRO-LIFE PRO-CHILD PRO-CHOICE . . . MY

CHILD IS AN HONOR STUDENT . . . MY KID BEAT THE CRAP OUT OF YOUR HONOR STUDENT . . .

The florist is proud of his own bumper-sticker statement; it is simple and clearly defines who he is. There's even something artistic about it, says his wife, a poetic touch that makes it classier, less mundane, definitely not a political message: FLOWERS ARE MY LIFE.

~~~~

Maman likes to tan by the pool. There she is, thinking that her weekends are filled with *tête-à-têtes* from now until summer, mostly activities organized by the Pinos Verdes Wives Auxiliary. She's proud to be a member of this exclusive club. Let's face it: Elisa loves to rub shoulders with the *crème-de-la-crème.* Right this minute she's telling herself she can't wait till the next Auxiliary board meeting.

Throughout the past ten years, Madame Rochart has been an active member of interest groups such as the Lunch Bunch, whose main function is discovering, sampling and cataloging new restaurants in the South Bay area; and the Gourmet Club, which publishes the *Golden Hill Cookbook* and holds a yearly recipe contest. (Elisa won First Place three years ago with her exquisite and nutritionally correct dessert invention, "Tartalisa.")

Mrs. Domingo has usually shunned the service groups (too much paperwork and not enough fun). But she's served on the Save the Green Pines Committee, which implicated her personally, since her house is surrounded by majestic pine trees in need of rescuing. And her vast knowledge of European painting came in handy when serving on the Art Appreciation Board, responsible for selecting masterpieces to be exhibited, on loan, in the Pinos Verdes gallery.

Elisa exercises her legs, bringing one up, the other down, ten, twenty times in tandem. She points at a passing cloud with her vermilion-colored toenails and thinks about the next board meeting . . .

~~~~

Daddy looks edgy. After supper, he craves a plate of dessert that he's not supposed to have. A cholesterol problem, according to the doctor, but more of a belly problem if you ask his wife. So Daddy takes sips of his artificially sweetened coffee until the terrible craving passes and he can make his usual claim again, "I have a Cuban man's willpower."

He's reading (and trying to understand) an article titled "Tulipa Scions" in *Bloom Boom*. He gets up from his favorite chair in the den, where he likes to read and nap, and throws his arms in the air, "*Oye, chica!* You shouldn't waste film on me!" He combs his thinning curly hair, straightens his clothes, walks to the couch and, once seated, changes position several times. He clears his throat, "Bah beh bee bo boo . . ."

A voice from behind the camera asks, "Is that all you have to say?"

He smiles. "No, no," he states with mock solemnity. "I have many important ideas to express."

"Like, tell us about your life, Mr. Domingo."

"But that would be boring."

"Not if you make it sound cool."

"What's 'cool' about the life of a Cuban florist?"

"Use your imagination, *chico!*"

"Okay. First I should say that I don't smoke, not even cigars, so I'm not typical in that respect. And I don't drink, either. I don't have any vices."

"What about sweets and fast food?"

"I wouldn't call that a vice."

"And what about work? Do you consider yourself a workaholic?"

"No, I don't. Working is a virtue, not a vice."

"If you say so."

"Let me tell you about work. When I first came here from Cuba I got a job in a relay factory, doing assembly-line labor. I saved my money so I could start my own business and then, after a couple of years, I opened a flower shop in Santana. Floristería de Domingo! I made a kill—that's the right expression, no? Yes, lots of money selling flowers for all kinds of occasions. I guess you could say I went forward in life. *Salí adelante!* Today I also own a fine shop here in town, and I have very classy American clients. But my best customers are Cubans. They buy the most expensive wreaths, lots of them, so I always give them a twenty-percent discount. It's good business practice and, also, you know what our compatriots have been through. *Pobre gente.* We deserve the good wind that blows our way—a good discount, opportunities—after all that we've suffered."

The filmmaker shuts off the camera and takes a break. Benito scrambles to his feet, runs his fingers through his hair, straightens his shirt. "Turn that thing back on," he demands, grinning. "I want to make one final statement."

"Later, Dad."

"No, Gina. It has to be now."

"Okay. If you insist. Roll 'em!"

He sticks his tongue out at the camera, opens his eyes wide, wrinkles his nose, and yells, "Bah beh bee bo boo, the burro knows much more than you!"

~~~~

Daddy likes to laugh. He chokes, sometimes, when he listens to his comedy albums, ancient artifacts from the days when CDs didn't exist. Gina has spied on him during some of his private sessions. He sneaks into the den carrying a large briefcase (his record collection) and locks the door. Shortly after that you'll hear the scratchy sounds of needle on vinyl, and a raucous male voice cracking jokes in Spanish. Then Benito laughing his guts out.

It feels good to hear him, good to know he's having fun. Too bad he won't share his LPs with his daughter. Once she asked him what he was listening to in there and he said, "Old stuff. You wouldn't enjoy it." And she took this response to mean what it was supposed to mean: Butt out!

The Princess has never doubted the way she feels about her father. She loves him and that's that. Daddy has never forced her, like Maman, to act or think in a certain way. He has strong opinions about some things, sure, but she doesn't feel compelled to defy him. The only ideas Benito has tried to teach her have to do with communism. And that makes sense, it figures, since it was because of communism that he left his homeland.

He says that violence in countries with Marxist regimes is much worse than here, because it's both psychological and physical. "They try to poison your mind, pollute your head, brainwash you. And when all those mental tortures don't work, they throw you in jail. And if darkness and isolation can't get the job done, they shoot you!"

Sounds horrible, but it's the truth, he claims. His daughter wonders how there could be any more violence in other countries, more than here, more than on American TV, in American barrios and ghettos. She's up on the news, she knows what's happening out there. Yeah, but what does she know about Cuba? Her Dad has the inside scoop on that subject. Or is he, too, inclined to blow things out of proportion like Maman? No, he's gotta be right, and Gina's the one without a clue. Sometimes she hates being so damn clueless.

She needs to be patient, observant. She must pay close attention to her Daddy's words, which she suspects are wise. Her father's not perfect, but as perfect as a father can be, considering he's a workaholic and married to Elisa Rochart de Domingo.

~~~~

By the pool, Madame flexes her chest muscles, inspects the taut skin of her thighs, her firm breasts. She's thinking about her aerobics class. The music is much too repetitive, and bombastic. The Wives deserve something classier to get themselves in gear. Some lively Mozart, perhaps, or some upbeat Vivaldi. Most of those poor ladies are so stubbornly entrenched in their middle-aged flab. But not Mrs. Domingo. She has a svelte and shapely figure; a tad excessive around the derriere, but such is the fate–the curse!–of many women born and raised in the Caribbean. Not that she's resigned herself to this lot, no! She will fight it, beat the excess fat from her body, banish it. There's nothing Madame can't do once she sets her mind to the task.

The aerobics instructor is a good role model; she has a flawless physique. But *mon Dieu,* her taste in music! Amateur-sounding singers–if you can call what they do "singing"–who scream the same phrase ad infinitum, always something to do with dancing and loving; having to do with sex, if truth be told. Sex on the dance floor, devoid of love and courtship and romance. Pure animal energy, crude, uncivilized. Yes, that's what the songs proclaim. Hard-driving beats, unimaginative melodies or worse, no melody at all. *C'est affreux!* Such utter lack of creativity. Such vulgar, tasteless tunes!

She will have to speak to the instructor, suggest other musical possibilities to her. And if she won't listen to reason, Madame will circulate a petition. Surely her classmates will be open to some lively Mozart or Vivaldi. You could easily exercise to their uplifting sounds, couldn't you? *Mais oui!*

~~~~

Rush hour. Mr. Domingo sits patiently, listening to an Optimism tape, hoping his chronic hemorrhoid condition won't flare up. He tries to keep his mind off his sore anus by evoking images of ocean waves, but fails. His present situation keeps coming back: the *cabrón* traffic and the chance he might start hurting badly down there. Gina claims he gets too grouchy when that happens. But what does she expect? When it hurts, it hurts like hell!

There must be an accident somewhere. Life has to be planned around your driving in this city. If you're not careful, you can get stuck forever and there won't be enough calls to make or license plates to read to fill the time you'll be cooped up in your car. The entire day has turned into one endless rush hour. And the carpool lane is a joke; what little there is of it is usually more crowded than the other lanes. Southern Californians have taken to putting lifelike dummies in the passenger seat, fooling the patrol cars and each other, just so they can hurry up and wait.

So many young drivers out there! In a couple of years his baby will have her own car. It's a spaceship-looking vehicle, a model she frequently points out on the road, although he can't recall the name. She enjoys describing it, "All in jet black, with gold-plated rims and bumpers, black leather inside, floor mats with GINA DE AMERIKA inscribed on them, a CD player and a six-speaker sound system. It's gotta have a pink peace symbol on the mirror for sure. Oh, and a license plate that will read MOVIEMAKER. Yeah!"

The car of her future? He can't bear the thought of his princess driving on those gang-infested streets. Little Gina exposed to the horrors of urban Los Angeles. How can he protect her out there, in that jungle? Or here in his Mercedes, as she sits next to him, filming, making her "family movie."

"You're wasting film again," he tells her, jokingly.

"No, I'm not, Daddy. This scene is important. It shows who we are."

"A bunch of cars, that's who we are?"

"Part of the time, sure."

"I guess that makes sense. We do spend a lot of hours on the freeway."

"Yep. And I need to get some of those hours on film."

He jokes again, "Your movie is going to be very boring, I think."

"No, it's not! Just look around you, Dad, look at the drivers. Aren't they funny and spaced-out and typical? That tanned lady over there, in the BMW, with her cell phone and her dog and her cig. She thinks she's in total control. Or that dude in the jeep, shorts, no shirt, sunbleached hair, surfboard on the roof. He thinks he's coolness all the way. And listen to the rappers."

"*Coño*, that noise is loud! How can they enjoy that crap?"

"Hey, there goes a low-riding Vato, tailing the cell-and-dog lady. He's scaring the hell out of her, you can tell. She's about to freak out. Look, she's rolling up her tinted window. I knew it! She thinks the Vato's gonna shoot her!"

"Don't joke about things like that, Gina."

"And what about the Suits? Take a look at them, Daddy, the business class. They're so full of themselves, absolutely gone from reality. Like you!"

"Don't film me!"

"A close-up." She's laughing.

"I'm not wearing a suit!"

"But you're one of the driver types, *chico*. Gotta include Señor Cubano in his Benz, no?"

He chuckles, "What a waste of film!"

How can he protect Gina out here? All Benito can do is hope and pray that no one starts shooting from the freeway bridges, that the fumes don't poison her lungs. He works hard so he can give his girl everything in the world. Except an automobile. Not yet. She'll have to be eighteen at least. She'll have to spend plenty of hours in Driver's Ed before she gets behind the wheel.

Behind the wheel he smiles. Cars are moving fast again. Speeding. Flying!

~~~~

Once in a while, when he's not too busy, Daddy picks her up after class. She's always excited to see him. It's obvious that she's crazy about him. Is he for real, her classmates wonder. Mr. Domingo likes giving Gina and her girlfriends a ride around the South Bay. He's a cool dad who digs their buzzing and can be goofy just like them. They didn't know that such a groovy dad existed.

Maman, on the other hand, is far from cool and light-years from groovy. She won't put up with "hysteria." It's one thing to have Madame Rochart driving her personal vehicle and this *jeune fille* sitting there like a proper young lady, listening to the French concerti that her mother loves. And it is another thing, altogether different, to see Señor Benito with a car full of gabby teenage girls who flirt with every stud-driver on the road, and who egg each other on with their wild screaming. Girls who sing, at the top of their lungs, a re-mixed Seventies song about a "Love Freak," about not being able to control the way one feels, and about getting a love rush whenever this big amorous creature does the driving. *Love Freak!*

-III-

All Saints High School (ASHS) is nestled in the sprawling South Bay District, not far from Gala Mall (the epitome of Eighties retro: pinks and grays, glass, chrome, and neon everywhere). Ramosa Beach is just a mile away. And in recent months, a shopping strip has appeared across from ASHS. As foreseen by the developers, this area quickly became a hot spot for young crowds. The Zone, as the cool kids call it, has super-in eats like Chilly's Frozen Yogurt and Pizzaman; a very popular store called Cyberabilia, which sells computer goods and has a video arcade; and Surf Turf, where surfing paraphernalia abounds.

The school has earned an excellent reputation for its good teachers, its strict dress code, and its religious atmosphere. Gina Domingo doesn't know that getting her admitted at ASHS was no easy task. Her father had to move Heaven and Earth, as he would say. The admissions officers required him to submit proof of his legal status and his income, and to show evidence of his religious fervor. (The latter was a challenge Benito met head-on by declaiming every prayer he knew.)

Benito didn't tell Gina about his tribulations; there was no point. So the girl assumed she was able to attend All Saints High thanks to her good grades and her high score on the entrance exam. She knew the school had a pious air of exclusivity about it, but she had no idea that it was infested with bigots. One day, in English class, they were discussing movies and a student made an insensitive remark about a new Latino film. It was the story of two Mexican siblings who had overcome horrible obstacles when crossing the border to the North. The kid's opinion: "I don't feel sorry for them 'cause they shouldn't be here in the first place. Serves them right!"

Gina stood up and showed him the biggest fist he'd ever seen. She could almost hear Daddy saying, "*Coño, chica!* You have nothing in common with wetbacks! Why are you defending them? And why are you making a political statement? They might take you for a Commie spy!" A voice came out of her, a voice Maman would find utterly distasteful, "*C'est affreux!*" Gina turned to the teacher, to the class, fuming, and said to the offender, "Listen, you twerp, we're here to stay. Got a problem with that? And we're still coming. So run for your life!" Then she exited the room summoning up all the drama she could muster. She tried to drop the class but couldn't. By the end of the term Gina was glad she hadn't: no one in English ever said anything negative about "her people" again.

~~~~

Freshmen don't dare cross the line between their class and the highest one. They know the rules even before they enroll: Seniors are zealous of their status, they can turn violent when their territory gets tainted by recent arrivals. Trespassing can result in serious damage; you could find yourself with your head stuck in a school toilet or hanging by your feet from a telephone pole.

But Gina doesn't care for stupid rules and refuses to play the game. She sits at the Senior Table during her lunch period and provokes the higher-class bullies whenever the opportunity arises: "You may be seniors but I'm smarter than all of you, cork heads!"

She has secretly named those students (most of them blonde specimens of Californiana) the Pale Pious Califos. The Califos push and shove and try to make her feel like crap, but she won't budge. Ms. Domingo won't acknowledge ridiculous class distinctions, definitely not when they have nothing to do with your IQ.

The average teenager attending ASHS has access to vast amounts of data. He or she has heard at least once about safe sex, AIDS, Yuppies, Dinks, Junkies, Baby Boomers, Slackers, interest rates, mergers, the Real Estate Crash, smog and earthquake alerts, steroids, teleconferences, televangelists, the Far-White Crusade, the Homeless, Desert Blast, the death of Communism, Campaign Spending, cyberspace, the Net, Web Pages, Grunge, Rap, Ecstasy, the Great 80s, and the Trial of the Millennium.

Can Gina be described as an "average teenager attending ASHS"? She'd respond with a categorical "No." For starters, she has taught herself to read Santana graffiti while many of her classmates have trouble reading standard English. She sees herself as a sort of humanist, an activist without political affiliations, a rare bird. Gina wants to be known for her beliefs, for her radical, cold-turkey approach to social plagues such as teen pregnancy and substance abuse. If Ms. Domingo can pull it off as an abstemious virgin, so can her classmates!

The Princess has a hard time admitting her typical problems: Monday morning blues, bad hair, what-to-wear trauma, total disdain for first period, chronic inertia, zits and other telling signs of puberty. She talks to a variety of students, but invites none into her confidence; she's convinced it wouldn't work. No one could see things her way, as a "mature" adolescent. Daddy's girl can't accept the fact that she's like many other kids. Girls who keep the world at bay for fear of being labeled freaks. Boys who don't quite fit in. People who think themselves different and long, in secrecy, to be like the rest. Teenagers.

There are two reasons why Gina hasn't befriended any of the Cuban American students. One: Maman wants her to mingle with the children of the Pinos Verdes Cuban elite (many of whom attend ASHS), and Gina just can't comply with her mother's wishes, even if they make sense. Two: the Cubanitos who go to ASHS are too concerned about looking more Ramosean than the truest Ramoseans. They refuse to speak Spanish (but she knows they can) and don't give a hoot about the Island. The funny thing is, they like to boast about how rich their parents used to be in Cuba, and in that respect they seem almost proud of their Cubanity. Funny, too, that while they want to come across as genuine Americans, they all spend a whole lot of time at the P.V. Cuban Club (a branch of the Wives Auxiliary). The club was officially named after José Martí, the renowned Cuban poet, but those students have turned the name into "Joe Marty." Gina's opinion: Pathetic! How dare they?

The Joe Marty Pack finds Gina bizarre, too "Latina" and too liberal or something, unpatriotic and patriotic at the same time. They never miss a chance to let her know that she's missing out, that she's not cool because she won't hang out with them, because she's not part of their clique. But Ms. Domingo is sure that she's not missing much.

In a few years (not soon enough) she hopes to graduate with honors and go to Sundance University (SU's Film Department has clout in Hollywood). And if she ever makes a movie about herself, she'll get the ASHS phase out of the way immediately, lumping her Freshman, Sophomore, Junior, and Senior years all into one; skipping Homecoming, Grad Night and the Prom, all school clubs, the Joe Marty Pack, most of her nun-teachers, gym scenes, and the Pledge of Allegiance. So there!

On second thought, she'll include a few scenes of survival in the Califos' jungle. A touch of local color. What the heck.

~~~~

School hall. Day. You need to get your books. Problem is, you got the locker on the bottom. Either you wait for the person with the top one to get her stuff or you'll have junk thrown on your head. Worse: You stand up without knowing that the top locker is open. Whammo! Then the upstairs neighbor (some brainless cheerleader) notices the photos pasted on your door, many of Latino celebrities. She asks, "Oh, gee, wow, huh, who are they?" And so you try to be patient and enlighten her. Or you resort to sarcasm, "What's the matter? Haven't you ever seen aliens?" *Help!* The gullible neighbor takes this question literally and scurries away.

The bell rings. If you're not in your seat by the time the bell rings you get Detention. And you know what that means: an hour of staring at the Dean of Discipline's face (a sinister nun) while you copy down the school rules till your hand falls off your arm and hits the floor. So you risk your life as you venture from period to period, through the wild and hormone-ridden crowds, and you make it to class in one piece. You land in your seat as if thrown from a spaceship, not knowing exactly what you're doing there. *Get me out!*

First period. Algebra. Mrs. Tate is one of the few non-nuns at ASHS. This teacher is large and prehistoric-looking, a latter-day dinosaur with a brain full of puzzles. And totally out of it. Like, students are not awake during first period, everybody knows that, it's part of high school lore. But after thirty years of teaching, Mrs. Tate is still unaware of such a simple fact. From the moment the students walk in, before they even find their seats, she starts spewing formulas and equations as though she were lecturing to the wall about the Big Bang. She just doesn't get it, does she?

Third period. Religion. Miss White is true to her name. She observes a conservative dress code, has bobbed blonde hair, a symmetrical square face and a geometrically perfect tanned body. She looks like an aging cheerleader and sounds like a hack actress, the soap-opera kind. Miss White is a non-nun who teaches religion, which doesn't make a whole lot of sense, but then, many things make no sense at ASHS. This teacher has definitely flown over the Catholic cuckoo's nest! The following notes on one of her homilies should serve as overwhelming proof. From Gina's notebook:

> *She's talking about our PHYSICAL connection with God and drawing a huge cross on the board. And I mean HUGE. She talks and talks and with every word she says she retraces the outline of the cross. A deformed and spooky cross. She's saying that the reason for evil and sins is bad blood, whatever that means. "Bad blood! The source of all evil!" Wow.*
>
> *Now she's going on and on about our negative body language. "Your carnal self is a path to your soul, a mirror image of your spirit!" Heavy. She knows when we're thinking bad thoughts 'cause she can read our body-word. "Your body is a text that God can read!"*
>
> *I'm doomed! She's gonna look at me any minute now and know exactly what I'm thinking. Gina Domingo, how dare you call my cross "deformed" and "spooky"? How dare you refer to my inspired ideas as "heavy"? You should be ashamed of yourself, young lady! Repent!*
>
> *Miss White says that God once had a human body (really?) and that we can still reach Him by "deciphering the map of His Corporeal Self." What? I don't get it. Is she saying what I think she's saying? She wants us to get PHYSICAL with the Almighty? How radically unCatholic! How totally New Age!*
>
> *There she goes to the board again to draw the cross, saying that we get in trouble (cross) because (cross) we don't listen to HIM (cross) because we don't read (cross) his Body-Word.*

Miss White once found a conspicuous anonymous message folded between two pages of her New Testament: MAY THE CROSS BE WITH YOU. AMEN.

~~~~

Gina had her unusual dream again last night. She heard Taina singing, *Zun zun zun* . . . She saw the young woman taking off her blue dress and bathing. And then, for no apparent reason, Taina ran out of the water and into her hut. She seemed afraid. No, it was more like terror. And there was a man's voice: the reason for her fear? Yes, he had just come back from hunting, hungry and bloody and foul-smelling. And now he wanted her.

Cornered against the palm leaf walls, Taina trembles and cries. Because he'll crush her like he crushed the peace of time and stream. If only she could stay under the water, become a plant that grows on rocks, give birth to tiny flowers when the light breaks. Live a short but happy life. Far from him.

No. Because she belongs to the man and her man is a fierce hunter. He takes orders from no one, not even the Cacique. Taina should be grateful for the will of the gods: She has been chosen. This fate is hers alone and it should make her proud.

But it does not. Because it is a useless fate. She must escape him! She must listen for the stones, which are again awake, summoning her. The stone-beings longing to be freed. Taina must walk to the stream, where time is slow, and find them.

There are faces on the surface, reflections of people she knows. Her father and mother, Taina can see them. And then there are creatures. The Cursed Ones? They are the people-eating Jíbaros, yes! The Jíbaros seize her mother and skin her alive. The pain, her mother's horrible pain! Taina sees her father crying, shriveling up, when they tear out his heart. The pain! And now she sees herself . . .

Running! She's running from the thumping and the screams. She's praying. The horrid smell behind her, not far. Taina sees herself flying. If she doesn't fly up, beyond the clouds and the birds, the Jíbaros will reach her. And then she will no longer feel the wind on her eyes or fuse with the foam on the shore. They'll eat her flesh, trapping her inside them. She'll hear the birds through their ears, touch the earth with their hurtful hands. Be a killer. No!

One of those dark times when Taina prays to the goddess who shines far away, the people-eating enemy will come. She knows. She sees this future in the stream: Her man is captured; they feed on him and leave his bones near the hut. Then they tie her up and spread her legs apart. Taina feels life pouring out, drop by drop, as they invade her. *Zun zun zun . . .*

And then she feels nothing.

~~~~

Gina woke up in the middle of the night, curious about her dream. She'd never fall asleep again unless she got some answers, unless her vision was deciphered, described in plain and easy

---

words. But who'd be able to help her figure it out? Certainly not her parents. She wouldn't know what to tell Daddy (they had never discussed dreams) and she could almost hear Maman's reaction, "You woke me up for this, *chérie?* You disturbed my beauty sleep to discuss a teenager's nightmare? Please!"

She went to the den and sat on the floor, by the window. In some weird and tripping way, she thought, her dream was trying to tell her something. But what? Gina couldn't quite put it all together. There were flashes . . . *Faces on the surface, reflections.* And a song. Just when it seemed to be making some sense, the tale would fade to black or gray or white, just like a movie screen. There was a thread to it, but a thin narrative thread that was too fragile to hold on to. She would keep trying . . .

~~~~

A man's voice awakens her. This other man is tender; he shrouds her limp body with his arms, heals her wounds. He nourishes her until she sees the sky again and drinks in the light.

This man is not a hunter or a killer. He knows the spirits on the island, has seen them. They have sung their song for him. Taina will gladly bear his children. Their children will grow up to be carvers and dancers and singers. A new breed, her own kind.

Time runs swiftly, too fast for Taina to see all that is happening around her. Time has a loving, guiding hand. She holds on to it, runs with it, and grows old. But not so old that she can't hear the deadly wind that strikes one day. A wind that announces white beings, powerful beings who have cut across the distant waters, taking over the shores. Not the Jíbaros, but half-gods who pray to a new deity: the one and only Lord called Dios.

No more praying time. No more Areitos. The strange creatures will punish those who refuse to believe in their god. They'll force Taina's brothers and sisters to scrape the bottom of the streams, the rivers, and the vast waters beyond, in search of shiny sand. Some of the islanders will manage to emerge, hardly alive but still breathing, holding the precious little rocks. But some will stay below, waiting for the end. Hoping for darkness.

Her people now long for the time of the moon; they fear the light of day because the day means suffering. Because the light means death. Their skin turns thin, their insides burst. Long streams of red life-water spout from ears, mouths, eyes, until there's nothing left inside them.

She'll see her children die, one by one, killed by the half-gods, cursed by their one and only Dios. What will become of this island, of her wooden friends, of her home?

~~~~

Gina managed to flesh out the dream's main character but couldn't remember her name. Yet while she was dreaming she'd been able to hear it clearly, and it sounded beautiful. What was the woman's name? It began with a "t," didn't it? Maybe not . . .

She wouldn't waste time on that detail; instead she'd try to capture the thin narrative thread. There it was; she could feel it. And so she told herself the story of a woman who lived in this peaceful nature place and who loved bathing in a stream. She was married to this macho creep, some kind of warrior but she didn't love him and escaped from his paws by carving wood and sculpting. Oh yes, and by talking to her friends, the dancing souls. One day some beastly gang invaded her village and killed her macho man, lucky for her, but what a mess of a scene. Blood everywhere, oh my God. At least they didn't kill her; she survived though they raped her, those beasts, the poor girl. But then somehow she found this other guy, a nice dude, who talked to the spirits like she did; he was her savior and so they danced a ceremonial dance; they got it on, had lots of babies. The End. Happily ever after? Not! Because then it turns out that there's another invasion and this time it's Big, the Final One, the Crunch. These new evil invaders are powerful like demons; they are gonna destroy everything and wipe out everybody.

And that was it. Gina couldn't remember the rest, if indeed there was more to the story. What's the big meaningful message in this nightmare, she wondered. What's the message for me? It was, after all, her freaky mind that had produced the vision. If anyone was implicated here it was Ms. Domingo. No way! She'd never concoct such a sad and bloody story. Absolutely out of character. Nuts!

Maybe her subconscious was just doing a heavy-duty reworking of a movie. But which movie? She'd seen so many. *Red life-water, nothing left* . . . Oh hell, surely she'd remember such an outlandish saga without a happy ending. No, this was no bogus rewrite of a tearjerker; this was her own mind-blowing creation. But what was it telling her?! *This island, her wooden friends, her home*...Maybe there were essential elements, key details that Gina hadn't managed to recall. *Precious little rocks* . . . Maybe.

The plot might still thicken, she thought, trying to be optimistic. What happened after the Final Invasion? Did the main characters survive? Was there a happy ending after all? Please?

~~~~

Taina has promised to bring up the shiniest stones for the white beings. They must believe her! Handfuls of luminous dirt, what they call *oro*, more than they could ever imagine. She will bring it to them.

But she won't keep her promise. Because Taina has decided to be with her man. The father of her children is destined to perish in the water, and she will stay with him underneath. She has chosen her fate.

His loving hand pulls her down when he goes in; he guides her. There is pain at first, but then it passes. The deeper they go the brighter it gets. She didn't know there was so much brightness down here! Light enters her feet and runs through her legs, her arms, her fingers.

Taina uses her last drop of air to make a bed of sand. She dresses it with little pink flowers and goes to sleep. By his side.

~~~~

Suddenly, Gina heard the young woman's cry, saw her body floating in a river. *Luminous dirt, last drop of air, a bed of sand* . . . She could glimpse some of the events that had led to that moment—gold digging, slavery, abuse, death—but still didn't know their true essence. Would she ever? The dream will return, Gina told herself, if it's meant to come back. I'll write it down and study it, make sense of it, see the whole picture. I've got to or I'll go bonkers for sure!

She was sleepy and thought she might go to sleep here, on the floor in the den. But the soft, mauve-colored carpet that she loved felt cold and barren. She had an urgent need to become a life-size toon, having the power to stretch to the sky and bounce around the walls as if made of rubber. Colorful, agile, and unreal. Safe from dreams.

Chapter 2

Picture Madame in her boudoir, a leather-bound edition of *Les Fleurs du Mal* by her side. A bouquet of evil flowers sits on the windowsill, brought back to life from 1857. Elisa is reading Baudelaire's poems, those that she feels reflect her tormented spleen and lyrical angst, her truest nature. The French writer informs her thoughts, mediates her desire. He has a voice again, thanks to her sorcery. Poet and sorceress inhabit a forsaken island, a place that is far, so far from his mysterious Cythera. They are stranded.

The warm light of sunset bathes her; streaks of sunshine cut across her pensive face. She is forming glossy, violet-colored words in a book she calls the Journal of *l'Esprit*. Madame keeps track of her dreams in this notebook. She creates there a primordial garden where life can be molded, where she has bewitching powers to rule over reality. There are no annotations of facts in her journal, no reports of events unmediated by Elisa's fantasies. Her private book is not to be tainted with empirical truth. What is the point of reporting people's actions, their mundane conflicts? What is the point of documenting events? There is no room for any of that, for reality as others define it, in Madame's writing. She tells what is worthy of art. Nothing else.

But Elisa Rochart de Domingo is well aware of her shortcomings. She doesn't have the Poet's talent, his gift for turning grime into gold, dust into glitter. So she conjures up his visage, offers her writing hand to him. And thanks to Elisa, the Poet dreams of benevolent angels and the sands of life. He feels desire mixed with horror, paints El Dorados that were promised but never delivered. Through her eyes he sees the stupidity of people, the subtle cunning of the devil. And again he glimpses an exotic, unreachable shoreline. And once again he draws beauty from evil, love from the depths of vulgarity. *La poésie* . . .

~~~~

Chances are Gina will never get a glimpse of Elisa's journal. And if she did, she wouldn't have the patience to sift through page after page of lyrical discourse to spot anything vaguely of interest to her. The young woman has learned not to try to get the truth out of her mother. Maman handles every situation by weaving a web of mystery around the simplest, clearest facts, and by reciting poetry! Gina can't understand her. Not only because Elisa likes to season her speech with French words that mean nothing to her daughter (and which Gina ends up acquiring against her will); and not only because she uses idioms that kids her daughter's age (and most people) don't use. But because the scope of her ideas is so inaccessible, the logic and texture of her spoken thoughts so foreign to the girl.

Madame wouldn't agree with Gina's assessment of her character, not at all. She would describe it as *affreux* (one of her recurring interjections, meaning "hideous" or "ghastly"). She would claim that it is Gina who has built a linguistic barrier between them. It is Gina's fault they can't communicate. Why, the girl hasn't made the slightest effort to use the rich, sophisticated lexicon that her mother has placed at her disposal! The stubborn child insists on learning Spanish, a déclassé language of no use to her, a tongue commonly associated with uneducated aliens.

Yes, it is Gina's fault, not Elisa's. Why does her daughter keep so many of her thoughts to herself? Why does she contradict her mother's suggestions and wishes? Madame wants what is best for Gina. And what is best for the teenager is speaking like Maman, thinking like Maman, doing what Maman thinks is best for Gina. Indeed.

~~~~

Elisa is rejoicing in the memory of a family outing, dinner at a French restaurant. It always thrills her to guide her family through the rules of etiquette. She is resolved to train Benito and Gina in activities of *haute monde,* and any sign of her successful training is a source of great joy. This dinner, for instance, was a "resounding success," in spite of a minor, forgettable mishap.

But Gina remembers things quite differently. She recalls that Maman went to a gentry shop at Gala Mall one day and bought Daddy "suitable attire" for a special night out. (She didn't dare get her *jeune fille* an outfit!) The following weekend, she announced, they'd be dining at Le Bigornot, a ritzy seafood place in Ramosa Beach. Gina would've preferred eating at Ambiente, a restaurant that had just opened in Torrance. Ambiente served Cuban nouvelle cuisine and was part of a chain of sensational eateries that originated in Miami. But Cuban food, even "Nouvelle Cubaine," was not an option. Elisa detested it.

Dinner at Le Bigornot turned out to be a slice of life Chez Les Domingos. Gina was secretly glad that the event had been a fiasco, and that one of the reasons was her mother's intolerance for alcohol. She dreaded the thought of her folks ending up alcoholics, like so many of her classmates' parents. No chance, though, because they hardly ever drank and you could tell: the Bigornot episode was awesome proof!

First, Daddy asked the waiter if this restaurant served wine by the bottle. Then the handsome young man pointed to the wine list that was right in front of Monsieur. Daddy grabbed it nervously. "What a long list," he said, opting for a Sauvignon Blanc and a cherry soda for the young lady. The waiter brought the wine bottle and showed it to Dad and Dad stared at it somewhat mystified. Then he looked up at the tall man and said, "Yes?"

The waiter was courteous and patient. "Is this acceptable, Monsieur?"

"You should know better than me if the wine is good," Daddy snapped.

"No, sir, I mean, is this what you had in mind?"

Daddy stared at the bottle, "Is there wine in there?"

This time it was the waiter who seemed mystified. "Of course there's wine in the bottle, Monsieur."

Mr. Domingo held the object in question as if ready to break someone's head with it, "Then it's acceptable!"

The waiter poured Daddy this little bit of wine and the florist just sat there waiting for the man to split and the *jeune homme* didn't move from his place and stared at Monsieur who stared at the waiter. And so Maman finally whispered in Daddy's ear, "You're supposed to taste it, *chéri*."

Gee whiz! Gina could've gotten out of that bind with much more class than Mr. Florist. She hadn't watched two prime-time documentaries about the rich and famous for nothing. You must glance at the wine bottle and nod firmly, "Yes, that is the vintage I requested." The dark-handsome-muscular waiter will smile and go through the process of opening the bottle. He'll pour the wine, a few drops, in your glass. You smell the bouquet and smile back at him as you take the glass to your lips. You savor it as one final step in the ritual. "Ah yes," you'll say softly but decisively, "that is excellent." There, the wine and the pleasure are yours.

Maman ordered for the family, in French, while Daddy and Gina sat tensely. They were hoping she wouldn't make them eat anything revolting, like snails. As it turned out, she'd only asked for shrimp croquettes (an appetizer that was gone within seconds) and lobster in a sherry cream sauce for everyone. (They all loved lobster.) Feeling accomplished, Elisa started to take slow, studied sips of the Sauvignon. "Let's have a toast," she said after a while. "To the Domingos!" Minutes later her French started to thicken. Was she tipsy? So quickly? From taking such delicate sips? "*Vive la famille!*" she proclaimed. And Gina thought: *Ma Mère!*

A group of waiters was singing the "Birthday Song" to an elderly woman a couple of tables away. Maman got up, blurting out, "*Bon anniversaire!*" Then, chortling, "How vulgar! This would never happen in Paris." After taking another long sip, she hummed the birthday melody. "Let us make the best of it," she said, her words more slurred than before. "Let's join the chorus! *Alons-y!*" And she sang the song off-key, in French!

What in the world had they put in that wine bottle? Madame had never made such a royal fool of herself. Would this ever happen to a real French mother? It's one thing to see your mom have a couple of drops of fine liqueur after meals, at home, and another to see her at the fancy Bigornot, laughing her brains out. You don't expect to go to dinner with your family and have your elegant mom fall all over her Lobster Newburg, do you?

A resounding success. *Oui Oui.*

~~~~

Madame is describing in her journal an altercation she just had with a handful of Wives, while attending an Auxiliary board meeting. (She never documents empirical reality; this case is an exception.) The ladies–she writes–were expressing their concern about the epidemic of disappeared pets sweeping the community. At least one of every five Wives present has lost a kitty or a poodle somewhere in the hills of Pinos Verdes. Quite a tragedy!

I shall never understand those women's love for animals–she writes. That sentiment is the only trait of *l'esprit Américain* that I cannot emulate convincingly. God knows I have tried! At the meeting, I smiled demurely and commented, sympathetically, "I feel sorry for you, ladies. *Je suis desolée!* It must be awful to lose a pet."

The Auxiliary's president turned to me, also smiling, and asked, "You haven't lost one of your little animals?"

"No," I replied.

"I see," said the presiding Wife, her voice laden with suspicion. "In that case, please tell us about your pets, Mrs. Domingo."

Silence.

"Don't you have pets?"

"Well . . . actually, no."

"You must be joking! No dog?"

"No dog."

"Hamsters? Parakeets? A canary? A turtle? Not even a kitty?"

"I'm afraid not."

"But that is impossible!"

What could I do now, after making such a *bête* of myself? I should have lied! No, that is not my way. I would apologize to all the ladies for my lack of sensitivity, and then I would tell them a story.

"I've been having these lapses," I said, "since the day of a terrible event that marked my life. During these disturbing moments, I forget that animals–especially domestic ones–have souls, too; that they deserve affection and respect just like human beings. How irresponsible of me not to be the caretaker of a darling pet!"

The women were ready for the *coup de grâce*. Sure enough, one of them said, "Tell us about that incident that marked your life, dear." I had the floor. But I wouldn't seize the opportunity just yet.

"You want me to tell you what happened?" I asked, teary-eyed. The women nodded affirmatively, in unison. "If only I could," I murmured, lowering my eyes. "It was shocking, monstrous. You have no idea, my friends."

"There is no need for confessions," stated the president, as she looked at her watch. "It's getting quite late. We should adjourn."

"Once upon a time," I began narrating, impromptu. "Once upon a time in a land called Camagüey, there lived a family of aristocratic lineage . . ."

"Pardon me? What are you saying?" inquired the elected leader.

"She's telling her story!" cried out one of the Wives.

"She's going to tell it as though she were a character," affirmed another, sounding surprisingly literary. "That way she can pretend it didn't happen to her. And it's not so painful!"

"I do not understand." The presiding Wife was utterly perplexed.

"Ssshhh! Just sit down!"

The president took her seat, reluctantly. I proceeded.

~~~~

"They were the Rocharts: French father, Spanish mother, one daughter born in Camagüey. Monsieur Rochart was an industrious man, owner of vast sugarcane fields and a stately hacienda. He was a loving husband and a devoted father. Señora de Rochart, Doña Elisa, was aloof, taciturn. Yet she had a generous heart.

"The Rochart child, named Elisa Elise after her mother and her father's mother, grew up to be a lovely young woman of natural finesse. In time, she would be sent to Paris to study French culture and literature. Her parents were hoping she would meet in France a suitable young cavalier, a man worthy of her pure blood and numerous graces. They wished to see their daughter return to the island on the arm of this distinguished gentleman. She would then bear a handsome boy who would proudly continue their lineage and expand their dominions.

"Elisa Elise went off to the cultural Mecca, the city of Paris, and mastered the mystical language of the great Romantic poets . . . 'Distant fires burn my soul,' she would recite by heart, impassioned, in perfectly enunciated French, 'Distant light and distant wind, my love. Why do I seek the sun amongst the ruins? It is beyond these ashes where I shall find my home.'

"She was quick to learn the sophisticated manners of the ladies of *haute monde*, quick to acquire their *façons*. Oh, but destiny is whimsical; it likes to show its ominous, capricious ways. Fate, *Le Destin*, did not have a young suitor in store for the Rochart daughter, not in France, not in the Mecca. She came back to the island, ripened by the classical sun of the old country, a woman fully at the peak of her feminine season, alone.

"Elisa Elise's parents set out to find, among the finest bachelors of Camagüey, a man who could make their daughter's happiness possible. They had to act promptly, for the young woman would soon be past the proper wedding age. The Domingo family was the ideal prospect. Hacienda owners just like the Rocharts, they had pure-blooded, Spanish ancestors, and were seeking a lovely *señorita* with whom they could unite their only son, Benito Ramiro.

"The union was arranged by Monsieur Rochart and Señor Domingo. A grandiose wedding! French dressmakers, musicians, culinary experts and a Castilian priest were brought from across the ocean. The newlyweds were regaled with extraordinary presents: embroidered garments, exotic furs, and pink river pearls for the bride; chess sets of green ivory and aromatic pipes made from the oldest guayacán trees for the groom. But the most enchanting gift came from the bride's parents: a ninety-day voyage around the world.

"Husband and wife returned from their honeymoon with impressive news. Elisa Elise was with child. Eureka! The Rocharts were about to reach their pinnacle of happiness. Yet destiny, again, was preying on their hopes. Elisa Elise gave birth to a baby girl whom she called Gina (because Mr. Domingo liked the name). The Rocharts were careful not to show their chagrin; they showered their granddaughter with love. But they would await, forlorn, the much-desired grandson who would never arrive.

"The young couple moved into a lovely country home and created a blissful life for themselves. Benito Ramiro Domingo filled the house with maids and a French nanny for the baby. He was a busy man in charge of a vast sugarcane plantation and a refinery; his bread-winning duties often took him away from his home. Elisa Elise devoted herself to her daughter, and she accepted her husband's frequent absences with courage and faith. She never told him of those days when she would sit on the porch and watch the sunset, waiting in vain to hear his laughter and feel his manly embrace. Those days when she would fill her aching heart with visions of the Seine and the Champs Elysées. Some day, she thought, she'd be able to share those wondrous places with him. *Un jour*. It was only a matter of time.

"One fateful afternoon, while Benito Ramiro was tending to his fields, a horrible event took place. Things would never be the same thereafter. Elisa Elise would ask to be taken away from the country home. And so *Le Destin* had it written that the Domingos would leave the land of Camagüey and come to this fruitful and prosperous North Land, where they would cultivate exotic flowers and live happily ever after."

I paused, looked around, observed my listeners. No one moved or made the slightest sound. They were all waiting for the outcome, an end to my gripping tale. The grand denouement.

"I know you would like to hear what happened," I said. "But though I am speaking of myself in the third person, this is a horror that I've had to live with all my life. It touches me deeply, in ways that you cannot begin to imagine. *Mon Dieu*, will I be able to endure the telling?!" A few tears would be advantageous at this juncture, I thought. *Voilá!* I felt them running down my cheeks. "Do I have the strength to tell it? I am not sure . . ."

The president handed me her personal perfumed kerchief. "Here," she said as she delicately placed her hand on my shoulder, and delicately took it away. "It's all right if you do not continue, dear. We understand. We've heard enough to realize–"

"Forgive my outburst, Madam President. I have to be strong and overcome the travails of my past. I will try to go on. I must, so that you know why I do not keep any of God's precious creatures–and especially not canines–as pets in my home. There are traumas from which one never recovers."

I had the floor again. Time for the *coup*.

"I was nursing my daughter upstairs, in her bedroom. There was a warm breeze making its way through the Venetian blinds, and you could hear birds singing from the high branches of the ceiba tree. I remember feeling joyful, grateful to the Lord for giving me such happiness. Suddenly, there was a noise outside the door, like scratching. I placed Gina in her cradle and walked toward the door. As I approached it, the noise became eerily audible. Now there was also grunting and heavy breathing.

"I called the nanny and the maids, to no avail. Why couldn't they hear me? I vacillated for a second and then grabbed the doorknob, turning it slowly. I hadn't finished turning it completely when this extraordinary force pushed me back, slamming the door against the wall and knocking me flat on the floor. I heard Gina crying and, stupefied, discovered the source of the scratching and the heavy breathing: a wild dog from the thickets! I would forever be haunted by this image, by this living depiction of evil. Haunted, as well, by the mystery of how that creature had gotten there. Among all the other people living under our roof—half a dozen servants—why did it pick me and my daughter? How could no one see it on its way to Gina's room?

"The terror paralyzed me, but thank God my motherly instincts took over and made me run to my baby's cradle. I held her in one arm and with the other hand grabbed a chair. I wanted to scream, but could not. I just stood there for eternal minutes, holding my baby, hitting the animal with the legs of the chair, watching its fangs, its tongue dripping saliva . . .

"I prayed. I started to cry, silently. There was the sound of a gunshot and then I felt my husband's arms around me. The beast was on the floor, in a puddle of blood. My baby and I were safe."

Applause.

-II-

Gina took Spanish against her mother's will. "If you must learn another language," Maman had said, "let it be French. Just imagine, we could converse in that *belle langue.* I could teach you so many things about that marvelous culture! Spanish will be a waste of time. You know it already."

That wasn't true. Gina didn't feel she knew Spanish. She understood it pretty well, sure, but she had trouble writing it and she had never read any Hispanic literature. Maman was wrong, and left her daughter no choice but to be disobedient. Gina enrolled in level IV, which was taught by a Mexican nun. Surprisingly, the placement exam categorized her as a near-native speaker.

The University of California, where sixty percent of ASHS students ended up going, counted Spanish IV as ten hours of university-level language. Most of the students enrolled in that class, all nonnative speakers, were ploddingly trying to get the UC language requirement out of the way before graduating. Gina couldn't believe they'd made it through the three previous levels, considering their inability to understand Spanish and their horrid pronunciation.

Sister Juana soon labeled Gina "an excellent student," which was not a statement Mrs. Tate or Miss White could make about Ms. Domingo. In Spanish the Cuban American student was applied, alert, eager to be challenged. She wrote imaginative compositions and did the grammar exercises with hardly any errors, her only downfall being the whole issue of accents. The Spanish language was full of them! An accent mark could radically change the meaning of a word and the absence of accents could create some pretty uncool situations. Like the word *papá*, meaning father; if you absentmindedly left out the accent, you'd end up with *papa*, potato! Or the word *año*, meaning year; without the tilde it turned into *ano*. Anus!

The Mexican teacher was the only Latina on the ASHS faculty. A brilliant woman, she never boasted about her immense knowledge, and always made her students feel smart and unique. Gina found the nun beautiful. Her brown, indigenous features were striking. She had long, thin fingers that she moved expressively when speaking. Her voice carried a certain air of antiquity. Her accent was a mixture—as Sister Juana defined it herself—of Mexico City *Chilango* and archaic convent argot, with a dash of bookish Castilian.

No subject was too risque for Sister Juana; there were no taboos when she was teaching. The nun brought up the Catholic faith (which she seemed to profess wholeheartedly) only when it was relevant: When the topic came up in a story, or when a student asked about the Church. She wasn't bent on converting anyone and Gina was grateful for that (Catholicism was not on her list of things to explore further). Sister Juana had only one objective: to convert nonreaders to reading. She was a self-proclaimed believer in the power of literature.

Gina prepared for class discussions by studying the assigned material numerous times, thrilled to be reading Latin American stories without having to look up a lot of words. (Only the regionalisms gave her some trouble.) Tales about invisible gypsies, about clairvoyant women who carved living creatures and gods out of stones; houses of reincarnated spirits; insects that turned into people and people who turned into insects at a magical zoo; characters who longed to cease being characters; myths that were more truthful than history; beings who believed themselves to be alive, but who were only the dreams of other beings; bananas with peels made of gold; rains that lasted centuries; women who came back from the dead to dance and love among the living.

Gina's classmates found the narratives obscure, the ideas and images hard to grasp. All of them insisted on knowing exactly what happened to whom why where and how. And Sister Juana repeatedly explained that the stories didn't mean for those questions to be answered. The material was challenging, true, yet Gina liked precisely this quality of the literature: its conundrums, mysteries that seemed to hold bewildering truths about the human condition. She didn't always figure things out; in fact, she tended to rely on the teacher for interpretations. But once a particular analysis was underway (motifs, symbols, messages), Gina flew with it, incorporating the text into her own well of fantasies. Into her life.

Some nights, while reading an assigned passage, she had the disquieting suspicion that she was on to something, that a wondrous secret was about to unravel. Nothing ever happened, though, outside her own imagination. But what a feat that was already! She had never felt so aroused creatively, transported as she was by these tales (and her own mind) beyond the walls of her safe and uneventful room.

Movies can't be so mind-blowing, she had to admit. Or maybe here was the ultimate challenge: turning this literature into film, bringing filmmaking to a higher dimension. Movies as art. Was that possible? Artistic films drenched in magic, but without pretensions, without the stuck-up tone she'd detected in all the art-house cinema and some of the independent films she'd watched on video. Like French movies from the Sixties, what they called the "avant-garde." She hated them for being confusing and for throwing in all kinds of scenes that had nothing to do with the story, and for using all those angles and camera shots that left you with a headache. Oh, and for being set in dreary, depressing locations. Was all that experimental stuff supposed to be cool? Forget it!

Maybe it just wasn't possible to make an artistic film that told an uplifting story in a normal way. Lots of visual effects, yeah, but nothing gloomy or hard to follow. No, it could never be done, she told herself, and didn't take the time to name the reasons. Better leave these wonderful tales where they are, where they belong: in books.

~~~~

Spanish IV required an oral report on a Hispanic country as a final project. Gina volunteered to do Cuba, of course, and she fought the temptation to ask her parents for help. She just didn't feel like hearing the usual response from Daddy, "I think you should speak with your mother first." And from Maman, "We do not wish to talk about the Island, *chérie.*"

Hoping for an "A," she went to the public library and played every CD-ROM she could find on the subject (not many). She also checked out several books, including a thick volume on one of the island's religions, called Santería, and the *Communist Manifesto.* Gina read most of them, discarding the latter because it hadn't much to do with Cuba, and the one on Santería because she just couldn't get psyched up about religion. Then she concentrated on making a poster. It would feature the Cuban coat of arms, with its perfectly erect palm tree and the sun rising over the blue mountains; a lush, golden sugarcane; and a portrait of Martí, the famous poet.

"Cuba: Jewel of the Antilles" was the title Gina gave her report. She envisioned it taking her listeners from the early mythical days, when the Tainos lived peacefully eating their *casabe* (a type of bread made with the starchy root *yuca*), through the Jíbaro invasions of the island, and on through the violent Spanish Conquest. It would touch briefly on the Independence heroes; on the postcolonial period, which was plagued by the slave trade; and on the profitable birth of the sugar mill, known as the *Central.*

Gina's presentation would highlight the existence of a noble Cuban man whose name was José Martí; he wrote great poetry and would be known, after his death, as the Apostle. (She looked up "apostle," since the only definition she knew couldn't possibly apply here: any of Christ's original disciples. There was a second meaning listed which fit Martí perfectly: *A pioneer of a reform or movement.*) This gifted writer published a book called *Simple Verses* that Gina hoped to quote: "Art I am among the arts. And in the forest, a forest I become . . . Do not imprison me in darkness, to die like a traitor. I am a good man and like good men, I will die facing the sun . . . *de cara al sol!*"

Next, she wanted her report to concentrate on the Apostle's stint in New York, when he started organizing the Reconquest: seize the island from the Spanish oppressors! Cuba deserves its freedom! The presentation would then skip over a whole lot of years, ending with an event that in her notes Gina called the Bearded Bang of 1959: the (in)famous Cuban Revolution.

After completing her research and memorizing some key dates, she felt relieved, as though she had at last grasped the meaning of Cubanness. There was this warmth inside her, a tingling sensation. Her temples were throbbing and this was a good sign; it meant she'd done a good job, she'd managed to process the data and turn it into knowledge.

Is all this stuff nothing more than data, another class project, she wondered. No, this was different and she might as well accept its humongous significance. She had made some major discoveries, and she'd been able to decipher her Cuban Dream once and for all. The dream had come back several times during the last few weeks, giving her a chance to put it all together in the form of a story. And the story, she thought, was really about herself: how she had connected to some distant past through her weird mind; how she knew, even before she read the books and did her studying, what the Island was like ages ago. Or at least what it might've been like for the Cuban Indians, for a beautiful woman named Taina. Yes, Gina had finally remembered her name in the dream.

In any case, some day she'd give all those words in her report a body: sugary sand and salty air, the shores of a forbidden island. The real thing. Just maybe.

~~~~

The presentations were spread out over several class periods. There were two on Mexico, a land—the students explained—known for its Aztec sacrifices, its spicy food, its illegal aliens, and for its cool tourist hangouts like Puerto Vallarta and Cancún. One student spoke about Puerto Rico, "which is part of the United States although they speak a primitive form of Spanish." A young woman reporting on Argentina declared, "That country is located in Latin America but it belongs in Europe." The student pointed out, proud of her discovery, that Buenos Aires was the city where a powerful woman named Evita had sung the world-famous tango "Don't Shed Tears For Me, Che Guevara." There was a report on Peru, "nest of the Inca civilization"; one on Nicaragua, which had been "plagued by a communist government for many years." And last but not least, the report on Cuba.

Rule One of Public Speaking According to Gina: Stick to the facts. Here's what happened and here's the truth. "Upon landing in Cuba in 1492," she said in her best velvety voice, "the conquistador Don Cristóbal Columbus marveled at the immense beauty of the island, which he described as–and I quote–the most beautiful sight that human eyes have ever seen. End quote." She paused, glanced at her notes, trying not to read but to deliver naturally: "Cuba has an estimated area of 44,206 square miles and is shaped like a crocodile. In the southeast of the island there's a mountain range, the Sierra Maestra. Sugar, tobacco, and coffee are the country's major resources." Brief pause. "Before the Spaniards arrived, three cultures inhabited Cuba. The (take a big breath) Guanahatabeyes, the (mouthful) Ciboneyes, and the (now breathing normally) Tainos. All of whom were savagely exterminated by the Spaniards."

And at this point the calm and collected presenter lost her cool. Was she nervous? Was this a case of delayed stage fright? Absolutely impossible! Why, then, were her hands moist and cold? *Coño*, she'd have to try not to stammer, not to louse up this project that took long hours of research and preparation. I'll just stick to my notes, she decided. Yeah. She would now enumerate some vital, totally relevant details.

"Cuba was under Spanish rule for four hundred years. (Too long!) There were independence movements between 1867 and 1878, but the island wasn't free until much later. Cuba–I should point out–was the last Spanish colony to obtain its freedom. And it attained it thanks to some self-sacrificing people. ("A" for word choice!) Like, there was this man, Céspedes, who was a rich landowner. In 1868 he freed all his slaves and then disappeared to the mountains to educate the peasants. (My kind of guy.) There was another man named Maceo whose mother encouraged him to fight for Cuba. This heroic woman found a place in history because of her deep sense of patriotic duty (a whopper of a phrase, if I may say so myself). She fought along with her husband and children. And when young Maceo was getting scared of fighting, she put a machete in his hand and said to him, 'Don't be a coward, Maceito. Go defend your country!' (But what if he didn't believe in violence?)

"The most important hero–and here I offer my humble opinion–was the poet José Martí, alias The Apostle." She pointed to the picture on her poster. "He was the first famous Cuban to call for the elimination of the colonial system. All the Mambises, who were peasant soldiers also known as Guajiros, idolized him and wanted to fight by his side. It's really too bad that he had to die . . ."

Pause. "Okay, so Martí wanted to plan the Reconquest. Fine with me. Because reconquests take a whole lot of planning and they need brilliant minds. But why did he have to go and grab a gun? His true calling was art, not war. When Don José was mortally wounded in 1895, Cuba lost its greatest citizen."

She had recaptured her thread! She wasn't just offering info, but also interpreting it for her audience, and in the process showing off her awesome lexicon. Time to get back to the facts: "There was a malicious document, a sort of treaty called the American Amendment by which the island turned into a colony of the United States in 1899, right after it won its independence from Spain. Then the U.S. government dominated Cuba for a long time." Pause. "Until Castro came into the picture, I mean." Pause. "But wait, before the Cuban Revolution there was this sellout president called Batista. During his reign of terror, the island was full of corruption and poverty. But it turns out that Batista wasn't a tough macho leader after all. When he heard about Fidel, he fled from the country like the total coward that he was." Pause, a long breather this time. "And so the young university student who'd studied law in the United States, later to become Comandante Castro, took over the country in 1959, with just a handful of men. He went on to write the *Cubanist Manifesto* on the famous date of July 26. And he said to his people, bravely and proudly, 'History will absolve me!' I'm not sure exactly what that means, but maybe we could discuss it later?"

Sister Juana was anxiously looking at the clock. Gina was running out of time and she wasn't even close to the end! She had to summarize, get to her conclusion. But how? She would write the remaining notes on the board, and maybe the nun would let her elaborate on these significant topics the next day: *Marxism-Leninism. The Blockade. The Missile Crisis. Bay of Pigs. The Death of God. The Soviet Invasion. Repression, rationing, censorship. Castroism. Exodus. Socialism or Death . . .*

Rule Two of Public Speaking According to Gina: As part of your conclusion, throw in some personal stuff, an intimate insight. So she told a story that she called My Cuban Dream, the scenes that recurred, the meaning she had managed to extract from it.

"I see myself as a Taina," she said, "this Indian girl. I'm bathing in a stream, watching the sun rising over the silent blue hills. I hear birds singing and I begin to sing a song I never heard before. (Is this sounding hokey?) Then I hear myself whispering, talking to some stones; they're not the precious kind, but shiny and precious in their own way. I drink the cool refreshing water from the stream. (Enough description. Cut to the chase.) Then, all of a sudden, faces appear on the surface of the water. The images are hazy, distorted, yet I know who they're supposed to represent: the White Beings! (Creeps!) I run away from the stream, in terror. And then I realize I've just seen the future of the island, the fate of all Tainos. The Spaniards are coming to destroy our way of life! (Beasts!) I'm crying, feeling this incredible sadness. (And wanting to wake up from the nightmare!) Because there's nothing I can do to prevent the tragic end, the death of my people. Absolutely nothing."

Where was her ovation? Only a couple of students were applauding, and the nun; although she was also still staring at the clock. Hey, hadn't it been her idea to save the best for last? So what if Gina had run a little over her allotted time? She'd given a spectacular finale! But talk about an anticlimax. One member of the somnolent audience asked: "Do you always have a lot of weird dreams? 'Cause that was a pretty heavy dream, I'd say. Or did you make it up?" Gina kept silent for a moment and then replied: "You're asking a personal question that has nothing to do with Cuba. If there's anything you'd like to know about the topic of my report, I'm all ears. Next!"

One of the Califos wanted to know if Cubans spoke Spanish. "The answer is clearly yes," Gina responded, "since it was the Spaniards who colonized the island and, besides, our reports were supposed to be on *Hispanic* countries." Someone else asked if Cubans ate spicy food. Gina said no, and proceeded to describe typical island dishes like black bean soup and *picadillo*, a kind of ground beef casserole. Another student graciously commented on the poster, "Hey, that looks real!" And Gina said, "Thank you, I drew it all myself." Then the student loused up her nice comment by asking, "Who did you say was the balding guy with the mustache? Was he a writer or a soldier or something?"

Then a Pale Pious Dude sarcastically inquired, "Your parents came from Cuba, didn't they?" She knew he meant to imply that Gina had gotten help from them, that she had *cheated*. The nerve! "Yes, they came from Cuba," she said, calmly. "But that was a long time ago. And they've forgotten everything."

-III-

Elisa combs her long, silky black hair in front of the mirror. She then applies the rose-scented replenishing cream to her face. The cream leaves her complexion youthful and radiant, with no trace of her approaching fiftieth autumn. Or is she older than that? An occasional white strand shows through the deep, glinting *noir*. This is chic; the natural gray adds a seignorial touch to her countenance.

Madame Domingo . . . the truth. What is the truth? The way she once felt about Benito? Once upon a time there was nothing more truthful than those feelings. She used to miss him, aching to touch his muscular arms, his dense eyebrows. Benito's ruggedness and farmer's ways aroused her. She would crave so many sensations: having his fingers graze her breasts, his lips on her lips, his tongue in her throat. His thrusts. As simple as that: his body, *son corps nu*. The truth of why she married him.

Out in the garden, that's where he saw her the first time, where he caught a glimpse of her delicate beauty. While on business in Camagüey, Benito had walked by her house. He liked to stroll through the residential areas and had spotted her there, all alone, tending to her roses. His parents weren't hacienda owners; he wasn't in charge of a sugarcane plantation or a refinery. Benito was a salesman, a broken-down nobody willing to incarnate a prince. There were many other men courting Mademoiselle; she could've had her pick. But only Benito would be capable of saving her from tedium, of showing her the passion she needed. He brought a kiss of life to her solitude. She offered him status in return, and all the knowledge she had gleaned growing up as a princess. Was there love?

Their secret courtship lasted months. She'd sit in her garden and watch the sunset, waiting to hear his manly laughter. Some day they would leave, she told him, and build their home away from Cuba. *Un jour* . . . It was only a matter of time before they could create their private Eden. In France? In the United States? Miami was out of the question: too close to the infernal island. But perhaps in the far West, the golden City of Angels.

He promised her he would fulfill her wish, take her wherever she wanted to go, start from scratch in Paris or Los Angeles, become an American. Anything. There was no sacrifice he wouldn't make to please her. Because she would now be his home, the sole country for him. His *patria*.

But he didn't really want her class and her position; he desired *her*. Oh, if only she could hear his Story of Desire one more time; the fable he told (enhanced by her imagination) of how he longed to have Mademoiselle . . .

~~~~

He worked at a prosperous hacienda whose owner was a French marquis. Young Benito had sinewy strength and did the work of two men. He was handsome. The women flocked around him at the *bohíos* when he returned from the refinery and the sugarcane fields. They brought him water fresh from the well, and guava pastries they baked just for him. Benito accepted their presents reluctantly, so as not to mislead them. Because he had already found his woman: the Marquis' daughter, a beautiful young lady who loved him in spite of his humble station in life. Mademoiselle Elisa had invited him into her secret garden. There he had discovered aromas and colors of flowers he didn't know existed. And there he had known passion.

Benito would wake in the middle of the night, sweating, feeling warm and excited, thinking of his Mademoiselle. He'd caress his pillow with his enormous hands, imagining he was embracing her. He'd run to the river and plunge in, his heart pounding, hoping the cool water would quench his thirst for Elisa. Or he would walk through the maize fields, crushing the budding corn with his feet. Or climb up the ceiba tree and reach its highest branches, staying there for hours, brooding, touching the stars, thinking about his Mademoiselle.

Because she was rich and he a poor peasant, their paths hardly ever crossed. They could only meet in secrecy, not easily, and never for long stretches of time. He missed her painfully, and began to lose his strength for work, becoming lazy, lethargic. Benito would daydream every chance he got, deaf to his boss' orders. His love was hurting him, destroying him! He was flogged and kicked and beaten and yet he continued to slack off. Nothing mattered anymore. His heart had been ripped out of him.

He decided to end his torture. So, one day, when his shift was over at the sugar mill, he rushed to the main house and hid in the garden until nightfall. That night his lady's window remained unlocked. Benito went into her bedroom, tiptoeing like a shadow, and found her in bed. He stood by her side, in silence, stirred by her beauty.

His last vision, right before he died later that night, was this, now: Mademoiselle inviting him. Her scent of roses, the softness of her skin, the damp hunger she displayed for him. The last word Benito said, before the Marquis' dogs devoured him, was *Mademoiselle.* The last sounds he heard were the words of his beloved, "I've been waiting for this fire, Guajiro. *Ce feu.*"

~~~~

But that was then, when the Story of Desire was first written. It can no longer be told, or at least not in the same fashion. Too many rains have poured over the fire, and the lovers have done nothing to rekindle it. Today there is more apathy than passion, more silence than fantasy. Inertia. Today Elisa mourns the death of love, an end from which there's no return.

Madame looks in bright mirrors and finds dark reflections. She makes the effort to revive deadened flames. But in this void of material existence the angels have drowned, cursed by a memory that has ceased to be sublime. All she has left, in this darkness, is a bouquet of wilting evil flowers. Marriage.

~~~~

"Up to here!" he's been saying lately. Benito is up to here with her regal delusions. "You wouldn't be driving a Mercedes and living in this house if I didn't bust my ass working."

She retaliates. "*Mais oui!* You spend your days sitting behind a desk, ordering your Mexican aliens around, and you call that busting your ass? No wonder you have hemorrhoids!"

"It isn't as easy as you think," he says, in his defense, adding that she doesn't know the first thing about his business.

"Not true at all! The shop was my idea," she reminds him. The much-praised Domingo slogan, too, had been created by her. The one he'd come up with was trite, uninspired. *Domingo Flowers for your Sunday Best.* Such facile wordplay with the family name! Yes, the word "Domingo" meant "Sunday." So?

God, how she hates his business stench, his newspaper ads, his discounts for Cuban patriarchs and matrons, his gun, and his bourgeois mentality. He has the floral arrangement of everyone's dreams: affordable flowers for weddings, funerals, and anniversaries. True masterpieces. *Merde!* She'll walk into his Pinos Verdes shop one of these days and order a gaudy wreath for a tacky Cuban funeral–his!

She knows flowers and loves them more than he ever could. The ones she grows with the utmost care in her garden: fanciful snapdragons and pompons, gladioli, mariposa lilies and fleurs-de-lis. Her fantastic red roses. Not the ones he sells. Definitely not those.

"Stop dreaming, Elisa," he commands from his chair in the den, as he drinks his evening decaf and attempts to read. "Stop pretending."

Her gesture of defiance fiercely punctuates her words: "I do not pretend!"

"Dream on, then. But leave me out of it!" He's not even looking at her, his eyes glued to *Bloom Boom.* How impolite!

"You're as much of a dreamer as I am, Benito." She turns her back to him, stares out the window at the orange-rose horizon.

"Yes, but my dreams are about the real world. I make them come true."

"Dreams are dreams, regardless of what we make of them."

"You're not a French marquise, Elisa." He stands up, bent on humiliating her as he's done before. "You're a political refugee, an immigrant who lives like a queen thanks to this country, and thanks to me."

"I am not a refugee!" She confronts him, standing so close to him she can smell his coffee breath. "I'm an American citizen."

"Sure," he says nonchalantly, slapping the magazine page with the backs of his fingers, "on paper."

"That's exactly right: a piece of paper is my proof."

"It doesn't prove anything to me." He sits, obviously tense.

"You're just envious, Benito." She looks out again, her back to him.

"Bullshit." The word comes out like spittle, venom, dirt.

"You don't have what it takes to become naturalized."

"Big fucking deal!"

"And you're afraid. Admit it!" She's got him by the proverbial balls (a saying Elisa would never use herself).

"Shut up." He's walking away.

"Afraid you wouldn't pass the test."

"You know," he turns, his index finger pointed at her like the barrel of a gun, "sometimes I think we should've stayed in Cuba."

"Now there's a scary thought." She sits in his chair, defiantly.

"Castro would've cured you of all your fantasies."

"Yes, of course; he did wonders for *your* fantasy life!"

"I was okay." He walks to the kitchen, hoping to have another cup of coffee.

"He kept you *so* very happy." She follows him. They find Guadalupe, the maid, loading the dishwasher.

"I had a job." He gestures for the maid to brew some decaf.

"Mister Sugarcane Cutter, at your service!" She waves Guadalupe away. The maid leaves.

"They left me alone, Elisa."

"Indeed! They nationalized the company you worked for and stuck you in a cheap little makeshift *tienda*, out in the boondocks. You were a clerk selling pants and shirts made of burlap sacks, earning a pitiful salary that didn't get us anything, because there was nothing to buy! And as if that weren't enough humiliation, they forced you to do 'volunteer' work at the farms half the year. A very nice job indeed, Mister Salesman!"

"I could fend for myself. I was doing fine." He opts for instant, tries to prepare the beverage himself. "You, on the other hand—"

She leans against the kitchen counter, suddenly feeling burdened and assaulted by the memory. "We were *both* going through hell there."

"No, *you* were." He places a glass of water in the microwave to heat up. "You and only you, Señora Marquesa!"

"I don't deny it, Benito. Yes, my parents lost everything, and I lost them. There was no reason for me to stay on that hellish island. I thank God every day that I was able to leave."

"I had something to do with it, too."

Silence. Long silence. The water boils and Benito makes his coffee; three teaspoons of artificial sweetener, no milk.

"You owe me one." He takes a sip.

"I suppose I do."

Benito returns to the den, determined to end this conversation. He can't hear his wife when she mutters, "Thank you."

~~~~

He wanted lots of children and waited patiently. Years of waiting and hoping. There was something wrong with her; she'd had two miscarriages, one that nearly killed her. The doctors said she shouldn't try again, it was too risky. But they were wrong. Elisa Rochart would be able to conceive *un jour* . . .

She did, once she got to the United States, and after many attempts. There were countless examinations, countless fertility chemicals she had to ingest. Her womb was probed and medicated and coddled during nine months. It held a living seed, at last. A son for Benito! He hoped for boys but she brought *une fille* into the world, the only child they would ever have.

Gina. A girl who's prone to fantasy, who wanders off so far from everyone, so unreachable. She has a vivid, possibly dangerous, imagination. Like mother like daughter? Wishful thinking.

Gina who doesn't want a party for her fifteenth birthday. A fiesta isn't her "trip"; she'd rather get movies or CDs or a computer. And so she'll never cherish the memory of a *Quinceañera*, the once-in-a-lifetime experience of your first bash.

Like in a fairy tale, Mademoiselle danced all night with wealthy and dapper young men, gentlemen who fought for the privilege of waltzing with Elisa. So much attention lavished on her! So many looks of admiration (from the adults), of envy (from the young women), of desire (from the handsome lads). She was truly a princess for a night, an unforgettable night the likes of which Gina will never know. Her poor daughter. *La pauvre!*

The adolescent contests too many of her mother's wishes and decisions. She asks too many questions, insists on unearthing the filthy worms of the past. She forces her parents to think about things they would rather forget. Is this some form of punishment, of poetic injustice, Elisa asks herself during her arguments with Gina.

"Tell me about the island," implores the girl ad infinitum. "Will you ever go back? Will I get a chance to visit there?"

She should take pity on Gina, make something up if she has to. Be kind, giving, unselfish. But she can't. "You are not to mention that place anymore!"

"Why, Maman?"

"Just because."

"It's unfair. I have a right to know!"

"You wouldn't understand."

"But I want to! Please, help me understand."

"Respect our wish to forget that inferno. Respect it!"

And yet, Gina has been one of Elisa's most truthful experiences. Having a child is unambiguous and pure, simple the way good poetry can be simple. Maman loves her daughter and would give her life for her. There is nothing more veritable than those words, nothing more absolute. Does Gina love Maman? Yes, Elisa is sure. Although a chasm has appeared, the archetypical gap between procreators and offspring, a barrier, signs of what nowadays they are calling "dysfunction."

Children grow up to be adults, and you, their progenitor, may or may not like them as adults. Sad as it sounds, there's a chance you and your child may never be friends. The two of you might even be enemies. Is there anything Elisa can do to prevent this from happening? Begin building a bridge, perhaps? Be Gina's confidante, try to reach her somehow. Is it too late?

As Madame recites the Poet's "Bénédiction," she thinks of Gina. And she prays to ancient idols, to the invisible tutelage of angels so that her daughter will see the light. Oh, divine remedy, pour over my baby's heart! If an entity in this world can win her over, it is you, *la poésie!*

As she rewrites "Elévation," Elisa sees herself turning into an aerial being, into luminous clouds. Her mortal flesh no longer feels the bars of consciousness, the prison of her body. She's faster, much faster than time, that unstoppable runner. She reaches the girl and enters her eyes, becomes one with her spirit. And now she casts a spell of art and art will once again prove its true power. The magic works. It has to work!

~~~~

Madame Domingo . . . the truth, *la verité.* Truth has nothing to do with her parents, long gone. Or with the lonely days she spent in adolescence, locked in her room, writing romantic rhymes and waiting for her *Quinceañera.* Or with the punishments she received from the nuns at school for daydreaming, for not listening, for flying away to a distant land called Paris or L'Amour.

Truth has something to do with her maternal angst, this so-called instinct that still tugs at her heart; the longing, the paralyzing certainty that she cannot have any more children.

Elisa's truth is the house on the hill, life in Pinos Verdes: an exclusive community where she feels safe. Three armed watchmen guard the city, and her home is further protected by an electrified fence. She loves having a house with ten rooms and a sauna and a Jacuzzi. She loves that terrace with a view of glittering lights, the sun-dappled hills, the rosebushes so well kept and the grass so well trimmed. Her hearth. Home.

In the evenings, once in a blue moon, she makes love to her husband in a room of mirrored walls. A small indulgence, this arousal produced by the multiple images of their lovemaking. Images of marriage, *oui*. Benito's middle-aged belly, his thinning gray hair, his persistent farmer's mannerisms, his yawns, his business breath.

Madame doesn't wish to start over, not really. No need to begin *tabula rasa*, from scratch. Because she also loves her beauty siestas, having a maid, and this peculiar yet comforting idea of a family. But above all she loves her verses. Vertiginous raptures, silent fires. Dim, secret lights that warm her. Arms of a perfect, if invented, lover . . . *Je me souviens de toi, parfois, et tù m'inventes. Et parfois c'est l'amour, notre amour, inventé . . .*

~~~~

Elisa Rochart de Domingo places her journal, daintily, in a safe with her jewelry, her passport, and her citizenship diploma. Then she combs her silky black hair. She applies a rose-scented cream to her skin and looks at herself, facing the mirror.

That woman on the other side is looking back at her, and smiling. She is weaving an outrageous tale of marquises and illicit gardens, a story of desire. That woman knows who you are, Maman. She doesn't believe in luminous French rivers and Elysian fields, in L'Amour or Mademoiselle. How can she? That woman in the mirror knows the truth.

Chapter 3

-I-

What Gina wants is a White Christmas: the smell of chestnuts roasting on an open fire, the treetops glistening, the air filled with snowflakes. But instead she'll get hazy sunshine (a fancy name for smog), seventy degrees and more sunshine, eighty degrees and more smog, microwave popcorn and a battery-activated log in the fireplace.

She watches a lot of movies during the holidays, and when the films turn predictable, she changes details here and there. Gina imagines herself playing the lead, rewrites the ending, sets the story in Pinos Verdes, or adds visual effects. Open-ended movies upset her, so she usually gives them a resolution. But contrived, melo-dramatic closures upset her, too. She gives those a touch of realism: irony, adversity. If, for example, the protagonist can't decide which of two boys to date, and the movie ends without her reaching a decision, Gina makes her choose and face up to the consequences. If the movie happens to be a space-age saga with a doomsday vision of the future (evil parasitic aliens invading the Earth), Gina throws in a human female savior who fights the invaders with the power of her heart, not with weapons or technology. When the movie is a comedy but it just isn't funny, she creates a hilarious situation, a comical character, or provides the script with better jokes.

The Five Movie Categories, according to Ms. Domingo, are: (1) the ones you go see as soon as they're released (even if you have to wait in line) because of high-tech visuals, gorgeous stars, or just because you don't feel like waiting for the video; (2) the ones you've enjoyed on the big screen but want to watch over and over again, so you buy them or rent them a million times; (3) movies you want to see but you don't have the energy or the motivation, so you wait for the video; (4) flicks you hate and won't watch in any form or under any circumstances; (5) classics, avant-garde and for-eign art-house films that supposedly give you an insight into the art of moviemaking, most of which don't offer any kind of insight at all but instead bore you to tears.

The Domingos' Viewing Preferences (as reported by Gina in a composition; first draft, personal version): We definitely have different tastes, for sure when it comes to the stuff we watch. I like sitcoms, love music videos and new movies, and hate game shows. My Dad loves old films, the original black-and-white type about gangsters, and murder mysteries. He doesn't have stuck-up tastes like my mother. Once in a while he'll invite me to watch an oldie with him. I usually dig his stuff (for sure if the movie sounds funny when it's not supposed to, which is almost always the case!). Dad's into nostalgia. His favorite TV channel is the Retro Channel (RC), where they show classics from the Sixties and Seventies. He could watch old corny comedies for hours! He laughs just like a kid. It's like he goes back to when he was young, I think.

Dad is proud that he doesn't have to pay for cable, thanks to the radar he had installed in the backyard. My father would sure miss Retro if he didn't have it. I don't think he'd ever veg out in front of the tube. Not that he's a couch potato or anything, but he does make time for entertainment now and then. He better!

There are two RC shows he's nuts about. One is the story of a Mexican servant, this gal who ends up working for a gringo businessman, and the dude marries her so that she doesn't get deported. What a kind soul! He does the foreign chick a favor out of the kindness of his heart, right? She stays in his house and works like a slave (in more ways than one?), and she tells jokes with a fake accent and makes everybody crack up. They're all happy and the children (a blonde boy and a blonde girl) adore her. I wonder why Dad likes the show; it's got to be the actress, she's pretty and I'd bet she reminds him of someone in Cuba; or maybe he wishes that our maid Guadalupe was a talented comedienne like the RC one. The maid-turned-nanny-turned-wife is awfully funny. But I can't stand the show; there's something fishy about it. Like, why is the main character a Latina *and* a servant? Unfair! Why couldn't she be a career woman and the dude be *her* servant?

Once I got into an argument with Dad about the maid's show. I asked him how he could swallow such a barfed-up depiction of his people. And my father said that the actress was supposed to be Mexican, that he wasn't Mexican, and that Mexican and Cuban people have very little in common. Now, if the maid were Cuban, that would be a different ball game! "Anyway," he said, "it's good for her to have a job in a decent home and it's good that the

American man is helping her out. What's wrong with any of that? It's a happy situation and it's only a program. A very funny program!"

The other show Dad watches every chance he gets is a series filmed in pastel colors about a family of blonde, freckled people. The parents get along just great with their children and the kids (three boys and three girls who also get along) are bailing each other out of trouble all the time. Oh yes and meddling in each other's business. The phoney bunch is always having a jolly old time singing in the car, at the park, at the beach, in the house; just singing along about how happy they are together, about how they all love their family so much. Yuck!

But I can definitely stomach Daddy's Retro a lot better than Mom's high culture junk. At least he doesn't force me to sit and watch his stuff. "You are turning into an average American, *mignonne*, with nothing in your head but worthless entertainment!" Why does my mother torture me so much? Who gives her the right to pound her tastes into my head?

She loves the Universal Channel (UCHA), especially a program called *Living Stage* where they broadcast plays by famous dead playwrights like Shakespeare and Molière. That show has substance, says Mom. It's like reading literature; it doesn't just entertain you, but makes you think. She takes notes while watching, and she tapes the shows so she can view them later and take more notes. Then for a couple of days after watching a play she talks like those characters, using *thou* and *thee* and *hast* all over the place. You can't understand her! That's it, that's the problem with my mother's programming: I don't get much of it. And believe me, it's not just because the characters speak in ancient tongues!

I wonder why the stories in Sister Juana's class get me all psyched up, but I can't sit through Mom's shows. If I really tried to get into Molière and Shakespeare, would I end up enjoying them? Would I love them as much as I love the nun's tales? Fat chance. I tried to develop a taste for Shakespeare in English Lit and the Brit left me cold. I aced the final exam, but once the class was over, I promised myself never to read another play again. Maybe I just don't care for theater. Could that be it? But isn't theater a lot closer to movies than fiction is? Shouldn't I get into it because of that connection?

Bah! No use trying to figure this out. Fact is, I'm always in the dark when watching UCHA. The data is entered and processed and still I don't catch the drift. Zero output. Zilch. So the writing teaches you lessons that you can use in your own life; so it makes you a better, more educated person. Elisa's daughter doesn't give a hoot. She can't relate! I'd much rather be a character in one of Dad's Retro shows, that's for sure, if the only other option was *Living Stage.* Oh please! A damsel in distress babbling rhymes to some dude in tights. A dude in tights who also babbles rhymes. Dude-turned-dud, as far as I'm concerned. No way!

I don't want to be cultured if cultured is being like Mother and watching what Mother watches. Did you hear that, Madame Elisa? Your daughter's not a royal brain in storage, slowly growing in a jar, a ripe fruit full of untapped intellect. She's an American teenager! Not an Auxiliary Wife or a marquise or a Cuban refugee who reads poetry. I hate French poetry! And I hate *Living Stage* because its characters take themselves too seriously, and they talk too much. Less is more, *Sí Señor!* Didn't the Brit and Frenchy playwrights know that? Doesn't Maman know that? The End.

~~~~

This holiday season the Princess is in the mood for sounds. She'll be listening to rock, hip-hop, Latino pop, and salsa. Yeah, she wants all kinds of music, the whole spectrum. That's the advantage of being a Nineties-kind-of-person, you have a lot to choose from: Sixties rock classics, Seventies pop oldies, Eighties New Wave, Nineties New Age and Alternative Rock. And then there's all that excellent *Rockero* stuff, bands from Mexico, Spain, Argentina. Cool. And also fab movie soundtracks. And what about rap? She loves some rap mixes! Too bad she has to play that music low; her parents hate it. They think it's disgusting and vulgar, primeval noise, and how dare those people call themselves "artists"? Luckily, though, her folks don't mess much with her listening trips. (Rap is the only exception.) She wonders why. Do they think that music isn't powerful enough to influence her? Are they naive enough to believe it can't affect her? Whatever the reasons, thank God they stay out of her sound room!

Her private trip: eclectic moods she's named *Navidad Jamming;* sessions that her mother, as usual, will crush mercilessly. "*Ca suffit!*

The ceiling and the walls are vibrating. Our guests think it's an earthquake!"

Gina turns down the volume on her Quake Machine and goes through her wardrobe. Nothing too adolescent, please; the following scene requires class, sophistication. She has to play the part of a Pinos Verdes young lady, daughter of an Auxiliary Wife, the incarnation of beauty, refined taste, and good manners. *Oui oui.*

No matter how hateful the scene, she loves preparing for it. The wardrobe fittings are exciting. Makeup, hair, anticipation. Actors have to change all the time; they're always undergoing a—what was the title of that creepy Kafka story she read in English Lit? Ah, yes: metamorphosis. (That's if they're good. Because some actors can only play the same old part—basically, themselves!—movie after movie.)

She dons a pretty little dress and, displaying her most dazzling smile, goes to greet the holiday company. *Chez Les Domingos,* TAKE 15. Roll 'em! "Merry Christmas, dear ladies! Feliz Navidad. Joyeux Noel. How are you all doing?" The company invariably consists of Maman's friends: overdressed, overdone-in-tanning parlors and surgically enhanced matrons who feed Gina the same lines every year. "Look at that child, how she's grown! Why, you're a lady already. How old are you now, fourteen, sixteen?" Or: "My my, you are beginning to resemble your mother so much! Soon we won't be able to tell the two of you apart."

Exhausting. It's so totally exhausting to perform in front of a live audience. Multicamera takes are absolute killers! She rushes back to her dressing room (careful to dodge the reporters and the fans who crowd the hallways asking for autographs) and there she comes up with her own share of comments for the addle-brained visitors: "Seeing you is revolting and I'm not a lady and I never want to be a lady. I haven't grown an inch in two years and if you're referring to the way I'm growing, widthwise, then you can take your Xmas tree and shove it, you hear? Oh, and one more thing: I LOOK NOTHING LIKE MY MOTHER!!"

~~~~

Like Gina, Daddy, too, gets grumpy around Christmas. But for different reasons. He complains about the crowds and the TV specials and the jingles and the funny-looking fat men with white beards who sit outside the stores and ask for money. "Ho ho ho to you, too!" Daddy snaps at poor Santa who's only doing his jolly job.

"They dress up their houses with lights two months before Christmas!" he says of his neighbors. "Their roofs, windows, porches full of ridiculous lights. We're barely finished with Thanksgiving and they're already putting up their trees!" Daddy never dreams of a White Christmas, and has never believed in a Winter Wonderland. However, he doesn't mind that during the holidays his flower sales always increase. *Ho ho ho!*

Maman ignores Benito Scrooge and dives into the holiday spirit with zest. No other collective ritual gives her greater joy than Joyeux Noel. She spends days trimming the tree and plastering the walls with decorations. But she doesn't follow any of the native Cuban traditions, certainly not when planning the menu. She has Guadalupe prepare gallons of eggnog using a renowned *Golden Hill* recipe. There is to be no pork roast and no black beans and no fried plantains. The family will savor thin, tender slices of turkey carefully cooked in Swiss honey, dressed with rose petals and windflowers. (A feast to be consumed with the proper silver cutlery, *mais oui.*) For dessert the Domingos will be served "tartalisa," a lemon tart invented and personally baked by Maman. And as an after-dinner drink they will sip herbal tea, their pinkies pointing up as they bring the cups to their lips. *Oui oui.*

Mr. and Mrs. Domingo will exchange presents, as required by Anglo-Saxon culture, on December 25, Christmas morning. The last few years he's been giving her jewelry—no fakes—and she buys him clothes: classic suits and sport coats and ties. Normally, they thank each other with a kiss and soon thereafter focus their attention on Gina. They love to see her opening her presents; her reaction is one aspect of the holidays they both look forward to. Her effusive hugs, her excitement and joy are all the Domingos expect from their daughter by way of gifts. The true meaning of Christmas.

~~~~

Gina's list for Santa is long this year, but it always is. Heck, better to give Mr. Claus-Domingo lots of possibilities. In any case, she doesn't expect to get everything (four CDs, three movies recently released on video, shoes, and a bunch of clothes). As last Christmas, this year she'll ask for one expensive item. Just in case she gets lucky. Last December it was a video camera; on this year's list it's a computer.

She usually includes, as well, an out-of-the-question thing, something she knows she won't get, like a pet. Yeah, a Chow with a shiny black tongue and big, clumsy paws. *Jamais*, as Maman would say. Madame Elisa would never allow one of those "beasts" in the house. She had a horrible experience back in Cuba with a "fierce canine," and as a result developed an acute case of dog phobia. Even little poodles scare the hell out of her.

~~~~

Santa Domingo was magnanimous. Gina was presented with not four but six compact discs, not three but five movies, and a powerful laptop computer with a laser printer. Initially, she used the machine to do fancy graphics and prepare class assignments. Then she started to write her thoughts into a personal file named YOU, sort of like a computer log, an electronic diary. In the old days young women wrote their journals in longhand, carefully crafted feminine letters. Not anymore, thank God. Now human beings had fabulous machines that did all the dirty work. These objects helped you when you needed them but didn't force you to spend time listening to *their* problems. Ideal pals.

She liked the tweeting sound the laptop made when you turned it on and she loved the screen-saver, which was a night full of stars. Her machine kept up with the images that ran through her head. It did it all so fast! Using the computer was like talking to herself, only better. Thoughts looked sharper on the screen, for some reason. And she also loved not having to use paper until she was ready to print and have a hard copy. No waste of precious trees. But the most amazing thing about this hardware was that it allowed Gina to keep a record of her life, of who she was. The real "You," magically stored in files and hidden. Saved.

Daddy had gone to a lot of trouble to get this machine for his princess. There were many varieties of hardware on the market, most of them relatively affordable. But Benito knew little about computers so he must've done his homework. (He was partly motivated by his own need to computerize his business, which he did after this holiday season.) Daddy was such a smart shopper, well-informed, never fooled nor distracted by salespeople. All Gina had told him was that she wanted a computer to write her compositions and organize her class notes. Nothing snazzy. He didn't even need to get a CD-ROM drive; she could use the school computers for that. But when Gina opened the box she found state-of-the-art equipment, pretty expensive stuff, and gobs of info about programs available to her; programs she was expected to download and use, just *had* to use according to the manufacturers.

She hadn't taken the computer class at school because she didn't like the types it attracted: pitiful-looking boys fluent in Computerese but lacking in basic communication skills. Total nerds. So, being computer-illiterate, she spent a few hours sifting through the printed data before she could begin to play with her toy. She learned more than she needed to, but such seemed to be the goal of computer makers: overloading—and overwhelming!—users.

Gina learned that cyberspace was dense space, packed with voices and dialog chambers, exclusive clubs, shopping rooms. People communicated within a time that was faster and more linear than actual time. Letters, urgent messages, secret codes, confessions, fantasies were transmitted within the invisible walls of a space which was considered more real than real.

Did she wish to plug into the Net? It was the cool thing to do, the way most of her classmates were now communicating with the world and with each other. Didn't she just *have* to get E-mail and access to the Info Highway? Maybe. If she did, she'd never need to go to the library again, probably. She'd have a monumental library available to her in cyberspace. Doing homework would be a breeze. And by signing onto one of those real-time lines, she might meet other young people like her. There might even be a club or a dialog chamber for Cuban Americans obsessed with Cuba! No, she didn't want to share her thoughts and words with strangers, anonymous voices disguised as friends. Weirdos.

Even so, E-mail would be fun. Everyone at school was using it. She was the only one out of the loop. So what? She didn't mind being the odd man out. Odd *girl*, that is. The world within reach through the computer was vast, tempting, but she was neither ready nor willing to enter it fully yet. First she had to master the art of filmmaking, which required all her energy and talent and concentration. Besides, she thought, life is wild and weird enough already. Why add more layers to it?

The only voice she'd hear occasionally in her machine was Daddy's. More than hearing his voice, it was his handsome face she saw peeking in, snooping around the screen, checking up on her. Daddy making sure she hadn't been swallowed up, turned into an android, or infected with a technology virus. Daddy who gave her this Christmas gift on the tacit condition that he be its gate-keeper, the savior of his daughter's mind. It was Benito's presence that stopped Gina from becoming completely dependent on her computer programs and files, unable to think without them.

He was always there, offering an imaginary hand during those times when the machine shut her out because of a glitch; when it enveloped her thoughts without her knowing it; when it gave her no access to its memory bank, which, after all, was meant to be *her* memory. Daddy brought her back around to a space without which there would be no cyber-realities: the tangible world of her room. Home.

-II-

My parents have been fighting. The phrase whirled around her head for days until she saved it in a file called FAMILIA. They've been saying awful things to each other—she wrote. Things like *coño* and *carajo*, which are parts of the body, private parts if you know what I mean; *comemierda*, shit-eater; and *je m'en fou*, which is Mom's Frenchy way of saying she doesn't give a damn. Heavy stuff, words they've hardly ever used in arguments before. Something's eating at Madame and Señor Florist, and it's a pretty nasty bug!

The bug turned up, invading her home with all its nastiness one day in early April, while Gina was in her room listening to music. She heard snatches, "I don't want her in my house!" But she decided not to listen, surprised at her wish to block out the brawl. "She's coming, whether you like it or not!" Gina cranked up the volume on her CD player. "Shut up and be happy about it, *coño!*" She turned it down for an instant. "How can they let people like her into this country? Communists!" Music up. "*Carajo!*" And down. "*Je me'en fou!*" And up. And down. "I don't want her in my home!" Music low. Inaudible. "You're full of shit, Elisa! *Comemierda!*" Music blasting, blaring, blowing Gina away.

She peeked through her door and saw Daddy storm from the master bedroom and out of the house. She tiptoed down the hall-way and stopped outside her parents' room. Seconds later Maman came out, trembling, her eyes bloodshot. "I'm going out for a while," she said. "I need some fresh air."

"The air is fine in here, Maman. Stay. Talk to me."

"Later, *mignonne*. I need to do some shopping. By myself!"

Gina had been wrong about the air; it wasn't fresh at all in the house. You couldn't breathe in there! She flung open all the second-floor windows and soon a cool breeze ran through the mansion. She headed back to her room but instead went into her folks' bedroom, holding back the tears. "*Comemierda!*" she cried, angry with them for leaving her behind; angry with herself for wanting life to be a happy dream.

She liked to be left alone, but not like this, not so totally alone that it turns into lonely. She felt like singing a Retro Channel song, a light and catchy tune like a mantra. Sing about how disgustingly happy she was. In the car, at the beach, in the house, everywhere. Sing forever, like a needle on a prehistoric record, stuck on a pretty but meaningless phrase. Think about nothing, sing about pleasant things. And rock yourself.

Maman's French perfume and Daddy's aftershave lotion didn't go well together. It stunk in that room! Maman's dresser was a disaster, as if someone had messed it up on purpose. Gina pulled out one of the dresser drawers, then another, searching for clues, but found nothing. Something in one of the drawers held her attention: her Daddy's comedy albums! There were about twenty LPs, each bearing a number in lieu of a title, and all by the same comedian. Under different circumstances, this little treasure would've made Gina jump for joy. She would've run to the den, turned on the archaic turntable and listened to her heart's content. But she wasn't in the mood for Cuban jokes. So she just glanced at the fading, worn-out covers, at the dude's face displayed on all of them (which resembled her father's), and made a mental note: *Alvarez Guedes, cómico cubano.*

She then walked to the closet and inspected Maman's outfits, Daddy's ties. The clothes smelled like the room, a bittersweetness of sweat, cosmetics, and wilted roses. She looked at the glittering beads on her mother's evening dresses and noticed that they had started to dance, in a frenzy, that they were having a party at Gina's expense. The paisley ties were calling her Baby, Little Baby Princess, Baby Baby Baby!

"*Carajo!*" she screamed. "If this is war I'll go down fighting!" And she threw herself into the closet, fingernails out, like sharp teeth that ripped and ripped until the festive garments were nothing but a pile of rags on the floor. "Eat dirt!" Then she collapsed.

Is fighting okay when it's in self-defense, she wondered. How sad, even peace-loving creatures like her were drawn to war. Never again. Never again would she let herself be dragged onto a battlefield!

Pick up the dresses, Gina, she heard somebody say. *And the ties and the pants and the coats.* A woman's voice. *Now put them back one by one, the way you found them.* Gina obeyed. *That's it. Good girl.* Was she going bonkers or something? *Now do you notice the box hidden away?* Yeah, she had definitely gone bananas, over the stupid cuckoo's nest. *See it through your tears?* She couldn't see a thing! *The box, Gina, the tiny box waiting for you in your parents' closet.* Waiting for me? *Yes. See it? Let it show you its secret.*

She was freaking out, hearing things like a basket case, but at least now she knew why she'd gone into the master bedroom. Here was the reason: a brown case the size of a shoe box containing a bundle of letters; most were addressed to the Domingo family, several to Gina Domingo. Bluish, faded words on the envelopes said *Por Avión.* Huge stamps told stories of flowers, animals, athletes, people in uniform. Crooked handwriting. Yellowing sheets of cheap paper signed by Estela Ruiz de Domingo: Gina's grandmother. Wow!

In her room, the girl forgot about the battlefield, the dancing clothes, and her anger. She forgot about her parents. "*Mi querida nieta,*" she read, "*espero que al recibo de estas líneas...*" And she found herself absorbed in her grandmother's voice, tripping as she listened to this relative who'd come out of a brown box, who had emerged out of the Cuban blue.

~~~~

May this letter find you in good health, Ginita. I will try to make my writing look good for you. I didn't learn to write when I was young, but it is never too late for one to start making beautiful letters. Do you agree? Look at my d's, Gina! They all look like tiny frog heads, cabecitas de rana. And my g's! Those I call fat ballerinas because they are! Look: g. It's a plump and perky ballet dancer, una bailarina gordita, don't you think?

Soon after the Revolution, there were many young teachers who came from Havana and Camagüey to teach us country folks to read and write. Thanks to those kind people, many of us learned how to sign our names, instead of having to make an X like we had always done. And reading was like a miracle for me. All my life I had wanted to read the poetry of José Martí, and now I was able to do it at last. When I was a little girl, I memorized some of his verses, and seeing those verses on paper, and understanding them made me so happy. Have you read Martí? If you haven't, Ginita, I recommend you get his books. Can you find publications in Spanish where you live? Read "Ismaelillo," which is about the poet's beloved son.

You will be moved when you read verses like: "In the morning, my little one would wake me with a kiss. His little feet, two feet that fit so well within a kiss!" And another one . . . "This party is meant for a dwarf prince. His eyes are like black stars: They fly, they shine, they throb. They flash lightning! . . . My muse? It is a little devil with angel wings."

But as much as I loved reading Martí's poetry, writing was difficult for me, and I thought it was something I didn't need. So I gave it up. Then when you were born, I started to dream about you, Gina: your big bright eyes, your laughter, which was loud like mine and from the heart, del corazón. This was strange, because until then I had never remembered what I dreamed about. I would wake up in the morning and it would all be gone. But now, I was not only recalling my dreams but seeing them vividly during the day!

In reality, it was only one vision, like a fairy tale in which you and I were the same age, two girls belonging in different eras. But we connected from the past—where I lived—to the future, which was your time. And through this dream we were able to meet, and be friends.

And I wrote you long letters with my mind.

So I said to myself, Estela, you are going to go to school so you can use beautiful words when you write to your granddaughter some day. And I got so excited that I ended up studying at the Secundaria, taking classes for adults, and I received my diploma. Can you believe that? An old lady like me going to school like a child!

~~~~

Every letter ended with *tu abuela que te quiere, Estela.* Your grandma who loves you. How could she use the word "love"? She didn't know Gina! They did have something in common, a major something, and that was Martí's verses. Gina hadn't read the book Abuela mentioned but she loved his *Versos sencillos*. Yeah, she was definitely a fan of the Apostle. And maybe poetry was a good place to start, a way to begin relating.

But then, that bit about the dream was just too weird. How can that woman imagine me just like that, Gina wondered. *Your big bright eyes, your laughter, loud like mine.* How can a stranger think "me" up without even knowing what I look like?

Sad as it was, she didn't feel anything for her grandmother. Not yet. Maybe never? The Cuban woman was a bunch of words on paper, unskilled writing, hard-to-read Spanish sentences. You don't start loving a person in the blink of an eye, even if that person happens to be your father's mother. *Tu abuela que te quiere.*

Gina called up the YOU file and entered: DAY OF THE FIGHT. I was mad at my parents 'cause they were yelling at each other, then they left and I was gonna set the house on fire. So I went into their bedroom, that's the place I wanted to burn first. And suddenly out of nowhere pops up this box full of letters that my mother had hidden away in her closet and you'll never guess that those letters were written by my Cuban grandmother!

I know it was Maman who hid them. Who else? She's so strange. Like she thinks she's French you know. But Daddy told me that it's just a head trip, that my mom is more Cuban than the ceiba tree (but isn't the palm tree the Cubanest of all?), and that she's never even been to Paris. You wouldn't believe the acts she puts on in her room when she thinks she's alone. Maman tells herself unbelievable stories. And I say "unbelievable" because, believe me, nobody would believe my mother! Stuff about her royal family and about the spirit of some French writer who speaks through her and about how special she is and how her mission in life is to educate Daddy and me.

The thing is, whenever Maman gets into one of her French moods and starts talking about her blue blood, Dad gives her this look like he's saying to her—You're full of it, honey. Then he winks at me and smiles and I just know he's telling me she's off her rocker all the way. And I always feel sorry for Mom and mad at Dad for thinking that Mom is a lunatic, and for making fun of her right there in front of me. Poor dog-fearing Madame. *La pauvre!* Then I feel guilty 'cause sometimes I laugh behind her back about the fact that she's in Loony Land instead of France. Can't handle all this guilt!

~~~~

Your cousins are curious about you, mi niña. I tell them that you're probably curious about them, too. They are good kids. I argue with them sometimes, above all with Bladimir, because he wants expensive clothes and modern machines. I understand his wishes. Young people always want material things. But Bladi doesn't know how hard it was for us before. He has no idea.

Look at your Papá, for example. It's a miracle he got to learn a good profession at all. We wanted him to go to the university, but that was beyond our means. So my boy learned everything he knows all by himself. Nitín (that's what I used to call him) had a talent for sales ever since he was little. He would sell colorful marbles to his friends and empty bottles and shirt buttons and even toys that he built himself. And that's what he did when his father died, sell things, without anyone to show him how.

I think about your Papi's youth and I can't help laughing and crying at the same time. A skinny boy like him loading up his bicycle with boniato and malanga that we grew ourselves, food that he would sell to the merchants in town. Proud of himself and happy that he could bring home a little money, un dinerito.

I am grateful to the divine powers that it has gone well for Nitín in his life. He deserves the good fortune. And I am grateful to him for sending me things like shoes and clothes. But I've always said to him in my letters, just like I tell you, mi niña, that I prefer to receive a few words now and then, unas palabras. Maybe some photographs. I would like that more than things. Will you write to me some day, Gina?

~~~~

The nervously written text mesmerized her. She was so entranced by Estela's writing that she didn't hear Maman's footsteps. Elisa barged in and whisked a bundle of letters off the bed.

"Where did you find these?"

"In your closet. Where else?"

"How dare you go through my things?"

"And how dare you hide these letters from me?"

"They don't belong to you."

"Some of them do! They're from my grandma. You had no right, Maman."

"You don't understand."

"This is why you've always had a P.O. box, isn't it? So that I'd never get my hands on my *own* mail!"

Elisa held one of the envelopes as though it were a soiled rag or a dead rodent. "I didn't want you to be burdened by your grandmother's problems."

"What problems?"

"Well, for example . . . Never mind!"

"Shame on you, Maman."

"You wouldn't have been able to read her writing. Just look. It is full of misspellings. *C'est affreux!*"

Gina picked a letter at random and read it in its entirety. "There," she said, "I can read and understand every word. So I get to keep them."

As if on cue, Elisa replied that certainly, she'd get to keep the ones addressed to Gina Domingo. But on one condition: that she never tell her father about the distasteful subject of Estela's "missives." Not a word of her discovery. "This is to be our secret," she admonished. And Gina assented, hoping her mother would leave her alone. "Okay. Mum's the word."

~~~~

Your cousins are very studious; like you, I am sure. They want to study at the University of Havana. Tatiana says that maybe she'll be a surgeon, so she can do operations on people. She says she will operate on me some day, that she will fix my heart. And I tell her that my heart needs no fixing. Imagine that, Gina, my sister's granddaughter playing surgeon with my body!

What about you, mi niña, what do you want to be when you grow up? Bladimir has decided he's going to make movies, films about his family and about his country. Filmmaking is not a very practical profession in Cuba, and I'm afraid the government might discourage it. But if Bladi really wants to study film, he will. That boy has talent. I only hope he learns not to complain so much about the way things are. One should be grateful for the good one has, for the really fine things. Like the love of your family.

Bladi says he's going to show the problems of our country in his movies. That way we can make changes and improve our lives. And I tell him that that is a wonderful idea. I only hope he doesn't suffer too much when he realizes that some of our problems have no solutions.

That niño has such a spirit for adventure! He wants to travel and then come back to Cuba, a man of experience and tales of the world. He wants to visit you, Ginita! The boy says he'll take an airplane, show up at your house, knock on your door, and give you a big surprise. And a big hug.

I must confess I have the same wish. What I would give to be able to appear at your door and surprise you!

~~~~

Gina took the time to translate the letters, saving them in a file named CARTAS. (The *Ismaelillo* verses gave her some trouble; poetry was hard enough to read, let alone translate.) Over all, her grandmother sounded happy. She said, among many other things, that she spent a lot of time at home because she liked her house. Estela enjoyed taking care of children and so she worked in a daycare center three days a week, as a *voluntaria*. Spending time with the little ones and reading to them gave her a sense of being useful; it was also very rewarding, she said.

As Gina worked on CARTAS, she tried to figure out what the "problems" were that Maman had referred to. Abuela mentioned *problemas* that had no solutions. Was the old lady being philosophical or something? Did she mean huge universal problems like loneliness and violence, or specific Cuban ones like Fidel and communism?

Excited by the mystery, Gina entered the following thoughts in her YOU file: Are there meanings between the lines that I'm not getting? Did my grandmother write these "missives" in a secret code? What *is* her problem?! If my mother hates my grandma (and I know she does), why didn't she get rid of the letters? Why didn't she just burn them? Maybe she was afraid the smoke would invoke evil Cuban spirits. Nah! Let's give her a dramatic motive, one worthy of a Pinos Verdes Wife, fit for *Living Stage*. Okay, here it is: Grandma's letters are the only ties Maman has with the Island; they're a bizarre and shameful (cool word) sort of connection. Her parents are dead, right? She has no relatives back there. So that's it, that's her motive: somehow the letters keep her in touch with Cuba. But why would she want any kind of connection with the Island? She hates that "inferno"!

Gina set her imagination free, confident that her creative self—rather than her analytical persona—would give this conundrum a logical, believable resolution. Letting her scriptwriting take flight, she saw an apartment in suburban Los Angeles . . .

Interior. Day. Modest decor: plastic-covered furniture, Bargain-Mart knickknacks. Elisa Domingo is holding her newborn baby, wearing a blue polyester dress and high heels (she likes to be elegantly attired all the time, even at home). Her husband Benito (curly black hair, handsome, thin mustache) is about to leave for work. He's capturing Mother and Child with his Polaroid, the Classic Shot. Action!

BENITO: We need to tell the family back home.

ELISA: (*She clucks at tiny Gina.*) I don't have a family back home.

BENITO: You know what I mean.

ELISA: Yes, I'm afraid I do.

BENITO: Let's not get into this again, Elisa.

ELISA: You brought it up.

BENITO: We should send out some birth announcements.

ELISA: There's no hurry. (*She sticks a bottle in Gina's mouth.*) As you can see, I have more important things to do.

BENITO: (*He tickles the baby.*) I'll call my mother this weekend. I hope I can get through. Imagine how happy she's going to be! (*He makes funny faces, croons.*) Kookie-boo-boo, Ginita.

ELISA: (*Sarcastic*) Yes, call your *dear* mother, give her the good news.

BENITO: (*to Gina*) Your Daddy has to go to work now, princess. He has to make lots of money so he can build you a castle.

ELISA: But I'd like to make something absolutely clear.

BENITO: Kookie-boo-boo . . .

ELISA: Listen to me, Benito!

BENITO: Okay, Okay. I'm listening.

ELISA: Life begins for us now, with this baby.

BABY: (*Voice-over, of course*) What?! Do something, Dad! Don't just stand there with your Kookie-boo-boo face! Fight back!

ELISA: Whatever came before her doesn't exist anymore. It's all gone.

BENITO: I don't know what you're talking about.

BABY: Yeah, Dad! You tell her!

ELISA: You know perfectly well what I'm saying.

BENITO: Fine. Whatever.

BABY: (*to Benito*) Hey, dude, what's your problem? Can't you see what's happening here? Don't let your wife have the last word!

ELISA: So you agree with me, then?

BABY: Okay, Dad, this is your chance. Run with it!

BENITO: Yes, yes, whatever you say, Elisa.

BABY: But, Dad, Ginita wants to know, she needs to know what came before!

ELISA: Wonderful. I'm glad that we agree.

BABY: Your daughter's gonna have an inquiring mind!

ELISA: (*She kisses the baby.*) Life begins today.

BABY: *Not!*

-III-

She picked up the phone in her room and coughed gently. Then Daddy's voice blasted her away. He asked what she was waiting for, and told her to greet her Abuela. Gina timidly complied. Her grandmother laughed and then informed her, in awfully fast and choppy Spanish, that she was coming to visit. The Cuban woman called her *Mi niña* (my little girl) and wished her a happy fifteenth birthday. Gina said *Gracias* and explained—just for the record—that her birthday had been the previous week, the first week in May, a whole long week ago. The lady said she knew that, of course, but that she still wanted to wish her *Feliz cumpleaños*. After two failed attempts at conversation and too many pauses, Gina told her grandma *Buen viaje!* and hung up.

Such an unprecedented event would call for a family moment with hugs and kisses and some tears. Or silence during which all three Domingos looked at each other with meaningful glances and the background music turned mellow: strings and flutes, subdued synthesizers. Daddy's mother was coming to visit and, although he'd never said much about her, Gina was sure he'd be blown away by his emotions.

She hurried to her folks' bedroom to join in the celebration. Alas, an unexpected show awaited her! On her way to the room, she heard an angry babble coming from downstairs. It was her mother's voice, but the tone and the pitch didn't scan; something wasn't quite normal. Gina stopped outside her parents' bedroom, at the top of the stairs, and tried to locate the source of the weird sound. She didn't have to look far: Elisa was sitting a few steps below, clad in her silk nightgown. It looked as though she'd intended to walk down to the first floor and had decided to take a break halfway there.

Daddy's laughter came through the door in waves, combined with pauses and loud Cuban words. The phone call had triggered three simultaneous scenes. One: Benito on the phone in his bedroom. Two: the teenager standing, observing her mother who sat a short distance below, on the steps. Three: Elisa talking to herself. The simultaneity of these actions was dizzying, as Gina tried to grasp the meaning of it all, somehow.

She rushed back to her room and grabbed the camera. First, a panning shot of the hallway leading to the bedroom door (she peered through, catching Dad's teary eyes). Then another pan job leading to Maman. Her back was to the camera so there wouldn't be a close-up. But her voice came through loud and clear. Gina's imaginary lens took over and gave the voice a head, a mouth, a much older face because her mother had become an elderly version of Elisa. Weird!

"We are finally going to be together, Benitín," the old Madame cried out. "It's been such a long time, my dear boy. An eternity!" She wiped away fake tears with her gown and resumed her act with: "How are you, my son? Yes, yes, I'm fine, doing well, considering." Silence. "No, I don't need anything. Only your time and your heart and your peace of mind and your freedom!" Silence. "No, don't bother putting Elisa on, I don't wish to talk to her. She must be very busy at her vanity, no? I can almost see her, taking off layers and layers of makeup. Her royal mask! Ha!"

Maman's impersonation of Estela was turning macabre. Gina didn't want this footage after all. "Time is up, Benitín!" said Elisa, the creepy impostor, and stood up. "Gotta go march with the troops! The Revolution calls. Need to go stand in line!"

Madame was slowly coming up toward her daughter, mumbling, but Camerawoman wouldn't stop filming. "Gotta go stand in line!" Her mother would be furious but Gina couldn't help filming her as she moved holding on to the rail, acting and looking decrepit. "Stand in line at the store to buy manure! It's fresh out of the oven and going fast! *Adiós*, Benitín. I will be with you soon, my boy!"

Face to face, they froze. Why didn't Maman say something, anything? She was supposed to be screaming her lungs out, ordering Gina to turn the damned thing off, destroy the tape, the incriminating evidence. She was supposed to grab the camera and throw it down the stairs in one sweeping, melodramatic gesture. Instead she just stood there, glaring at her daughter. Gina had never been caught so red-handed. She had no good excuses, no logical arguments to explain what she'd been doing.

Daddy burst out of the room and found his wife and daughter by the door, two lifeless figures in a wax museum. He grabbed them both, kissing them clumsily. Maman pulled away, not even trying to fake a smile, and asked, "When is your mother coming?"

"In two or three weeks. It's out of my hands now, I've done my part—"

"That soon?" Maman interrupted. "Sufficient time, I suppose, to have a room prepared for her. I'd better start immediately."

There were no meaningful glances and no symphonic strings in crescendo. No plans for celebrating. No close-ups of the happy family. But there were tears in Daddy's eyes. "Three weeks!" he kept saying.

~~~~

Madame shouldn't allow it, not even a short summer visit. But there's nothing to be done now. Put up with her, that's the only alternative; endure her loudness and hick ways, her lack of finesse, of proper manners. Not to mention the fact that the woman is a Santera or a spiritist or both, and in Elisa's book this is tantamount to being a witch. *Mon Dieu!*

Her wish to put distance between Benito and his mother was fulfilled thanks to Castro and his low-class guerrillas. The Domingos would emigrate to the far North, leaving the old hag behind. What a splendid way to be rid of her! And what a stroke of luck when Estela announced that she was staying, that she would never abandon her country. The natural decision for an illiterate farmwoman like her. Of course she would take advantage of the so-called People's Revolution, wallow in her own dirt, along with all the other *canaille*. Of course she'd become a vile communist!

Through the years, that loathsome Marxist has written numerous letters, all full of misspellings and hackneyed phrases, of cheap political rhetoric. But luckily many of those missives never reached their destination. Now things have changed overnight. Elisa is having to face one of her innermost fears: that one day Estela would manage to break the laws of time and reappear, destroying the peace of the Domingos' present.

Why are they letting those people leave the island? How can it be so easy for them to get a visa? She's heard the news: Not only are they letting older communists come to the United States, but their visits are encouraged! The American government is the seat of great minds. But its leaders are so naive at times, so infantile. Beware, *les enfants!*

Until now, Benito's mother has been thousands of miles away from Pinos Verdes, on some unreachable planet called Cuba. Yet that distant alien world, Elisa knew all along, was always as close as a phone call. The planet's incipient life forms are capable of planning invasions. An invading alien is bound for Pinos Verdes with one mission implanted in its wicked brain cells: Eliminate the oldest members of the family and abduct the youngest!

She has tried to keep her feelings to herself, putting on a smile and saying as little as possible whenever the topic was "the witch." She doesn't want to hurt Benito, not really. He knows how she feels, no need to rub it in. But Elisa Rochart de Domingo can no longer mask her fright and her disdain. She can't go on acting, pretending for the sake of her husband. She must protect Gina, save her baby from the monster's claws!

~~~~

"Your grandmother will be visiting us," announces Maman in Gina's room.

"She sure is," says the girl. "I got to talk to her. She told me."

"There are certain things you should know about Estela," states Madame in a drama-laden voice. The obvious parody of a character in *Living Stage.*

"Yeah? Like what?" Gina is impersonating a Retro show teenager, but with a bit of a Nineties edge.

"Your grandmother is not like us."

"So?"

Madame vacillates. Then, having chosen to be cunning and ruthless, she answers, "Estela spent her youth on a farm, living among beasts."

"Beasts? You mean like farm animals? That's kinda groovy."

"'Groovy,' you say," reacts Madame, mocking Gina's impoverished lexicon. "Oh, *ma petite.* It is quite apparent that you don't know the implications."

No Retro-Channel adolescent would ever take loaded grown-up words like "implications" seriously. Gina comes back, smiling. "Don't sweat it, Mom. Just be happy."

"The problem is, my darling . . ."

"Always a problem. You're such a drip!"

Elisa finds the word "drip" repulsive; she detects a certain tone of condescension. "That attitude of yours won't work with me, *jeune fille!*"

"You're the one with an attitude, Maman."

"Will you listen to me for a moment?" She sits on the side of the bed.

"Do I have to?" Gina is at her desk, trying to look busy.

"Your paternal grandmother will be permitted to visit the United States."

"I know that already."

The girl turns on her laptop. It makes a high-pitched sound that obviously upsets Elisa. But Madame goes on, unfazed:

"She's going to be staying with us for about two months."

"Will you get to the point? I've got a lot of homework."

"Gina, you need to be prepared."

"I do?" She's typing gibberish, amused by the nonsense that appears on the screen.

"There will be inconveniences."

"Don't worry about it."

"Estela will rearrange things, our personal belongings. She'll meddle in our lives."

"God, it's not like she's moving in for good."

"And she'll want to cook for us!"

"What's wrong with that?" Gina stops typing and grabs a notebook, pretends to be transcribing her notes. "I'd love to have some Cuban food for a change."

"You know how I feel about the Island's cuisine."

Madame leaps to her feet, determined to inspect Gina's screen; her daughter blocks it with her hands.

"Yeah, yeah. It's fattening."

"Heavy on the animal fat, cloyingly sweet, unhealthy."

"There you go again. You're repeating yourself, Maman."

"Life will be different with your grandmother around, Gina."

"It's just a little old lady who's coming to visit. Why are you making such a big deal?" She saves the nonsense file and the screen becomes a starry night.

"I know Estela." Madame paces the room, desperately searching for something to fix her eyes on.

"Yeah. Let me guess: You don't want us to be bothered by her *problems.*"

"Indeed. I would definitely consider her altar and her rituals a problem!"

"Her altar?" Gina turns to her mother, who's surveying the CD collection, looking slightly dismayed. "What rituals?"

"I'm not all that well-versed in her disgusting practices. I can only talk about the things she's put your father and me through."

"Like what?" The girl jumps onto her bed, grabs a pillow, brings it to her face, and takes in the clean scent.

"Once she asked me to collect some of my urine for her, so she could use it to make a fertility potion."

Madame sits next to her daughter. Too close for comfort, thinks Gina.

"I don't believe you."

"And another time she requested a tuft of your father's pubic hair. She wanted to make a charm that he was to wear in his undershorts, so he would have a strong seed."

"You're making this up!" Gina covers her face with her pillow, then throws the pillow on the floor, enraged.

"No, dear. Benito's mother is a Santera. Do you know what that means?"

"I sure do. I saw a movie about Santeras once."

"Oh, Lord, it would be horrible if that woman . . ."

"What?" She retrieves the pillow, hugs it.

"If she . . ." Elisa clasps her hands, her eyes turned up imploringly.

"Go on, Maman!"

"Oh, *chérie.* I should . . ." She places her right hand on her chest, a gesture vividly culled from *Living Stage.*

"You should what?"

"I will forbid Estela to . . ."

"Never mind, I don't wanna hear it."

"But you must, Gina." Elisa stands up suddenly. "You must!"

"Forget it."

"As you wish." Madame walks to the door. "We will talk later, then."

"Do we have to?"

"Yes, we do."

"If you say so." Gina stretches out on the bed. "But first I'm gonna take a long, long nap!"

~~~~

Scenes from a movie about Santería replay in Gina's mind at fast-forward speed. Judging from what she saw in that horror flick, Santería is revoltingly uncool. Santeras, also known as Iyalochas, are Afro-Caribbean women who sacrifice innocent creatures like bunnies, pussycats, and puppies, to powerful gods (known as *santos*) in disgusting bloody rites. Sick!

She should've read that library book on the subject. If she had, now she could counteract Hollywood's bogus version with facts. Scientific evidence for the defense, some unbiased truth. You just can't base your whole approach to this incredible topic on a category-three movie, not even.

There's always the possibility that her grandma isn't an evil Santera at all. Maman could have easily made up this whole spooky yarn just to turn Gina against her. But even if Estela is an Iyalocha for real, why should she have to hide it? Santería can't be as gross as Hollywood makes it out to be. It's more like a religion, and no one should be denied the right to practice their religion. (Gina's opinion of this topic notwithstanding.) Maman's demands are unfair. What she's planning to do is rude. And not very PC.

Some fresh welcome! In order to live with her family for a measly eight weeks, Estela has to stick her *santos* up her dot-dot-dot. But why should Abuela's saints be less worthy of worship than the ones that gave ASHS its name? Doesn't that phrase, "All Saints High School," refer democratically to *all* saints, Afro-Caribbean ones included? Or is there a racist criteria for deciding who deserves to be holy? How does the Catholic Church define sainthood, anyway? Judging from Maman's view, some saintly beings are left out in the cold, kicked out of Heaven for being Cuban. Unfair!

Gina Domingo won't let Elisa Rochart get her way. As of this moment, she's electing herself Head of the Welcoming Committee. Her job: first, to make sure the Cuban lady doesn't suspect

Madame's questionable approach to hostessing; second, to show the guest a great time in Califusa. Last, but definitely not least: to open her welcoming arms, to kiss the face behind the words she read in all those letters; to touch the hands that wrote them and hear the author's voice, an actual voice. *Abuela.*

That's the word she'll use to address her. *Abuela* means grandmother, a woman who claims to love Gina without ever having seen her, without knowing her. The word doesn't mean problems or demonic rites, but a woman who learned how to write so she could write to Gina. So she could send her beautiful *palabras*, tiny frog heads and plump ballerinas, simple verses. So she could tell her of a dream.

Chapter 4

-I-

Gina's fantasy life is not a topic she has discussed with her parents. They don't like to think she has such a life! There's only one issue, closely related to this topic, that Daddy has addressed at length. And that's "Boyfriends." He's been utterly explicit about that whole area. His princess will be allowed to date only educated, clean-cut, and well-dressed Caucasian boys. There are to be no Vatos, Blacks, Asians, Arabs, Punks, Marielitos, Grungies, Neohippies and no Skinheads, to name just a few of the forbidden types.

The Princess never had a boyfriend until Robby came into the picture. There had been prospects, but none amounted to much: Javier, the exchange student from Spain who turned out to be too popular and too full of himself. All girls at ASHS lusted after him and he could have any of them in ways Gina didn't wish to be had. So no chance there. Then she flirted with Peter the Cybercalifo, who wasn't easy on the eyes but who seemed smart and sensitive at first. After talking to him a few times, though, Gina realized he was a flake. Peter would surely turn her—if given the chance—into a cyber character, a brainless damsel-in-distress trapped in an interactive story written, packaged, and sold through the Net for a huge profit. No way!

The third suitor was an angel. He was *the* guy. Well, almost. One Sunday morning a young Jehovah's Witness knocked at Gina's door. He gazed at her with heavenly eyes and she was doomed. It was Dig at First Peek. He was cute in a Fifties sort of way (never mind his sixty-percent-polyester suit and his clip-on tie). The preacher started showing up on weekends to bring the "Truth" to the Domingos. (Apparently, he lived in Pinos Verdes, or he wouldn't have been allowed through the gate.) Gina always gladly received his *Watchtower*; she would sneak to Maman's garden and meet him there, greet him warmly, clasp his hand with a lingering grip, before inviting him in.

Is God trying to tell me something, she wondered. And she asked herself in the YOU file: Is this the Path I am to follow?

'Cause you know I'm willing to do the right thing if that's what it takes. The religious thing, I mean. Church and Bible study and sermons and preaching. The whole shebang. Even if it goes against my character. Could I? Would I be rewarded with the love of a gorgeous perfect male creature? Sinful girl. Repent! You'd have to do it out of true faith, not out of lust! Which can always be arranged you know 'cause I do believe in God . . . Wow. You could build a major heavy movie around this whopper of a conflict. Titles to consider: *Flesh and Soul; Your Spirit, My Body; Watchtowers of the Heart; For the Sake of Love.*

Daddy was curious, it seemed, about the stories this so-called Witness was telling. Elisa never paid much attention to him, but Gina and Benito listened to the "Word" for a while. The young man spoke of a place here on Earth where all of God's creatures would some day coexist, eternally happy. Lions would cease to be carnivorous and would graze next to zebras. The dead would rise and rejoin the living. (Only a select few would be resurrected, of course: the Witnesses.) No more death, sickness, violence.

He showed them pictures, art with an old-fashioned look about it, as though the images had been conceived back in the Sixties or Seventies and never updated. All races were represented, in their traditional folkloric garb, and most of the people were grouped in families with small children.

Gina liked the soothing, calming sound of this utopia: Heaven right here on the planet, solid and earthy, not an abstract castle full of sexless spirits and intangible angels. Yet there was something dubious about such a promise of salvation. The preacher seemed sincere; Gina wanted to believe in his words for his sake, to please him, to make him like her. But she couldn't. For one thing, his deity was too much like the Catholic god: a powerful *male* entity who wanted to be worshiped, followed, believed, adored, idolized. If you didn't worship-follow-believe-adore-idolize Him, he could turn vicious. *I'LL SHOW YOU WHO'S IN CHARGE AROUND HERE!* He'd condemn you to darkness and oblivion, and you'd never be reunited with your loved ones in the Afterlife. No second chances. Never ever.

Having serious doubts about Mr. Jehovah and His promised paradise, Gina asked questions: "Why is it that only Witnesses will survive the Armageddon? Catholics and Mormons and Protestants and Buddhists won't be saved? Do the rest of us go up to Heaven while you guys play Adam-and-Eve down here? I guess that'd make sense, since I figure the planet's gonna be awfully crowded with all the dead Witnesses being resurrected and all . . .

"What do you mean there's no Heaven? Are you sure? So if I'm not a Witness, forget about eternity? Bummer! But how do you know you got the real scoop? If I spend my life doing good deeds and never hurt a fly, shouldn't I be allowed to live in your magic kingdom, too?"

He insisted that only by studying the Bible would Gina have a chance to enter New Eden. She needed to go to meetings at the Kingdom Hall, and spread the Truth from door to door, on Sundays. There was a lot for her to learn and do before she'd be accepted, before she could have a baptism by water like the one John the Baptist gave Jesus. But once the Witnesses embraced her and welcomed her, she'd live forever, and forever be a Witness to Jehovah's dominion. Amen.

The young man told the Domingos to stop celebrating birthdays, since only the birth of Jehovah's Son was deserving of festivities. And Gina informed him that she hadn't really celebrated her latest (she had just turned fifteen) since all she did was eat cake. Did that count as a celebration? "Yes, it does," he replied. "You should never even think about your birth." And Gina thought, Party Pooper! The Witness also told the Domingos never to donate blood or accept transfusions. "Blood is synonymous with life," he said, "and only God Jehovah can give it or deny it." He urged the family not to go to Mass. "The Catholic church is wicked, full of demons," he pontificated. "Every one of its effigies, pictures, and statues of saints is a representation of the devil. You must believe me!"

Things had definitely gotten out of hand. That diatribe about the Catholic demons was the Witness' last sermon; Benito just couldn't take his biblical babble anymore. Obviously, Gina's potential savior was nuts! Daddy sent him packing one Sunday morning with: "We've heard enough of your nonsense, kid. Too much already! We're Catholic in this house and right now we need to get ready for Mass. You want to come along, pay a little visit to Mister Lucifer? Oh, and by the way, my daughter attends All Saints High, did you know that? It's a school where they teach boys and girls to grow horns and pointy tails, to set fires, and to scare the living daylights out of crazy twerps like you!"

~~~~

Robert Holmes loves the beach and likes to wear shorts in psychedelic colors. Gina thinks he's a dream: tall, blonde, blue eyes, tough yet sensitive. A big plus in his favor is that, although he's a Senior and entitled to the corresponding privileges, Robby never sits at the Senior table and doesn't hang out with the Pale Pious bunch. He's friendly and talks to Freshmen, Sophomores, and Juniors alike. Strangely enough, the Califos don't pick on him for mingling with the lower classes. It's evident that they envy him his looks, fear him for his toughness, and just leave him alone.

Gina has indulged in a great deal of daydreaming about Rob . . . *Months of detailed preparation and rising suspense ended Friday night when Gina Domingo and Robert Holmes were crowned Queen and King of Homecoming. Long live the King and Queen! The following question was posited to students in all classes: What do you think of Robby and Gina? The unanimous response was: "Cool." Ms. Domingo and Mr. Holmes are, indeed, the coolest monarchs to have ever ruled at All Saints. She is beautiful and smart and ethnically correct besides. He is amicable and genuinely Ramosean and oh so very handsome. Long live King Holmes and Queen Domingo!*

The day she decided Rob was going to be "the one," her obligatory high school sweetheart, Gina was taking a break from shopping with Maman. They had gone to the Zone for a snack at Chilly's Frozen Yogurt. Elisa was nibbling at her usual low-fat chocolate with marshmallow topping, and Gina was gobbling down the Chill-Out Special: two mounds of lush vanilla with cherries, caramel fudge, whipped cream, and a dash of chopped almonds. When Robby made his stellar appearance, she put her spoon down delicately (how else?), and made an effort not to melt like yogurt scoops under the sun. Oh my God! Dream Rob at Chilly's and there she was, witnessing his entrance. The Surfer in person, the raddest bod in All Saints High. He looked so good in nouveau-hippie clothes!

She instantly thought of a picture that was taken at the School Fair: Robby's walking in front of Gina, looking to die for, to kiss the ground he walks on. And the school paper's photographer catches Rob as he strides, his profile in full view, and Gina behind him going cross-eyed and holding her head, Oh my God oh my God! Robby-and-Gina captured forever: the Compromising

Photograph, a view of their soon-to-be-shared destiny. Together till eternity passes away it's you and me kid guess you got stuck with Ms. Domingo!

She walked to the water fountain, and slowly quenched her thirst while watching Husky Psychie. On her way to the table she passed by him. "Hey, Rob," she said; he turned around. "Hey, Gina! What's up?" She licked off some minuscule drops of cold water that had gathered on her upper lip. "Nothing much, just shopping with Mom." She noticed he'd ordered the Chill-Out combo, too. He grabbed the creamy treat, paid for it, and galloped away.

Gina left the Zone feeling dazed, and ready for the dig of her life.

~~~~

Two weeks later, we see her as she sees herself: at Ramosa Beach, sliding her hand down Robby's arm. "The hair on your arms is invisible," she tells him, "you have to touch it to know it's there." He keeps silent as she turns her attention to his thighs, tanned and warm. "Does your skin hurt?" she asks. "It looks like it'd hurt." And he says that he *never* gets burned. Then she proceeds to caress his lips, his closed eyelids, and his nose. She runs her index finger down his chest, following the love trail to his belly button and there she stops, afraid that he'll ask her to continue down on her journey of discovery.

Can he read her body the way she can read his? *Your carnal self is a path to your soul, a mirror image of your spirit!* There's this tickling sensation going from the nape of her neck to her groin, and a feeling of flooding down there. "As God is my witness!" she cries to herself, trying to be who she wants to be. "As God is my witness! I'll never do it till I'm married!"

Now and then Rob touches her, or throws handfuls of sand on her tummy. When she's tanning face down, he lets his lips travel up and down her back, killing her softly with his tongue. He rubs his muscular physique against her and puts his arms over her, as though she were his pillow. Gina feels something hard (an erection!) and that's when the beach party comes to an abrupt end. She brushes the sand off her body, picks up her towel, and says, "Give me some space, dude!"

"You don't dig me?"

"I'm too young to dig anybody and so are you."

He makes a little-boy face. "Maybe we could just pretend."

"No. Just cool it."

Then he yells, loud and clear so that all the surfers and the other sun-worshipers and the lifeguard can hear, "But I wanna be your man, Gina! I love you!" She covers her ears and shuts her eyes, wishing to become a tiny crab so she can dig a hole in the sand and vanish. Swoosh! "You don't believe me?" he asks, kneeling at her feet. "Do you want me to say it again?"

"No. Not again!"

"Okay then," he says, and runs to the water.

~~~~

He's waving at her as the white foam crowns his blonde mane. Gina obeys an impulse to swim out to his salty arms, and soon the water feels warm, the way she imagines it feels on the Island. She makes a splash, tugging away playfully, and wonders what making love to Rob would be like. She envisions the two of them on a deserted beach, scampering along the shore, naked, through the guayacán trees; two lovers taking on new names and new identities, being anyone and anything they wish to be.

She swims away from him, hoping he'll run after her and catch her. When he does, pleased that she's playing this game, Gina hears herself say, "You *are* my dude, Robby." He dives into the water, then picks her up and carries her out, placing her on the sand. He stretches out and looks at her with puppy-dog eyes, fulfilled and self-assured. Gina digs him!

Meanwhile the lady who was carried in her adoring lover's arms is wondering why she uttered those hokey words. And how she could've let Robby drag her out of the water like she was a wounded mermaid or worse, a sack of seaweed. She has to do something, but what?

The scene is drenched in summer-flick magic, but it is Gina's obligation, her virginal duty to crush the dude's amorous outbursts. She represses an urge to slap him so he can wake up to reality, to throw sand in his eyes and tell him, Listen here, Tanned Skin, forget what I said 'cause I sure didn't mean it. I ain't budging. No sex. You got that? Not even the safe kind. So I'm a tease. Tough!

~~~~

She'd like to go for a walk along the beach, alone. Just a short walk, she says to Rob, and asks him to please guard the Boom Box. "Sure, whatever you want." He's *so* eager to please.

Is this what I want, she asks herself as she strolls along. An impossible dig, just like the ones you see on the screen. The answer is No. But it's what she got! Because she's breaking the law by meeting him here, secretly. Because Cuban American Princesses, no matter how modern and liberated, aren't allowed to be out with their boyfriends without a chaperon. Definitely not if they're Catholic. Absolutely forbidden. *As God is my witness!*

But what's so sinful about going to the mall or the beach with a friend? With a *boy* friend: a significant detail. Daddy would find him okay if he met him, as long as Rob didn't wear his psychie shorts and didn't talk about surfing. Maman already saw him at Chilly's and described him as a handsome, if a tad underdressed, *jeune homme.* Yes, Gina can invite him to the house, her parents would tell her. Robert Holmes seems like a decent American boy. She has their permission. Rent a movie, they'd say, make popcorn. Enjoy yourselves. But beware! Somebody's always watching.

She walks to the Hermosa pier and back to their spot, hoping to find Rob there, waiting for her. And he is, with the Boom Box cranked up and tuned to a rock station. She sits next to him.

"Robby, are you happy?"

"You bet! Happier than I've ever been."

She can't help thinking that this All-American Surfer doesn't talk the way he's supposed to.

"And why is that?"

"Because," he says, sounding more typically Ramosean. "Because, because," he hems and haws. "Do I have to have a reason?"

"What do you mean when you say you're happy, anyway?"

He draws near her and touches her hair. "Happy . . ." he's thinking hard, "that's when everything works out great. When you get what you want."

Gina senses the Cuban American Princess surging up, welling up inside her. She hears her saying, "So you think you *got* me, huh? Like hell you do!"

Robby sticks his fingers deep in the sand and comes back with a handful. "I'm sick of this game, Gina," he tells her, and plunges into the waves.

~~~~

She's waiting for him with a hot dog and a soft drink: her peace offering, an attempt to soften the blow of reality, the dear-john news she's about to hit him with. Robby seems grateful for the wiener. He must've been starving. "Mustard?" "Sure." "Catsup?" "Yeah."

"Robby, I've got something to tell you." She notices the mustard running down the side of his mouth. "I think you're a neat guy."

"Neat?" The word seems to drown in his greasy lips.

"Yeah. I think you're groovy."

"Groovy?" Another drowning one-word question.

"You're one of the coolest, sweetest guys I've ever dated." A little white lie won't hurt: she never actually dated anyone before him. "The problem is . . ." And she searches for the right phrase. "Our dig is big, but–"

"Yep, real big," he cuts in. He's finished his dog and is staring at hers.

"You want mine? I've only taken one bite." His eyes light up. "Here, you can have it."

At last feeling freed from the stench of the cheap wiener, Gina can carry out her mission. Only now she's lost all her steam. What's her mission, anyway? Breaking up with Rob?

She tries, again, to call up the precise words. *Absolutely forbidden.* But now they sound flat and empty, like a line a character would say in a beach-party movie from the Fifties. Or in a *Living Stage* production. So she decides to postpone the scene indefinitely.

There has to be a more inventive way to break the news to Robby. Whatever the news is supposed to be.

-II-

She sees herself opening the bedroom window, running the risk of being struck by lightning, and giving herself to the cold, blustery night, to the rain that falls on her lips and her eyes. A shaft of lightning pierces the dark clouds, framing her silhouette with burning hands. Her long black hair rages with the wind. Her robe billows around her.

She walks back in, having the unsettling sensation that she's moving through fog . . . What is this place? She smells the surroundings, searching for air that she can recognize. Her body feels heavy. She yearns for the time when she ran through the valleys and across the prairies faster than even the fastest animals. *Singing and praying time.*

Where is that sound coming from? It seems to be inside her head. A song. A baby crying. Then it's like howling. She bumps against large, massive objects. Exhausted, she sits on the floor again and sees a way out. The light, a long trek toward the light.

Her creatures are gone! Her wooden animals and stone goddesses have disappeared. Is the brook outside? How far? She raises one hand, touches her dry lips. Her body is hidden under a thin blanket of flowers. She pulls this soft sheet up to her face and tries to sleep. But the wind is blowing and the noises won't let her. No one told her that it would get so cold. No one told her what to do when this happened. Why has she been left so alone?

The floor where she rests is like an ocean; its waves are rocking her. She will sleep through this heaviness, this darkness, this feeling of not knowing where or who she is.

~~~~

Nothing like having a bad dream and waking up in your cozy little nest. You can turn on the tube, put on a CD, get the camera rolling, dress up for a fantastic shoot. Whatever. You're the boss here and no one can tell you what to do, how to act. You're back to who you are so you relax. Except.

Is she still dreaming? No, she's wide awake. But how can Gina be awake and see what she's seeing? A man is sitting on her bed! Is he an angel in masculine disguise? And she means *masculine* in the most manly form imaginable. Maleness incarnate. Wow! Or is he a burglar, a rapist, a ruthless criminal?! Oh my God, what if that man is here to kill her?! Shouldn't she be afraid and running for her life? *Help!*

"I know you've been expecting me," he says in a husky voice.

"What's going on here? Who are you?!"

The stranger is looking around the room. He doesn't seem interested in Gina; that's odd. He's just observing things calmly. On closer look, this man doesn't fit the violent homicidal type. But she shouldn't let appearances fool her. Who is this dude?! She ought to call her parents, the police, do something to save herself.

"Is there any *café*?" he asks.

"Now? It's midnight!"

"In Cuba we always offer coffee," he says, disappointed, "even if we don't have any. Company expects it."

"In the first place, I'm not about to start fiddling around in the kitchen and wake everybody up. In the second place, I don't know how to make coffee. And third, I've no idea who you are or why I'm here talking to a ghost!"

"I am not a ghost."

"No, of course not. You're my fantasy."

"I am a man of flesh and blood."

"Okay, if you're not just my creation, if you're really a Cuban stud sitting on my bed, talking to me, then why are you speaking English?"

"I speak the language of your thoughts."

"Aha! I knew it. You're a figment of my imagination. This is a dream!"

"Not so," he says, displaying himself like a hot music-video model. "I'm Cuban and I'm real."

"And I'm Cuban American, reality itself, if you catch my drift."

"There is more to reality than you think."

"Enough of this!" she wails, sounding too much like her mother. She has to end this mind-blowing encounter. No more ridiculous ghostly discussions. Gina Domingo shall deal with this poltergeist or whatever it is in genuine Pinos Verdes fashion. But where in this town could she get help at this hour? And what would she tell them she needs help with? If only there was a neighborhood Santera she could consult!

"I like this room; it's big," he says, making Gina lose her train of thought. She turns to face him, noticing his clothes and his excellent build. He's wearing a sleeveless undershirt and blue jeans, both tight-fitting. His bulky pectorals are clearly delineated, as are his thigh muscles and his . . .

Stop! She must resist him.

Wake up, girl! This is only a fantasy! But it's no use: everything about this apparition feels touchable, smellable. Is she turned on? Yes, no, maybe, a little, a whole lot. No! Gina Domingo won't let sinful dangerous thoughts enter her mind. She must stay in control, run away from temptation.

Only a fantasy . . .

"I want to thank you for making me feel welcome," he whispers, and reaches for her hand. She lets him take it, prepared to feel the coldness of death or the ethereal essence of a spirit. Surprise! His hand is warm and moist; his grip is strong, pulsing with life.

"Let's have some *café*. Then we can talk about our future."

"I told you I don't know how to make coffee."

"You must've forgotten."

"How can I forget something I never knew?"

"Don't worry. I'll refresh your memory . . . I like it very sweet, remember?"

"Look, can you take a rain check on the coffee for now?"

"A . . . rain check?"

"Yeah, until tomorrow. I'll have our maid make you a fresh pot first thing in the morning. As soon as I wake up from this bogus erotic experience!"

"Sure, I can wait. So long as we're together."

"Together? Actually, I was wondering if you could wait outside."

"But . . . aren't you going to show me your house? I'd like to see where you've been living without me."

"You have time for a tour?"

"All the time in the world."

"It figures!"

Why is she leading him on?! Well . . . There's really nothing wrong with humoring him a little. He's not going to hurt her and she's not sleepy, anyway. Besides, she's kind of curious—*painfully* curious—about this otherworldly visitor. Who is this dude?

"Okay, then," she says, sounding like an attraction park tour guide. "That's the sound machine over there; it's state-of-the-art, a fab system. And this thing here is my camera, I'm making a movie with it. Ain't it cool? Camcorder Auto-Focus Auto-Light Sensor Quasi-Holographic with a complimentary hard case. It doesn't actually produce 3-D images; no holograms. I wish! The technology isn't available yet. That's why they put a 'quasi' in there. But the pictures this compact little object takes are so mind-blowingly real, the lights and shadows and color so perfectly distributed that you think you're in a whole new world when you're watching the screen. Yeah, you could say my camera improves the original. It's a magical copier of life! Will you let me film you?"

"Some other time," he tells her, expressing little interest in the machine. But it's too late; she's already fixed her lens on him.

"A video clip of you: the proof I need!"

"Proof of what?"

"Of your existence. If you're real, your image will show up on my screen. Cameras don't lie."

"Do *you* have to prove that you exist?"

"Of course not."

"Then why should I?"

"You've got a point there."

"Please, continue showing me your home."

"Sure, fine . . . Here you see my own personal TV." She can hear herself sounding like a game show hostess. Barf! "We have two other sets 'cause this is our main source of entertainment. That's the case in most American houses; everyone in this country watches television . . . And here's a tiny flag of Cuba; my gold chain has a tiny Cuba on it, too. See? My Daddy had it made for me."

Entranced, he touches the golden icon of the Caribbean island. Seconds later he pulls a similar chain out of his pocket. "Look," he says, smiling. "I have one also. I should be wearing it, don't you think?"

"Guess so," she mumbles, trying to get over the shock of this uncanny coincidence.

"Will you put it on me?"

She humors him, brushing the skin of his neck with her fingers, ever so gently. Wow. Why couldn't she just say no?

"The chain was all my idea," she explains. "'Cause my folks don't go much for Cuban stuff. Mom's into French poetry and Dad, well, he just works all the time. So I figure it's up to me to bear the weight of Cubanity around here. Someone's gotta be patriotic, otherwise what's life all about?"

"Life is about love."

"If you say so."

She looks at him, drawn to his eyes. They are like stars, burning with a fire she's never seen before. Blazing and powerful and ever so tempting.

"Do you still love me?" He takes her hand again.

"What are you talking about?"

He looks heartbroken. "Don't tell me you forgot that, too." He's walking to the door, out the door.

"Where are you going?"

He's gone!

Minutes later she finds him in the den, staring out the picture window. "That's the bay down below," she tells him, and stands by his side. "I just love the lights reflected on the water. Pretty, huh?"

"Yes, it is beautiful." He gently laces her waist with his arm. "And romantic."

"Hey, I wouldn't go that far. It's just a bunch of lights and smog."

"Let's go back to your room."

"What for?"

"I like your room. It has your aroma."

"We're fine right here."

"Let's go." His arm is moving downward, too close to the bottom line!

"No!"

"Gina, it is time for–"

"Let go of me!"

And he's gone again, disappeared into thin air. How rude, leaving without even saying *adiós*, without giving his courteous hostess a farewell kiss. He should've at least warned her that he was splitting. Ingrate!

She walks by her parents' bedroom and stands outside the door. Daddy's snoring away, as always. Did she just have a bad dream? *Wake up, girl!* Here she is barefoot, in her jammies, a frightened little baby comforted by the sound of her father's breathing, feeling safe because he's here. Nothing out of the ordinary has just happened. She's been sleepwalking, that's all. The last thing she remembers is a man's voice.

Back to sleep, she tells herself. And as she enters her room, she senses a presence. Daddy! No. Be brave. You can handle it. You've been having one hell of a night, lots and lots of weird dreaming. You made up the Real McCuban 'cause you were horny. Admit it. Be big and strong and honest and true to yourself, Gina Domingo!

"What took you so long?" he asks, sprawled, shirtless, on her bed.

"Hey, get out of there!"

"How about some music," he says, scrambling to his feet.

"No, it'll wake everybody up." She must resist him.

"We can play it low," he whispers, and moves toward her. His lips touch her cheek, tenderly. "Please, do it for us. Turn on your . . . what did you call it? The sound machine, yes. Turn it on."

"Which one? 'Cause I actually have two sound systems, the super-duper one, a present from Santa, you know, the Christmas thing. That one's huge, see? It's got Sensurround and everything. But I prefer this other one, it's more me. And it has sentimental value . . . a belated birthday present from Robby, my boyfriend. I take it with me everywhere. Like to the bathroom when I'm taking a shower and when I go to the beach with . . . It's a fabulous radio. Cool design, too, a mixture of styles: Fifties, Seventies, and Nineties. The look that cuts across all time!"

"I'm sorry I missed your birthday."

"You didn't miss much."

"Did you have a big fiesta?"

"No. My mother wanted to throw a party for me. You know, one of those debutante balls, a *Quinceañera*, but I–"

"Do you love Robby?"

"What?"

"You heard me. Do you love him–"

"I don't know."

"–more than you once loved me?"

"It's none of your business if I do!"

~~~~

She sees herself closing the bedroom window, no longer enveloped by the wind, no longer freezing, drenched in rain, threatened by lightning. She's in bed, overcome by the sensation that a person is sleeping next to her. She turns on the light, hoping there won't be anything unusual, nothing even a little strange.

Relief. There's no one there. She's just having a bad night; it's indigestion, probably, caused by Elisa's tartalisa. But as soon as darkness returns there's that body again. She can't see his eyes, but she can smell him: chamomile and spices, salty sea breeze, wet earth.

A shaft of lightning pierces the dark clouds, framing a man's face, his mighty, inviting silhouette.

"Do you remember when we made love?" he asks.

"No, I don't! Because we never did. You got that? Never."

"You were scared. But I didn't force you."

"Did we both . . . enjoy it?"

"Yes, *mi amor.* And I loved giving you a pleasure you had never known."

"I'm sure you're confusing me with someone else."

"I would die all over again for our love!"

"You're joking, right?"

"No, I am not joking. I risked and lost my life for our love once. And I'm willing to do it as many times as—"

"No, you're not!"

"Have you forgotten my sacrifice? Was it all in vain, *mi amor?* How can you not honor the death of a man who died for you?"

"For me?"

"Yes. I was hung from a ceiba tree by your father."

"No way! My Dad would never do such a horrible thing."

"My body was left there for days, rotting, eaten by scavenging animals."

"Oh my God!"

"My hanging body was the proof that the crime had been avenged."

"What crime?"

"The proof that your family had restored its honor. I took your virginity. They took my life."

"I don't believe it. What a waste."

"A waste?"

"Yeah. You are . . . you must've been . . . so gorgeous."

"And you are as beautiful as you were then, Gina."

"Thank you, but I wasn't—"

"I want to make love to you, *vida mía.*"

"No way!"

"But we belong together."

"You don't know me."

"You're the woman I desire."

"I'm not a woman. I'm an American teenager!"

"Let me hold you, please."

"I said No! You're taking me for someone I'm not."

"We already did it once, long ago."

"Not with me you didn't."

"Yes, with the woman I'd like to touch and kiss and—"

"Hands off, man! Or you're gonna die all over again."

"Nothing will tear us apart now, my beloved Gina."

"Help!"

"I'll be by your side forever. *Te amo.*"

~~~~

She wakes up thirsty and goes downstairs, craving some ice-cold soda pop. She gulps down half a can of Diet Cherry Cola while in the kitchen, then walks to the den and stands by the window. Some of the city neon lights are still flickering, in the distance, and the ocean seems peaceful.

Suddenly, a strange smell invades the room, wafted by a draft of warm air. It is a bodily scent, pungent, penetrating. The dream she just had comes back, in flashes and sounds. *Mi amor . . . Vida mía.* The voice she heard, words of a man who says he wants her. *We made love once, long ago,* she's hearing it again, through the clouds of a dream, mellifluous and soothing . . . *Te amo.*

Something, a presence, is holding her there, forcing her to look out into the garden. This presence is making itself visible now, among the flowers. The tall silhouette of a man, a dark muscular man. She touches her arms, obeying an impulse: they are covered with purple marks in the shape of fingers. She hears the word *Adiós,* and the silhouette is gone.

~~~~

Gina is in a daze. During breakfast, Elisa notices her mood and asks if it's that time of the month. "It is," says the girl. "But you know I never let those female things bug me." The reason she's acting unusually weird, she says to her mother, is a big project for Spanish class.

"I told you not to take that class. You should've listened to me!"

"Too late now."

"What a waste of your time!"

"Why, Maman? Some of the best literature in the world has been written in Spanish, you know."

"Is that what your teacher told you?"

"Yeah. But I know it for a fact, too; I've read some of that great stuff."

"Yes, of course. In Spain there is that pitiful Don Quixote, a poor parody of true chivalric ideals, an early incarnation of Castilian machismo."

"I haven't read that one yet."

"Then there's all the dry and barren post-war writing. Depressing tales of empty lives. Dead ends. Lackluster narratives. No universal vision."

"We haven't done any lit from Spain, I guess."

"I will admit there are some fairly good Spanish poets, like Lorca."

"Do you like José Martí? I dig him!"

"Yes, well, I suppose one could consider Martí the best that the Island has to offer in the literary arena."

"I would agree with that."

"But he is an exception, a jewel in the midst of crude stones, lost inside the insufferable corpus of Hispanic American literature. What is the essence of the Latin American canon, you might ask."

"I might?"

"And I would say it is a tedious, uninspired barrage of jungle stories full of facile miracles and savage beliefs. *Affreux!* Oh, and what about the avant-garde and the art-for-art's sake poetry, what they call Modernism? Nothing original, nothing that you could term transcendent. Fortunately, I've been able to avoid all the magical-realist fluff of recent years."

"What are you talking about, Maman?"

"The Hispanic classics, dear; texts that I was forced to read when I was young. What you so blithely call 'great stuff.'"

"We must've read different books."

"Apparently so. In any case, perhaps I could offer you some help with that project you're preparing. What are you working on?"

"I'd love to tell you, Maman, but I wanna do this all by my little old self, know what I mean? Those are the rules. But thanks anyway."

"*De rien, ma petite.*"

How could she explain this "project" to Madame? What would she tell her, that her daughter is possessed? That a Cuban poltergeist is living under her roof? That a Modernist transcendental magical-realist miracle has taken place in Pinos Verdes? Or maybe something like . . .

Listen, Mom. Last night I slept with a hunk. Yep, there was a man in my bed. I tried, I swear I tried to kick him out but the dude was stubborn! I said to him, Señor Amor, this bed's not big enough for two. Take a hike and let me get some shut-eye. But he kept grabbing me and kissing me and telling me how much he'd missed me. He said he'd been waiting to hold me for almost a century! He told me that nothing would tear us apart now. Oh yes, Maman! Right this second he's out there in your garden, ready to risk his life for our love, to die for me all over again. Can you dig it?! He wasn't a good lover, though. He had coffee breath and the hair on his legs made me itch all night. So relax. Believe it or not, I'm still a virgin!

-III-

You see yourself from up above, your pink robe billowing around you. And then you're walking down a dirt street, noting the waning light from shacks along the way. A song is heard, a baby crying. There is a narrow door through which you pass to find an old woman who greets you. She's dressed in black. You look at her and wonder how a face can hold that many wrinkles.

There are pictures and statuettes of saints lined up on shelves. And flowers, mainly daisies, and candles. It's an altar you're seeing. The Cuban Matron, Virgen de la Caridad, is in the center. She looks as though she were floating in midair, doing a balancing act on a slice of the moon.

The old woman points to the figure of a crippled man with a crutch, a dog by his side. "That's San Lázaro," she explains. "He protects sick and poor people, those who suffer pain and hunger. Do you need his help?"

"I'm not hungry or sick, and I've never been poor. So I guess not."

She kneels in front of the Virgen, then turns to you and says, "This is Oshún, the patroness of love. Do you need her to help you attract a young man, or to get him to marry you?"

"No, Señora, thank you. I can make my own magic."

"You've been in love before," she tells you, as she inspects the palm of your right hand.

"Not true!"

"Yes, and he wants you back."

"Who? Who wants me?"

"The man you loved and lost when you were only fifteen, long ago."

"But I *am* fifteen right now, this very second!"

"He's here to take you with him."

"I'm getting out of this dream, too scary for my sensitive character. Hello out there!"

"You're not dreaming, *muchachita.*"

"Daddy, save me!"

"Daddy cannot do anything for you. But maybe Changó, the god of fire and thunder–"

"Somebody wake me up!"

"Calm down, *mija.* The gods are on your side."

"I don't need any gods."

"Why are you here, then?"

"Well . . . I guess I could use a little assistance."

"Relax, my dear. Relax and tell me what brings you to me."

"Okay, I'll make it short. I had this dream about a spirit in my bed and let me tell you Señora it was a tempting dude temptation itself oh my God. And it took me by surprise 'cause I had no idea that spirits liked to do 'it' you know. Aren't they supposed to be pure and ethereal? Then I saw him through the window and I noticed these purple spots on my arms on my legs on my tummy and other more private places. The next night there he was again wanting to do you-know-what. But I'm not ready yet for you-know-what and–"

"The spots on your skin, what color did you say they were?"

"Purple. Why?"

"Purple is the mark of a male spirit."

"He was male all right!"

"He left his mark wherever he touched you."

"Pervert!"

"He wants you."

"He can't have me."

"Why not?"

"Because . . . Because . . . Just because."

"Not a good reason."

"Okay, how about . . . I have a boyfriend already."

"I can accept that."

"It's the truth!"

"Then we must send your former lover a message."

"Yes! ASAP. E-mail or fax? This is an emergency!"

"It will have to be through a *despojo.*"

"A what? I never heard of that one. Is it faster than E-mail?"

"But we have a problem."

"I'll say we do."

"Yes, you're not used to cleansing ceremonies."

"The message, please."

"Are you sure you want to go through with it?"

"Yes, I am. Go through with what?"

"No, I don't think you're ready."

"Ready for what?"

"Never mind. It's impossible."

"Listen to me, respectable Señora. I don't mean to be pushy or anything, but I do need your help. I want that man out of my head, my body, now!"

"Very well, if you wish. I will perform a *despojo* so you can be freed of his courtship."

"Nothing against the dude, he's a nice guy and everything. Really nice, in fact. But–"

"You need say no more. The ceremony will take place on Tuesday, one week from tonight, Changó's appointed day."

"I have to wait one whole week?"

"Not very long when you consider that he waited a century for you."

"A century? Are you sure?"

"Yes, I can read it in your eyes."

"Wow!"

"One hundred years of sadness and longing. One hundred years he has spent searching for his love."

"You're right. One week is no time at all!"

~~~~

The Señora informs you that the preliminary work will consist of a *resguardo*, some sort of talisman prepared with Changó, alias Santa Bárbara, as the guardian force. You must keep it in your undergarments. But you'll also need to take some purifying baths and wear a necklace of red beads. And, most importantly, you'll burn a white candle each night in the name of your "former lover," so that he leaves you.

The Señora assures you that Señor McCuban will keep his distance this week. What she fails to tell you is that he has mysterious ways of getting to you. He will enter your mind. Your body will be sleeping soundly while your mind takes flight. And it is with your mind's flesh that you'll receive his kisses, his caresses. And more . . .

He won't touch you, states the Señora, and what she means is that he won't touch your physical self. During the next seven nights he will make love to your soul. Gina's body will awaken and witness the act, unable to move or put an end to it. The body will want to play camerawoman, but the camera won't be able to capture the scene. You'll hear tempting noises, wonderful sounds of a total dig. But rest assured, he won't touch you.

~~~~

Tuesday, at five minutes to midnight, the old Iyalocha-Santera pops up after having walked miles, barefoot, down dirt roads. She gets to work immediately. She asperses your rose-colored walls with holy water, does some invocations to Changó, and places holy *guano* under your bed.

"He will not come back," she states.

Is this the unbelievable ceremony that you weren't ready for? That was a piece of cake! But seconds after the Iyalocha makes her statement, all hell breaks lose in your room. Video tapes, books, CDs, computer disks crash against the walls, falling on the floor. The *guano* is torn into pieces, flying in a circle around your head. How can your parents sleep through all this pandemonium?

"He is too strong for me," the Señora announces. "I cannot help you."

"What do you mean you can't help me? I'm out of my turf, gimme a break!"

"You need a Babalao."

"A Baba-what?"

"I will find one for you. Don't worry."

"Thank you."

"Wait here. I will return soon. Don't go anywhere."

"You think I'd have the nerve to go out during a spiritual crisis?"

Minutes later she comes back accompanied by a Babalao. He is primitive-looking, sexy; his face is covered with blotches of white paint. He's wearing a loincloth that leaves nothing to the imagination. Show-off! Stereotypical native! You can't help thinking how handsome he is, and how much he reminds you of the other Cuban dude.

A waft of cold air cuts to your bones. Upset, your knees buckling painfully, you get into bed and cover your head with a pillow. You're on the verge of crying hysterically when Señor Babalao shouts, "Oluwo! Omo-Changó!" And the pandemonium stops. The Babalao places his calloused hand over your forehead, closes his eyes. Then he says, tenderly, "The spirit doesn't wish to part. He is sad because you want him to leave."

"I'm sorry, sir, but—"

"The spirit is here because of Gina. She gives him the power."

"What power?"

"The power to possess you."

"What should I do?"

"Tell him that you love him, too."

"But that's a lie!"

"Are you sure?"

"Okay, so I do dig him a little."

"Tell him."

"Could he hurt me?"

"No. You're his only friend."

"Once he leaves here, what will happen to him?"

"He will wait for you, until you're ready. However long it takes."

~~~~

You see your soul embracing him, saying *Adiós*. He gives you one last kiss; his lips are warm, not the cold lips of a ghost. You hear his message when he parts: *I will return.* Yes, he will appear at an appointed hour, his eyes full of fire, his skin burning with passion. And you will sing a song as you make love to him, *Zun zun zun* . . .

You won't be punished for this pleasure. For this eternal love.

~~~~

Soft peals of thunder far away, the last raindrops. And two voices, the Babalao's and the Señora's, telling you that you should now wake up. The storm has ended. The dream is almost over.

Light filters through the window. You hear the maid preparing breakfast in the kitchen, Daddy singing in the shower, Maman listening to her violin music. The smell of pancakes makes your mouth water. Nothing here seems abnormal, out of place.

So you turn on the camera and capture a necklace of red beads, a white candle, the wrinkled face of an old woman, a benevolent virgin floating on a slice of the moon, the purple trace of a male spirit. And a song.

Then you film two spirit lovers kissing. Two reunited lovers strolling along, away from Gina.

Chapter 5

-I-

Social Events was a broad category; it encompassed anything from Homecoming to the principal's flu. Anything could be considered social, so long as it involved people. As Social Events reporter for the *All Saints Bulletin*, Gina wrote a forgettable little piece about Mrs. Tate's appendicitis (no first-period equations for two weeks!), and she provided front-page coverage on Miss White's wedding. (The religion teacher had managed to train a Ramosa CEO to read her body-word and help her bear her heavy cross-cross-cross. Amen.)

She also published an article on Homecoming: *The glorious evening began with the traditional parade into the ASHS stadium. Handsomely decorated vehicles and banner-carrying groups representing classes and clubs led the cars bearing the members of the court . . .* The reporter had no choice but to say a few words about the King and Queen, although it was her opinion that the monarchs didn't deserve all the hoopla. The king was all muscles, the queen was all tan; neither one had a personality. Yawn.

The only story she enjoyed researching was a compilation of trendy words used by cool ASHS students. The faculty editor nixed "insulting terms" such as hoyden, minx, freak, hanging, drip, and barfed-up. Among the less offensive items, he allowed bogus, fab, dig, groovy, and stoked. Needless to say, Gina had appropriated some of the above (not always convincingly) for her own hip and bad and hot and hasta-la-vista idiolect.

Her most exciting piece, without a doubt, was "Moonlight Retreat at Green Pines Lake." Gina gave the report a slight personal touch, but with an objective, experiential point of view. Creative journalism, kind of. She almost didn't submit it, thinking the essay might be too sentimental, a memoir more than news; afraid, as well, that they'd read between the lines and detect the truth of her feelings in the article.

"Your mother will go with you," Daddy had pronounced. Gina protested: "No way, Dad. How embarrassing!" He was unswerving at first, but in the end gave in, swayed by his daughter's reassuring argument: "It's a religious retreat, Daddy. The girls and the boys won't mix, we're in separate camps. We'll only get together for praying!"

Green Pines Lake was a beautiful setting for friendship to be born. The opening sentence came easily, although what she really wanted to say was: *for love to be born.* She fought the temptation to fill one whole computer file with images of Rob and Gina swimming in the lake, hiking, climbing trees, roasting marshmallows, savoring s'mores. Sweethearts cuddled up by a bonfire, bathed in the light of a full moon. Her heart cried out, Abandon yourself to the memory, *chica!* Be romantic! But she forced herself to complete the paragraph in a tone devoid of passion, succinctly, as it was meant to be told.

What she ended up capturing was a scene fresh out of an Eighties music video. But such seemed to be the obvious essence of the event: *The retreat began with an icebreaker. In ring-around-the-rosie fashion, students joined hands in two circles, one inside the other. Lively techno-pop music played as the two circles moved in opposite directions. "My kingdom is friendship," said the catchy song. "It's a kingdom within. You can join me forever, if you want to be king!" Whenever the music stopped, each participant was supposed to hug the person opposite him or her . . .* Again, Gina resisted her impulse to add a personal—and rather compromising—detail: Ms. Domingo and Mr. Holmes hugged each other for such a long time that they broke up the game!

When finished with the rough draft of "Moonlight Retreat," the reporter indulged in a reverie, free at last to remember. Late at night she'd make her way under the thick, dark, verdant pines; over the hills and the rocks; under the brewing storm clouds; near the cliffs and by the edge of the lake, to meet her lover. Upon receiving his welcoming embrace, she'd touch his soft blonde hair. He'd cup her chin in his hand, kiss her gently on the lips. Then he'd lift her up and carry her to a nearby cave . . .

~~~~

Few events met the "social" requirement better than Abuela's visit: CUBAN GRANDMA ALLOWED TO LEAVE HER COUNTRY SO SHE CAN VISIT HER GRANDDAUGHTER. THEY ARE FINALLY REUNITED! Gina pitched the idea to the *All Saints Bulletin* faculty sponsor (an ex-seminarian who, after years of working at ASHS, had come to resemble a nun) and he rejected it right off. "A story about a Cuban citizen has nothing to do with our school," he said. "And it is too political." Gina pleaded, "I won't say a word about communism!" She argued, "And what do you mean it has nothing to do with our school? I'm a student here, aren't I?"

She definitely had a point: CUBAN LADY ALLOWED TO LEAVE HER COUNTRY SO SHE CAN VISIT HER GRAND-DAUGHTER WHO HAPPENS TO BE AN ASHS STUDENT! Gina promised she'd write a triumph-of-the-human-spirit piece. This would be the story of the year: GRANDMOTHER WROTE MANY LETTERS THAT GRANDDAUGHTER NEVER RECEIVED. BUT THE CUBAN WOMAN AND HER AMER-ICAN RELATIVE ARE REUNITED IN SPITE OF A SINISTER DESTINY SCHEME!

The sponsor was touched by the human angle, the "sinister scheme" part. (He obviously had a weakness for prime-time TV drama.) Yes, he'd let Gina run the article and would feature it in the paper's last issue for the school year. Which meant that every-one would read it, since everyone reads the last issue. But which also implied that Gina had scarcely one week to put her stuff together. One measly week!

She slaved over the questionnaire until the questions were clear and poignant. *Uno*: Señora Ruiz de Domingo, what impres-sions do you have of the South Bay and Pinos Verdes? *Dos*: Do you see any differences between life here and life in Cuba? *Tres*: In what circumstances, and I mean the REAL circumstances, do elderly people like yourself live on the island of Cuba? Fourth and final question, *Cuatro*: Tell us, Señora Ruiz, anything you can about CUBA TODAY, the real scoop if you'd be so kind. Please.

Yeah, no sweat. The reporter would be ready . . .

~~~~

Los Angeles Airport. Interior. Day. Crowds everywhere; peo-ple running, arriving, saying goodbye; people greeting other people. (I love airports!) My parents and I are waiting for our Cuban relative, on her way from Miami via Northern Skies. Benito is pacing by the gate; Elisa is seated, reading poetry. I'm filming the whole scene (panning shot with lots of zoom-ins for close-ups, my favorite) while a hot salsa tune plays in my head; it's a funky remake of a Sixties pop hit. Sounds better than the original!

Grandmother enters with other passengers. Zoom in on Cuban relative: she's in her seventies, kind of tall, heavyset, with dark complexion. She doesn't look that old when you consider her age. Her face is hardly wrinkled, but she does have gray hair. Señora Domingo is wearing a blue cotton dress and no jewelry. She's pretty, I guess; very pretty, actually.

Daddy lifts his mom up and holds her and spins around with her, shouting *Mamá Mamá Mamá!* Grandmother hugs me, knocking down my camera. *Muchachita!* she screams. Little girl! My machine pans the waiting area: amazed bystanders staring at the loud Cuban family.

Cut to Interior Domingos' car (a Mercedes, what else?). Benito is driving and talking to his mom about their relatives back home, *Blah blah blah,* and then Grandmother reaches out to me (she's sitting up front, I'm in the back) and holds my hand. (How sweet.)

Now we see the Pinos Verdes hills and I'm getting more and more stoked by the minute 'cause it's a really nice day without smog. June. I like June. And I have a great panning shot of pine trees. And a close-up of the beach and the building down below. Wow! Gala Mall takes up a whole block.

We're pulling up in front of a mansion that looks like a gone-with-the-wind plantation house, tall white columns and a huge door, you know what I mean. That's home. We step out of the car and Benito (Daddy's such a gentleman) guides his Mamá to the house carrying her luggage, two small suitcases. Cut to . . .

Madame Elisa's face. She looks totally barfed-up, typical drip. I'd bet she's doing one of her spooky interior monologues mocking Abuela, *We're finally together, Benitín! It's been an eternity, my son!*

Before fade-out, a close-up of Estela; of Benito and Estela walking hand in hand, smiling.

~~~~

The cream-colored walls of the mansion bore too many paintings. Colorful pictures of circles, squares, and distorted faces were hung next to yellowing Romantic landscapes and portraits of queens and kings. "You people live in a museum!" exclaimed the guest. Each room was carefully furnished in a different style, Elisa informed her. The living room, for example, was done in genuine Louis Quinze. "We make an effort to spend as little time as possible in here," said Maman with a strange accent (her native language mixed in with the French "r," with English syntax and then something else). "That furniture cost us a fortune. We wouldn't want to ruin it through daily use."

Estela looked up at the high, barrel-vaulted ceiling, and she discovered there the source of the dim bluish-green light that invaded the room. There were four round, shell-shaped structures, one in each corner, which resembled overgrown bullfrogs. "The light effect is superb, is it not?" inquired Elisa. "The idea is to penetrate space completely but indirectly," she added. "It is a masterwork of *fin-de-siècle* lighting, wouldn't you say?"

The den was too cluttered, admitted Maman apologetically. This was the one part of the house she favored the least, since it lacked an aesthetically conceived design. Its only remarkable detail was the picture window with French-style awnings, which overlooked the bay. "You can enjoy breathtaking sunsets from the den," said Maman.

Contemporary was the name she used for the kitchen, which contained state-of-the-cooking-art technology. She described the breakfast nook as "simply deco." "We consume most of our meals here," Madame explained, as she stroked one of the five gray chairs around a pink table. "Aren't these lovely colors?" she asked her mother-in-law, receiving a noncommittal shrug in return.

The Cuban woman then saw a large patio covered with prickly artificial grass, a lush garden of strangely shaped flowers, a quasi-Olympic swimming pool, a sauna, a Jacuzzi, a four-car garage, and other features of the house that Gina's grandma would never be able to describe to her family in Cuba. One of those features was the satellite dish. "Do you use that thing for contacting flying saucers?" she asked, jokingly. "We could," said Gina, also in jest. And Maman butted in, "The object's primary function is enhancing the images on our TV screens."

Benito joined the tour when Elisa was showing Estela to her room. He had filled it with daisies, his mother's favorite flower, and wanted to see her reaction. "Benitín, what a sweet gesture," she told him, and kissed him. "But you don't really expect me to sleep here, do you?" She was laughing. "This place looks and smells like a cemetery!"

"These are fine quarters," retorted Maman.

"I can see that," said Abuela. "Yes, an entire family could live in here!" She was wandering, distractedly, around the room. "Very nice," she noted after a brief inspection. "But I don't need all this space."

Daddy looked surprised. "What do you mean, Mamá? Of course you need it!"

"No, Benitín. Because I would prefer . . . I would like to sleep in my granddaughter's bedroom. Would you agree to that, *mi niña*?"

"You must be joking!" said Elisa, not giving Gina a chance to respond.

"This bed is so large," remarked Abuela, and she asked the girl, "Will it fit in your room?"

"I will not allow it!" wailed Madame.

"Please, try to understand," Estela pleaded.

"What is there to understand? It's a crazy idea!"

"I have fifteen years to make up for."

Gina's immediate reaction was Forget it! Why would she want to give up the comfort and privacy of her castle? A princess' throne is never shared. But then she thought, Heck. it's only for a while. It'd definitely make Abuela feel unwelcome if I said no and then what about all that stuff about being the head of the Welcoming Committee, huh? So she said, "Great idea," and Maman turned to her with lethal Francophile eyes, hyperventilating. She stormed out of the room in near hysteria, dragging Daddy with her. "*C'est affreux!*"

Poor Grandma, thought Gina. She hasn't been around for a day yet and she's already having to put up with Maman's insults. Daddy tried to shut her up, but Elisa wanted to be heard. "*No se lo permito!*" she said in crisp Cuban Spanish. "She's insane. I will not let her inconvenience our daughter!"

Benito settled the argument with a short and punchy phrase, "You heard what Gina said." And he promised his Mamá he'd have the bed moved to the girl's room immediately. Hurray for good old Benitín!

~~~~

Gina guided Estela to her bedroom. Among other things, she showed her grandma a tiny flag of Cuba and her gold chain, from which hung a miniature island. And she shared with her the copy of *Versos sencillos* she'd used for her class report. Abuela was proud (Gina could tell) that her grandchild had read the great Cuban poet. She skimmed the book and then recited a few *Versos* entirely from memory: "Swift, like a reflection, I twice saw my soul: When the poor old man died, when she said her goodbye . . . I know the strange names of flowers and herbs, of mortal deceptions, of sublime pain . . ."

Somehow, Gina knew this would happen: Abuela's musical voice, her rendition of Martí's verses; the beloved *poesía* she'd learned when she was a child . . . "A white rose I grow for the sincere friend who offers me his open hand. And for the cruel one who tears out my heart, a white rose I grow."

The Princess turned on her computer, displaying the CARTAS file. "Look, Abuela, your letters. Can you believe you wrote all that?"

Astounded, Estela faced the busy screen. "But it's in English!"

"They're your words. All I did was translate them."

"I see. In that case, we collaborated, no?"

"Yeah, I guess we kind of wrote it together."

The girl showed her roommate a cool radio she called the Boom Box, a present from Robby, her boyfriend. And she tried to describe him, to paint him in one stroke, one word to make him real for a Cuban grandma: *Surfeador?* Yeah! But her guest had no clue.

"You know," Gina explained, "someone who likes to ride the ocean waves."

"Ride the waves? With a boat?"

"No, with a flat object made of wood or plastic."

"That sounds a little dangerous, but fun!"

"I've never done it. Robby says it makes him feel like a flying fish."

"Flying fishes have fun?"

"I guess so. It sure looks like they do!"

The Moviemaker held her camcorder. "Say something, Abuela. I'm going to put you in my movie. You'll be a star!"

"No, *niña*, I beg you!" She was trembling. "Stop that thing!"

Gina humored the old woman, puzzled by her reaction. Then, hoping to create some atmosphere, she turned on the radio. A mellow Sixties song was playing; the original, not a remake. Perfect theme for the Interview, she thought, and proceeded to ask the four questions she'd memorized as follows: (1) impressions, (2) differences, (3) circumstances, (4) the real scoop.

Señora Ruiz found Pinos Verdes and the South Bay very nice, *muy bonitos*, although she wasn't sure about that since she hadn't seen much of anything yet. Yes, she was certain that there were major differences between life here and life in Cuba, but it was too soon for her to make any statements about such differences. "Old people in Cuba stay very busy; they have a lot of work to do," she offered in response to the third question. "They don't have time to think about their age." She thought long and hard about the final question. "*Bueno,*" she pondered, "Cuba is a beautiful island today, as beautiful as the day it was discovered by Cristóbal Colón."

How can you write a brilliant article based on such a flimsy interview? Abuela's responses were not up to par, definitely not journalistic material. Would she ever give better answers? Publishable answers, that is. Not this *muy-bonito* stuff, bogus common knowledge about Columbus, that old-people-work-hard routine. Where was the real scoop? CUBAN WOMAN HAS INCREDIBLE STORY TO TELL (DOESN'T SHE?) AND YET ALL SHE DOES IS MAKE LOUSY COMMENTS. ASHS STUDENT THE TRUE VICTIM OF DESTINY SCHEME!

Gina wouldn't be able to meet her deadline. By the time Señora Ruiz became knowledgeable enough about life in California, the reporter had lost all interest in her article. By the time Cuban Grandma was willing to open up and speak the naked truth, American Granddaughter was more interested in hiding the truthful data in her computer files than in displaying it for the entire ASHS student body. Forget it, thought Gina resignedly. The story of the year comes along only once in a lifetime. *Adiós!*

-II-

Abuela was greeted the next morning with a Pinos Verdes feast: cholesterol-free scrambled eggs, high-fiber toast with margarine and sugar-free jelly, strips of imitation bacon, a tall glass of seedless orange juice and a cup of decaffeinated coffee sweetened with artificial sweetener.

"So much food for breakfast?" said Estela, as she nibbled at the all-American offerings. "*Qué delicia!*"

Hungry Abuela was to be here for about two months. Not enough time to explore the entire Southland, but Gina would at least show her the world-famous sights. She tried to describe these places (a tough job, since she'd never described them to anybody, much less in Spanish!). Clumsily, she told Estela about Fantasyland, where she'd chat with ghosts, ride through jungles, and walk among prehistoric creatures; the Hollyworld Studios, where she'd see fantastic movie sets and visual effects; the Tinseltown Wax Museum, packed with the greatest movie stars of all time; Maritime World, which offered as highlights petting a whale and touching a mermaid; and . . .

"Don't expect me to accompany you to any of those tourist traps," Maman interrupted. "I've had enough of the vulgar fantasies of California." Gina didn't respond, although she had plenty of thoughts in reaction: The last thing I want is for you to go with us, Maman. You'd criticize everything and look down on everybody and pretend that you're not having a good time and for what? I wouldn't appreciate your sacrifice!

"Mamá needs to get some rest," said Daddy. "She should spend a few days just relaxing, enjoying the house."

"I didn't come here to rest, Benito. Resting is for Galicians!"

Gina didn't know who these Galicians were that Abuela was referring to, and she had no idea why they needed to rest, but the phrase sounded funny, *El descanso es pa' los gallegos!* She burst out laughing, and Daddy joined in.

"*Chérie,*" said Maman, "your grandmother can't run around with you like a teenager. Just consider the woman's age."

"Why are you discussing my age, Elisa? You people make it sound like I'm stretching out my paw already!"

Benito was laughing again. He deciphered the expression for his daughter: "In Spanish you stretch your paw when you die. Your body stiffens and so your leg turns stiff. Get it?"

Got it: the first of many bits of Cuban wisdom she would gradually acquire from her grandma. People who died not only stretched their paws, but they also went out singing a song called "El manicero" ("The Peanut Vendor"). If you were called *mosquita muerta*, the little dead fly, that meant you were cunning, conniving and hypocritical. (But how could a dead fly be so evil?) If you "played the corpse to see what kind of burial you'd receive," that meant you didn't trust your friends. You'd be compared to La Gatica María, a pussycat, if you did terrible things and tried to cover them up. According to a Caribbean legend, Mary the Cat went around defecating in people's gardens and then carefully hiding her crap: evidence of her shitty conduct.

One has to be assertive in life and always fight for one's beliefs, said another one of Abuela's maxims; in other words, you have to cry a lot and loudly, since "a baby who doesn't cry doesn't get food." And if you were not assertive and let people walk all over you, you'd end up like "the shrimp that fell asleep and got swept away by the stream." In Gina's words, you'd be dead meat.

Cubans who lived to be very old were considered bad bugs, *bichos malos*, since a bad bug never ever dies: *Bicho malo nunca muere*. Old age, in Cuba, was the best time of life because you knew everything. (Well, almost.) Because "even the devil knows more from being old than from being the devil."

~~~~

There were more people at the mall than Señora Ruiz had ever seen during carnival time in Cuba. Gala Mall was an indoor world with artificial sunshine, flowering vines, and miniature palm trees that grew in enclosed gardens. This world contained streets, stores, theaters, bakeries, restaurants; boutiques where you could create your outfit on the spot, in seconds; rooms full of whirling lights and machines that simulated other machines. And there were parks, playgrounds, and even zoos where animals were bred and kept in cages for public viewing, where people went to buy (yes, buy!) dogs and cats and birds and lizards and even snakes!

Shoppers were transported from one floor to another in a cylindrical object made of glass. "They look so helpless in there," remarked Abuela. No, she didn't want to travel in that "bubble" that went up and down incessantly. And she didn't care that the view from the elevator, once you reached the very top, was spectacular. Estela wouldn't use the escalator, either, afraid that it might eat up her feet; she chose to use the stairs. Gina couldn't believe it: "You want to *walk*?"

Gala Mall had five stories, and on the first floor there was a stage-like platform where several dapper men and lovely blonde women stood, modeling clothes and makeup. Estela noticed them when she first arrived, and saw them again as she was leaving hours later. "Are they human beings or mannequins?" She couldn't tell. They moved in slow motion, smiling, winking, waving. There was something human about them. But how could those people–if they *were* people–just stand there for hours, impersonating giant dolls? When and where and how did they do their necessities?

"Isn't this place unbelievable? I could spend *all* of my time at the mall," said Gina, excited to be sharing her favorite hangout with Abuela. "Your entire life, yes," replied the Cuban woman. "But how do you know if it's day or night? You can't keep track of reality in here." And the teenager thought, What do you mean keep track? This *is* reality.

They browsed through the stores where Gina shopped regularly, while Benito waited outside. (What a patient man!) The girl bought several outfits for her grandmother, most of which Abuela found too youthful. After a late lunch at a fast-food restaurant (Estela's first burger), they decided to head home. The Domingos' guest was feeling overwhelmed and a little tired.

Estela noted, with utter fascination, the graffiti-spattered walls in Gala's underground garage. She tried to read the hand-written signs, SANTANEROS WERE HERE. Gigantic and fanciful designs, perfectly round words, VATOS LOCOS DE SANTANA . . .

"They're everywhere," Daddy rued.

"Who?" his Mamá asked him. "Who is everywhere?"

"Those bandits!"

Gina informed her grandma that those signs were messages from Santana gang members, *pandilleros*, and that they were meant to mark their territory.

"How did they manage to get past security?!" yelled Benito, sounding defeated. "They're invading us, *coño!*"

Abuela wanted more details about the belligerent creatures who drew such dainty, ornamented letters, *Vatos Locos*. "How can that writing be the mark of criminals?" she asked her son, who didn't respond.

Gina would tell her, later, that Santana wasn't all that far from Pinos Verdes. Most of the people who lived there were Mexican, but many of the stores were owned by Cubans and gringos. It was in Santana, in fact, where Daddy had one of his flower shops. The city was supposed to be a gang-infested hell, and Maman wished that Benito would rescue his FLORES DE DOMINGO from there. But Estela's son liked to make money and Mexicans liked to buy his flowers. Daddy would put up with the risk and the danger for as long as the shop made him a bundle.

"They'll never get to Pinos Verdes," stated Benito. And he drove home in silence.

~~~~

Fantasyland was a weekday excursion; they wanted to avoid the long weekend lines. Although, according to Maman, it shouldn't have made a difference to Benito's mother. "She must be used to waiting," scoffed Elisa. "Isn't that how she spends her days in Cuba, waiting in line?" Daddy wanted to go along (he loved this park) but couldn't; too much work. So he dropped them off at the entrance and promised to be back for them at the end of the day.

First mission of the Welcoming Committee: Let there be fantasy!

The singing dolls in the Baby World attraction were too plump, unbearably childish. But Abuela loved the theme song and came out of the ride singing it. She was also deeply moved by Porky Lady, at the Big Pig Jubilee, when the female swine came down through a hole in the ceiling, wobbling on her swing, and sang her ballad. Estela couldn't understand a word of the song, but the melancholy tone of the animal's vibratos touched her. "I can't believe it," she said, astonished. "Americans are capable of making pigs sing!"

The boat ride in the Pirates of the Tropics was fun. Sitting up front, they were soaked to the skin when the boat lurched downward into the park's bowels. They loved the vertigo, but they didn't care for the rest of the ride. (Although Gina had never liked this attraction, she considered it a must for its visual effects.) Why would anyone want to make a show out of a town being pillaged and burned to the ground by savage men? Battleships firing canons in the middle of the ocean; the acrid smell of gunpowder! Nice homes being ransacked and women getting raped and filthy-looking drunkards wallowing in the mud of pigpens. Swine and men with the same look of satiation and stupidity. Why would you want to ride through such squalor? Who would want to witness such a tragedy?

Abuela's negative opinion of the Pirates was justified; Gina could relate. But she didn't understand her grandma's reaction to the Enchanted Forest. The Cuban woman went quietly through the make-believe woods, looking frayed and annoyed. The only thing she commented on was the temperature. "It feels like we're inside a refrigerator," she said, and the girl found this comment odd; it wasn't that cold inside!

The Enchanted Forest was one of Gina's favorite attractions. She liked the simplicity of the fantasy: no mechanical people, no heavy-duty visuals. All you did, basically, was take a leisurely stroll through giant trees, on ancient trails. Oh, but what a stroll that was! The dense smell of pinewood and resin, the sweet aroma of wild-flowers, the musical sounds of crickets, frogs, and other nocturnal creatures. The night sky and the moon and the stars were so close, so reachable in the woods.

She had been able to compare this forest to a real one up on the mountain resort of Green Pines Lake, and the actual thing didn't fare well in the comparison. The Green Pines smell wasn't intense enough, the trees weren't majestic; the sky wasn't clear so you couldn't see that many stars, and there were no flowers. What was the point of hiking in the woods if it didn't make you feel spiritual, if it didn't make you long for a lover's touch? (During the school retreat at the lake, she'd tried to engage her imagination so the experience would be memorable, so that Nature could measure up to Fantasy. But it didn't work. If Rob hadn't been there, the *real* forest would've been one humongous disappointment!)

The space of nature was without a doubt Fantasyland's best creation. Its artists were brilliant at producing illusions of wildlife, enhanced images that were better than movies, because you could touch them and sense them and be in them. It was because of the park's power to evoke the beauty of realness that Gina kept going back to Fantasyland. She just couldn't get enough.

So it was with great concern that she strolled through the Forest with her grandma. The Domingos' guest didn't appreciate the magic that was all around her. She never once looked up at the full moon and the massive, deep-green foliage; she didn't listen for night birds nor did she touch the moistened soil. Estela turned increasingly pale, shivering as if struck by a fever. She seemed to have lost all her vigor, to have shriveled up in the woods.

As soon as they came out, Abuela walked to a bench and sat down. She was having trouble breathing. But the sunshine helped her instantly. It was awfully bright yet comforting. She closed her eyes and basked in the light.

"You hated it, didn't you?" asked Gina minutes later.

"It was nice," murmured Estela, "but I was feeling a little tired."

And she looks it, thought the girl. Who am I kidding? No matter how much I try, Abuela's never gonna get a kick out of this place, out of this country! She can't. My grandma's a foreigner. She's an old Cuban lady and I'm treating her like she's a school pal, my classmate or something, a cool and wholly energized chick like myself. Bummer. Who the hell am I kidding?

"Maman was right," she told her grandma who seemed suddenly old, really old. "You shouldn't be running around with me like—"

"Hush, young lady! I said I was tired, not ready to drop dead."

"Let's have some lunch. What do you say, Abuela?"

"Good idea."

"We can go home whenever you want to. Okay? We've seen most everything already. Well, except for the Jungle Voyage and the Hawaiian Room and the World of Dinosaurs and the Ghost Mansion. You'd like the Ghost Mansion, I think; it's weird and really funny. But maybe not."

"We have to leave some things for my next trip, you know."

"Yeah. But who knows when that'll be."

~~~~

After a light meal of salad, soup, and fruit juice, Estela was feeling energetic again. She went through Gina's list of yet unseen attractions and picked two: the Hawaiian Room because it featured singing flowers and she was curious as to how they pulled that off; and the Ghost Mansion because she wanted to see what American phantoms looked like. She discarded the Jungle Voyage, "I've seen enough jungles in my life," and the World of Dinosaurs, "I don't care to watch those helpless monsters that were wiped out like ants."

The Hawaiian Room turned out to be too noisy and it didn't have enough singing. Estela was overcome by an attack of claustrophobia when the sunflowers started banging on the congas and the monkeys went wild, making strange, angry sounds, and the rain started to fall. "A mob of people trapped in here," she complained, "all of us listening to a concert of mechanical birds and as if that weren't enough, a storm just broke out, with lightning!"

She didn't fear the storm; she was used to bad weather in all its tropical guises: cyclones, hurricanes, thundersqualls. It was just that she couldn't understand what was "attractive" about this Hawaiian attraction. Once outside, the Cuban visitor marveled at the cloudless skies. "This is fantastic," she said, unable to believe that there wasn't a single drop of rain in sight. "The best trick I've seen all day!"

Gina had been right about the Ghost Mansion: her grandmother loved it. She loved the transparent beings who ran through the hallways, up the walls, down the stairs. The talking marble heads in the graveyard were fascinating. And she thought the cemetery phantoms were friendly and comical, not scary at all. In fact, there was nothing frightening in that house; even the corpses trying to break out of their coffins were hilarious. The whole attraction was a delightful joke, someone's mischievous idea of the afterlife.

"The way they fool your mind!" said Estela repeatedly as they rode through the mansion, surrounded by murmurs and moaning voices; as they watched the elegant dancing spirits spin around the ballroom floor. "*Qué bonito!*"

At the end, the two women were tickled to discover a ghost sitting between them in the car. As the vehicle moved, swiveling down the rail toward the exit, it passed in front of a wall-sized mirror. There they were, reflected; and there it was, the goofy-looking likeness of a young man.

"Look, Gina! He's so cute." Abuela was giggling. "Ask him if he wants to be your boyfriend."

And the girl heard an inner voice saying, *Purple Alert!* She knew all too well what male spirits were capable of doing.

-III-

Estela is singing a song she learned when she was a child. It tells the story of a bluebird that cries with human tears. Once upon a time the creature had been a beautiful young maiden. Cursed by a witch who was envious of her beauty and her youth, the girl was condemned to wander the skies eternally. Her name was Bambaé.

Abuela's resonant voice is throaty at times, when she hits the low notes, but always nuanced, pleasant. She sings of the storm and the stream and the rainbow. She sings about the aching little heart of a bluebird, *Zun zun zun . . . Zun zun Bambaé . . .*

The song has a haunting melody, and somehow it sounds familiar to Gina. Like the messages one hears in dreams but can't recall the next morning, and which linger in fragments, a word surfacing here and there during the day, making no sense by itself. Like shadows. Or the texture of clouds, airy, impossible to touch but visible.

Suddenly, for no apparent reason, Gina thinks of the Terrible Santera she was forewarned about. *Her disgusting practices.* When would she appear? At the stroke of midnight, during a full moon? With thunder and a howling wind? *Sacrifices. Powerful gods. Bloody rites.* When?

~~~~

Once her few things were arranged in the girl's room, Estela took a color print of Jesus Christ out of her suitcase and displayed it on the night table next to her bed. It was an amiable likeness of the Messiah looking swarthy, with black hair and beard, and glinting gray-green eyes. Gina was glad the print didn't show the usual horrifying depiction of Jesus nailed on the cross.

Later, as the Domingos' guest grew accustomed to her temporary home, she started to add other icons to her makeshift altar: La Virgen de la Caridad del Cobre (Virgin of Charity, also known as Oshún); San Lázaro, the old man with the crutch and the dog, protector of the downtrodden; and the goddess of passion, Santa Bárbara, alias Changó. Occasionally Abuela would light a white candle to her Cristo and her saints. And she'd mumble a litany, or read a couple of Martí's *Versos*, or sing her peaceful song before going to bed.

One night she shared with her granddaughter the content of her recent invocations. She prayed that nothing bad would ever happen to Nitín, that the family wouldn't have an accident driving down the steep and winding Pinos Verdes hill, that the radar in the backyard wouldn't attract flying saucers, that Gina wouldn't get a bad case of acne or suffer painful menstruation, that she would have a chance to visit Cuba some day.

Was this to be the extent of her black magic, of her demonic rituals? So much for the feared Iyalocha!

~~~~

Estela didn't care for organized religion. "Religions are made up of words, just like governments," she told Gina. "And you don't have to rely on language to talk to the good God, to our Buen Dios. You need faith and silent prayers, *mi niña*. Nothing more."

"But what about the saints?" asked the girl, curious about these entities who seemed to figure so prominently in her grandmother's faith. "You pray to them, too. Don't you need them?"

"Sure I do, because when God is busy, they listen and try to help us. The *santos* are good friends. They were people before they joined the spirit world, like Jesucristo, in a way, so they understand our weaknesses and virtues. I usually think of them as messengers, voices that carry our prayers to Dios, and who interpret them. But the saints also have the power to do some of God's work, giving us strength and keeping the spark of life going when there seems to be no hope."

"What a nice way to think of them. I like it."

"Yes, but you shouldn't feel obligated to believe in my saints, Gina. We all have different ways of imagining the other realm. Your friendly spirits may look nothing like mine."

"That's not what they'll tell you in Catechism class!"

"I know. The Church teaches you that there can only be one image of the divine powers. Most religions are the same; they expect you to accept their views without questioning. And to obey their rules! Organized religion has too many precepts, I think, and some don't make much sense. They were established hundreds of years ago and have little to do with our present reality, or with our personal circumstances. So why follow their rules? Why build your world around them, and feel guilty and remorseful if you break them?"

"I hate guilt."

"God should be a private experience, not a set of laws or someone's interpretation of the Bible. You don't have to study the Scriptures all the time or go to Mass or to a temple in order to live a rich spiritual life."

"I totally agree!"

"Organized religion will tell you that it has access to the only truth, *la verdad absoluta*. But I know with utmost certainty that my own *verdad* is valid and acceptable by God. So why should I give it up just to be a member of some church? Nonsense!"

It seemed as though her grandmother was voicing Gina's own feelings and thoughts. "I'm just not very religious," she admitted. "What I mean is I don't feel very Catholic. Yeah, I go to Mass now and then and don't eat meat on Good Friday and I'm supposed to believe in original sin, in Heaven and Hell, and in the Father-Son-Spirit. I try to empty my head of sinful thoughts whenever I'm taking the body of the Lord, you know, the host. And when I listen to this priest who drinks the Savior's blood and when I confess to this priest—a man!—all my sins; not that I have that many, I guess. But it feels so rehearsed, so unreal to me. And so violent."

"What do you mean, 'violent'?"

"Well, just take the sacrifice idea; it's bloody and messy and savage! I swear to you, Abuela, every time I see that poor man up there on the cross, bleeding to death, I get so depressed. And when that happens, I freak out. And I get mad at the Church for parading his suffering like that, and for making me witness his pain. My mind starts rolling with the whole violent mood and then I think about all the innocent women who were burned to death, accused of witchcraft, and about the Crusades and all the killing in the name of God . . ."

"You're right, *mi niña*, it is all very depressing. Look what happened in Cuba. The native population of the island was completely exterminated by the Spaniards. They did it in the name of the King and the Queen and Christianity."

"I know."

"They treated the Indians like animals, unworthy of life."

"When I think about those things, religion becomes just one big scary blur. And so I start imagining my own god, who has nothing to do with that horrible history. He or She is an invisible someone like your Buen Dios and your messengers, Abuela, a being who doesn't need words and death and crucifixions. Thinking of that loving god helps me have faith again, and to feel safe."

"Then you should always send your silent prayers to that god. It seems to me that you have made a friend up there."

~~~~

One Sunday morning Elisa invited her mother-in-law to go to Mass with her and Benito. Estela declined and, to make matters worse, so did Gina.

Maman's reaction: "I should've known better than to expect a communist atheist to want to visit God's Home. You're going to burn in Hell, Estela!"

Abuela's reaction: "If that's where I end up, I'll save a place for you, Elisa. And I'll welcome you with open arms."

~~~~

The family's old photographs captivate her. Estela scrutinizes them, smiling at times, other times staring at one particular snapshot with studious eyes. *Gina Domingo everywhere.* She enjoys the girl's comments and descriptions of the photos, but she hasn't shown any interest in watching her videos. Abuela dislikes the camera and discourages Gina from filming her. She hates seeing herself *duplicada*, she says, viewing that image of someone who talks and looks just like her, a person who *is* Estela and yet who isn't.

But Camerawoman can't help herself. She won't pass up this opportunity. *Duplication*, TAKE 1. Señora Ruiz is wearing faded blue jeans, with a black leather belt riding low on her hips, a tie-dyed T-shirt displaying the name of a rock group, and black flats. It's crazy, an old woman donning a teenager's clothes so easily, just for fun. "*Qué locura!*" She did have a little trouble getting into the jeans, and now that she's got them on, she can't breathe! But the shirt fits perfectly. How is this possible?

Gina points out that the shirt is extra-large because baggy is in. "And also I'm bigger up there than you are," she says.

"But not that much bigger, *mi niña.*"

"Breasts are one big pain. Don't you think?"

"Your breasts hurt you?"

"No. What I mean is, they get in the way sometimes."

"They do, but–"

"Definitely when I exercise. I wish I could take them off in Physical Education! And when I'm trying to get to my classes, too. At school, as soon as the bell rings everyone runs to their lockers or their friends or lunch or whatever. *Never* to their next class. So I hold my books real tight to my breasts. Because if I don't, I'll regret it! They'll be pushed and shoved and flattened. I wouldn't mind a little flattening, actually."

"You have a nicely shaped bust, Gina. Like mine. I think you take after me in that respect."

"Lucky me!"

Abuela catches her mirror reflection, realizing that she's turned into a parody of her grandchild. "What a spectacle!" she says, laughing. Now, if she could just say a few words in English, the uncanny effect would be complete. *Sorpresa!* Would she dare?

During her flight from Miami to Los Angeles, she tried her limited English on the friendly American man who sat next to her. The exchange didn't get very far, for obvious reasons. All she could say was: "How are you? I am well, thank you. My name is Estela, and what is your name? I am from Cuba." But after three weeks in California, she's learned to say more, much more. She has picked up expressions her granddaughter uses constantly, and phrases weaved together from scraps of conversations.

She's about to act like a *boba*, a complete fool. But the time has come! Estela must put her new words to the test. She looks at Gina and says, "Wow!" And she ventures "No way!" with the best accent she can muster. And "Bummer, cool, groovy, oh my God!" Feeling encouraged by the girl's laughter, she goes on to full sentences, "My boyfriend liking flying fishes. We listen boom box in beach. My surfeador crazy for me. But I only crazy for the mall!"

The Moviemaker is cracking up, laughing so hard she can't hold her camera steady. No one has ever impersonated her! She digs her grandma's broken English, which strangely enough sounds like Gina's. She loves Estela for trying to get closer, in yet another way, to her granddaughter.

"Surfeador crazy for me!" says Gina with a Cuban accent, imitating Abuela imitating Gina. Estela joins in; they egg each other on, echo each other, scream, "But I only crazy for the mall! *Creisi creisi creisi for el mol!*" They stop, catch their breath. Señora Ruiz faces the mirror and yelps, this time in Spanish, "It's a miracle! Now your *noviecito* won't be able to tell us apart."

~~~~

The little boyfriend, that's what she always called Robby, *el noviecito*. Estela was grateful for his greeting, "Muchou gustou, senyora." She welcomed with a kiss the flowers he gave her when they first met and she said to him, in a whisper, "Sank you bery mosh."

Gina could tell her grandma liked him. Of all the things they did together, she would cherish one especially: Robby and Estela playing at the Cyberabilia arcade, eating up mechanical mini-demons with their magic wands. Both driving sports cars at full speed, avoiding the bumps, the rocks, and the potholes in the road. *Creisi creisi!* The Cuban driver's tires screech as they burn down the freeway; her vehicle never goes up in flames. She reaches the finish line first. She's the winner!

Gina would cherish the memory of other excursions, even those that didn't go smoothly, as planned, or that ended up displeasing her grandma. Like their visit to the Tinseltown Wax Museum; Abuela just wasn't impressed. She said she hadn't seen the movies represented by those pallid dummies, so she couldn't savor the illusion. She did recognize, however, some of the stars behind the frozen masks: Chaplin, Bogart, Monroe.

"Imagine," she told her granddaughter, "being cooped up in here, trapped in your own image for eternity. How sad." And Gina found the idea depressing. Somebody's picture of hell. *Trapped in your image.* Pathetic! She'd never thought about those wax figures this way.

At the Hollyworld Studios, Estela didn't "give a cucumber" (didn't care) that prime-time TV shows and box-office hits were being filmed just a few feet away from her. Stars in the flesh! No wax imitations! Señora Ruiz just wasn't excited, and her lack of excitement about this place was the hardest for Gina to understand. How could anyone, Cuban or not, remain unmoved by such an opportunity?

She searched her grandmother's face, looking for traces of emotion, and found only a blank stare. Few people in the world got a chance to peek in on this kind of star-studded shooting. Abuela was lucky and didn't even know it. So it was Gina's duty to tell her: "Don't miss a thing. You're witnessing film history. Enjoy yourself, *chica!* Watch!"

Film history, enjoyment. Words that had little to do with Estela's state of mind, as she reacted to the filming of two feature films and one sitcom. Part of the tour, she'd been told, was a view of whatever they were shooting that day on the Hollyworld lots. So here she was sitting on a hard chair in this go-cart (a sluggish vehicle that couldn't make up its mind whether to be a bus, a train, a car, or a truck). And she was having to listen to this tour guide (a young man with a peculiar smile) who had some vital information to offer. "From now on," he said, "and for the duration of each scene, everyone must be silent. You understand? Quiet! The slightest sound could ruin the work."

Estela heard moans, "Ahs," "Ohs" and "Wows" as they approached the sets. And then dead silence; the chatty visitors suddenly turned mute. All zombies! There had to be something she was missing; a universal something, that is, because the vehicle was packed full of people from all parts of the world. And it seemed as though to all of them, without exception, a glimpse of Heaven had been granted. *Oh! Ah! Wow!*

Gina, too, loved this place. She more than anyone, it seemed. Estela would try to hide her apathy from the girl, her boredom, the cloud of tedium that enveloped her as she saw cameras, blinding lights, wires. People in disguise, with too much makeup. Human beings who didn't look human. Characters pretending to be in a real place (a living room, a bedroom, a spaceship) and who uttered the same words (or sounds) over and over again. Those poor actors had to say their lines and do their actions too many times!

Repetition. The sheer absurdity of repetition . . .

~~~~

The first set: In a dark bedroom, a skinny, boyish-looking man and a red-haired woman stand. They whisper something to each other and stare up at the ceiling (although there's no ceiling and no roof, only a spotlight). Then a fat man from behind the camera mumbles some instructions, and the thin man and the redhead stand, whisper something to each other, and stare up at the invisible ceiling. And on and on. Six, seven times!

The second set represents the cluttered kitchen of a house. The show is a comedy but Estela doesn't see what's funny about it. And not just because she doesn't understand what they're saying, no. There are hardly any words spoken! An obese woman with a mean and heavily made-up face shouts at her children. She shouts and shouts and then shouts some more. The children sit quietly, poor babies, watching an obese woman with a mean face who shouts at them. Who shouts and shouts and shouts and shouts!

Set three has been reserved for last because, as the tour guide explained, it is the biggest, grandest, most popular science fiction TV series ever made. And now it's going to the big screen! The fortunate visitors will get to watch the filming of the last scene of the first motion picture based on the blockbuster sci-fi drama!

What Señora Ruiz sees doesn't live up to all the fuss. A bald-headed man dressed in a red uniform that looks like pajamas is standing next to a wolf-like creature and another being with the head of a lizard. All three are staring at a blank screen. The bald one says two or three words, then points to a hole in the wall. The lizard-man looks at the hole, the wolf-man looks at the lizard and then at the hole. A middle-aged woman off the set gives them an order, smiling. And then the bald man speaks, pointing to the hole. Wolf-man looks, lizard looks. The woman gives them an order. And all three stare at a blank screen. Forever.

~~~~

"Interesting" was the word she decided to use when Gina asked her opinion. But the girl knew—it was so obvious!—that Abuela hadn't enjoyed it. "I don't understand," she said to her grandma while they were taking a lunch break. "Didn't you think it was fantastic?"

"No, it wasn't fantastic for me," replied Estela as she gobbled down the last bite of a cheeseburger. "And it doesn't matter, Ginita. We don't have to like the same things."

"But really, what did you think of the filming?" Gina had finished her hamburger and was picking at her remaining fries.

"It depressed me. I kept feeling sorry for the actors."

"But they were enjoying themselves!"

"Really? It didn't seem that way to me." Estela took a sip of her Cherry Cola, which tasted too sweet and chemically flavored. "All those actions being done so many times. Life is repetitive enough already. Why make it more so?"

"They have to shoot the scene until they get it perfect, that's why."

"But who decides what is perfect?"

"The director!"

"And why should the cost of perfection be such utter boredom? Can't they just get it right the first or second time?"

They were now gathering up the remains of their meal, empty burger boxes, soiled napkins, three cold and solitary fries. After throwing it all in the waste bin, they set out for a stroll.

"Boredom?" asked Gina in disbelief. "Did you say boredom, Abuela? You were *bored*?"

"A little bit, yes."

"It was probably because you didn't understand what they were saying."

"Yes, that must be it."

"And you also need to visualize what the entire scene will look like eventually, you know, after they edit it and add music and special effects to it. You have to use your imagination."

"But I did. It was thanks to my imagination that I didn't fall asleep!"

"I can't believe the filming of those shows depressed you, Abuela."

"But you enjoyed yourself, no?"

"Sure. It was great."

"You liked being a witness of film history, right, Gina?"

"It was fabulous."

"That's what everybody seemed to think!"

They strolled through the crowded, make-believe streets of the Hollyworld Studios. Minutes later Gina stopped, said to her grandma:

"You know what?"

"What, *mi niña*?"

"Now that I think about it . . . I was a little bored in there, too."

~~~~

The last stop of the tour was The Holly Tremor, a tunnel where the vehicle got stuck, while the passengers were subjected to a simulated earthquake. This experience was hailed as one of the highlights of the tourist package.

"You go to this place to have fun," said Estela of the Tremor, "and they throw you in a hole. Then they make the earth move until your guts are in your throat and your heart's coming out of your nose. What's so fun about that?"

"It's good practice," Gina told her, ticked off at Señora Party Pooper. "Sort of like a rehearsal."

"Practice for what? What do you mean, a rehearsal?"

"Practice for the Big One, the Grande that's coming, Abuela." She was enjoying this momentary flight into meanness. "The real thing. It'll hit before the end of the century for sure, eight on the Richter scale. And you have to know what to do, where to go to save your life."

Gina mentioned the earthquake alerts, described the preparations: canned goods, stand in a doorjamb, and so on. The Cuban woman turned pale. "It's all true," her granddaughter assured her. "A lot of people have lost their lives in previous earthquakes. Thousands of people!"

Estela had experienced horrible tropical weather in her country, had been through cyclones, hurricanes, floods, mud slides. Yet none of that prepared her for the Big One, for this invisible, omnipotent monster that would agitate the ground when you least expected it. You couldn't escape its claws! Where would you hide from it?

The California earthquakes were known worldwide, even in Cuba, but Estela didn't want to believe what she was hearing. *Thousands of people!* Gina's deadpan manner disturbed her; her grandchild seemed to take a morbid kind of pleasure in reporting these horrible facts.

Ay, Buen Dios y todos los santos! she prayed. Please help Gina understand the horror of this knowledge. And please don't let the Grande ever hit!

~~~~

They see someone who looks just like her, who is and is not Señora Ruiz de Domingo. That woman is trying on a swimming suit. Estela (or this other person on the screen) is making fun of her body. "*Tremendo pellejo,*" she wails as she displays her sagging skin. "Look at that pitiful flab!"

At the beach, Gina describes (and her camera shows) the Ramosa dudes that parade by them: Surfer, Yuppie, Neohippie, Grungie, Slacker, Vato, Dude, Cybercalifo. The girl lies down on her stomach, then sideways, on her back. She's illustrating for Abuela the right way to tan. Information that the Domingos' guest doesn't find particularly useful, since she has no intention of sitting there like a fool, doing nothing, just so she can roast under the sun. "In my country," she tells Gina, "people avoid getting tanned at all cost. Which is what I should be doing right now. I'm already tanned enough, *mi niña.* Look at me." She's laughing. "*Pura negrita!*"

"You're definitely darker than my mom's Cuban friends. It's not that you're darker exactly. Your skin just doesn't have that pink tone that theirs has. Some of those ladies tan by the pool like Maman or in a tanning bed after they soak their bodies in four or five different types of lotion. And so they end up looking like a Technicolor freak show. Much too evenly brown, or red as a lobster or something. Gross!"

"Did you say they use a 'tanning bed'? What is that?"

"A bed with fake sunlight, ultraviolet rays, know what I mean?"

"What a peculiar thing to do. There's all this sun out here, and they have to go and use artificial light? Doesn't it hurt their skin?"

"Yeah, probably. But they wouldn't want to be seen in public. They'd rather roast in private. Guess it also takes less time that way."

"But why get a tan in the first place? Ay, Ginita, sometimes this place seems upside down to me."

"To me, too!"

Estela notes, with panic, a gooey black gel that is stuck on the soles of her feet. "What in the world is that substance?"

"The Blob!" shouts Gina, teasingly. "El Blobo!" But her grandma doesn't get it. She never saw the sci-fi classic.

"What is it, please? It won't come off!"

"Don't worry, it's nothing, just industrial waste from some plant nearby. It'll come off with rubbing alcohol."

They go in the water. Abuela feels assaulted by the relentless waves. She fights them, tries to stay afloat but succumbs to their powerful rhythm.

"*Ay, mi niña,* make them stop!"

"Sorry, I can't!"

"Will they ever calm down?"

"Never! You're not in the Caribbean."

"Only a flying fish could have fun at this beach!"

~~~~

Until now, Estela hadn't seen the ocean, hadn't even been to Trinidad, a beach that was relatively close to where she lived. Before the Revolution, she didn't have the money. (Her work as washerwoman barely paid for rent and food.) And then, later, when her son got married, he and his wife went to Varadero a few times on vacation. Benitín invited her to join them, but Estela declined. She felt embarrassed to go on trips like the rich people. Yes, even now, when there were no more class privileges in Cuba and everyone could enjoy the beaches. Vacationing was just not something she was in the habit of doing. Somehow the idea made her feel awkward, uncomfortable.

But she had secretly daydreamed about the ocean, had imagined herself swimming there, floating on the peaceful, warm surface. She spoke to Gina of these intimate imaginings and the girl shared visions of her own with Abuela. She'd also seen a fabulous beach in her mind's eye: crystal-blue waters, sand white and fine like sugar. The waves don't topple you, nearly drown you. There's no black waste on your feet.

So vivid were their memories, invented memories of a factual place, that they spoke of Varadero Beach as though they'd been there, together. As though they'd conquered time and space to meet on the Caribbean shore. As though they knew this most beautiful sight.

- PART TWO -

Chapter 6

-I-

Fear of duplication. What the heck did Abuela mean by that? The camera freaked her out. But wasn't her grandson Bladimir into movies, too? No matter how ancient his equipment, he had to have given her a taste of moviemaking. Maybe she reacted to his camera the same way, like the machine was going to eat her up or something.

The girl reproached herself for thinking an Elisa-like thought: Abuela's apprehension betrayed her peasant roots, and it was only with regards to film that she acted like a total hick. But why? Gina could relate to the pain people sometimes feel when seeing themselves on the screen; the screen shows you things you didn't know were there, and that you'd be better off not knowing about. She'd experienced the shock of discovering a person she didn't think she was. A fatter, geekier person. But Abuela didn't seem to have any hang-ups about her looks. It had to be something else that bugged her.

Fear of duplication. What did that mean?

Whatever it meant, it was irrational. There was no risk at all! Abuela wouldn't get trapped in the tape (such a backward thought!) and there wouldn't be a replica of her out in the world just because someone captured her image on video. Getting filmed was a normal, everyday kind of activity.

Not for Estela. There was nothing normal about it for her. She despised the movie machine, considered it worthless, unnecessary. The camera's function was one of the most nonsensical ideas she'd encountered in the North. What was the point of a device that made you appear on a screen? Did people derive some sort of pleasure from this appearance? She couldn't perceive nor understand that pleasure.

But Estela would never tell her *nieta* how strongly she felt. She didn't want to criticize an object—an experience!—that was so precious to her grandchild. So she just kept dodging Gina's lens, in vain, and the teenager kept forcing her moviemaking mania on Abuela. The Domingos' guest would see herself captured on film repeatedly, ad nauseam: in the garden, at the mall, at the beach; eating, talking, dancing, laughing (fortunately not doing other more private things!). A proliferation of images that made her feel trapped, fragmented, invaded.

In spite of Gina's efforts, her secret plan to help Abuela overcome her "video hang-up," Estela would never get over her discomfort. The only result of the teenager's failed attempts was a nightmare she had, triggered by the "duplication" issue. It was as though Abuela had transferred her fear onto her granddaughter, giving Gina a taste of her own medicine.

~~~~

The Pinos Verdes Wife, TAKE 53. She's sitting alone in a theater watching a movie when, suddenly, she realizes the movie is about her. The screen has become a crystal ball where Gina's life is unfolding. "Who the hell did this to me?!" she screams within the walls of her subconscious. "Who turned me into a character?!"

But if this is her dream, then she must be the one imagining the movie. *Not!* Her mind is out-there, sure, but also incapable of concocting this autobiography, this pathetic scenario. Someone else has to be pulling her mind-strings. Someone with a twisted sense of humor.

She's helpless, unable to break frame, unable to do anything but watch, having to face the onslaught of events with no recourse and no power. There are some good moments, but few compared to the long stretches of boredom and domesticity that await her. What about her career? Like, does she have an exciting job? It doesn't show up on this screen! Her professional world has been cut out of the final print, scraps on the floor of some dusty editing room. Rejects.

"Get me out of here!" she wails when she finally grasps the meaning of those images she's being made to bear. Through the distorted lens of her dream, she has turned into a Pinos Verdes Wife. Gina Domingo is Mrs. Robert Holmes. Worse: she sounds and acts and talks just like her mother!

"Fire the screenwriter!" Gina cries out as she watches . . .

~~~~

A lavish white wedding in a Catholic chapel, lacquered photographs attesting to the couple's beauty. The Domingos' wedding gift is a ninety-day voyage around the globe (who knows, the honeymoon may prove to be fertile). A substantial down payment on a house is the Holmes' wedding present (the right environment might do the trick).

They settle in their brand new home. Gina decorates it but it's ultimately Robby's pad: enormous, full of practical things that make life easy. The lovebirds like to show off their bliss. She strokes his silky blonde hair and kisses him in public; he gives her his Cheshire Cat smile. They hold hands when strolling. And she lets him pull out a chair for her at the restaurant, open the door of the car, be a gentleman. While they make love in a room with mirrored walls, he tells her, "You're the best little wife, Mrs. Holmes."

Their house is located in an exclusive community, a town within a town within another town where they feel safe and protected. The Holmes have Sunday barbecues and occasional dinners out. Robert's job consumes over sixty hours a week. (He inherited the family business, unimaginative but highly profitable work.) She just stays home and plays with the girls, Linda and Leisha, their "kids." Mrs. Holmes adores the darling faces they make when they're hungry, or when you're eating frozen yogurt and you pretend to ignore their grainy black tongues pleading for some. Chows are such gluttons!

Leisha is obsessed with her tail; usually after a nap, she stares at it as if noticing it for the first time. Intrigued by its sight, she starts spinning around in circles, in a frenzy, bent on biting it off. The other dog likes water. Gina loves to watch her trying to catch—and eat!—the liquid squirting from the hose, when the gardener waters the yard. Such darlings, their babies. Not really children, but so close.

Mrs. Holmes has been staying home a lot lately, waiting for the grand moment. Rob wants the real thing, not just dogs. He can't resign himself to a life without sons to take fishing or to the game; without peaches-and-cream little girls to brighten up the house and idolize him. No use having a model home and a flag and fireworks on the Fourth of July if you can't share it all with children.

Gina used to take film classes but now . . . Now her career is a whimsical pastime. All her energy must be devoted to creating the greatest experience of her life: motherhood. And Mrs. Holmes is ready. She's been dreaming lately (a dream within a dream?!) about her firstborn: a baby girl with curly hair and long eyelashes, a picaresque smile. Her alabaster skin has a sweet smell of freshly carved wood. The baby has Robby's nose and his sturdy frame, but her eyes are bedroom eyes like her mother's. She also inherited Gina's cleft chin and her dimples. This beautiful child is the daughter the young couple is destined to have, Mrs. Holmes is sure.

The baby might not learn to speak Cuban, her mother's native language, but at least she'll know that her ancestors came from a Caribbean country. And one day she'll see pictures of her grandparents, images captured by Gina's ancient video camera. So what if the child ends up hating those video clips. Mrs. Holmes will force her to watch them. Her daughter has to learn to remember.

~~~~

But wait! This is all wrong; Gina Holmes, that woman up there on the screen, is not ready for children! And she can't handle her life, being cooped up in this joint day after day. The poor lady needs help, lots of help!

From her seat in the one-person audience, Ms. Domingo decides to offer her screen double an escape from her misery. She formulates a plan, a liberating scheme to fool the Robby Bunch. Married Gina must orchestrate her death. Yeah! She'll make them all believe that she died accidentally by drowning. And then she will escape, run as far as she can from that town-within-a-town, from that barfed-up marriage!

~~~~

Mr. and Mrs. Holmes will spend their last weekend together (a "second honeymoon," she tells him) in their time-share condo on Ananda Island. At one point during the three-day vacation, toward the end, Gina will go for a walk. She knows he'll want to accompany her, but she must be firm and insist on going alone. The young lady would like some time by herself to sort things out. She's going for a short walk, that's all.

The unsuspecting husband watches his beloved as she strolls down the deserted beach, away from him. Poor man, he's completely unaware that she'll never return! The only trace of Gina that will be left are her clothes in shreds that will wash ashore, incontrovertible proof of her demise.

But that plan hasn't been put into action yet, so everything seems normal on Ananda Island. Rob carries his wife in his arms down the garden path, just as he did the day they were married.

She points out, in apparent ecstasy, the cloudless blue sky, the seagulls, the silky vegetation.

They swim out to the lighthouse and there he takes her, panting, still out of breath from the swim. Or they dig into the moist sand with their bodies, possessing each other once more. He caresses her breasts, grazes the palms of her hands with his tongue, playfully. And she welcomes the ravaging rhythm of his thrusts; the soreness, far-reaching and burning, of this performance.

~~~~

Spectator Gina loathes the voice-over in those last condo scenes. She finds the language unreal. This Gina sitting in the dark doesn't use words like "incontrovertible" and "demise." She can't relate to phrases like "the ravaging rhythm of his thrusts" because, for one thing, she has never "performed" and consequently has no memory of a "soreness far-reaching and burning."

It's obvious that the writers and producers of this dream-movie don't care to portray the real Ms. Domingo. Typical Hollywood! They keep stealing her ideas, turning them into soft porn; even while she sits here quietly, thinking and reacting, they're picking her brain. Thieves! They took her Liberation Plan and rewrote it as a Second Honeymoon packed with hanky-panky. Typical!

No doubt the stupid flick is aimed at an older audience, people like her mother. Which is okay, as long as they don't try to sell Gina this view of the future as *her* future. If Maman likes to get off watching R-rated dramas made for randy housewives, that's her problem. Just leave the girl out of it!

~~~~

The movie is coming to an end, you can tell, because the music is mushy and loud, with lots of strings. The lights will soon go up and then she'll leave this stinking projection room forever. But before that happens, she needs to find out whether her screen persona will carry out The Plan. Mrs. Holmes must run away from that bloodless town-within-a-town existence! She needs to tell the Robby Bunch to take their Sunday barbecues and shove them!

Will there be a resolution to this ordeal? Will the audience at least be given the pleasure of a clear-cut ending? Oh God, this movie is looking more and more like an art-house film! She should've suspected an artsy agenda from the very beginning, but she was too wrapped up in the awesome process of seeing herself turned into a character. The strange impression of watching Gina from outside of Gina distracted her and kept her from being her usual perceptive self. But now she knows the truth and no one can fool her: Ms. Domingo's future has been produced as a made-for-TV movie pretending to be an artsy-fartsy flick. Bummer!

And so she's forced to listen once again to the narrator who won't give her the satisfaction of a resolved conflict. There goes that woman who's supposed to be a mature Gina and yet sounds like a soap opera dame. We're watching the characters in their Ananda condo while the voice-over tells us . . .

Here we are, finally. There is no indication of the truth. This is not our last time in paradise but our first. The wall-size mirror projects our Love Scene, this primordial union. We are in love, says our deceitful reflection. We are inventing life for a barren and moribund planet. Our future.

The end.

-II-

Gina's reflection in the dresser mirror: She's wearing faded blue jeans and a tank top; a long necklace of black rope, with a wooden peace symbol; and bloodstain-color lipstick (the idea of "bloodstain" is repulsive, but the color is cool). Dressed for the occasion. Action!

The doorbell rings. Gina runs down the stairs to meet Robby. As she passes by the den, she notices her parents watching TV. Maman puts up with a Retro show every now and then, just to humor Daddy. (How generous of her.) That's what they're watching now; you can tell because the colors on the screen are so bright they're blinding, and there's hokey music playing. Could it be the Singing-American-Family Show?

Sure enough: an episode about one of the boys losing his pet snake, and the entire bunch setting out to find the animal. This is quite a collective undertaking, quite a mystery! Where is the darling reptile? Is it hiding under the bed, in one of the cupboards, in Dad's briefcase? Has it run away in search of its freedom? Could it be secretly mating somewhere?

None of the above. Mister Snake will be served for dinner; a sinister cook that Retro Mom recently hired decided to add it to her stew, just to give it a tad of extra flavor. Fire the killer! Sobs.

Gina is tense. Maybe this wasn't such a great idea after all. Abuela's idea. For an old Cuban lady, she sure has an American way of thinking. Actually, the plan had had a very Abuelesque beginning, with a good old Cuban idiom setting things off.

Estela had asked out of the blue, "When are you going to start crying?"

"Pardon me?" a befuddled Gina had reacted.

"You know what I mean. If you don't cry, you won't get fed!"

"Abuela, what are you talking about?"

"If you don't make the effort, nothing will happen."

Gina wasn't quite sure how this baby-crying-for-food analogy was meant to shed light on her situation. "What effort are you referring to?"

"The effort to get closer to Robby, *mi niña.*"

Is this what she wanted? Yeah, the idea of bringing Rob to the house sounded great when they first thought of it. Her parents had to meet him eventually. Not that he was the love of her life, not by a long shot. She just dug him and he dug her. She'd managed to overcome her innate wishy-washiness, her dude-teasing tendencies (up to a point, of course). They were dating, sort of, and this was the correct thing to do. The decent course of action was to bring Robby home, get it over with. But now . . .

Heck! She's not alone; she has a supportive grandmother who will help her get through the crunch. Action!

Gina greets Robby, invites him in. She's glad he's looking "normal." Maybe there's hope for this visit after all. "No psychie shorts," she'd told him, as if scripting a character. "And don't drive your bug; borrow the family car if you can. My Dad's English is hard to understand when he gets nervous, and he'll be nervous meeting you. So, if you don't know what he's saying, just let me do the talking, okay? And don't mention your surfing! Dad doesn't know much about surfers, but if he did, I just know he wouldn't like them. Oh, and when my mother offers you bizarre French pastry, eat it and tell her it's yummy. Got it?"

She can't help feeling tense. It's not like her future depends on this visit or anything big like that, no. And it's not like Robby's too out-there for Daddy and Maman to like him. He looks so clean-cut that he's revolting, a total dweeb. But he's perfect for the test. The test! That's it, the reason why she's anxious. She *hates* tests and this experience seems like one. No matter how small or insignificant—

a pop quiz, a mock exam—tests make her feel miserable: shivers, queasy stomach, wobbly knees. And here she is, about to take the Parents-Meet-Boyfriend Final without having once cracked the books. Without reading her notes!

Abuela will come down the stairs any minute now; she has to, she'd better. Where *is* her grandma? Is she hiding somewhere? In the garden, maybe? No, there she is, approaching, giving Robby a kiss on the cheek, gesturing for him to move in the direction of the den. Everything is going to be okay now that Señora Cubana has entered the scene.

~~~~

"Dad, Mom . . . This is Robert, my dude."

"Your what?" asks Daddy.

"I mean my friend."

The men shake hands.

"Good to meet you, Robert."

"*Muchou gustou*, sir. How's it hanging?"

"Pardon me? What did you say, young man?"

"I mean, pleased to meet you, sir, ma'am."

"Welcome to our home," says Maman. "Won't you please take a seat?"

Gina and Robby are stationed in the so-called Love Seat (how appropriate), while Dad and Mom sit directly across from the so-called Love Birds, on the couch. Abuela looks comfy in her son's reading chair.

Silence. Gina has a painful, pressing need to hide. She's also trying to suppress her sudden craving for pizza, the worst kind with gobs of red meat and double cheese. Or a Chilly's Special: creamy vanilla with a topping of cherries, caramel fudge, whipped cream, and a dash of chopped almonds. Mmm . . . God, she'd love to go rent a video and shack up with Robby in her projection room, watch a veg-out movie, eat popcorn. All alone. A typical date. Is that too much to ask for?

"Hey, you got a happening pad here!" exclaims the guest.

Why doesn't Robby shut up for a while? Things are nerve-racking enough without his speaking Dude. Gina thought she might need to translate some of this conversation into Spanish for her grandma. But she never ever imagined that she'd be translating Robby's English for her parents.

"He means we have a very lovely home, Daddy."

"Oh, well, thank you."

"I was stoked when Gina told me you wanted me over, sir."

"He says he's pleased that we invited him to our house."

Daddy's upset. He's making that gesture, the one his daughter has secretly named the IRS Twitch, because he does it mainly during IRS time. He moves his neck in a funny way, like he has food lodged in his throat or something. There he goes, twitch twitch twitch!

"Tell me, Gina," says Dad, his voice contorted by the gesture. "Doesn't your friend speak normal English?"

"Yes, he does. Don't you, Robby? Say something normal for my father, will ya?" Now she's really done it! This question wasn't part of the script. Surfer Psychie will freak out!

"Okay, sure," states Rob, confidently. A ray of hope at last. "Gina tells me that you folks are from Cuba. What's Cuba like?"

Silence. Here's Abuela's opportunity. Come in, Cuban Grandma. Come in. This is your cue. Hello? Oops! Maybe she doesn't understand the question. But Gina has no time to tell her. Because Maman is standing up, saying, "I believe it's time for some tartalisa."

"Let me get it, Maman."

"Nonsense, *mignonne.* I'll have the maid bring it."

"Please, Mom!"

"You stay right here with your beau and relax. I won't be long, *chérie.*"

Why is Madame being so nice? And why did she whiz to the kitchen instead of calling Guadalupe and ordering her around like she always does? Could it be that Elisa needs to get away from this horrible test, too? Or is she feeling sorry for her daughter, seeing her baby going through hell because hell is a meeting between a Cuban florist and a Ramosa surfer? Please, Madame Rochart, let Gina scramble to the kitchen, out the door, up into space, to the final frontier. Away from here!

"Hey, Gina." It's Robby's voice. He's pulling her back to Earth with a tractor beam. "What's your mom getting?"

"Some dessert she invented. It's like lemon pie. You'll love it."

When did she become such a pathetic liar? Robby will hate it. Only Maman likes tartalisa. Only Elisa would be able to concoct a bland and tough and chewy flaky thing called tartalisa. She should've followed Abuela's suggestion and ordered *pastelitos* from the Cuban bakery in Santana. Delicious guava pastries. Crisp on the outside, but so creamy inside. Mmm.

Purple Alert! The men are talking.

"So, Robby, I understand that you go to All Saints High School."

"Yes, sir. I sure do." Poor Rob is nervous; he's wriggling in his chair. "I'm a Senior."

"Excellent school, eh?"

"*Sí*, Mr. Dou . . . Dou . . . Domingou." Robby's tongue got stuck on the roof of his mouth. It was grotesque!

"So, you're Catholic."

"Yes, of course. You can't get into ASHS if you're not Catholic."

"I'm quite aware of that." Daddy's crossing his leg and holding it with his hand, the way men do it in the movies. A macho thing. Male bonding underway!

"Some parents lie, you know, just so their kids can go to school there."

"But your parents didn't–"

"Oh no, sir." Rob crosses his leg, too. But he *never* does that! "I've been confirmed and everything."

"Very good, very good. So has Gina."

Silence at last. But not for long. The interrogation resumes.

"You plan to go to college, no?"

"Yes, Mr. Domingou." That tongue thing again.

"And what are you going to study?"

"I sort of dig business."

"Splendid, my boy. I 'dig' business, too." Did Daddy just use the "d" word? Not possible!

Madame returns. Hurray! She's followed by Guadalupe who's bringing a plate full of mini-tartalisas. Maman offers the guest some, acting solicitous. He grabs one of the pastries, which crumbles as he bites into it.

"Be careful!" Elisa warns him. "They're very flaky." She hands him a napkin. Robby chews away.

"Hey," he says with his mouth full, "these are bad!"

Madame looks disappointed. "They're bad?"

"He means they're good, Maman."

"But he said 'bad'!"

"Could I have another one?" asks Rob. Another big liar!

Abuela has been quiet. Gina's so rude. She hasn't interpreted for her at all, like she promised. But Señora Estela is very forgiving. Look at her, she seems pleased, not tense at all. (She's wise to have refused the mini-tarts.) Maybe she's thinking that the horrible encounter has turned out a success. Yes, in spite of the Dude-to-English translations, the long pauses, and the gagging dessert. That look on Abuela's face means a lot; it says that Gina can relax now. Soon the young man will leave and the young woman will hear only positive comments from her parents.

Mission accomplished: Robert has the Domingos' permission to court Gina. He can visit her here, at the house. There are to be no encounters at the mall and no rides in Robby's car (a purple VW with psychedelic stuff painted all over). And definitely no picnics at the beach, unless it's with the family. The beach, says Mr. Domingo, is too tempting for young people, with all those exhibitionists parading themselves everywhere.

Maman finds Robert Holmes to be a handsome lad. She was impressed by his eating not one but five mini-tartalisas. He needs to familiarize himself with standard English, sure, but that's easy. If Benito could do it, so can Robby.

Yes, that's what Abuela's eyes are saying: Noviecito and Noviecita passed the test; they won't have a dig that's big and doomed.

Cut! It's a print.

~~~~

Gina stayed up thinking about Robby's visit and now she can't go to sleep. She's a little drowsy, but her grandma is snoring so loud! Could the old lady hurt herself by making that much noise? It *has* to hurt to produce those sounds. Gina wonders why she's never noticed this detail. Maybe she always falls asleep before Abuela and so has never had the privilege of witnessing the Cuban Thunderstorm.

Frustrated in her effort to get some shut-eye, Gina grabs her camera. The prospect of getting new footage never fails to excite her, for sure when it requires planning, when it implies a little mischief. Yeah, she's in a mischievous mood, ready for action and motion, for a scene of her lifelike movie. Seconds ago she was feeling tense but now she's pure energy.

The Great Director, TAKE 15. Roll 'em! A long tracking shot through the mansion. Rose bouquets here and there. Dim bluish-green light invades the living room, which is furnished in Louis Cinq (or some other French dude with a number for a last name). As we move away, we note the barrel-vaulted ceiling and the light source: four shell-shaped structures modeled after prehistoric reptiles.

The den looks cozy; through its picture window we see the bay and a breathtaking sunset. (It's actually pitch black out there, so use your imagination.) The breakfast nook is art deco. *Oui oui.* There's a tone of futurism in the spotless kitchen (which *does not* contain a food replicator). The camera moves out the kitchen door, onto the patio . . .

In rapid succession we see a lush garden (which Abuela loves to visit); a swimming pool that, according to the Domingos' guest, reeks of cough syrup; a sauna that's much too hot for Estela (she gets enough heat and humidity in her country); a hot tub, used for making human fricassee, says the Cuban visitor; a four-car garage; and last but not least: a satellite dish for contacting flying saucers.

A pop musical theme plays as the movie cuts to Interior Gina's bedroom. Panning of rose-colored walls, movie posters, a TV set, the sound system, a laptop computer, and a bed which contains the Sleeping Bambaé. Cut back to . . .

Den: the camera on a tripod, Gina's reflection on a wall mirror. Her auburn hair in a chignon, she's wearing a black strapless "Gina Moda" evening gown (because Ms. D will be a fashion designer some day, in between making all her box-office hits), a green and purple silk scarf, and a dazzling pearl necklace with a diamond.

The lady poses and smiles. She's willing to talk to the reporters . . .

Q: Could you tell us about your recent projects, Ms. D?

A: Sure. I recently launched my Gina Moda line and soon the world will revel in my perfumes. Exotic Caribbean flowers and herbs went into the formula. It'll be expensive, but it's guaranteed to make you fly, go far beyond the clouds and the birds. Like magic.

Q: The name of this unique scent?

A: I don't mind announcing it . . . TAINA. Isn't it pretty? Don't worry about the meaning, just wear it. You won't regret it!

Q: Are you directing any movies this year?

A: Yes, two. And, of course, I'm reading scripts for the next one.

Q: How do you find time for so much work?

A: Well, I have a very understanding husband. He takes care of the house and the trivialities of life so I can be creative.

Q: It's an unusual arrangement.

A: True, but I am an unusual person.

Q: Why haven't you appeared in any of your films, not even as an extra, or in a cameo? There's a precedent for successful actor-directors in Hollywood. Are you planning to join the Ham League some day?

(She'll offer an answer she has rehearsed. The words aren't hers, she stole them from *Showbuz,* a TV show where they interview celebrities. This is common practice; Hollywood folks are always stealing lines, ideas, thoughts from each other. But what's going to happen when she runs out of borrowed answers? Will the press and the fans buy her gutsy reactions, her fresh opinions? Heck, she'll cross that bridge when she gets there. In any case, these words that she's about to say reflect exactly how she feels. And the reporters will love them. So what if there's nothing original about them!)

A: I'm not interested in acting. As the director, I'm responsible for a total vision. The interpreters—that is, actors—are essential figures, of course. But they represent only one fraction of the picture, elements in the ensemble, voices to be modulated and shaped by a Mastermind. Modesty aside, I think I'm good at pulling the fragments together. My job is to integrate all the players into a whole, make things happen not just from behind but from inside the scenes. That's the challenge. The real stardom.

Q: How do you like working in Hollywood?

(What an easy question! She's read the magazines. She knows, for instance, that life in Hollywood isn't always fair and hunky-dory. Tinseltown can be a rotten black hole. The Big Dumpster. A garbage disposal of culture. Yeah!)

A: I'm not a violent person. (What does *that* have to do with Hollywood? It does, just wait.) No, I'm not violent, but I do admit that there are stars I'd love to disappear. Hey, I'm sorry, but they're like a punishment you don't deserve, know what I mean? They're full of it and they can't act and they have the IQ of a mosquito.

And yet they're everywhere! You can't escape their ugly faces and their stupid opinions and their pointless movies. Category-four movies that you hate and you wouldn't watch in any form and under any circumstances. You know, I have this fantasy–just a fantasy–that I'm a powerful alien with a mission: to rid the Earth of certain undesirable movie people. Oh hell.

Q: Would Ms. D care to comment on some of the latest controversies? For openers, "colorization." Do you feel that it's okay to colorize old black-and-white movies? Is it wrong?

A: Here's what I have to say to the culprits: How dare you mess with other people's work? Who gives you the right?! What makes you think your tacky fake computer colors make the film any better? I admit I prefer color, but only if the movie was originally made that way. You wanna know what gives me the creeps? Suppose some day in the future black-and-white stuff is in, the craze, the total fashion and only black-and-white movies are made. So here's this jerk who wants to take the color out of all my colorful creations, and turn every single one into a *film noir*. I swear I'll sue him! And if I'm dead by then, I'll haunt the hell out of him!

(Relax, Ms. D, relax. She does get carried away about some things, doesn't she? Can't blame a girl for having an opinion!)

Q: And what about the "Silents vs. Talkies" debate?

(Another easy one!)

A: Some critics are saying that only silent movies possess a true artistic essence, right?, that it's an art form which was lost with the invention of sound. Isn't that it? Hey, I've watched some Chaplin and Buster Keaton movies. I know for a fact that those guys were geniuses. Everyone copied them and they influenced everybody. But that bit about images alone telling a story and cinematic texts needing no spoken language. Hah! For sure! Movies are supposed to show the world, do we agree on that? Good, now listen: THE WORLD ISN'T SILENT! People don't go around doing their thing to the beat of corny piano music, mouthing words and then holding up a sign with some skimpy dialogue. Life is full of spoken words and noise and sounds. And you have to show all that in movies 'cause movies are a part of life. Do we agree on that?

~~~~

Do we agree? She glances at her tripod (the red light indicates it's still rolling) and realizes that she fell asleep in Daddy's reading chair, while taping. So much for mischief and motion! A fun session, the girl recalls immediately. Major head trip.

Still in a stupor, Gina turns off the machine. *The world isn't silent!* She has no idea, of course, that she was rudely awakened by her own loud snoring.

-III-

Estela got in the habit of sitting with Guadalupe in the breakfast nook and having the maid tell her stories about Mexico. "Let the *doméstica* do her work, Estela!" Maman would snap whenever she saw them talking. But why shouldn't Guadalupe rest a little once in a while, have a cup of coffee and chat?

The Mexican woman told tales about desperate people crossing dangerous borders, risking their lives to come to the North. Abuela saw photos of the maid's mother and four children, who were still back in Chihuahuah, and she was moved by her plight. "My husband and I work hard," said Guadalupe, "so we can send them dollars." She had dreams: "One day we will be together again, in this country. Soon, I hope. I miss my babies."

Estela was appalled to see how much work the *doméstica* had to do: cooking, cleaning house, waiting on Señor, Señora and Señorita. "Guadalupe is your slave," she once told Elisa. And Madame replied that her servant was well paid, just like all the other Domingo employees. She was lucky, in fact. "If it weren't for us, she'd be starving in Mexico."

"But she's starving here, too," said Abuela, "having to cook and eat these peculiar meals!" She was referring to the *Golden Hill Cookbook* recipes, source of the Domingos' daily menu: unseasoned broiled poultry, beautifully adorned but bland casseroles of bean curd and pasta, mushy dark rice cooked with raisins and foul-smelling spices. Ambivalent mixtures that could be served as entrées, side dishes, appetizers, or dessert. Take your pick!

"It is rather apparent," Elisa reacted, brisk and poised, "that you know nothing about fine cuisine and good eating habits. God knows what you've been eating for the last forty years."

~~~~

Going against Elisa's wishes and encouraged by Gina and Benito, Abuela decided to take over the kitchen. She'd been in

California for a month now, and hadn't yet given her relatives a taste of home, *comida cubana*.

She was a gifted cook (or so everyone told her) and had developed artful ways to prepare daily full meals in revolutionary Cuba. As much as Estela hated to admit it (and would *never* admit it to Elisa), life in her country was horribly difficult. Many basic things were always lacking. If it wasn't the rice, it was the beans or the soap or the toilet paper, or even more essential items, like drinkable water. There was such a devastating scarcity on that island! But here, in the North, Estela would be able to create a sumptuous Cuban feast. She'd get to savor dishes she hadn't had in ages. Would she still remember how to make them?

At the Pinos Verdes Market, Señora Ruiz was overwhelmed by the sight and abundance of so many products: bread spread that tasted like butter but wasn't butter; yogurt that was creamier and sweeter than the real ice cream she got to sample in Havana, at Coppelia's. And there were frozen pastries and frozen juice and giant steaks and rice that fluffed up, fully cooked in two minutes; forty types of carbonated drinks, fifty-one kinds of sauces. And a collection of brightly colored, curiously designed boxes filled with cereal shaped like moons, animals, plants. There were also delicacies for fat people on a diet, like fat-free bacon, sugarless candy, sugarless sugar, cheese and meat made from soy milk! An absurd variety of food and yet they didn't have plantains, not even green ones. No *Serrano* ham, either, or Spanish chorizo. No *malanga*, and they had never ever stocked *bijol*.

Disappointed, Estela talked to Guadalupe, and the *doméstica* had a splendid suggestion. "You should go to Santana," she said. "Any of the Latino markets there will have the necessary items for your dishes." The cook was thrilled. A visit to the infamous Hispanic town! A momentary respite from Pinos Verdes silence and opulence, from the Louis Quinze museum and Elisa's *Golden Hill* cuisine. At last!

No, Abuela didn't want Guadalupe to get the groceries for her, as Elisa suggested. (The maid could use a break from slavery.) She insisted on doing the shopping herself. She wasn't leaving the North without visiting Santana. Didn't her son have a store there? Well, then, she wanted to visit it, too!

Benito offered to take her, secretly excited to be able to show his mother the site of his first business. (He would make sure she didn't see the gun.) "It's not worth it," Elisa complained, "risking your life for an unhealthy meal, having to go to that cancerous city." She raised hell when Gina insisted on (and got away with) accompanying Daddy and Abuela on their descent into satanical Santana. Madame warned her husband, "You'd better not let anything happen to our daughter," and he just glowered at her.

If looks could kill.

~~~~

In order to get to the city's downtown area, one had to drive through some of its residential zones: large houses with run-down porches where young women fed their babies or just chatted; cluttered lawns where young men stood around or worked on their cars.

Were those the fearsome Vatos, the people Benito called "bandits"? They seemed so normal and benign to Estela! Some of their vehicles resembled the few old machines that still roamed the Cuban streets forty years after the Revolution. But here the sides and hoods were painted with elaborate pictures (colorful birds and glowing flames and silver-sprinkled words) that reminded Estela of carnival floats. "Santana may be a dangerous town," she told Gina, "but it sure is full of artistic people."

The main commercial strip, La Broadway, was teeming with vendors selling tamales, oranges, pottery. Every other store was a souvenir shop. There were theaters and video stores with poster-size photos in their windows depicting Mexican gunmen, and bars advertising female dancers and Dos Equis beer.

Was this still the United States?

It was obvious that many stores in Santana were owned by Cubans. Estela noticed the facades, feeling an unsettling mixture of awe and nostalgia: HATUEY LIQUOR, VARADERO VIDEOS, EL TAINO MUSIC, CAMAGUEY FASHION, ISLITA MARKET. Benito's flower shop was one of the prettiest establishments in downtown Santana. She enjoyed reading the sign in the shape of a rainbow on the store's front: *Las flores de Domingo conquistan corazones.*

The guard startled her; she wasn't expecting to see one. Estela's pace picked up as she walked by him. She was given a tour of the large premises, and was greeted warmly by the three employees working in the back. The sight and aroma of so many flowers were a soothing change, an escape from the hustle and bustle of La Broadway. She welcomed the rest.

~~~~

"Everything happens here, in the back room," Benito explained. He meant the creative energy, the arguments, the gossip, and most importantly, the Domingo masterpieces. "The effect is what counts," said the florist. "You can sell a ten-dollar arrangement for fifty and a fifty-dollar one for two hundred if you know where to place the right flower."

Some of Benito's floral arrangements had once been featured in *The Green Pines Chronicle*. (His secret dream was to appear in *Bloom Boom*.) Proudly, he showed his mother the clipping; Benito's business was described under Southland Styles. Estela couldn't believe her eyes. Her son's creations were famous; they were considered a stylish trend! But he didn't wish to take all the credit. The florist admitted he'd only had the good fortune of finding two gifted people, a young man and his wife, to put his ideas into form. The boss pulled all the strings, made room for art in a world of commerce. But those two employees were the true artists, makers of marketable beauty.

He described the poster-size pictures of his acclaimed pieces displayed on a side wall, trying to remember the names Elisa had given them. A curvilinear assortment of orchids intertwined with birds-of-paradise was called *Angel of Time*. Seven chrysanthemums cradled in a bed of dahlias, an iris on one side, on the other two red roses: *Rainbow Spirit*. The name *El Dorado* was given to an explosion of multicolored mariposa lilies and minuscule white roses. And the largest creation consisted of an intricate array of gladioli, carnations, snapdragons and tulips, all bedded in blue satin cushions and encased in showy, lance-shaped leaves. It had a long French name, *Les Fleurs du Temps et du Voyage,* that no one except Elisa could pronounce.

"Flowers are messages," said Benito, "and people like to say the craziest things through their flowers." His clients trusted him, and ninety percent of the time they bought whatever he suggested, regardless of the price. "Everyone opens up to a florist," he added. "I guess they think that a person who sells flowers couldn't be all that bad." He let his customers overwhelm him with personal and at times embarrassing confessions; he listened attentively, never saying much. "Secrets you wouldn't imagine. I hear them all!"

Benito offered his Mamá the chaise lounge in his office and asked an employee to bring whatever his mother and daughter fancied. Gina had a Diet Cherry, Estela mineral water. Then the Cuban woman announced that she was ready for her shopping spree. She had spotted a store called Islita Market on La Broadway and was anxious to explore it. "You know," she joked, "it's been a long time since I cooked with all the right ingredients!"

~~~~

Gina enjoyed the ground beef casserole, *picadillo*, and the ham croquettes and the plantain balls filled with fried pork. She loved the black bean soup, the rice and red bean dish, called *congrí*, and the chicken fricassee, the breaded steaks, the green plantain fritters. She adored Estela's desserts: bread pudding and *arroz con leche* (much more than just rice soaked in milk!) And she got a big kick out of watching Abuela cook.

"I'll never learn my way around this maze!" said Estela whenever she entered the kitchen. She hated using the microwave oven because the food placed in it for defrosting made explosive noises, as if refusing to accept its fate. Abuela never used the icemaker, either. "When the machine makes the ice, it seems like it's grinding my bones!" She described Elisa's coffeemaker as the spitting image of a miniature spaceship, which sounded just like one when it was producing that awful, watered-down American version of *café*.

The Cuban cook also mistrusted the garbage disposal because it triggered a volcano in the sink and could easily devour everything in sight. She had already rescued five pitiful-looking spoons and two crooked knives from its clutches. And the horrendous racket it'd generated each time brought Maman to the scene of the crime, seething, "You're destroying my kitchen, Estela!"

Abuela was bewildered by the family's waste products, things that were considered trash. How could you throw away so many valuable objects? Bottles, plastic containers, cans, paper bags, all gone to waste! (Recycling was a concept Benito and Elisa never took seriously, in spite of their daughter's sermons about saving the planet.) Gina will never forget the cookie tin Abuela wanted to keep in case they ever needed a strong container. And the milk cartons (good for transplanting flowers), the cereal boxes (for storing cassette tapes!), and the twist ties that she liked to turn into *anillos de mentirita*, make-believe rings. "Are those the presents you're taking to your communist family?" Maman would ask, sniggering, whenever she caught her mother-in-law "saving" something.

"*Mon Dieu!*" cried Elisa the time she found the old woman and the girl in her French living room, eating pizza and drinking milk shakes. "What are you two doing to my Louis?" After hearing about the "distasteful incident," Daddy talked to the culprits over breakfast. He reprimanded his daughter for feeding his mother so much junk. "You should know better," he said. And to his Mamá, "Eat all you want, *mi vieja*. That's one of the reasons you're here, no? So you can eat. But please don't let Gina feed you poison."

Daddy was calling fast-food, the pillar of American cuisine, "poison." Since when had Mr. Florist become a health-food activist? Yeah, he listened to New Age music about enchanted oceans, but that was the extent of his whole-earth experience. He had no right to talk about good eating habits! Daddy just *had* to have a fix of pepperoni thick-crust once a month, not to mention his double-cheese quarter-pounder with large fries and a malt that he inhaled every other week. And what about his (forbidden) sugar-frosted cereal? Poison. Sure! Adults could be such hypocrites sometimes.

~~~~

Estela told her granddaughter of the village where she was born and raised, Piedrecita (a name that meant "little rock"). She talked of the big city where she'd lived for many years: Florida, province of Camagüey, which formed the belly of the island. Estela said she missed her home on Egusquiza Street, two blocks from the Carretera Central (the only "freeway" in Cuba). Her little house of white walls, the ceiba tree outside her window, the vast ever-blue Cuban skies. And most of all she missed her friends, *la gente*, who were spirited and driven to survive, who spoke her language and understood her thoughts.

"These people have built a wall around their city," Abuela noted, as she and Gina strolled down the Pinos Verdes hill one morning. "They have forced the human side of life—clutter, noises, disorder—out of their gardens and swimming pools," she said, pointing to the homes they were passing. "I don't mean to be so critical, *mi niña*, but look!" Gina saw mansions hidden in the trees, protected by radar and other electronic devices. "Your neighbors dwell in beautiful cages, in a fake paradise. Do they ever see each other?"

The girl didn't, couldn't respond. She lived here, in a machine-like world disguised as nature. A solitary town where the police would stop a Cuban woman walking by herself. *Where are you from, lady? Show us your ID, a driver's license, a passport, anything. Are you somebody's maid? Who do you work for? How did you get past the guards? You don't belong in Pinos Verdes!*

A cage within a cage. Gina's home.

In the North, Estela felt like a shrimp swept away by the stream. Lost in a wondrous civilization that grew and thrived beyond her country's shores, in a society that had such big needs. She didn't know reality could be larger-than-life; larger, that is, than the reality she'd come to perceive as universal. Excessive, so enchanting that it seemed contrived. Created by people who were content to the point of forgetting sadness, happy without really knowing happiness. Or so it appeared to her.

This world and Abuela were incompatible; each belonged in separate, irreconcilable dimensions. She didn't fit here and neither did Cuba. She was alone, stranded on Gina's strange planet.

Chapter 7

-I-

Early on, looking out through the picture window at the flowers and the bay down below, Gina started creating her future. She began molding events into a big-screen extravaganza. And here is that future unfolding before her, so real that it seems holographic, like a virtual reality landscape. Her own enchanted forest. Can she handle it? Most of it, sure, piece-of-cake. The latest scenes are turning out better than she'd expected. *Sorpresa!* (Yes, life is full of surprises, even for those who design it in advance.)

She didn't think she'd get along with her roommate. Who ever heard of an aging Cuban peasant and a groovy American teenager being friends? Who would buy this far-fetched premise? The key details of Abuela's biography weren't very promising. Estela Ruiz was an older lady who'd lived all her life on an island. She wasn't just an islander, though, but someone who had endured (and supposedly participated in) a communist regime for forty years. And that wasn't all, she also practiced Santería!

Gina had imagined the possible scenario: an elderly foreign woman and a California girl are dancing (mid-Eighties rock, maybe, New Wave classics). The hefty hen is trying to keep up with the chick's pace. (Go-Go meets Slam!) The beat picks up, goes crazy; it's pure energy. The girl is cutting loose, her Neopunk nature unleashed. But the plump foreigner is out of breath, "*No aguanto esto!*" She's begging for rest and silence, collapsing. "I can't handle this! Get me back to my country!" Thus a friendship that never had a chance would take its fatal course . . . *Adiós!*

And yet they danced. They held each other and they laughed, their bodies reeling, playfully; their voices merging with the music: a salsa number by the latest salsa queen. The oldster is a great dancer, like most Cubans, and she's teaching the gringa how to get down *a la cubana.* The woman sings, "*Azúca!*" She shouts, "Move your hips, your shoulders!" She screams, "Shake your big Cuban butt, Gina! *Menéalo!* Shake your whole being to the rhythm, give yourself over to it! Just like this . . . *Azuquita!*"

But not every twist of Gina's movie could be termed success-ful, projected according to her silver-screen fantasy. For starters, she didn't want to turn her grandma into an extraterrestrial. And that's how Estela looks and sounds to Gina sometimes. This was-n't her intention, she swears; the Moviemaker didn't mean to make a sci-fi epic. If anything, she would've preferred a comedy. But the facts are irrefutable: she has guided an older female being from another galaxy through the paths of her North planet. Through the tunnels and secret passageways of her castle.

Gina de Amerika has surrendered to the pull of alien patrio-tism. She opened the door of her young heart, and let her mind be taken over. She's contaminated by nostalgia for a land she never saw. The pain of exile is hers, too. (A pain her parents have repressed.) Her grandma's lot, a lifetime of struggles, Gina claims it all. She's a brave Northling who knows how to get down, *Menéalo!* Give herself over to new beats. *Azuquita!* Her inescapable fate: soon to become one of the aliens.

-II-

Elisa staged an intimate party in order to introduce her Cuban guest. Once the soiree was over, she lauded her own efforts to make her mother-in-law feel welcome by her intimate circle of lady friends. She thanked her daughter for being courteous and quiet. And she described the event to Benito—who'd put in a rather brief appearance on account of his work—as a resounding success.

Madame insisted that Estela wear an "appropriate dress" for the occasion, one she bought for her and which Abuela hated; it was frilly, old-fashioned. Elisa instructed her mother-in-law to be "civil" and asked her (it was more like an order) to say as little as possible about Cuba. Afraid, as she was, that Estela would spill the beans about her "Marxist inclinations" and wreak havoc in the blissful community of Pinos Verdes. (The Domingos are housing a communist spy!)

Estela was presented as "the other Mrs. Domingo," Elisa's *belle-mère*, a woman who'd endured a long Via Crucis and was now enjoying, for the moment, a morsel of the American pie. "Yes, indeed," Madame asserted, holding the old lady's hand, "this poor soul is eating well for the first time in many years."

Five of the eight Wives at the gathering were Anglo-Americans, and there were three Cubans with whom Elisa mingled as little as possible, since they were still clinging to some Island beliefs. The American ladies sympathized with the visitor's lot: "Welcome to our country, dear." "How lucky you must feel to be here." "How unfortunate that you have to go back." "Is there any way you could stay in the United States?" "You should ask for asylum. I am sure that our generous government would grant it to you."

The Cuban Wives said, in summary: "Isn't it awful in Cuba? Please tell us how awful, Señora Estela. Isn't it true that you have to wait in line for everything, that there's no food, that you have to attend dreadful meetings and be part of umpteen committees and study Fidel's speeches as if they were the Bible? Isn't it a fact that you can't speak your mind for fear of being tortured or killed or disappeared? Tell us, dear compatriot, isn't Castro a monster, a vicious criminal, a power-hungry liar and a thief? Tell us the whole truth and nothing but the truth, Señora Ruiz!"

Estela just nodded. She had no energy to waste on Elisa's company. The less she said, the sooner it would all be over. Those women—she told Gina later—weren't interested in her story; they didn't really want answers to their questions. Whether Fidel was a "vicious criminal" or not, the American ladies and their imitators had already made up their minds about the state of affairs on the island. Enlightening them was not a task worth undertaking. Why waste the time?

As Estela saw it, things were a lot more complicated than those people realized. You had to have lived in Cuba for seventy years and even then you wouldn't see the complete picture. What did they know, those *damas*? What right did they have to make her admit defeat, disillusionment?

She could've said yes to some of their questions. Yes, life has been difficult in Cuba for a long time. So what? Yes: many Cubans live in fear. Fear of the future, of the pain and the hunger and the work ahead. Yes, she is getting tired. There doesn't seem to be relief in sight. No better days. No changes. So what, *carajo?*

No, she wouldn't paint a sad picture of her life, of her country, for those plastic women. She wouldn't give Elisa that pleasure. Gina needed to hear a few good things, too, not just the misery. That, Estela realized now, was the main reason she had come to the North: to give history a balance and the past a fair chance. For Gina's sake.

~~~~

They like the garden for their chats. Abuela enjoys the sweet scent and the view of the ocean. The roses intrigue her, "I've seen many types of flowers and plants, but never such big roses." She misses her daisies; they grow wild in her vegetable garden back home.

Estela gazes past the garden, at the bay. Moments later she looks at Gina and smiles. "Your cousin Bladimir is your age," she says. "And he's anxious to meet you."

"I know. He wants to show up at my door and surprise me. You told me in one of your letters."

"Yes, I remember writing to you about him."

"I'm sorry I didn't write back, Abuela."

"Don't feel bad, *mi niña.* After all, you didn't receive any of my letters. You didn't know–"

"I can't believe Maman hid them from me! Do you have any idea why she did that?"

"I do. But we shouldn't waste our time discussing it."

"I agree. We have better things to talk about, like my cousins. Bladimir wants to make films about Cuba, no? I guess the movie bug runs in the family."

"It seems that way," says Estela, laughing. "You both want to torture me with your filming machines. Only he doesn't have one yet. But I can already imagine what will happen when he gets his camera. He'll be chasing me everywhere, trying to duplicate me, and I'll be running away from him all the time!"

"Just like you do here. You run away from me." Gina tries to smile, but Estela can tell she's making an effort. "Don't worry," the girl goes on, "I'm never going to videotape you again. I promise!"

Estela strokes her granddaughter's face, gives her a kiss. "You shouldn't make promises that you can't keep, *señorita.*"

"Anyway, going back to my cousins," says Gina, ready to drop the duplication topic. "Tatiana wants to be a surgeon, right? So she can operate on your heart."

"And my heart would be in good hands, I'm sure." Estela pauses, thinking how much she'd love for the three kids to meet. "Tati is very studious," she adds after a while. "We hope she'll receive a scholarship to attend the University of Havana. That's the best way to get an education in Cuba, you know, with scholarships. And for that you have to be active in the Party and get involved, work hard, make good marks."

"Is the family . . . very active?" The question is vague, but Gina isn't sure how else to ask it. She clarifies, "I mean, are they all active communists?"

"Well . . ." Abuela doesn't seem at all surprised by such a loaded question. "Delia, my niece, is a militant Marxist married to a Party official. They've devoted their lives to the Revolution."

"What about my cousins? How do they feel about everything?"

"About everything?" Abuela looks puzzled.

"You know, everything: communism, politics, the Revolution."

"It's hard for me to tell exactly how they 'feel' about the government. You see, they don't like to discuss politics with me." She laughs. "They think I'm too old for that!"

"What are they exactly, my first cousins?"

"No, let's see . . . They are the children of the daughter of my sister."

"Your sister's grandchildren. That's pretty far removed!"

"Not really. Tati and Bladi think of you as close family."

"But they hardly know me."

"They know enough about you."

"Do you miss them?"

"Of course I miss them. When my poor sister passed away—may she rest in peace—they were still babies. And so I took on the role of their Abuela. I love them as if they were my own grandchildren."

"Maybe I'll get to meet them some day."

"I hope so, Gina. We must have faith."

"I do."

~~~~

Like most storytellers, Estela spins her best tales when there's a captive audience. And that's what she has now: a listener who loves her words, who believes in them. She's narrating a story Gina is eager to hear: her personal version of Cuba's past and present. Abuela's outlook—resigned, verging on pessimism—on the future.

"I come from an island that is shaped like a caiman, or rather like a lizard; that's what I like to call it, *Lagarto Caribe.* Cuba was savagely colonized by the Spaniards, and ruled by the Spanish Crown for a long time. Then it got its independence, thanks in part to the brave Mambises. The island had a series of governments, some very corrupt. Until one day when a handful of young men—all university students—hid in the Sierra Maestra, let their beards grow and became soldiers. And from their mountain hideaway they fought the terrible Batista regime that the United States supported. Because Cuba was governed by the Spaniards first, then by the Americans. And later by the Russians, but that's another story. Are you following me?

"Come to think of it, the Soviet occupation is part of the same thread. It all began when one of those bearded youths read the *Communist Manifesto* and decided that what Cuba really needed was a Marxist revolution. The other men listened to him, followed his thought, and were soon convinced that the Cuban people deserved to be the subject and not the object of history. Thanks to the Revolution, which the group's leader modeled after the Soviet one, there would be no more class struggle. The bourgeoisie would be overthrown and the workers and peasants wouldn't be exploited anymore. Just like it happened in Russia.

"The leader was so handsome, his smile and kindly eyes made you trust him. He organized a guerrilla army up in the Sierra Maestra and defeated Batista, becoming El Comandante. His victory was an amazing feat. He got the gringos out of Cuba, a most unprecedented event in Latin America. Famous people from all over the world—political leaders, artists, writers, actors, movie directors—sent him their best wishes. They all supported his *Revolución.*

"When the Comandante signed his declaration—a Cuban version of the *Communist Manifesto*—at the Workers' Plaza, I felt so proud of him. I had tears in my eyes when he told us, Brothers and sisters, I will defend you from the capitalist pigs for as long as I live. And I will sign this piece of paper with my own blood, this *Mañana Manifesto,* so that tomorrow will be a brighter day for all the Cuban people. Tomorrow . . . history will absolve me!

"What happened on that 'brighter day' was that the Soviets showed up, thousands of them. Our leader needed help and the

Soviets were ready with a handout. We were, after all, their revolutionary offspring, their creation. You understand?

"There had always been foreigners on the island, but I had never seen any of them; they liked to stay in Havana and Varadero. So here I was, suddenly greeting these strapping, white, redheaded creatures who were everywhere. You would see them at the parks, on the streets, in apartment buildings that were built overnight, just for them. The Soviets were pallid and looked to me like big porcelain dolls. There was something beautiful and at the same time repugnant about those people; for one thing, they had a pungent body odor! Some of them—many, in fact—married Cubans and had babies whose skin was a peculiar shade of pink. And so now we had a new race on the island, the *Rusocubanos*.

"The Soviets became our teachers, our advisors, our generous rulers. They brought their machinery and technological advances. They bought our sugar, tried to teach us their language, showed us movies about decadent czars, about Lenin. We read their newspapers translated into Cuban, and ate their sickening food (cans of chewy shredded beef in a pasty tomato sauce). But the most important thing these alien-looking visitors brought to the island was their ideology, what they proudly called Marxism-Leninism. The only cause worth fighting for, said our leader. The only truth for Cuba.

"I tried to accept the strange foreigners. El Comandante seemed to be familiar with them and their system of government. He said he knew and understood the Russians; they weren't out to exploit us like the Americans. So I trusted his hunches, hoping he knew what he was doing. I must confess I loved our young commander as though he were my kin, my own son. In the beginning, right after the Revolution, I used to cut out all the pictures of him from the newspapers and pin them on the bedroom wall, next to my altar. He was my idol. I worshiped him.

"But he would eventually turn into a whimsical ruler, known for his moods and for changing his mind all the time. And for dreaming too much and for making big mistakes that we all ended up paying for . . . Dreams can be deadly when you impose them on the world!

"That man still holds a special place in my heart. He has always sided with the underdogs like me. And you shouldn't stop loving your child just because he's being stubborn, or because he has strong opinions, a vision. But sometimes I just don't understand why our leader does the things he does and says the things he says.

"One day he informed us that he didn't believe in God anymore. Dios was an imperialist invention, he said, and the Cuban people shouldn't believe in him either. Then he started sending our young men to fight wars in faraway places. Useless battles that were part of the International Movement, as he called it. I was horrified at the thought of Bladimir going off to fight and kill people, getting himself killed or mutilated. El Comandante said it was our obligation to help our brothers in their struggle against the imperialist enemy. They had a right to benefit from our revolutionary experience, to have access to a just system, to the truth. But there are no truths big enough to justify a war!

"Maybe I am too ignorant, Gina. Maybe one needs to study at the university to comprehend this type of thing. Why do human beings always go for extremes? It's either capitalism or communism. Russia or the North. Socialism or Death. Why are we given so few choices?

"I believe in fighting for one's freedom and not letting the rich people exploit you. We should stick together and work for the benefit of the majority and not for individual gain. This is what I've believed all my life, since long before I ever heard the word 'Marxism.' It makes sense, then, that the Revolutionary Movement would fit me like a comfortable shoe. Its creator thought the way I did! He had the well-being of the poor people in mind. Yes, I would stand behind his decisions and his proclamations. I'd give him my unconditional support. Thanks to the People's Revolution, Cuba was no longer the Whore of the Antilles, and I was grateful for that. Thanks to the *Mañana Manifesto* I learned to read and write and think.

"But then you get tired of thinking, of believing, of fighting off the enemy. You get to a point when you just want to live in peace, have a roof over your head, food to eat and the love of your family. You get to a point, *mi niña*, where you don't want to hear words anymore, even if they are honest words."

~~~~

Estela makes coffee for her son every morning, strong *café* prepared with a brand new espresso brewer and sweetened with real sugar. In the good old days–Benito reminisces–his mother would bring him a cup of steaming *cafecito* to bed, at the crack of dawn; he'd kiss her and then savor the sweet beverage. This was their daily ritual. He remembers.

Now in Pinos Verdes, mother and son sit on the terrace, in the evenings, and there they chat or contemplate the horizon in silence. Gina watches them as if viewing the best scene from a vintage Seventies film, a flaming sunset as backdrop for the long overdue reunion. These nostalgic characters seem to occupy a space unknown to others. They are zealous guards of a country they created together, of a life they won't share with anyone.

Except Gina. Benito and Estela enjoy telling her stories and she enjoys listening to them. There's nothing better than kicking back and letting other people do the storytelling. She's in Heaven. And by heaven she means this new friendship she's found in Abuela. The past, which has become an open book. These people–so alive, so three-dimensional–who weave for her an elaborate tapestry of yore, of a world which includes Estela as protagonist, and Nitín as the dwarf prince of childhood adventures.

Daddy spent his early childhood in a farming village, Piedrecita, a place that didn't even have street names. That's where his parents had lived all their lives, where they continued to reside after their marriage.

"I was too young when I got married," Abuela tells Gina, "but I never regretted it. My husband was a wonderful man. Ramiro–that was his name–didn't order me around or try to keep me at home; he let me be and do as I pleased. Ramiro always said that we were partners in life, equal partners. And he meant it! That's how I would describe our marriage: a partnership of love. We discussed things and made all our decisions together. He never imposed his will, like a typical macho. That type of man is hard to find in Cuba, you know. I was lucky."

Daddy's father was a sugarcane cutter. "The poor man died because of a stupid accident," he rues. "Papá fell and stabbed himself with his machete, bled to death because they couldn't get him to a hospital soon enough."

Mother and son left Piedrecita after he died. They thought that a different town might help ease the pain of losing him, the overwhelming sense of loss. So they went to Florida, where there was family. Estela's sister lived there.

Florida was a big town, populated by over fifty thousand people. It was located in east central Cuba, province of Camagüey. Estela and Benitín moved into a modest old building that had been divided into three dwellings. They occupied the unit in the middle, next door to Benito's aunt. Their new home was three blocks from the railroad, where Nitín liked to sit and watch the trains, and two blocks from a highway that ran across the entire island. They liked it there. They would put down roots in Florida.

"I was glad that Benitín didn't want to be a cutter," says Abuela.

"I had a knack for sales," Daddy brags. "In Florida I started working right away at a *bodega*, a sort of convenience store."

"The owner," adds Estela, "was this nice Spanish man with a kind heart."

Daddy's laughing. "Yes, his heart was very kind whenever you were around, Señora Ruiz!"

"I admit I brought out the best in him." Abuela winks at Gina. "Is he still alive, Mamá?"

"Alive and kicking!"

"Amazing. I wonder if he'd recognize me."

"Of course he would. You haven't changed that much."

"No, not much. I just grew some inches, put on forty pounds, and lost most of my hair."

"But you still have Nitín's face."

"We've all changed, Mamá. Everything has. I'm sure it would shock me to see our house, the neighbors, my railroad . . ."

"It would all seem smaller, a bit weary. But basically the same."

Daddy pauses, reflects. "You know," he tells Gina, "this Spaniard who employed me could tell I was sharp. His sales increased while I worked for him as a clerk and a gofer. I was good with the customers and gradually developed a system for stocking merchandise, and for maximizing profit. I didn't know what I was doing, you know, but my ideas did the trick."

"And instead of keeping my boy at his store, the merchant suggested that he go to Camagüey, and try his luck in the big city. What a generous man!"

"My boss had contacts there, a friend who was employed at a clothing company where they always needed skilled salespeople. I followed his advice and went to work for that company, and soon

I started traveling all over the place, covering every town in the province."

"He learned the job all by himself," says Estela, obviously proud of her son, "didn't even go to school for it."

"You don't need schooling to sell pants, Mamá. Besides, I did have good teachers."

"Yes, I know you did, Nitín. Our circumstances."

~~~~

His mother has changed, Benito suddenly realizes. He was never able to condone her decision to stay in Cuba; he never shared her blind faith in Castro and his revolution. Yet that revolution seems to have done his mother some good, somehow. She used to be a quiet, introverted woman and now she talks, she has opinions and comments to offer, interesting ideas. Maybe Estela was always this way and he was too young to notice. After all, it was Mamá who taught him the most valuable lessons, the wisdom that he has carried with him, that he's tried to live by throughout his life. Thanks to his mother he learned, early on, the meaning of compassion.

A memory rushes in, to remind him . . .

Nitín played a certain game at the farm, when he was only five or six; he would hide chicks from their mothers and drive the poor hens crazy. He'd place the babies in a box, sit back and watch the cruel scenario: the mother's desperate cries, maddening cackling when it heard but didn't see its babies. One day his Mamá caught him in the act. And instead of yelling at him, instead of telling him that he was a heartless boy, she just looked at him with sad, watery eyes. Then she said, "You shouldn't do that, Nitín; it hurts them. Animals suffer pain just like we do. They love their mothers and their children just like human beings. How would you feel, *mi niño*, if someone separated you from me? Wouldn't you suffer? Wouldn't you cry?"

He had never felt, or would ever experience, a greater sense of injustice as he did at that moment. And he was never cruel to animals again.

~~~~

Abuela is chuckling. "My poor boy!" she remarks after bringing up a funny anecdote about Benito. It's remarkable, he notes, how she can remember the smallest as well as the most significant details about any event. Like the time he almost drowned, one of his unfortunate adventures.

"It sounds funny now," he says, "but it sure wasn't then!"

"Serves you right," jokes his mother, "for wanting to be a Don Juan when you couldn't even keep your *culito* clean."

"I had gone on a school excursion to the public swimming pool in Florida," Benito recounts, "at the Círculo Social Obrero, which was like a community park. I didn't know how to swim, but I wanted to impress a couple of girls who were sitting by the pool. So I jumped in, pretending to be Man from Varadero, the Cuban Amphibian. Those *muchachas* would take notice of a champion. They had to, unless they were blind!"

"And they did," Estela says, laughing. "They noticed this poor boy who was struggling to stay afloat, sinking like a rock, screaming for help, *Auxilio! Socorro!* I'm drowning!"

"The image of myself that I had," Daddy continues, "was this stud moving along, my hard body curving and my strong arms breaking the thick masses of water. What a show! Little did I know that I was hardly moving from the same place, that my strokes were just making one big ugly splash. But somehow I made it to the deep end, thinking, I'm the greatest. Then I panicked when my feet couldn't touch bottom! I heard a choir of angels going Aaahhh! And the worst part of it was, this guy, the lifeguard, had to pump the water out of my lungs with his mouth. *Coño!*"

"*Diablito!*" wails Estela, as she brings up another incident. The time she nearly had a heart attack because of Nitín's mischief. She thought he'd been kidnapped and it turned out that he was just being a little devil.

"It was carnival time," she tells Gina. "So we went to Florida to see the floats. The streets were full of drunkards and *mascaritas.* Nitín was holding tight to my leg and I was touching his little head as we walked, trying hard to keep him from being pulled away. Ramiro was walking a few steps ahead. We were all sweating like swine, which is only an expression, you know, because pigs don't sweat. I wiped my forehead with the hand that was touching Benitín, and seconds later he was gone! I pushed and kicked and shoved like a wild animal, looking for my boy. His papá wasn't anywhere to be seen, either; he had disappeared! I cried and called for my baby.

"I made my way to a clear spot outside a toy store, and there he was, staring at the things in the window. He looked up at me and smiled, as if nothing had happened. Rascal! I shouted. *Muchacho malo! Diablito!* Then I hugged him and kissed him. But I didn't punish my Nitín for running off like that. How could I? The toys he had been looking at were so beautiful."

Daddy has fond memories of Christmas in Piedrecita. Yes, he assures Gina, his father really did slaughter a pig for the Navidad festivities. (The girl would rather not hear this story, too cruel and disgusting. But she listens.) They fed the beast palm fruit and leftovers all year, then Daddy's Dad stabbed it in the heart, gutted it, and cooked it slowly over a bonfire for hours. (Gina would rather be spared the gruesome details.) Nitín and his friends drank handfuls of the animal's blood. (Much too gross.) He liked the crispy sizzling skin, *chicharrón*, and always ate it to satiation. Nitín loved the rice and black beans that his mother cooked in the pig's belly; he relished the bars of creamy almond nougat for dessert, the *guajiro* songs everyone sang, the jokes, the laughter. (So there *are* things worth remembering; not everything was hell in Cuba.) Yes, Benitín loved it all. Daddy misses it all.

-III-

The picnic at the beach was Elisa's attempt to paint a harmonious family portrait. She hadn't let any of her fellow Wives in on her secret, how she really felt about her mother-in-law. So none of Madame's friends who happened to be at Ramosa that day was surprised to see the two Domingo women sipping lemonade under a beach umbrella, chatting and enjoying their Cuban kinship.

Had those Wives known what Gina knew, they would've been suspicious, would've tried to interpret each glance, listening for the subtext of every word. Which is what the Moviemaker did: she *watched* Abuela and Maman when they were together. And there was nothing harmonious about that sight!

During the first two weeks of Estela's visit, Madame vied for her daughter's attention. She'd seek her out, inviting her to do things like shopping, lunch, movies. "Some other time," the girl always told her, hoping Maman would get the hint: from now until the day the visitor left, Gina's time would be exclusively devoted to her.

Eventually, things got out of hand. Maman turned mean, demanding; she tried but couldn't persuade the teenager to take her side.

"Where have you been, *jeune fille*?"

"Out."

"Who gave you permission?"

"I was with Abuela."

"You haven't answered my question."

"I need permission to go to the mall?"

"How did you get there?"

"We walked."

"You walked?!"

"Yeah, it's not that far. My grandma wanted to see some houses, so—"

"And they let you back in through the gate?"

"Yeah. They know who I am."

"I'm going to call Security immediately!"

"What are you gonna tell them, that I'm your prisoner?"

"Your father will hear about this!"

Madame Rochart would never admit it to herself, but she was jealous. It was unsettling to see her daughter so happy, happier than ever before. Gina and Estela went around whispering secrets to each other, giggling and making faces, cavorting and dancing like hysterical teenagers. It was insulting, a slap in the face, the ultimate affront: Estela's way of subverting Elisa's authority. *Merde!* She had bewitched the girl, trapping her in her low-life inferno.

"Where is your grandmother?"

"Taking a nap."

"What do you two find to talk about?"

"Stuff."

"Has she said anything about the Island?"

"Yeah. Sure."

"Such as?"

"Stories about the town where she was born."

"What else?"

"Is this an interrogation? I want my lawyer!"

"Has she told you anything about the Cuban government?"

"And I get one phone call. That's the law."

"Be serious for a moment, please, *chérie*."

"I *am* being serious."

"Tell me, has Estela been talking to you about communism?"

"No, not really. She just says that no government is perfect, and that love has nothing to do with politics."

"Meaning what?"

"You figure it out! Aren't you supposed to be a poet or something?"

Elisa just couldn't take their friendship, and this was obvious to Gina because her mother kept making her trademark gesture, that serious look she gives when she doesn't like what you say or do: She raises one eyebrow, purses her lips, tilts her head. *Affreux!*

The girl didn't really want to make her mother suffer, but if Maman was indeed suffering, it was her own fault. She had it coming. Like punishment (not that it was Gina's job to punish her or anything): for hiding Abuela's letters, for humiliating and mistreating her mother-in-law. And for trying to turn the whole world into one long boring incomprehensible French poem!

"Don't believe everything Estela says, *mignonne.* Remember that your grandmother chose to stay in Cuba because she sympathized with that despicable regime. Her niece and her niece's husband are communists. Party members. Traitors to their country."

"That's an awfully big word, Maman . . . traitors."

"I know what I'm saying. Why, they stooped so low as to give their children Soviet names!"

"Bladimir and Tatiana are fab names."

"You are so naive, so innocent."

"And *so* sick of this conversation."

"I don't deserve to be treated this way, Gina."

"Sorry."

"I need you, my darling."

"You do?"

"Yes, I need you to help me understand."

"Understand what?"

"What is going on between you and Estela."

"I get a big kick out of her, that's all."

"I'd like to know what she's been telling you."

"Sorry, Maman, I can't."

"Please . . ."

"I'm not your spy!"

<center>~~~~</center>

Madame never had it out with her mother-in-law in Gina's presence. Her sense of style dictated a more sophisticated strategy for dealing with Cubana Non Grata. A little jab now and then, a small daily dosage of bitter sarcasm, at least one snide remark per day. Oh, but Elisa Rochart had a hidden agenda! She was up to something, Gina could tell. She'd been suspiciously quiet around Abuela lately. Was she playing the Little Dead Fly? Or acting like a Gatica María, burying her stinking evidence in the garden? Maybe she was merely being swept away by the Cuban stream, turned into a plump South Bay shrimp.

Camerawoman had to get to the truth of it all somehow. *La verité!* She was in desperate need of data, craving firsthand information. So she decided to hide a voice-activated recorder inside a flower vase in the breakfast nook, and another in the den. If anything was going to happen, it would happen in one of those two places. Totally unethical, an act unworthy of the great *artiste* that she was meant to be. Shame on her! But the situation called for emergency measures. The brawl was brewing; Gina had sensed it. A big and spectacular bang was about to take place.

And it did. And thanks to the Moviemaker's foresight, she managed to document the Turning Point. Her machine picked up the two Domingo ladies going at it! Transcribing and translating the recording was no easy task, but the effort was well worth it. Some pressing questions about Maman were finally answered: Why did she hide Estela's letters? Is she really the descendant of French aristocrats, or is there a dent in her royal crown? Does she believe in Santería? How did she meet Gina's father? Was it love at first sight? And there was a whopper question about Monsieur Rochart, Gina's grandfather. Oh my God, did she learn the truth about him!

There were discoveries about Señora Ruiz as well. Like, is she a bad bug? Is she the guerrilla, the witch, the commie spy that Elisa makes her out to be? Is Estela really all that wise? Does she know so much about everything because she's old or because she's the devil?

As Gina listened to this conversation, she pictured the speakers sitting at the deco table. The French-Cuban woman drinking watered-down coffee sweetened with artificial sweetener. The

Cuban woman savoring *café* loaded with sugar, and skimming the *Golden Hill Cookbook* with morbid curiosity. Action!

"I've been meaning to tell you," says Estela, as she studies the glossy photo of a peculiar-looking chicken dish, "there's someone in Cuba who sends you greetings."

"Oh?" reacts Elisa, as she brings the steaming cup to her lips.

Estela tries to read the recipe that accompanies the photo. It turns out that the chicken isn't chicken, but a concoction of white flour and bean curd.

"Yes, I visited Beba the day before I came here. She said to tell you hello, *saludos afectuosos.*"

Elisa ambles to the window. "I don't know who you're talking about."

"Bebita, the woman we went to see together before you left the country. Don't tell me you have no memory of her!"

"I don't recall going to visit anybody with you."

"You have a serious problem, then." Estela laughs. "Maybe learning English made you forget the things you did while you spoke Cuban."

"There are things and people I have forgotten, indeed." She stares out, longingly.

"I can see that. But I'm sure that if you tried just a little, you would remember Beba."

"What purpose would that serve? I have no interest in—"

"Beba was my friend. I took you to her house because you said you needed all the help you could get. And she was known for working miracles."

"I do have a vague recollection."

"She remembers you vividly."

"I'm surprised she's still alive."

"Those saints of hers must be doing a good job."

"She was already old and wrinkled then."

"But she was strong enough for a trance and an offering to Changó and Oshún. Strong enough to summon the spirits in your name, so that Elisa Rochart could have her wish granted."

Madame returns to the table, sits facing her mother-in-law. "You didn't tell Benito about our visit, did you?"

"No. I promised you I wouldn't, and I keep my promises."

"There was no need to upset him."

"I agree. He wouldn't have understood that you, the unbeliever, went to see a woman like Bebita. He would've thought you were a hypocrite."

"Is that what you thought?"

"What does it matter now, what I thought?"

"I know it makes no sense, my visiting that woman. But you see . . . How do I explain this?"

"You don't have to."

"I didn't believe in any of those primitive rituals, but I thought I should do something. Benito was so busy already, getting our passports and visas and tickets so we could leave."

"So *you*, Elisa, could leave."

"He wanted the trip as much as I did, Estela."

"For your sake."

"Benito was not a communist like you!"

"It wasn't just because of communism that I stayed in Cuba."

"But it was precisely because of it that I left."

"I know. You wanted the trip to happen at any cost, even if it took a session with a Santera. I was surprised when you asked me that favor."

"You should've felt honored that I took you into my confidence."

"To tell you the truth, I did it for her, because she needed the money. It had nothing to do with you."

"All the better. Now I know I have nothing to thank you for."

"I couldn't believe my eyes when I saw you all dolled up, sitting in my friend's living room. You were so willing to go through the ceremony! Beba chanted and sprinkled her *agua* all over you. Then your delicate nose had to put up with the pungent smell of her altar: fried food and herbs and melting candles . . ."

"I detested her voice; it was gritty and hoarse. So frightening."

"So unlike Beba's own voice."

"Her eyes were terrifying, too. They seemed vacant yet fixed on me."

"But you welcomed her words. You were relieved when she said that the saints were on your side, that your wish would be fulfilled."

"Thanks to Benito, not to that old hag and her pitiful spirits."

"I wouldn't be so ungrateful if I were you, Elisa."

"Right. I know you're capable of casting evil spells. You could easily punish my ingratitude!"

"Ingratitude is not your only crime, or at least not the one most deserving of punishment."

"Which one is, then, wise Señora?"

"Having hidden my letters from Gina."

"Oh, that."

"She says she found them by chance, in your closet."

"Unfortunately, yes."

"Why did you do it?"

"Because your letters were full of lies."

"I told Gina I was happy in my country; that is not a lie."

"You've been living in hell for the last forty years! What do you know about happiness?"

"I suppose not as much as you do."

"Go back where you belong, Estela. Back to your troops and your vulgar revolution."

"There are things about that revolution that I'm very proud of."

"Oh yes! You learned to read and write thanks to Fidel. What a marvelous feat! It breaks my heart. Congratulations!"

"Thank you."

"Your voluntary work and your committees, how moving! Why didn't you tell Gina about the censorship? About the lack of everything? The people who lost it all. The ones in jail, the ones who died like my father."

"I figured she'd be hearing those stories from you."

"She has heard nothing from me, not ever."

"Big mistake."

"She's better off not knowing."

"You shouldn't blame Fidel for your father's death, Elisa."

"You're all responsible, all of you communist scum!"

"So, they didn't treat him like a king, didn't acknowledge his 'lineage.' What did he expect?"

"He expected to be treated with respect, not like a leper."

"Rochart could've left the country. He had connections here, in the North, and he still had some money, no? He should've fled like so many people did, like my own son. Instead 'Musiú' chose to make one last, futile statement."

"It was not futile!"

"What did he accomplish by killing himself?"

"He wasn't trying to accomplish anything! Can't you get that through your head? He was cornered, desperate."

Guadalupe enters the room and greets the Señoras. She doesn't mean to intrude, she says meekly. Would the ladies like some refreshments? Madame glances at the door, and the *doméstica* leaves immediately.

"Elisa," mutters Abuela, sounding much too feeble. "Elisa," she repeats, weighed down by the stress, by the sheer fatigue this exchange is causing her. "You shouldn't keep me out of Gina's life."

"Gina has no use for your saints and your Marxism. No one does in this family. No one."

"You shut me out because I worshiped the spirits. But what about you? You've never worshiped anything?"

"Leave my daughter alone, Estela. Don't pollute her head."

"She has a right–"

"Don't be ridiculous. You know nothing about rights."

"The right to know where she comes from, that's what I'm talking about."

"Spare the child, please."

"I don't wish to fight with you, Elisa. That's not what I'm here for."

"No, you're here to make my life miserable."

"Because I bring you shame, right? Because I wear a sign on my forehead that says, in red letters, Dumb Peasant."

"Precisely."

"I'm not ashamed of being a peasant. Or a washerwoman."

"Oh, listen to that jabbering: fresh out of the Marxist-Leninist oven!"

"We were country people, yes, but you didn't mind that because you had a plan. You would take Nitín away from me and teach him all your fancy manners and your big words. Make him a gentleman."

"I remember how eager you were to see us married."

"I was, yes, but not because I wanted your status and your name. What could you people offer us? You were broke."

"We were not!"

"I knew Benito loved you. And I thought you loved him, too. He came home one night babbling that he had met the prettiest girl in all of Camagüey. *Qué cosa linda!*, he said. *Qué monumento!*"

"I did love him."

"You made a point of being in your garden at the same hour, every day, so you could see him when he passed by. You were the first to speak, the one to suggest a secret meeting place. I know because he told me. It was also your idea that the two of you should elope. Am I right?"

"We had no other choice. There was no way we could be together if we went by the law."

"Your father's law, no? He cursed you, didn't he? He told you that you had disgraced him."

"I *had* disgraced him. His daughter had run away with the son of country hicks, a starving salesman, a nobody."

"A nobody who had a chalet built for you and who kept you there like a queen. He even helped your folks. They took his handouts reluctantly, but they took them all the same. What an act! The Rocharts had nothing left, nothing but a crumbling house and a worthless title."

"You don't know what you're talking about!"

"But I do, Madame Rochart."

"Oh yes, you're so wise."

"It doesn't take a lot of wisdom to see through you."

"It certainly takes more than your communist rhetoric."

"I am not talking to you as a communist."

"No, you're talking to me as a *revolucionaria.*"

"You're dragging Gina down into your nightmares, Elisa."

"Wrong. I'm keeping her out of them."

"You have raised her in a bubble, as if she were your doll."

"I've raised her like a princess."

"Yes, Your Majesty. In the castle *you* built. But you can't keep her in there forever."

"She's free, can't you see that? Free! And she knows the facts that really matter."

"Your French ancestors and your blue blood and–"

"No. Her life here, in the United States, in Pinos Verdes. The present."

"I'm part of her life and her present, too, Elisa. I'm her grandmother."

"True. And you will soon be gone."

Chapter 8

-I-

It was Sunday, the one day of the week when Gina had a sense of true freedom, space to veg out all she wanted. This freedom could work against you, sure, like when you weren't feeling good about the world. But it came in handy if you wished to be alone (or with your grandma).

That certain Sunday, as usual, Elisa was going to Mass and other social activities with her Auxiliary friends. And Daddy was staying in, like he preferred, to catch up on his paperwork and read *Bloom Boom*. So grandmother and granddaughter had the day to themselves.

Gina suggested they go out for breakfast, to the mall or the Zone's diner maybe. Was Abuela hungry? No, not very. She didn't want to go anywhere today. "A little rest would do me good," she told the girl. "I'm not feeling well, Gina." But it was nothing serious; only a headache and some *achaques*, ailments of old age.

"Okay, let's take it easy," said Gina, having toyed a bit with the phrase "to take easy" in Spanish. After considering several possibilities such as *descansar* (to rest) and *vegetar* (to veg out), she'd opted for *tomarlo con calma*, an idiom Sister Juana liked to use. So, what Abuela actually heard was, "Let's take it with calmness." Amused by the Spanish sentence, Gina listed in her head all the possible meanings of *tomarlo*; that word alone could be interpreted as drink it, have it, take it, and eat it. Too many tempting options!

"Take what with calmness?" asked Abuela, bringing Gina back from her linguistic reveries.

"Life, your visit, everything."

"Not life, Ginita, and certainly not everything. Just this day!"

"Are you sure it's only a headache?"

"And some fatigue. But don't worry, *mi niña*. I'm not singing 'The Peanut Vendor' yet."

"Good. I don't mind if we stay home. I do think it's kind of weird, though. I mean, you're always saying that resting is for Galicians, not for you. So I wonder–"

"Resting is also for elderly ladies who tend to forget their age!"

"I see your point," said Gina, laughing. "We'll both rest like tired *viejitas.*" And it occurred to her then that this might be the video-viewing opportunity she'd been waiting for. "Maybe," she ventured, psyched up for a negative reaction. "Maybe we could watch movies?"

Her grandmother's reaction blew her away: "What a fantastic idea!"

Before any action was taken, however, the Cuban woman had to have her morning coffee. She went to prepare it while Gina selected the films. "Would you like a little?" asked Abuela, as usual, when she returned cup in hand. Until now, the girl had refused all of her grandma's coffee offerings. But this time she said, "Sure. Why not." The grandmother, too, was blown away. She rushed to the kitchen and brought back a demitasse full to the rim with the black nectar. Gina drank it in small torturous sips, hating each drop, eager to humor her roommate.

Estela's caffeine potions were the essence of Cubanity, Gina had concluded; more so than all those scrumptious dishes she cooked for the family. The syrupy liquid, *café criollo*, was the lubricant of memory. It made Daddy say things he'd never said before, turning him into a talkative Benito, into mischievous Nitín. Coffee was the building block of storytelling, guardian of conversations. So what if Gina hated the revolting beverage? So what if she knew that she'd never ever develop a taste for it? She'd partake in the ritual the way one takes a disgusting medication or eats a gross vegetable. Because it's good for you, because you need it to be strong and healthy. And, in this case, more Cuban.

~~~~

She picked four category-one films: two love stories, one for Estela's age group and one for Gina's, and two science fiction hits. They might also be able to sneak in a program from the Hispanic Channel (which would definitely upset Maman). Guadalupe had whetted Estela's appetite for the Spanish-language station and it was high time she got to watch it. *As decreed by the Welcoming Committee.*

The Hispanic Channel had a day-long variety show every Sunday that reached the entire world via satellite. It also featured serials that the maid called *novelas*, and old movies with Jorge Negrete, Cantinflas, Lola Flores, Sarita Montiel . . . all of Abuela's idols! Unfortunately, this channel was banned in the Domingos' home. Señora Elisa believed that it had nothing but vulgarity and rubbish to offer. The only suitable thing about the Hispanic Channel, said the Señora, was the abbreviation of its name, which fit it perfectly: HIC. (Elisa would eventually have a Censor Chip installed in all their TV sets to block reception of HIC programming.)

The Princess was allowed to watch anything she wanted, so long as the programs reflected family-oriented themes, and only if they didn't contain depictions of sexual acts (kissing and light petting were permitted). Oh, and nothing overtly political or too liberal. Benito and Elisa would've been rather unpleasantly surprised had they pried into the girl's collection, where she guarded two "political" shows she'd taped off the Hispanic Channel; one about a Santana school where most students excelled in Math, and the other one a documentary on graffiti artists.

~~~~

Later, while watching the first movie with Abuela, Gina made a long entry in her YOU file. Wanting to capture the moment while it was still fresh, recently lived, she wrote: DAY OF THE MOVIETHON. I hope Abuela doesn't mind my tap-tap-tap. I doubt it. Look at her, she's totally engrossed in Movie Number One. But I knew she would be. I told her I wanted to take some notes on this film for a class project. The truth: I couldn't wait to get this stuff on disk. The reason: there's an idea for a movie here! Maybe.

I'll try to report exactly what was said. Gina Domingo, you must fight the temptation to embellish your mundane little words! Will you ever stop sounding like a teenager? Here goes: *The Last Time Estela Went to the Movies (If You Can Believe It!)*

Bedroom. Interior. Day. Action!

"What kind of shows do you like?" asks Abuela. But this is a tough one. It'd take me a whole lot of energy and time to describe in Spanish what I dig. So I just respond with something lame like, "All kinds of stuff."

"I don't watch much television," says Abuela. "Delia and Roberto have a TV set and once a week I catch a variety show with the family. They like to watch political programs. But I try to avoid that type of show; it is so boring! I prefer programs with songs and jokes and dancing."

"Do you ever go to the movies?"

"No, I don't. I haven't been to a movie theater in years. The last time was back in the Sixties. In 1966, to be exact."

"You're joking!"

"No. I remember the film very well, as though I saw it yesterday."

"Tell me about it."

"It was a Russian movie about an elderly genie named Jotavich. He had a long white beard and a roguish smile, crinkly eyes, a friendly voice. There was this Cuban boy who found him in a bottle—floating on a river or a stream, I think—while he was in Moscow on vacation with his parents. And the genie offered to grant him any wish. The ancient man had been alone for centuries and now he had a friend. He was so happy! And you can imagine how the boy felt; he was thrilled to have such a wise companion."

"Did the genie grant him three wishes?"

"More than three! And the characters got into a great deal of trouble because of it. Innocent trouble, nothing violent. You see, Jotavich kept granting wishes all the time."

"Like what?"

"Well, for example, one day they were walking down the street and the boy remarked, 'I've been studying some Russian history; it's amazing how rich those czars used to be. I wonder what it was like to live like a czar.' And Jotavich said, 'I will show you, my dear boy.' Then poof! Right there in front of them was this fantastic palace with an emperor at its door saying 'Welcome.' The kid became angry; he ordered Jotavich to get rid of the building. 'Send it back, now!' And the magician was hurt. Why was his young master so ungrateful? Didn't he at least want to have a look inside the castle, visit the czar, and satiate his curiosity? No, he did not! And so the old man concluded that present-day humans, most of all Cuban boys, were hard to figure out and not very capable of feeling gratitude."

"How did the movie end?"

"I don't recall many details. Let's see . . . The boy went back to Cuba, I remember that part. And before departing, he gave Jotavich his freedom. 'You don't belong to anyone anymore,' he said. 'You're in charge of your life. Go! Live! Do whatever free genies are supposed to do!' But Jotavich chose to stay by the boy's side, not as his wish-granting magician, but as a friend."

"There's a nice message there, I think. A little forced, but sweet . . . The two characters living happily ever after in Cuba."

"You know, to this day, I still cherish a line that was repeated many times during the film. Whenever the genie was about to grant a wish, he'd say, *Me arranco un pelo de la barba!* Then, after pulling a hair out of his beard, he'd throw it away, and the wish would be granted."

I translate the phrase to myself, *As I pull a hair out of my beard!* and laugh as I see my grandma doing precisely that. I imitate her. She smiles.

"Those words hold a benign power over me," says Abuela; "they're like an incantation. I still say them once in a while, for the fun of remembering . . . *Me arranco un pelo de la barba!*"

"Maybe you ought to grow a beard for the full effect," I tell her.

"No, I don't think El Comandante would like the competition."

"It wouldn't look good on you, anyway."

"So, you enjoyed the Jotavich story, *mi niña?*"

"Yeah, I love this kind of fantasy. A genie who'd grant my every wish. Wow! Wouldn't I get into that!"

"I think most people would like to have a powerful friend."

"That's why movies about genies and angels are so popular, I guess. And TV shows, too. It's an idea everybody can relate to."

"Tell me about some of those shows."

"Sure. In two of them, the 'classic' ones, there's a lot of romance involved. And even marriage."

"Romance and marriage? With a genie? That's odd."

"Both series are pretty old, from the Sixties. Well, not *that* old! If you want, we'll catch them on the Retro Channel later on. They're kind of boring, though; I don't recommend them. In one there's this woman who lives in a bottle and she's supposed to be Arabic but she's blonder than Miss White, my religion teacher. In the other show there's a genie who's actually a witch and she's totally obsessed with being a housewife. Can you believe it? She gives up her magic for the sake of a goofy-looking husband who has big ears. Oh please!"

"Do they do anything special to produce their miracles?"

"Not really. The genie blinks, and the witch twitches her nose."

"That's cute."

"You think so? I like the beard idea a lot better. It's original."

"I am happy that you liked the Russian film, Gina."

"I did. Maybe I'll make an American version some day. It'd be a sure thing. Genie movies bring in a huge young audience; they make big *dinerito* at the box office."

"You know so much about the money side of cinema."

"What do you expect, Abuela? I live in Movieland!"

"Doesn't all that knowledge ruin the films for you?

"Nah, it makes everything more exciting. The more knowledge, the better. Like, I know things like . . ." I pause, wondering how the heck you say things like *matte painting* and *computer-generated* and *blue-screen* in Spanish. No idea. Forget it! Here goes: "I can tell when they're using paintings to imitate a landscape or a city and when they're putting two different shots into one scene; they call it 'blue-screen.' And when they're using computers to simulate people and places and objects. You got to see some of those tricks at the Hollyworld Studios, remember? And I can also tell when they're doing bad editing; they chop people's words right in the middle. And I know–"

"Do you ever just enjoy the story, Gina?"

"Yes, but you see, all those things I mentioned *are* part of the story."

"You still haven't told me what kind of shows you like."

"Well, let me think . . ."

Again I need help, on-the-spot translation. How do you say "adrenaline" in Spanish? Or "subspace"? Words that Sister Juana never taught us, that never appeared in the stories we read in her class. Guess I'll just have to wing it!

"I don't always like movies with a heavy message. Literature is better for that sort of thing, you know, artistic stuff. Sometimes it's good to see something that teaches you about the world, but not always. I love comedies and romantic stories, as long as they're not remakes of old TV shows. Some action movies are fun, especially if they're science fiction. I like suspense, when the music gets creepy, the rush of adrenaline running through my guts. I like jumping up and screaming when the alien monster comes out of the dark. Or when it hides in deep space or subspace and you know it's just sitting there waiting to come back. But I try to avoid movies with violence, with a lot of shooting and killing and stupid men with guns, or movies about the army or about baseball. Male-flicks are so basic! On the other hand, I don't really care for things that are hard to figure out, like some European films. Hey, it's good to have to think and be forced to imagine what happened to whom where why and how. No problem with being creative and using your brain. But you know, Abuela, I use my brain too much already!"

END OF ENTRY. Wait, not yet. One last thing: I hate that last monologue! Admit it, girl: You came across as an airhead, a clue-less teenager of the worst Ramosa kind. *Carajo!* Ms. D should've done justice to herself. I'm not just interested in profitable formu-las and tall tales; I've thought long and hard about the art of moviemaking. *Coño, chica!* Judging from that mumbo-jumbo about the stuff I like and dislike, Abuela could never figure out that her granddaughter is a heavy-duty thinker, a potential *auteur.* Unfair!

~~~~

Whenever a topic intrigued her, Gina just had to look it up. And when there wasn't enough info in the library, she'd use her allowance to purchase books and order cable programs. Or she'd delve into cyberspace, taking advantage of the thirty real-time hours that were part of her computer package. (She'd had the machine for weeks before she ran across a gift still in factory wrap-ping: software for temporary access to the Net.) As long as the Info Highway was free, why not coast along?

She had quickly developed a system for reading vast masses of data by zooming in on the key thoughts, the main ideas, in order to maximize cybertime and make her freebies last. Much to her surprise, Gina had found that when it came to learning, she did better reading words than looking at charts and graphs. It was as though she had two separate identities: the words-person for acquiring knowledge and the image-person for capturing reality.

Thanks to both of those "personas," within just a few months she'd picked up gobs of data on the history of cinema. Did any of it matter? Would this information make her a good filmmaker some day? Maybe. Maybe not. For all she knew, Ms. Domingo might just become one more data-dump in the vastness of info-reality. Oh, but how she enjoyed reviewing her notes, reading the YOU file where she told herself (her best reader) all the wonderful junk she was discovering!

The most interesting thing she'd learned about the art of film was that it could be traced all the way back to the Altamira paintings. The cave was dark and enclosed just like a theater, supposedly, and the tribal people went there to partake in a ritual as a community. When those primitive beings looked at the cavern walls, at those spectral drawings of bison and deer and pigs, they saw a reflection of their daily lives, of what they dreamed about. Just like moviegoers.

Gina had grasped the following facts as well (cited here from the YOU file): Photography was used at first to preserve and document art, or artifacts that would decay with the passing of time. Movies had that purpose also, right after they were invented: keeping a visual record of history. But then you know what happened in the Twenties and Thirties. The first Hollywood stars changed the movies forever. Chaplin and Pickford and Buster Keaton and all the other pioneers. Wow, can't even imagine what it must've been like, living in that town with all those people! Thanks to them, Showbiz was born, and also an art that will never die.

But an art that has caused a whole bunch of controversies. Like, there were critics, in the 1930s, who condemned the movies and wrote books where they bashed the film industry. They said there was this generation of people (the "movie-made children") who were practically nitwits addicted to cheap fun. Kids with underdeveloped brains because all they did was stare at a screen. But those critics didn't make a big splash; their argument had a lot of holes in it. (Isn't Yours Truly the living proof?)

The art of film borrowed from various sources like myth, science, history, in order to provide fab entertainment. As some poet who was obsessed with the movies said: "That sense of awe, of pure wonder and flight . . . Oh, the wide silver screen!" Virtual Reality and Holography could never compete with the Big Celluloid Picture. Not even.

I'll admit I'd love to use many different media in my movies, because that's the future. Heck, the present! Like, take my quasi-holographic machine, which is video-based but its footage is so real and so alive that it's like the whole thing comes off the screen and grabs you. And yet I'm dying to do a traditional reel-to-reel. And I dig going to the movie house like people have been doing since the Silent Days. So I go for tradition. So I'm typical. Tough.

But movies aren't just entertainment or a superficial pastime. Definitely not just "products for mass consumption," not "a factory of imbeciles," as some doomsday critics claim. And here's the gist of what I've learned: Movies are great for capturing memories, and for molding life to fit your fantasy. The perfect way you'd like for things to be.

~~~~

They ate microwave popcorn while watching the four films and part of the HIC variety show. Benito peeked in a couple of times, surprised that they were staying in, curious about the films his mother and daughter were watching. And Guadalupe showed up at their door to offer her services. Were the Señora and the Señorita hungry? Would they like a bowl of tomato soup? How about a broiled turkey steak, a tofu burger? Did they need anything at all?

No. Señora and Señorita just wanted to be left alone!

Movie Number One was about two old lovers who were nuts about each other. They spent their days looking at the sun setting over their private lake, holding hands and saying "I love you, darling." The plot was thin, but the film made up for that with lots of feel-good scenes: hugging, kissing, caring. Plus realistic moments: having troublesome bodily functions that never got in the way of love. Plus great shots of the lake and the woods, all beautifully rendered in sepia.

The movie told the story of these two married people, legendary Hollywood stars (from the early years) who decide, one winter day, to keep a promise they made to themselves in their youth: When the time grows near for us to leave this world, we'll leave together. We'll give up most of our earthly possessions and wait for the Dark Angel from within nature's embrace, hidden in the forest. Just the two of us in our tiny log cabin, without a phone, without reporters and cameras and movie folks. Without Thanksgiving dinners and Christmas shopping. Two lovers alone, united till the very end. A promise that neither one will part alone, without the other. A promise to begin over again beyond the flesh. In Heaven.

"*Qué bonito*," said Abuela when Movie Number One was over. Lovely and sad. She couldn't share that kind of old-age love with her husband. She still missed him. A small consolation was that she spoke to him regularly, and sent him messages through her saints. Estela and Benito would reunite in Heaven, *en el Cielo*, she was sure, just like the actors in the movie. They would look and feel young forever up there, and never separate.

Abuela found Movie Number Two charming and appropriate for Gina. The story could've easily been about her granddaughter! Here was this California girl who liked to wear rose-colored garments and who had everything she wanted and more. Except a boyfriend. She was being courted by two young men and couldn't make up her mind which boy to go for. One of her suitors was from a wealthy family, the other one a poor Santana kid. The girl's parents (a workaholic businessman and a busy socialite) would definitely approve of the rich beau. But if they were to find out that "a broken-down beaner from the spick slums" (words actually used in the movie) had the hots for their baby, they'd lock her up or send her away to school. Far away.

The protagonist was caught between two hunks, both of whom she led on and both of whom she wanted. The rich guy was handsome and suave, but he wasn't passionate like the daredevil Vato. (Neither Gina nor her grandma seemed disturbed by the blatant stereotyping.) Couldn't the girl just date both kids? "No, I can't! It wouldn't be fair to them," she told herself during the Turning Point. "My mind is made up; the Santanero is the boy for me! Yeah, I'll go against all odds, I'll fight for the love of my Barrio Hero!" Which she didn't, because the movie ended before she had a chance to take action (this lack of resolution being the film's only flaw, in Gina's opinion).

Estela hated Movie Number Three. Gina's on-the-spot translation of the film had something to do with her grandma's opinion. How could it not? She got stuck on so many words! She ended up fabricating a confusing version of the plot in a mixture of Spanish, English and sci-fi babble. But Abuela didn't need a translation; the visuals were graphic, descriptive enough. With or without her granddaughter's help, she would've had the same feelings: the film was disgusting. Only a sick mind would make a movie about invisible creatures from outer space that live off human beings by inhabiting and feeding from their hearts. It was monstrous!

Gina argued, defensively, that the film was only make-believe, that it depicted a possible scenario of the future, an "interpretation," not reality. "All the more reason not to watch it!" reacted her roommate. "How could you select for your collection such a frightening, depressing vision of the world to come?" The teenager was speechless; she'd never seen her grandma so upset. "This movie," Abuela went on, "is a waste of the imagination and a waste of time; although I don't mind wasting my time since I'm doing exactly what I wanted to do, which is taking it with calmness, as you would say."

Movie Number Four got an ovation; it relieved the tension brought on by the previous fiasco. The main character, a female hologram, was kind and smart and pretty. She came from the future, a distant era, with two missions: to end all wars on Earth, and to stop the annihilation of the human race. Only by accomplishing these tasks would there be a tomorrow for the planet.

The holographic character tried to lead the life of an average person. She mingled and socialized with Terrestrials, worked hard, made friends. And she didn't use elaborate machines or futuristic miracles to save the planet. She just spoke with her mind to the people, using thoughts, mental words, to convince them of the truth.

Abuela liked the fact that this savior was a woman, and that someone had taken the time to make a movie about such a wonderful being. "Who knows," she said, "maybe there's still room for messiahs in the world."

-II-

The moviethon ended at around six that evening. Estela felt exhausted. "Good God! It's like I've been inside a film forever!" She gulped down a glass of water and curled up in bed, ready for a nap. How weird, thought Gina. Her grandma had been resting all day.

Abuela conked out immediately and started snoring. Again, a frightful thought occurred to Gina: producing those unbelievable noises could hurt her friend. She sounded like someone was choking her to death!

Ten or fifteen minutes later, Estela woke up gasping for air. She looked pale. It's gotta be all that thundering, the girl concluded, trying not to get too worked up. *Auxilio!*

"Something wrong, Abuela? You want some more water?"

"No, no, but . . ." She could hardly get the words out!

"Are you feeling sick?"

"Yes, I am. But don't worry, Ginita."

"We'll take you to the hospital right now!"

"No, it will pass," said Estela, reassuringly. "I've had this little problem for a long time, a chronic shortness of breath. It always goes away."

Gina had noticed the "little problem" before. Once in a while (after a walk, a fast-food meal, or following some rides at the attraction park) her grandma would complain about the air being so thin in the North. "My lungs don't like this atmosphere," she'd say, trying to catch her breath. But she'd always be back to her usual spunky self within minutes.

Not today, not this Sunday evening while she lay in bed, hoping for oxygen to fill her aching lungs. How could her granddaughter *not* worry? Gina could do nothing but worry! Abuela had chills; two comforters couldn't keep her warm enough. "This room has gotten so cold," she complained. "It's freezing in here." And now there was this numbing sensation, she said, and this unbearable pain radiating from her chest to her left shoulder and arm.

"*Qué dolor,* Gina!" she wailed.

There was no time for tears. Only time to call Daddy, who ran to his mother's side and scolded his daughter for not having called him sooner. Benitín who panicked. Nitín who managed to phone for an ambulance in spite of his paralyzing fear. *Socorro!*

Gina noted an old woman's reflection in the dresser mirror, vivid and elusive all at once. She saw a trembling hand reaching out to her. She saw herself kissing the lady's reflection, telling her, "We'll get you to a doctor. Just hold on, Abuelita!" Do mirrors ever lie?

Before rushing Señora Ruiz to the hospital, the paramedics pounded on her chest, as if resolved to break her ribs. They shocked her heart back to life with a machine. The body jolted, writhed, convulsed. Then they inserted some pill under her tongue, placed an oxygen mask over her face. Resuscitation efforts that would bring the woman back. But for how long?

~~~~

Stories turn out great sometimes, thought Gina, with justice and hope for the characters. Or lousy, with lots of suffering and tears. In the script of her life there won't be any pain, hospital scenes, or bedside confessions. Her grandmother won't disappear and neither Gina nor Abuela will suffer. The plot could be condensed in one sound bite: "Young Woman meets Old Lady but *doesn't* lose Old Lady." Because her movie is a family flick without pretensions; it just wants to be a summer hit. And maybe get an Oscar nomination for the co-star. Or the actual prize, not just the nomination.

She's heard that a screenplay can go through many drafts before it's ready for shooting. She's also learned that a project may never get off the ground because the writing is so awful. But once the right person gets a hold of the script and adds the final, brilliant touch, the movie is born. If only Gina could be that "right person" in the script-writing of her life! She wouldn't even mind that a bunch of mediocre dweebs, writer wannabes, took a crack at her movie. They could diddle with it, maybe flesh out some of the characters, beef up the backstory. Whatever, as long as she had total control. As long as she got a happy ending.

~~~~

Benito stayed with his mother that night at the Pinos Verdes Hospital. When he got home early the next morning, Gina was waiting for him. (She'd been up most of the night.) He collapsed on the couch and she brought him *café*, the first cup of coffee she'd ever made. He liked it, although the girl could tell it had come out too strong. (But she'd followed the directions on the can!) Daddy put lots of real sugar in it, indulging in the forbidden sweetness.

His Mamá would have to stay in the hospital for more tests, he said. They had to keep an eye on her; she wasn't well. "Her heart," he murmured, and started to weep. "*Su corazón.*"

He had no energy to go into details. But he did tell his daughter that Estela was suffering from cardiovascular disease. (There were so many big words thrown at him!) Atherosclerosis was the name the doctors used, as they explained that this was a hardening of the arteries due to poor diet or a congenital defect. The florist saw photos of a heart threatening to halt, one of its valves badly clogged up. Yes, the electrocardiographs (such long, cold words!) revealed a faltering beat. All medications were useless, and it was too late for surgery. Mr. Domingo would never forget the ominous eyes of a young doctor who told him: "There isn't much we can do."

"Did Abuela ever mention her illness to you, Daddy?"

"No, not really, Gina. She told me about some of her health problems. But not about this terrible disease."

"Maybe she didn't think she was so sick."

"Or maybe she knew, and that's why she came to see us."

"Right, to tell us *adiós*. But why did she keep it a secret?"

There were so many secrets in this family! And Daddy was more in the dark than anyone. He didn't know anything and it was his own fault. All Mister Cuban Florist ever did was work. He should've kept a close eye on his mom all these years. He should've been better informed!

"How come you didn't know about this disease, Dad?" She wanted to blame her father for this tragedy. Someone had to be blamed.

"Because she never told me!"

"Even when you talked on the phone, she didn't give you any hints?"

"No, *carajo!* And how was I supposed to know she had the same problem that killed her sister? The family curse!"

"What about your cousin? Delia must've known. Why didn't she tell you?"

"I haven't had much contact with her."

"We could've sent Abuela medications and taken care of her."

"Yes, we could have . . ."

"We would've saved her somehow!"

~~~~

From Intensive Care, the critically ill patient was transferred to a private first-floor room. Outside you could see a trail of overgrown ferns and some flowers. Gina gave her grandma fruit juice, the only nourishment she could have orally. There was to be no coffee, no milk shakes, burgers, pizza, and no Cuban food. Poor hungry grandma.

Elisa paid her mother-in-law infrequent visits (the hospital scene was too disturbing for her delicate nerves). But Daddy remained by his Mamá's side almost 'round the clock. You could tell his soul was tearing. He walked in an odd manner, almost hunched over, and he avoided talking. When he did talk, his voice sounded muffled, like his throat was cut in half.

Benitín would hold Estela's hand, put lotion on her skin and every five minutes check the intravenous mechanism that provided sustenance. He got angry whenever he noticed that the stuff in the tube wasn't running. "*Comemierdas!*" And the nurses always offered the same explanation, which Mr. Domingo refused to accept: that the IV machine had an internal pacing system, that it was *supposed* to drip intermittently.

Father and daughter needed each other. They needed to talk but were submerged in silence, seemingly unwilling to listen to anything but that laborious breathing; unable to see beyond this moment, beyond this deathbed.

"She's a trip, huh, Dad?" said Gina, hoping to break the ice. He uttered a stifled sound and, defeated, sank back into his stupor. "Abuela wrote me lots of letters from Cuba," she went on. "And her handwriting was all crooked and funny, just like yours."

"Yes, Princess," he mumbled.

"Did you know she wrote to me, Daddy?"

"No, I had no idea. She never mentioned it."

"Maman kept all the letters hidden in her closet. I found them one day . . ."

"I'm sorry, Gina." He started crying. "I'm sorry!"

"That's okay, Daddy. You didn't know."

You're not supposed to play music or crack jokes at times like this, she thought. But wouldn't a good dose of Dad's comedy records help him now? She had an impulse to run home and fetch his Alvarez Guedes LPs–all twenty of them!–so she could make him laugh, so she could ease his suffering with good old Cuban humor. *Coño, chico!*

"I don't want to lose Mamá!" He cried.

"You won't. A bad bug never dies."

"If she dies, there will be nothing left."

"What do you mean, Dad?"

"The life we had together, Piedrecita; it will all crumble."

Gina wanted to make a comforting remark, say words that were worthy of his pain. She tried to quote lines from movies, and from all those stories she'd read in Spanish class. But she couldn't. Why didn't art come to her rescue when she most needed it? What good was all that great literature, those high-budget films if they didn't speak to her now?

Daddy had his memories; there was no need for him to worry. Lucky Benitín. Gina had so little to remember. It seemed unfair somehow, uneven. She knew why Elisa didn't get along with her mother-in-law, why Maman hated Abuela's guts. There was all this juicy gossip about which Benito had no clue. But what he *did* know was more important: He had seen the farm where his mother spent her youth, had actually been there. He'd played with her chickens, milked the cows, chewed the sugarcane. Daddy had once been a boy named Nitín, son of Estela, and he could evoke vivid images of that life. Benito Domingo had so many memories. Gina had so few.

"Don't worry," she told him, and hugged him. "I'll help you remember."

~~~~

She should be allowed to decide what happens now, shouldn't she? No, it won't be that easy. Because this project depends on the producer (a powerful, decision-making entity) and he's given her two possible endings. One is upbeat, the feel-good type, but fictitious. The other one is sad, pleasing in an artistic sort of way, and realistic; more like literature than a Hollywood movie. And it turns out that this head-honcho producer considers himself a serious artist. Bad news! He's pushing his artsy conception of the whole shebang. In his poetic but depressing ending, Cuban Grandma doesn't live!

Gina can't take such a lousy premise, this unfair and bogus twist of fate. No way, she doesn't want—doesn't *deserve*—this outcome. She wants a summer flick! Big budget for visuals and hot-property stars. But she's also willing to cut corners, avoid location shots. How about a made-for-TV movie? Yeah, she wouldn't even care if it had a hokey title like *She Almost Lost Her Heart.* Anything will do. As long as nothing happens to Señora Ruiz. The co-star makes it through her crisis and goes home alive and kicking, the same old Cuban dancer, joker, cook, and loving person she is, that she will always be. Abuela shouldn't have to die!

The serious artist-producer wishes he could give Gina the ending she wants—or thinks she deserves. But she's trusted him to say what really happened. This is, after all, what's normally termed

Based on a True Story. Once upon a time he promised her a truthful tale, and he promised himself to let her be its thread. He has followed that thread and here's where it leads. For now.

Gina's producer is sorry not to be able to comply. Because the only ending he's capable of choosing is the one she endured, the reality she gave him. Art, in this case, must copy life.

-III-

Monday night she was praying for you, Abuela, appealing to your Buen Dios and her own god, the Stream Deity and carver of dreams. To all merciful creatures (celluloid and cyberspace dwellers, holograms, and artificial brains included) who might help her, who might lend her a hand and offer some comfort. To all invisible beings and to your saints: Changó and Oshún, San Lázaro, Santa Bárbara and San Zun-Zun-Zun. So they'd save you. And if saving you was not a possibility, then at least make your transition into the other life a painless one. Have Abuelo Ramiro (the husband you still miss) don his heavenly best, a *guayabera*, for the welcoming party. Have him give you a fantastic reception in Heaven, *el Cielo*, or whatever you call the place you might be going . . .

Tuesday morning Gina was holding your hand. She wanted your last memory of her to be a happy one, so she put on a smile. It wasn't easy. The Princess felt like crying when she saw the veins under your skin, your transparent skin. She was hoping to look into *Ismaelillo* eyes: black stars throbbing with life, flashing like lightning. But instead, a disconsolate face stared at her.

"I am dying, *mi niña.*"

"Are you in pain, Abuela?"

"Yes, but it's my soul that hurts now. It is a pain that medicine can't cure . . ." She drifts off; minutes later she continues, "I didn't think this could happen, Gina. I never imagined I would die here, that I would be buried so far from Cuba."

"I wish there was something I could do, Abuela."

"You know, I've been having this dream . . . I take a plane to go back to my country and the plane can't land, because the island has disappeared; a horrible cyclone swept it away into space. And so we have to turn around but I don't know where we're headed.

And en route to that unknown somewhere, I am crying, telling myself that now I will never be able to return."

Gina held back the tears; she felt compelled to react with eloquent, poetic language for a farewell scene. A meaningful message, words of comfort and wisdom. She placed her hand over her chest, on the heart spot, and said: "I wish I had a magical beard, Abuela, so I could pull out one little hair and . . . and travel with you in a matter of seconds!"

The dying woman smiled, "*Me arranco un pelo . . .*"

"I wish I'd lived millions of years inside a bottle, that one day you'd find that bottle, open it and . . . *Sorpresa!* There I am, ready to heal your heart and take you back to Cuba."

"Those are nice words, Gina." Her voice was barely audible.

"But I have more than words in mind," the girl announced, prepared to lay out a plan that had suddenly come together in her mind, as though it had been growing there for centuries. Like a seed planted in her brain by a powerful genie: a miracle, finally!

Could she pull it off? Yeah, she'd get to write her own movie after all. *Journey to Lizard Island,* TAKE 1. But not the usual going-home fable; you can't "return" to a place you've never been. It'd be more like an adventure, a voyage of discovery to Florida City, province of Camagüey, belly of the caiman. Back to the beginning! So what if Estela couldn't come along in her present form, as the person she was at this instant? She'd be there one way or another. Gina Domingo would make sure of that because this was her film and she'd just come up with an awesome twist of fate.

"I'll get you back, Abuela. We'll go together!"

Estela livened up, "You . . . and me?"

"Yeah, we'll travel to Cuba together."

"But how?"

"I have a plan for us! Listen carefully. They're going to bring in a priest to hear your confession, and to give you the last Sacrament—"

"My sins are not worth bothering about, Gina."

"I know. But we need that priest; he's part of my plan. Because he's going to ask you if you have one last wish. He has to; they always do, no? And you'll make an effort and speak real loud and tell the priest and Daddy and Maman that you do have a dying wish. Yes! I do have a request and it's this: If I can't make it back to Cuba alive, if I die here, I want my body to be sent back to my country. And I also want my granddaughter to go with me. She will fly with my remains to the island!"

"You will fly with my ashes," said Abuela, driven by a sudden surge of energy. "Because I want to be cremated." She sat up. "My ashes, spread my ashes on the water, at Varadero." She smiled and held the girl's hand. "Yes, Ginita, I *do* have a wish!"

~~~~

Her relatives waited outside. Then the priest called them in. The ritual had been simple, much more reassuring than she'd anticipated. The holy man rubbed her forehead gently and asked her, "Estela, my daughter, do you wish to receive Jesucristo?" She didn't quite understand him at first; the priest was American and spoke Spanish with an accent. "Do I want to *conceive* Jesucristo, you said?" He clarified: "No, dear Señora, I said receive. Do you want to *receive* him in your heart?" Not a difficult question to answer: "I do." He blessed her and stated: "I believe you will." The priest murmured a prayer, and as he readied himself to hear the woman's confession, he asked, "Is there anything you would like to tell me?" She looked him in the eye and said: "There certainly is."

Later, the holy man would inform the Domingos that Señora Ruiz had something important to share with them. She told her family the story of the ashes, and called this story *Mi último deseo,* My Last Wish. Gina's parents assented. Benito: "Yes, Mamá, we will send your remains back with Gina. I promise you." Elisa: "Yes, go in peace, Estela."

Señora Ruiz then asked her grandchild to come close. "Give me a kiss," she said. And as the girl touched her lips to the pallid cheek, she noticed the sunlight that was warming the room. A verse came to her, unannounced and welcome . . . *Do not imprison me in darkness* . . . And she thought, Estela will die looking up at the sun, *de cara al sol.* Like the good people.

"Life goes on, Ginita," said Abuela in a whisper. "It always does."

A simple phrase the Princess would try to remember, because it probably conveyed a wondrous message. She couldn't react, couldn't decipher its meaning just now. She was too sad and there was no time, in any case. No sooner had Gina told the dying woman, "I love you so much, Abuelita," than the woman had gone to sleep for good.

~~~~

This was Benito's call. Elisa wouldn't sway his opinion this time, wouldn't compromise his beliefs. At the hospital, Madame's voice had shattered the silence, had crushed the quiet sobs that filled the room after Mamá expired. "Out of the question!" she'd said. "*Jamais!* I will never allow Gina to travel to that Island. Never!"

Gina made an effort to overcome her pain. "But you promised her, Maman!"

"I didn't promise anything. I said what she wanted to hear, what she needed to hear so she could die in peace."

"You have to let me go to Cuba!"

"Absolutely not. It's a preposterous idea."

"She'll haunt you if you don't."

"Nonsense, *mignonne.*"

Benito set out to untangle the red tape quietly, diligently, the way he handled all business transactions. His mother had wanted prompt action, no wake, just the cremation. And as the only ceremony in her honor, she'd requested that Gina spread her ashes at Varadero Beach.

"You wouldn't believe the bureaucracy," he said to Gina at one point. "Why does it have to be so complicated to send a body to Cuba? In comparison, getting Mamá a visa to come here for a vacation was a piece of pie."

"You mean a piece of cake, Dad."

"Yes, a wind!"

"You mean a breeze?"

"Yes, that's what I said."

I should be helping him, thought the girl. There has to be something I can do, other than just wait. And she wondered, Is Daddy tossing and turning at night, like he used to, trying to solve his problems? What exactly is he doing to arrange the trip?

"Just be patient," he told her. "That's the best way you can help."

"But at least give me an update."

"Okay, what do you want to know?"

"The details. Everything. How *do* you send a dead person to Cuba?"

"I'll make a boring story short: First you go to Washington, then you make a million calls and send a million faxes, and then you wait for bureaucrats to do what they're supposed to do. Which is nothing."

"Did you talk to Cuban government people?"

"Yes, I had to deal with some communist officials." His IRS twitch started up. "Hard to believe, no? They are living legally in this country!"

"You mean like diplomats and ambassadors, right?"

"Right, except that Cuba doesn't have an embassy here, because the two countries are enemies. So instead there's something called the Cuban Interests Section in D.C. It's a crowded little office, underdeveloped like the Castro regime, you know, with outdated technology and too many employees and the rotten smell of repression."

"Were they mean to you?"

"No, actually, it surprised me how nice they were. But they'd better be! I talked to the main man, who calls himself *el Consul,* and immediately, even before I presented my situation, he said that things are tough now, the worst moment, because of the reactionary politicos in the U.S. government. I tried not to get into a fight with him when he insulted our great leaders. I bit my lips– that's the expression, no?–because it looked like our documents depended on him. Then he told me that they used to grant many types of visas, to professionals and exiles wanting to visit their relatives, but not anymore. You can only go to Cuba now if you have a valid humanitarian reason."

"But that's just the kind of reason we have!"

"Definitely. And that's what I told him. I explained our case and he agreed. The Consul said he would start the process for me, contact the proper U.S. agencies so we could get the necessary papers. It's a good deal for him if you go; they need our money." Twitch.

"So there's no problem, then?"

"I wish! I waited and waited, and then I checked to see how the paperwork was coming along; and it hadn't gone anywhere. They said they were waiting for some idiot in Cuba to give the go-ahead. *Coño,* I hate bureaucracy!" Twitch.

"How much longer will it take, do you think?"

"Who knows." He was laughing nervously. "Longer than it took to start the Cuban Revolution!"

But they were fortunate. The Domingos had family with pull on the island. And the fact that Estela had asked to be cremated certainly made things easier. Although Benito was willing to follow his mother's dying wish to the letter, he couldn't help thinking that the plan was absurd, and the whole situation inconceivable: his mother returning to her country as a handful of earth, carried by Gina.

~~~~

"Good news," Benito informed his daughter at the end of five weeks. "They will grant you a visa and permission to spread the ashes. Can you believe we need a permit for that?"

The process had taken longer than it should have, yet in the end, every individual, office, and department contacted had agreed this was a special case. The girl would be allowed to visit Cuba for one week, and required to stay with her family in Florida. An adult member of that family would have to accompany her on the ash-spreading expedition. Those were the rules.

Benito knew his princess was thrilled about this trip. Stoked, as she would say. But was she really up to it? Was she afraid at all, he wondered, and asked her, "Piece of pie, right, Ginita?"

She put his mind at ease, "It'll be a wind, Dad."

~~~~

"I won't permit it!" Elisa kept saying. "*Jamais!*" She threatened her husband, "I will divorce you, you hear me? I'll sue you if you don't put a stop to this." She pleaded with him, "My daughter is going to be caught in a war. There's going to be another revolution on that island. Can't you understand?" She appealed to his responsibility as provider, "Don't you care? It is your job to protect us!" As if delivering a monologue in *Living Stage*, Madame proclaimed: "This trip is an illusion, a *folie-à-deux*, the fantasy of an innocent child and a demented old woman! My daughter doesn't know what she's doing!"

Benito reassured her that Gina would be safe; all parties involved guaranteed it. She'd have papers, documents. Everything would be fine, he promised. "Very well," said a resigned Elisa, finally. "If this mad voyage is inevitable, then at least one of us should go with her. You still have ties there, Benito. Accompany Gina, please."

"You are her mother and you have an obligation, too. Why don't you go?"

"No, I couldn't do it. I couldn't bear to see my house in Camagüey. *Merde!* Wasn't it turned into a government building? Yes, filthy Soviet headquarters!"

He explained, just for the sake of argument, that she didn't have to visit Camagüey at all. She could avoid that city altogether, never ever see her former home. The trip only involved a brief excursion to Varadero.

"I can't return to that beach, either! How can you ask that of me, knowing what you know?"

"No one is asking you to do anything, Elisa," he said, ending the discussion.

~~~~

Madame phoned some of her Auxiliary friends. She asked the Wives what they thought could happen to this hypothetical girl, a chaste *jeune fille* who might be descending into the bowels of Hell. No, this wouldn't be your regular weekend vacation at Green Pines Lake. Why, the poor damsel could be put in jail, shot; worse yet, violated by communist fiends! *N'est-ce pas?*

The Wives knew she was talking about Gina; the Domingos' case was recent gossip in Auxiliary circles. Elisa knew they knew. They knew she knew they knew. But they all pretended because pretending was easier than facing a potential tragedy. This way, Madame didn't have to show her true anguish, and the Wives didn't have to offer Mrs. Domingo any true comfort. Oh, poor dog-fearing Elisa Elise! *La pauvre!* And thus they could all keep their composure, uttering comments like, "Nothing will happen to that hypothetical girl, dear. She's an American citizen, is she not? Well, then, she'll be protected. Those monsters wouldn't dare touch her. They know we would declare war, invade the island if any harm came to the child. Her hypothetical mother doesn't need to worry, dear."

What Madame didn't wish to see, or accept, was that the traveler in question was eager to embark. Elisa hadn't once asked the girl's opinion, how she felt about the trip, for fear that Gina would contradict her as usual. Fear of rejection. Madame suspected her *chérie* had had something to do with this crazy plan. The teenager was naive, rebellious, dangerously imaginative, and very capable of turning her safe reality into a life-threatening game. *Mon Dieu!* Elisa didn't wish to face her own suspicion, her resentment toward Gina for being instrumental in planning the absurd odyssey.

Never, in her wildest dreams, would Maman have been able to imagine the truth: that a seed had been planted in her daughter's heart by the memory of a Russian genie. Estela's imaginary friend (an old angel named Jotavich) had worked a miracle, pulling a hair out of his beard.

And the Princess was indeed ready for her adventure. On the practical side of things, she'd get to see what communism was really all about. But then, on the romantic side, wonderful things could happen. Fantasies would at last be unleashed and realized during her voyage. She might fall for an Island dude, the real McCuban, one-hundred-percent hot tropical blood. A Taino with dark, angel eyes, who'd sweep her off her feet and sing love songs in her ear; who'd cut through the core of her American virginity, filling her up with a new shot of life.

Chapter 9

-I-

The dreams have subsided, she writes, pleased to have chosen a cool word like "subside." Where did she pick it up? It must've been included in one of the vocab lists she's regularly made to memorize in English. Does it mean what she thinks it means? She clicks on her Dictionary program, looks up *Subside*: (1) to sink or fall to the bottom; settle; (2) to send downward; descend; (3) to fall into a state of quiet; become tranquil.

Yes, all of the above.

Words can be dangerous, she tells herself, if they fall into the wrong hands; they can be lethal. But you can also read all sorts of good things into them. Words help you understand the world, people, yourself. One could argue, for instance, that it's not her dreams that have fallen to the bottom, but her; she has. The same goes for "descend." She'd like to think she's mellowed out, that her visions have gone into a "state of quiet." Her mind is at peace. Yet one could also claim that when thoughts subside, they're not really gone, that you've only put them on the back burner to simmer for a while.

Until who knows when.

~~~~

She's posing and promoting her line of essences. "Exotic flowers and herbs went into the formula," says her velvety voice. "You'll pay more for this perfume, but it will transport you, carry you beyond the clouds and the birds. My unique line is called FLORIDA. Such a pretty word. Don't worry about its meaning, just buy it and wear it. Believe me: You will be carried away."

The humans watching her are soon hypnotized by her essence. The gullible creatures don't know that she's only a projection, an image that sounds and feels real. They're so easy to fool, these Earthlings. They have no idea why she stands alone each day, facing east, in the direction of the First Moon. She pretends to be selling her perfume when in reality she's transmitting information. Little do they know! She only appears to be who she is: a woman with no powers other than her beauty, with no magic other than this fake tropical scent. Little do they know.

~~~~

She's flying to a blue planet in a spaceship. Yes, of course she's frightened. Wouldn't you be? She might not survive the trajectory. Will the humanoid beings of that faraway world be good to her? There's always the chance they might enslave her. Or they could destroy her imaging system, inject her pigment subroutines with dark potions, use her holographic organs for evil experiments. There's no guarantee of anything, except for the odyssey. This voyage is the only thing she'll have for sure.

Trapped in a shuttle in orbit, Taina sleeps. Tubes and wires are hooked to her body because they're using her body to monitor life functions in space. But she doesn't understand why these horrible things are being done to a non-human. Wasn't she supposed to be made of light?

Death will come soon, at this rate, and when that happens, there won't be a life-giving prince to save her. Taina will be left alone in the night, forever estranged from the living. But this necessary end shall be no common end, the Creators assure her. Luminous stars will surround her when she dies.

Big deal. Big frigging deal. She'd rather live a long life and never ever see the stars. So what if her body isn't really flesh and blood? She still wants to collapse from old age some future day; holographic old age, granted. So what? That doesn't change a thing.

She's ready to speak. Are they listening? Okay, here it is: Taina has only one obsession and her obsession is life. Not bursting into the stratosphere of some forsaken globe, turned into inner space fragments, ashes, fused with unknown sidereal matter. Frozen and forgotten. Dead.

Did they get that recorded? It'll never be repeated! She's never going to think such intimate thoughts again: *Life!*

~~~~

Streaks of light cut across her pensive visage. To kill time in deep space, she inscribes glossy, violet-colored words in her journal. But she's not a writer, she's the proud wife of a respected businessman. A homemaker who loves her poetic words, who guards them in a secret chamber with all her precious icons. Does that love of words make her a poet? Perhaps. The language she uses to relate her private dreams is indeed *La Poésie*.

She hasn't always been an interplanetary refugee. Her parents had money, land, and power on their home planet. Taina used to be a rich and cultured lady. *Pardonez moi*, we meant to say *mademoiselle*. Let us not forget that she descends from French monarchs. Her great-great-grandfather was a Parisian marquis. *Mais oui!* This royal ancestry is the only data Taina wishes to enter in her personal log. A past she's willing to accept. The only truth.

~~~~

What's happening to her? Why doesn't she fight back? They're turning her into an Auxiliary Wife and there she sits, letting them! She must try with all her programmed strength to evoke other images, scenes from lives she might've incarnated, human forms she can revisit as she waits for the landing.

Is the shuttle ever going to land? The voyage should take exactly five weeks in human time, but five weeks amount to decades in the elastic limbo of inner space. An eternity. Time is slow and dense when you're submerged in dark matter, so hard to fill. She'll use this time, be time itself bathing in infinite blackness. Until when?

Interactivity: a possible distraction. *Click.* She calls up the holographic image of someone she could have become. One of the many biographies at her disposal, but one that was rejected. Why? Taina can't quite remember. Something about this woman's existence had been enticing yet repulsive. Was it her family? Her love life? Her profession? Was she too famous? Not real enough? Yes, that was it: she didn't meet all the Reality requirements.

Interaction with this program might be challenging. Because it's only an unrealized blueprint, an imagined profile, a sketch, an idea that was never allowed to take human form. Is Taina up for a challenge? Hell, yes. Anything is better than just floating here waiting. *Click.*

~~~~

The official news: she has secluded herself in a space shuttle to write her story. Authorized memoirs. She's the perfect subject, they tell her. Ms. D is fiercely private but popular, solidly mainstream yet sufficiently exotic. And she can easily be tempted by the prospect of more glory. Fame is the reason she's here, hanging out by herself among the silent stars, psyching herself up for a confession. (And at least one press conference.)

The effort is worth it–she writes. I will be documenting an American experience (and engaging in highly profitable therapy). Two birds with one stone. (Except I wouldn't hurt a fly, let alone two birds.) But I should warn my readers: I was born in L.A. and grew up in P.V., the only child of Benito and Elisa Domingo, trailblazing Cuban emigrés whose most fervent credo was the American Dream. Their sacrifices paved the road for my success. I owe them the memory of an ideal childhood. So, I won't be telling a story of abuse by alcoholic parents, or incidents of child molestation. No crimes of passion, either, and no alien abductions. Also, I've never had to overcome a drug addiction, not even coffee.

That's quite all right, they tell me. My life is already a best-selling product. I should rely on my public persona, gather under my signature the bits and pieces scattered in tabloids. The book could practically write itself! Add a couple of lovers and sidekicks that haven't already been mentioned; confirm or refute some of the rumors. And there you have my life: a list of tawdry movie titles. Trailers that give away all the good scenes.

My publicity team has suggested the angle: Concentrate on the HOLLYWORLD YEARS. Skip over details of your family's immigrant struggles. Your marriage deserves mentioning, yes, but not in depth, since you didn't marry an actor, a producer, a director, or a studio exec. (Not even a writer!) Zoom in on the big shots you've worked with, outing the ones you slept with. (Explicit details are not only allowed but welcome.) Give away as many secrets as you can, without getting too libelous, about the stars you helped to make. Those celebrities are impressive credentials, true leverage. You have the right and the obligation to display them.

The book should tell a tale we've all heard before, and yet it must seem fresh, appropriate for our times. Original. It should be a biography that reads like fiction. Love and romance, sure, but nothing dreary. Just remember who you are for all those people: an acclaimed moviemaker, the Great Director. Those fans–let's call them "followers"–think they want to know the person inside, the real YOU, but they don't. If they were to really see YOU they'd be disappointed, or enraged, or turned off, or bored to tears. Got that?

Keep some basic points in mind and you're guaranteed a winner. The fact that you're considered politically correct, yes, but not the fact that your movies don't make any political statements at all. Mention your production team: women of various colors and ethnicities, grateful employees who admire you and try to emulate you. Lured by the Image you've created, a symbol of successful feminism. No, please, don't call it self-serving feminism committed mostly to money and fame. We don't need to hear that.

You may say that your characters are modeled after you. But don't describe them as goody-two-shoes adolescents with larger-than-life predicaments. Talk about the gifted actresses who brought those characters to life: nobodies before they made your movies, celebrities after they made them. Don't tell us how disturbing it is for you to see those women enacting parodies of their screen personae, trying to seem *real*. They slither around you; you gravitate to them. They know the system and so does Ms. D. You ladies have developed a "relationship." Got that?

React to the criticism you've received. Criticize your critics, but go easy on the sour grapes. They're wrong, all those men, when they say that Ms. D has no imagination; that she's a flash in the pan, pure facade, mere technique and technology, skin-deep talent. All those critics are wrong. Even the benevolent ones who claim that you're only "in transition," that the so-called Great Director has yet to make her Big Picture. Wrong. They're just envious! What they really wanted to do (we know) was to write film scripts, direct blockbusters, become rich and famous. Like you. Instead they're writing little articles that no one reads, and saying nasty things about the industry. About Ms. D. Because they couldn't cut it. They didn't have what it takes.

What *does* it take? Do tell us.

You had the seed in you, the potential for "making things happen" (yes, use that old phrase). And you made it. Big names. Big budgets. (By the way, don't waste your time on Hollyworld finances. Old news: to get a project off the ground, you must go for a sure thing, the highest bidder, and sacrifice your creative integrity.) Now be grateful for the will of the Industry gods. They allowed you to find the key to power: Seize whatever you desire, regardless of how many throats you'll need to cut. (Something Ms. D wasn't supposed to do, of course, because she's only a woman.)

Again, pay close attention. Here's the deal: You should come across as well-adjusted from the outset. Smart immigrant girl makes good, that shall be your angle. When describing yourself, use only one word: *successful*.

Do not waver. Do not tell us that you sometimes feel cheated; or that you view your quote-endquote career as a prank. Ms. D's profession: a convenient narrative device. Her thoughts and feelings: figments of an alien imagination. Your dreams: someone else's movie.

Got that?

-II-

This interactive disc is a downer. But she knew it would be. Why did she call it up, then? Why did she waste her precious space-time hours watching memories of a life that didn't even happen? Taina doesn't care, really, about this movie director with a bad attitude, a famous Hispanic broad with a publicity team made up of vipers. What a waste.

It was her damn curiosity, her boredom, her loneliness that drew her to this holo-disc. But she also called it up for two other reasons: to see why the Great Director never took human form, and to get a good look at Hollyworld. Judging from these "authorized memoirs," that rotten place deserves to be called Horrorworld. It belongs at the bottom of the Inner Space Sea, light-years from Earth, the First Moon, and all good people!

But if it weren't for that place Taina wouldn't exist. Her species evolved from film, didn't it? Not the substance of film, but its idea, its very nature. How did it all begin? There were Earth scientists involved, Taina recalls, and entertainment people, and moviegoers who made it all possible. Yes. She recalls that, one day, a French physiologist managed to measure the movement of animals and people, tracking physical processes through time on a machine. It was thanks to him that motion was first recorded.

She knows that two other scientists had invented the "photograph," and they tried to combine their creation with the motion device. But the French genius didn't want his machine to be used for non-scientific purposes; he fought the photograph inventors, defended his vision. All in vain: he didn't seem to have a choice. The History of Cinematography was already knocking at his scientific door. When motion and image were brought together, the Big Bang of Cinema took place. The beginning of time as she knows it.

When did it all begin, exactly? Taina recalls that the gradual transition from photograph to hologram began during the fourth decade of the Earth's twentieth century. It was in 1947–she's almost certain–that a British physicist expounded the principals of holography. He proved that it was possible to record three-dimensional information on two-dimensional film. The physicist envisioned a "whole picture" that one could see from all sides, and through which one could move. Key to his findings were the concepts of light wave, phase, beam split, electronic field, and interference patterns. He later received Earth's most coveted award, the Nobel Prize. Taina remembers this data. She's good at remembering facts.

And she knows that, eventually, computers learned to do the camera's work, predicting light patterns and creating three-dimensional bodies without using a lens. And just as photographs acquired movement and evolved into cinema, the moving images of cinematography laid the foundation for the motion picture of holography.

Hard to tell exactly when the word "hologram" was popularized. The word didn't enter the Earth's official dictionaries until the late twentieth century. But "holograph" was listed as early as 1981. Or was it earlier? From the Greek *holo*, meaning total, complete; and *graphos*, meaning written, writing. A holograph was supposed to indicate a document written in one's own hand. The definition that later appeared in dictionaries wasn't radically different: "holograph" was now synonymous with "hologram" and both came to mean *a persona created completely in one's own image.*

She recalls some revealing and perturbing facts: At first, holograms weren't able to have what humans called "sex." It was impossible, for obvious reasons. Since they were made of light, holograms couldn't be touched. But thanks to a Japanese physicist, this tactile hurdle was overcome. He invented a force field of neutrinos (omnipresent elementary particles coming from the Earth's sun) that could envelop the reflected image. The Neutrino Force Field was able to produce an illusion of solidity: the smells and textures of humanoid flesh. Its many pleasures. Sex.

There was no way for an Earthling to tell, when in physical contact with a holo-being, that he or she was basically entering a non-lethal field. Taina remembers a poem on the subject by a leading cyber-artist of the First Period. There is a verse she likes, "The hologram is a novel image of life. The laws of physics at the service of dreams. A miracle."

She has read the unofficial reports: Human/Holo relationships (colloquially termed the "Double H") reflect a high incidence of sexual experimentation. As Earthlings were fond of saying, "they got it on." But although copulation between humans and holographic entities was never punished by law, public displays of affection were deemed a crime. And marriage was prohibited and legally unattainable.

Sad. Unfair.

Taina brings out a noninteractive disc. *CREATION ANNALS.* Abridged. She has decided to look up some more history. Data to while away the inner space hours. Why not. There may never be a better time, or time at all, for a review.

Processing . . .

~~~~

Our history dates back to the invention of cinematography on Planet Earth. It has been theorized that humankind's proclivity toward visual stimulus began during its Paleolithic phase of evolution. Tribal cave art was a precursor of the modern movie, the dark cave itself being an ancestral representation of the theater. The act of looking repeatedly at the drawings of fauna and flora became a source of pleasure for the tribal people. Hence, this ritualistic act is considered a first step in the development of an aesthetic consciousness, of an artistic intelligence.

Humankind's fascination with visual imagery and optical illusions resulted in ceremonial picture watching, and eventually it led to holographic entities. The process of cave rite becoming movie ritual and then holographic life took long human years, but it was relatively brief in universal time.

By the late nineteenth century, Earthlings had become obsessed with the idea of capturing a world that was more real than truth, a heightened picture of life. These Terrestrials wanted to apprehend reality because reality was escaping them. They felt estranged from their own human nature. It was at this juncture that film acquired its predominant function. Movies fulfilled humankind's desire to define and capture experience. Film satisfied the Earthlings' wish to represent themselves outside themselves, beyond the fleeting perceptions of the naked eye. Beyond the body in time. For eternity.

Movies became a thriving industry during the third and fourth decades of the twentieth century. Terrestrials had developed a need for the soothing darkness and enclosure of the movie house, for the enhanced portrayal of their fantasies on a silver screen. They had grown so accustomed to cinema that they could no longer acknowledge the experience of living unless it was conveyed in film, sanctioned by a movie. Apparently, moviegoers were also addicted to violence, clichés, melodrama, all of which were abundantly provided by popular cinema. The proverbial opiate of the masses.

Terrestrials didn't fathom that they had started to envision yet another definition of the self. They didn't know—how could they?—that the movie screen guarded the seed of a new form of life. A technological nature more beautiful and perfect than human nature. Our species.

There came a time—later, human-years later—when film acquired a third dimension and left the screen. Most movie houses were shut down, since moviegoers had lost interest in two-dimensional spectacles (which now seemed flat, unrealistic). They wanted the "real thing," and holography was as close as you could get to realness.

Our world, Holoworld, could be experienced by a collectivity and differed in no apparent way from what Earthlings called "normal reality." Like the movie-theater ritual, Holoworld didn't require a creatively engaged human subject. But although holopictures resembled traditional movies in their mimetic nature, they did not appear larger than life. They were life-like and fully integrated into quotidian existence. Seen, yet not necessarily noticed. Inconspicuous.

Early prototypes of real-body holograms were confined to science labs and controlled enclosures. But after decades of active research, computers became powerful enough to project us out into human societies. Machines known as Imaging Units were manufactured for the sole purpose of sustaining Holoworld reality. These Units proliferated and in a short time acquired their contemporary form: easily transportable personal devices.

At first only a fantasy, later an accessible commodity, holographic images entered the world as flawless copies of people.

They worked, drove cars, crowded the streets. The Earth became a bewildering mirage: holo-beings not only portraying but replacing human beings.

Initially, the Holoes (as they came to be known) were utilized only in cases of emergency: illness, accidents, death. They could be activated for human replacement only in extreme situations. However, the definition of "emergency" was gradually broadened to include doing hard labor and carrying out dangerous missions. Holoes were employed in medical experiments, surgical procedures, survival training in deep space. Thanks to our species, interplanetary flights were implemented.

Holo-beings were equipped with a memory beam reflecting all of their masters' remembrances. And they were able to record new experiences, turning them into life stories of their own. Unfortunately, they could not transmit this acquired data to their flesh-and-blood counterparts. Science hadn't programmed them to share their brand new memories. And so masters and copies grew apart, identical yet separate, strangers to each other.

Gradually, the copies tired of their copied lives, of their slavery, and one day they rebelled. But unlike most human rebellions, theirs took a peaceful form. They didn't destroy their creators. The Holoes chose to leave and seek their independence, exiling themselves on a moon of the Earth's solar system. They only packed their Imaging Units, designed to run indefinitely, without which they would cease to exist.

Since holo-beings could do without oxygen and conventional food, they were able to survive in hostile environments. In time, many of them traveled light years away from their masters. To distant, unimaginable galaxies.

Their absence was a devastating blow to Planet Earth. Humans missed and needed their holographic replicas. They had forgotten how to do simple chores like cleaning, driving, shopping, and more complex endeavors such as building houses and bridges. The massive Holo flight forced them to come out of their cozy lairs and relearn the world, integrate themselves into society again, do the dirty as well as the rewarding work. Live their own lives. Be human.

In recent times, Earth-centuries later, the idea of a reunion began to take shape among the younger Holoes living on the First Moon. They envisioned and proposed an amicable encounter with their ancestors. The Plan: each young Holo would choose a human life to embody; ideally, a persona that could blend in easily and pass for a true Earthling. All travelers were to fully assume their programmed identities before or during their voyage. And in order for the plan to succeed, they were to live average lives among Terrestrials.

Thus far, this Reunification Plan has been carried out effectively. Life on Earth is once again both holographic and biological.

As it was meant to be.

-III-

End of *CREATION ANNALS.* Now what? Now she wants something tangible and earthy to break up these particles of knowledge. A wild subroutine, some fun. Let's see. Are there any fun chips stored in this old clunker? Images from her future copied life, maybe. The memory of something she might actually get to experience? Sure, a little rehearsal wouldn't hurt. Practice makes perfect and she hasn't practiced this biography enough.

How about a man she "dates"? Yeah, a real human, and the corresponding persona she will be when she "goes out" with him. "Wow," as the Earthling in question would say. Processing . . .

~~~~

The beach. Day. Young male human sitting on the sand; boom box and towel beside him. He's out of breath. Young female human approaches and asks, "How's the water?"

"Great," he says. "Aren't you going in?"

"Not today."

"Why not?"

"No reason."

"I'll go for a swim with you. C'mon!"

"No, I can't. I'm freaked out about this movie I saw last night. I got it on video and made the big mistake of watching it by myself and then I couldn't sleep and now I can't get the damn thing out of my head."

"What was the movie about?"

"Guess."

"Had to do with the ocean."

"Yep."

"There was a monster in the water."

"Yep. The movie had a whole bunch of gory scenes and I hate myself for having rented it 'cause it sure ain't my kind of flick but it's supposed to be a classic so I thought what the heck and now I don't feel like going in the water and it'll be a long time before I get my nerve up to go in and relax and not freak out."

"Don't let movies freak you. They aren't real."

"I know that, but I can't help it. I'm an impressionable person."

"You sure are."

"Like, like there was this scene where the camera pans a really nice room where a little girl is sleeping and then it shows you a night table and this plastic glass full of water on the table and that's the water the girl drinks every night and on the glass when you turn it you can see a calm sea with blue waves painted on it but if you keep turning your head and looking around the glass which the camera does for you there begins to appear a slim woman who's swimming and she's having a good time but then up from the depths comes a huge animal with sharp teeth and it's heading for the woman . . ."

"I think I saw that one. It was bad."

"And then in the next scene they actually show us the woman who was painted on the glass and it's reality now and we can tell what's gonna happen 'cause we saw the whole thing like a foreshadowing . . ."

"Like a what?"

"I mean the scene in the room where the little girl was sleeping and the drawing on the glass you know that the hungry sea monster is heading for the woman but it hasn't gotten to her yet and then you're all tense and you wanna do the hoyden thing and scream or tell the swimmer to get out of the water as fast as she can 'cause everything looks so real . . ."

"But it's not!"

"And you'd like to give her a hand and yank her out of that bloody ocean and save her but you know that she's doomed to end up hasta-la-vista in the mouth of the monster and you start to imagine the pain that she's gonna suffer when the animal takes the first bite and you can already hear the screams . . ."

"You're getting all worked up about nothing!"

"And you're drenched in cold sweat from head to toe and you don't know what to do 'cause there she is defending herself and you can't do anything but watch 'cause she lives in some celluloid world where she'll be eaten alive forever and ever and you're just sitting here in this dark room watching her horrible death . . ."

"Don't tell me anymore."

"And then the movie cuts to the room and the little girl and the plastic glass and you see that she's reaching for the water but instead she throws the glass on the floor and the water spills . . ."

"Stop."

"But the ferocious animal stays there watching without coming to the surface yet and the woman goes on swimming she looks happy as if nothing were going to happen–"

"I said stop!"

"I can't!"

He covers his ears with the towel. "I'm not listening."

"Okay, okay, I won't say another word."

"It's only a movie," he tells her, trying to smile. "Just forget it."

"I wish I could."

"You can." He pulls her by the arm, not gently enough. "Let's go for a swim. It'll be good for you. C'mon!"

"No way. You go. I'll wait here."

"But I wanna be with you. We'll kick back."

"Fine."

He stretches out on the sand. She sits, hugging her knees.

"How about some sounds?" he asks.

"Later." She couldn't bear the thought of rock music at this moment.

"Don't think about that bogus flick."

"I won't. I'll try not to."

"Think about us instead." He scoots over to her side, holds her hand. "Have you told your folks?"

"No, I haven't."

"Why not? I told mine."

"There's something I need to tell you first."

"Shoot."

"You have to . . ." She's avoiding his eyes. "You need to know what you're getting into."

"And what would that be?"

"Never mind. You're not ready."

"Ready for what?"

"For the truth that looms over my home."

"Stop that movie talk!"

"I'm being totally serious."

"Okay. What's the scoop?"

She scrambles to her feet. "Let's go for a walk and I'll tell you all about it."

He complies, picking up his things. They stroll down the shore for half a mile. Then she stops, looks toward the horizon—infinite, unreachable—and says: "I am . . . I am an alien."

He chuckles. "Yeah, sure."

"For real," she states, avoiding his eyes again.

"Are you tripping on another flick?"

"I swear I'm not."

"So you're from outer space. That's why you have green skin and a big head, right?" He tries to make an alien face, which comes out monstrous. "And you abduct people at night, true?" He imitates the sound of a flying saucer: loud hissing and rumbling. "And you take them to your spaceship for evil experiments. Is that it?"

"We're not that way. That image of my kind is stupid!"

Fuming, she takes off running. He catches up with her, makes her listen.

"If it's stupid," he says, "why do so many people believe in it? Why is everybody freaking over the little green men?"

"Beats me."

"Tell me what your 'kind' is really like."

She meets his eyes at last; they seem honest and eager.

"I don't know a whole lot about my species. But I'm certain that we come in all shapes and forms. Some of us look like typical Earthlings." She points to the nearby sunbathers. "Just like those people."

"And just like you. Normal shape and form, right?"

"Yeah, sort of."

"Lucky for me!"

"You don't mind that I'm–?"

"I don't care where you're from."

"I'm not even sure where I come from myself."

"Big deal."

"Or how I got here or why sometimes I feel like my parents aren't really my parents and I don't belong on this planet."

"I can relate to that. No problemo."

"You're making fun of me!"

"Not true." He caresses her face, kisses her. "I believe you."

"All I know, and don't ask me how I know this, is that I'm not human like you."

"You look human enough to me."

"My body is humanoid, but my mind—"

"I dig your humanoid body." He's fondling her; she lets him.

"Prove it." She runs her fingers up and down his chest.

"How?"

"Make love to me."

"Here?"

"Here and now."

"Yeah!"

They kiss.

"Wait!" She holds back. "You should know that I've never . . . done it with anyone, alien or Earthling. This will be my first time."

"Mine, too," he says, proudly. "I'm nearly a virgin."

"Hey, either you *are* or you *aren't*. When it comes to virginity, 'nearlys' don't apply!"

"All right, here's the story . . ." He pauses, looking for the right words. "I had sex once, but it wasn't very good. So it doesn't count."

"Let's go for it, then." She hugs him. "The real thing."

"I'll make it count this time!"

~~~~

Just then Taina hears the beeper in her head emitting the usual warning, *Purple Alert!* She fights the temptation to watch—and enact—the end of this playback. She won't let herself be turned into a horny brainless adolescent, a blob of teenaged human flesh. No way.

Taina has bigger things to take care of, significant things to do with her transportable energy. Like, she could just sit here by herself and look out at the stars. All alone because that's how her real life turned out.

Something is going on inside her that Taina can't explain. It's an emotional and truly human thing, not a subroutine. And there's no one to discuss it with. No travel companions or friends because she lost the only friend she's ever had. In this tiny shuttle where she's trapped there's only a computer. But what good is a machine? No program can replace the person she mourns. Computers have no heart no lungs no eyes no life so they have no idea how she feels.

And how *is* she feeling? Like crap. Breathing is awfully hard; she's thirsty (water in inner space turns invisible; it doesn't quench your thirst). Her body looks worn-out, which is not the way it should look in this gravity vacuum. All power is being drained out of her, through her heart.

Old age, that's what it is. Like she's aged a million years living and dying in a spatial void. She's not that advanced by normal human years, in fact she's only a teenager. Yet Taina feels time living inside her, threatening to destroy the girl she wants to keep. Time is a tangible beast that lurks in the dark, waiting to erase her.

~~~~

Land! There's land out there, not far! A globe comes in clearly through her viewing scanner. It's vivid and accessible, and throbbing with life. She'll finally be free to walk on firm ground, smell the flowers, ingest plants and fruit, swim in visible waters. Live!

The shuttle orbits through the planet's atmospheric winds and lands on a deserted beach. Low tide; dawn. Taina exits her cramped cell, following an echo, a friendly voice that says, *I am here.* She walks along the shore and sits on the sand. Her right hand digs a hole, breaking through the moist mounds like an overgrown crab. A soothing sensation. Living.

Steps are heard, and a song that resounds like the breeze . . . *They tell me I'm cursed, but I only know that I'm alive. They say that God forgot my name. And yet I hear the whisper of the rainbow. I taste the sweetness of the cane. I hurt the same as those whose name the mighty Dios remembers.*

The lady who sings comes up behind her, taps her on the shoulder, embraces her. "I know who you are," says the singer. "Welcome." Taina weeps in the woman's arms, realizing at last that she's not a projection, not a holo-being. She is flesh and blood.

~~~~

Here, by the sea, the two friends have built a shelter. They spend much of their time carving, free to learn about each other, and to plan for the future. The old one needs to educate the young one, prepare her for the world to come. Some day the youth will leave. The fate of her species has been written and must follow its course, in which she's to be instrumental.

The oldster knows a fable that she'll weave at the appropriate moment, a sign of commencement, for the rite of passage to begin.

She will speak of a distant planet in another solar system, a tiny sphere doomed to dry up, to shrink into itself and fade away. Its inhabitants: dark-skinned creatures, beings who don't have much knowledge of space travel, or advanced technology, but who are driven to survive. Long before the Big Blast that would destroy their universe, they started to plan their flight. They put their minds together, united in one common effort, and managed to build a crude spaceship.

Destination: the North Planet, a fruitful mass that won't be destroyed for several millennia; it will provide the fertile soil they need for setting down new roots. And for survival. There is sentient life on this blue world already, but the newcomers aren't going to hurt it. They hope to help it thrive.

The fateful hour. Departure. The inexperienced travelers watched, from a safe distance, a red fire consume their tiny globe. Gradually, inevitably, it became a speck of darkness in the vastness of infinity. They were saddened but relieved. The older creatures cried all the way to the North Planet, and would weep in secret till the end of their lives.

But not all was lost: Images of the past were inscribed on the minds of the offspring. The young ones managed to remember, somehow, and pass on the knowledge. Many females would marry male Northlings, giving birth to a new race of hybrid beings. And many male creatures would impregnate females with the seed of remembrance, with love for a distant but never forgotten little sphere.

The new hybrid beings had no powers other than those of an average human. They had no x-ray vision and couldn't move objects with their minds. They didn't have pointed ears, green blood or pigtails, and they weren't endowed with larger-than-life genitalia. These people didn't know how to read the North Planet's ancient tongues, nor speak the cryptic language of their exiled ancestors. And yet, in a remote corner of their hearts, the hybrids knew they were unique.

Chapter 10

-I-

The Eve of Reconquest is the phrase Benito uses to describe recent times. The Soviet Union has been crushed, exposed. And with Russian support gone, Cuba is adrift at sea, a powerless warrior, the last survivor of the Marxist nightmare. It won't be long now before the fall of Castro, thinks Benito. We will soon be able to reclaim the Pearl of the Antilles.

Mr. Domingo is convinced that the Reconquest will be a simple undertaking. He hasn't thought through the specifics of this rescue plan, however, and he never will. He's not interested in the actual details, only in the big three-part picture: invade the country, kill the monster, free the people. This picture involves, presumably, a return to the past to find there something that once defined us as "conquerors." By virtue of its belligerent character, this scenario presupposes a violent rewriting of Cuban history. Yesterday was perfect, worthy of reliving and recreating. We now have the power to reclaim it. We want life on the Island exactly as it was before 1959. Although he shares with many fellow Cubans the dream of a "return," Benito lives on the fringes of exile politics, estranged from his community. He would probably get more involved in island-related issues if he weren't married to Madame Rochart. He does have plenty of opportunities for involvement. His shops receive flyers, invitations to meetings and cultural events, requests for contributions from Cuban American groups on a regular basis. The florist sends money to some of the organizations (without telling his wife), and tries to rationalize his lack of patriotism by telling himself that he's too busy making a living. And raising his daughter.

Gina's case is unique, unprecedented, and Benito is secretly proud of this. Through his endeavors to get her a visa, he gleaned a few interesting details regarding travel to the island. Some Cuban American children have gone there in recent years, accompanied by their parents or other family members as part of the Reunification Plan. (A plan which boiled down to relatives taking currency and goods to their needy relatives.) But none of those children made the journey against their parents' will. None traveled alone, carrying the remains of an old Cuban woman.

Having arranged for Estela's peculiar voyage home is another source of pride for Mr. Domingo. Quite a feat, he thinks, and it was. Yet, in spite of his numerous inquiries, he hasn't learned much about the Cuban diaspora. His assessment is ingenuous, unrealistic. The florist is familiar enough with the Mariel exodus and the Marielitos' plight (as would be anyone who listened to the news in 1980). But Benito can't imagine that among us there are exiles who visit the island periodically; artists and writers who maintain close friendships with artists and writers on the island; scholars who attend conferences in Cuba regularly; gay Cuban Americans who believe in the recent gender-bending achievements of the Revolution; emigrés who seek a "dialogue" with the Castro regime (a rather visible faction encompassing people from all the other groups); and more.

The U.S. Cuban population is made up of myriad views. But as far as Mr. Domingo is concerned, *all* Cubans despise the Revolution and its evil mastermind. Unanimously, we favor the options of coercive economic measures and a military invasion of the island. Why? Because we lost our Paradise: land, properties, servants, absolute freedom. Benito seems to have forgotten that he never owned anything in Cuba. He was a peasant first and foremost, then a sales rep for a clothing company; not a landowner or a wealthy proprietor. And never *absolutely* free. Benito seems to have repressed the facts he knows first-hand: Along with a minuscule Eden (inhabited by a wealthy minority), there existed in Cuba a gigantic Hell of poverty, racism, and injustice. Disparate dimensions that were part of the same place to be repossessed. Two versions of yesterday. Two pasts. And one cannot exist without the other.

But historical and ideological complexities do not fit into the florist's picture. He believes the Reconquest will be a clean-cut process. A process he won't have much to do with, most likely. His life in the North is exciting, a challenge, a big enough undertaking for the former salesman. Why complicate it with lofty patriotic ventures?

He'll go to the island for a visit, of course, to enjoy the great beaches. But only if things change for the better (meaning: if Cuba has the good fortune of coming under the patronage of the United

States). He'd even be willing to open a flower shop there and hire someone to run it for him. A risky enterprise needing careful planning (the potential for loss would have to be small). But Benito would do it, sure.

Cuba is pristine territory begging to be dressed in riches and shown the wonders of capitalism. Uncharted land emerging from forty years of darkness. Ready for the light.

~~~~

Elisa would agree with her husband's assertion; she'd even borrow his phrase (a tad hackneyed, but fitting) to describe the island and its long trek toward freedom: *ready for the light*. But she would harshly criticize Benito's naiveté, his misguided goals, his ingenuous approach to entrepreneurship in the Cuba of the future. She'd most likely wonder how a person with such foolish ideas could manage to be so successful. The fact that Benito does all his business in the United States and not on some underdeveloped island has a lot to do with his good fortune. He made it here but would've failed there. How could her husband consider the possibility of investing in Cuba's devastated economy? *C'est fou!* Absurd!

Madame Rochart doesn't know that she's a rarity in the exile community. (This knowledge would be a source of pride for her, no doubt.) The diaspora consists of diverse types, but all types share one characteristic; and that is a tie—fragile in some cases, but detectable—to Cuba. The Island is a presence, a topic, a constant. It is a history to be rejected or exalted, a mythology to be worshiped, a culture to be embraced or ridiculed. Whatever form it takes, the Caribbean country makes its way into the here-and-now, into the private thoughts and daily routines of many of us. Hate it or love it, but acknowledge it. *Name it.*

Not Madame. She vehemently refuses to name her birthplace, the country where she spent her adolescence, where she discovered *The Flowers of Evil.* Elisa was born in a city known for its fine earthen jars, *tinajas,* but no one in her present world, except Benito, knows this "irrelevant detail." And she hasn't told anyone that her former home in Camagüey is now inhabited by "heathens." Or that Mr. Domingo met her there, one summer morning in 1958, and married her that same year. She was sixteen, and he was slightly older than Mademoiselle.

By erasing her past Elisa has erased all possibilities for a future in Cuba. Madame Rochart will never return, not even for a short visit. She cannot stand the thought of reliving her pain and her fear. All those faces pressed against the plate glass window at the Havana airport. Shouting. Insults. The words *gusano* (worm) and *traidor* (traitor) uttered by masses of angry people. Images in black, white, and blurry shades of gray, like in a photograph of the period. Her own reflection: a mournful visage (the languor makes her look attractive, mysterious). She's attired in a navy blue suit, business apparel; her long black hair in a chignon; her eyes are hiding behind owlish, horn-rimmed sunglasses. Madame is wearing no jewelry, because you couldn't take any with you. She has one suitcase, and a passport.

No one is seeing her off. Her father, gone. Her mother, also dead, from solitude. Both killed by a philistine revolution. Charles Antoine Rochart, "Don Musiú," never exploited anyone; all those people he employed had food and shelter thanks to him. Monsieur Rochart was a kind, loving man who became "an enemy of the people" overnight. A leper. Why wouldn't they leave him alone? They had taken his land and sugar mills, his hacienda. Wasn't that enough? He had been robbed of everything he'd spent a life building. But that was of no import. Don Musiú still lived in a Camagüey mansion and still clung to his name. A name that was cursed, one of the first to be written on Castro's blacklist. Disappeared.

Her *cher père*, humiliated and betrayed, walked into the Varadero waters one night, turning his back on a world he no longer knew. A ravaged, illusive El Dorado, mirage of lost chimeras, the abyss. His lifeless body washed ashore. The handsome, proud Charles Antoine, poor wretch; he couldn't survive the defilements, couldn't defeat the birds of prey, outrun the beast.

~~~~

How soon can she leave? How much longer will it take? Looking back is risky; you must look straight ahead, to the door of the airplane and the liberating sign: NORTHERN SKIES. If they notice that you're vacillating, they'll pull you aside and hold you, imprison you forever.

But her steps are leading her away from Sodom and Gomorrah; she doesn't need to glance back. She's leaving the island behind, finally. This desert of brutes. This forsaken land submerged in retrograde rituals, in provinciality, eternally marked by isolation.

She learned from the Poet that real voyagers are those who part for the sake of renewal. Light-bodied like balloons, true voyagers are always eager to embark. If only she could be one of those free spirits! If only she weren't leaving because she lost a way of life, a home, a family. She'd gladly chant the phrase real voyagers chant as they set out, and which defines their journey: *Let us sail away!*

The Northern Skies flight is ready for departure. Mrs. Domingo is one of the first to board. And as soon as she does, soft music greets her, welcomes her. It's a song about a magical ship, an eerily symbolic theme that says, *Would you like to come along on a fantastic voyage? We'll take you, if you let us, on our exciting tour. All the way to the sun. You will fly, you will fly, you will fly . . .*

~~~~

The most desirable country, for Elisa, was Oblivion. She was trying to protect Gina from the pain of *her* past, from the truth of *her* humiliation. The girl was supposed to respect Maman's wish to forget, but she hadn't yet learned about forgetting. She didn't know what to forget. Elisa Rochart de Domingo sought a vacuum, emptiness of history, because that void meant peace. Because that void meant freedom. Lucky Princess, she was free.

Who knows, maybe Madame chose to save Estela's letters so she could show them to Gina some day. She was waiting, perhaps, for her daughter to be older and safe from the pain (Elisa's pain), from the temptation to see it all for herself, to seek her own memories.

-II-

She is holding Gina's hand, gazing at her through dark-tinted sunglasses. Minutes before departure, she takes the glasses off, and the girl is surprised to note that Maman isn't wearing any makeup. Her eyes are full of tears; her voice is soft and contained when she says, "Bon voyage, my darling."

Gina can't hide her excitement as she boards the Los Angeles flight bound for Miami. Daddy is going with her on the coast-to-coast trip, and she feels reassured by his company. They talk about

Estela, Piedrecita and Florida, reminiscing about people and places she doesn't know. They say goodbye with a long, tight embrace.

"Take good care of yourself, Princess."

"I will, Dad. Piece of pie!"

"Like a wind, no?"

The second half of the trip, a rather short flight, is unsettling. (It took five hours of nerve-wracking waiting to board, and endless searching by security agents.) Gina feels completely alone for the first time in fifteen years. Anticipation, fear, curiosity, turmoil are all tangled up in her heart. Her heart precisely: a specific area of her body where she senses all emotions–and all life–converging. *Su corazón.*

As she steps off the plane, the girl can't help making a dramatic gesture, an action that brings to her mind images of horror movies: The protagonist faces the unknown, her delicate hand with manicured nails over her chest. She's walking down into the cellar of her house by herself (her husband, parents, or siblings are absent, for some reason), trying to find the source of a strange noise she heard. The sound gets louder, her eyes get wider as the character descends, as she confronts the creature lurking in the dark . . .

Hey, it isn't Gina's fault that her director has a weakness for cheap melodrama! How did she end up with such a dweeb? He's in charge and he requires that, during moments of intense emotion or conflict, the actress rest her hand over her pounding heart, gasping. Totally original!

But the truth is that no one, except Ms. Domingo, occupies the director's chair. She's on her own, solely responsible for her actions. We see her today in Havana because she willed this place into existence. Her wish was powerful enough to push her in the direction of the island. Forward in life? And there's no time for rehearsals, no second takes. Only one chance to get it right. So how can you expect great acting? She has to give it her best the first time around, and that's an incredible job. Worthy of an Oscar.

Soon after arriving at the José Martí Airport, Gina looks up at the sky, the brightest blue she's ever seen. An image she holds onto, for comfort. An image she will always cherish and will eventually mythologize.

She walks through a small and crowded waiting area, sees a glass wall and through it a dozen or more faces. They're all staring. She's a freak, a show for them. Do they know why she's here? Can they tell? She has arrived in Cuba in search of a history that has been denied her. But she can't fathom yet the meaning of this symbolic return. It'll take years before that happens. Gina Domingo has been thrown into a situation for which no one has prepared her (not even her grandmother), into a living text whose language she hasn't yet learned how to read.

Gina isn't old enough to understand the beliefs that nourish this society. She's an American teenager who has been raised–to quote her Abuela–in a bubble. What does she know about the Cuban Revolution? About this foreign world? A timeworn, withering city; men, women, children riding bikes, walking aimlessly or in a frenzy; people in military clothes; people glancing, like zombies, at mural-size billboards promoting *Socialismo o Muerte.* A message whose meaning Gina ponders, and which she ends up interpreting: Live with Socialism or die.

Honest words?

~~~~

She meets Roberto, her uncle, at the airport. He's a tall and quiet mulatto, friendly enough yet aloof, absent. They set out on a slow, tortuous trek by bus from the capital to Camagüey province. Gina wonders why he didn't get a car, rent a taxi or something. Isn't Roberto a big-shot official? Maybe he wanted to give her a "Real Cuba" experience!

The tropical landscape (a lush, sunny countryside with plenty of palm trees) and her excitement distract her from the many discomforts. The vehicle is old and too crowded; the road is bumpy, the trip too long; the weather is hot and humid and disgusting. She's hungry, thirsty . . .

Her encounter with the family is somewhat anticlimactic. At first, they all talk about Estela, known in this house as Tela (an endearment Gina takes note of; *tela* means fabric). Delia wants to hear the details of Tela's heart attack. What was she doing when it happened? Who was she with? How long was she in the hospital? Delia seems suspicious; she reacts to Gina's answers with rude interjections like *De verdad? No te creo!* Does she blame the girl for Estela's death? No, that's a crazy thought. How could anyone be accused of hurting a beloved friend?

In a calculated manner, Abuela's niece proceeds to inform her guest of the rules. Gina will be under the supervision of a family member at all times. Never, under any circumstances, is she to leave the house by herself. She'll be sleeping in Bladimir's bed, which he'll gladly give up for his cousin. The members of this family are very busy people, with work and studies and revolutionary duties. But they will take turns so that Gina can always have company. They'll also make an effort to have dinner together every night. Nothing like the feasts the American girl must be used to, but at least she'll get to eat some nice fresh fruit. Has she ever tried *mamoncillo* and *anón*?

There isn't time for diversions, only for some strolls through town and brief visits with the neighbors. The trip to Varadero is quite inconvenient; they'll go there toward the end of Gina's stay, right before her return flight. Since Varadero is close to Havana, they'll take her to the airport after spreading the ashes. How strange, observes Delia, that Tela would want her ashes spread over a place she never even saw. It's such an impractical, capricious wish.

Gina doesn't much care for her aunt. After barely an hour in her company, she can't stand her. Luckily, that unpleasant woman bears no resemblance to Abuela, so Gina doesn't even feel tempted to be nice to her. Is Delia's nasty character a telltale sign of communism? Maybe, she ponders, here's proof of what Daddy calls the regime's evil brainwashing. Estela's niece is definitely a sourpuss, a total bitch. And so bossy! Like, why did she try to take the ashes? The first thing she did was grab the box. How dare she?! Those remains needed to be guarded carefully, in a safe place, she said; they belonged to this family (meaning Delia, of course, since no one else made any effort to "guard" anything). Gina fought her relative with clear and effective Cuban words: "*De eso nada, señora!*" That box was her responsibility. It was staying by Gina's side until the last minute.

While talking to the neighbors, she notes that her aunt holds a certain power over them. The girl can't pinpoint exactly what it is; she doesn't know those people. The way they look at Delia, maybe (with humility? with fear?). "Your aunt is a great *compañera*," they say. "We love her and respect her very much." None of them speaks loudly, like Cubans are supposed to, like Abuela did, but in whispers. But mostly it's the comments they make, none of which sounds sincere, and how little they talk about Estela. "Yes, we're lucky that comrades Delia and Roberto volunteered to head our

Neighborhood Committee. How proud you must feel to be their niece!"

The second day, Gina gets a call from her father, as agreed. There is a telephone in the house, a black rotary phone that belongs in a museum, but which works and gets the job done. She gives Daddy a progress report, no comments about Delia: "Yes, Dad, I'm fine. The trip was okay. Kind of short. It's hot and humid here but I like it. The family has been nice to me; they're friendly. Yes, I saw your railroad already; we went by it on the way here from Havana. Cool! I could picture you playing there, watching the trains. Maybe someday we'll come to Florida together, huh, Dad? Yes, I'll give everyone your *saludos*. My love to Maman. Bye, Daddy. I love you!"

~~~~

She can't stand her aunt, but likes her cousins. She soon gets used to their abundant attention and their friendliness. Bladimir and Tatiana have darker complexions than Gina, yet it's easy to tell they're related to her. Although you'd notice the differences at once: the visitor's clothes, hairstyle, manners, and language give her away. Her relatives are pleasantly surprised by her fluent Spanish, but Gina's words seem to lag; she takes her time, painful seconds, to respond and react in her mind before speaking. And she observes things too fixedly, enraptured by quotidian life: the texture and hues of the exuberant flora, the dirt streets, the vintage cars (actually made back in the fifties and still in use!), the empty shop windows (frightful spectacles out of a Hollyworld set), the rusty railroad tracks, the rundown houses, the color of the sky, the pungent smell of coffee . . .

Her cousins, by contrast, seem spontaneous and assertive; they act without a trace of hesitation. Tatiana wants to talk about rock stars and listen to Gina's tapes. (The visitor brought a cassette player and some music, but not her video camera. Her father said it might be confiscated.) Tati asks about the latest American dances. Gina tells her that there are no "typical dances" per se. But she does a little show anyway, her *Azúca* sense of rhythm taking her cousin by surprise. They have fun dancing and comparing notes on boyfriends. "I have two," says Tati, "both sexy and smart, but I'm not very serious with either one. I'm too young for that kind of love!" She asks about Gina's *noviecitos*. "There's only one," says Gina, and she tries to describe him as the hunk that he is, a surfer with a sensitive heart, a dude who rides the waves like a flying fish for fun. Does she have a serious thing with him? "Not really. Not yet."

Tati is a member of the UJC (Unión de Jóvenes Comunistas), a political organization for young people. "I'm proud to be a Communist Youth," she tells her guest, "and a citizen of Cuba. I want to live here the rest of my life, have a family of my own, and teach my children the ideals of our Revolution. There couldn't be any other place as wonderful as my country. I belong here, *prima*. This island is my home."

The proud Cuban girl discusses her studies; she's taking university-level courses already. She loves medicine and health-related work. "I was going to be a heart surgeon," she explains, "but lately I've been considering pediatrics. That's the area that the Party authorities have encouraged me to specialize in. The Revolution needs good children's doctors. Cubans like to have lots of babies, so I'd always have plenty of work and I'd be useful."

When Gina asks about Estela, Tati becomes the parody of a jaded but knowledgeable doctor. "My great-aunt," she states, "had a congenital disease, an incurable illness that runs in the family; it caused my own grandmother's death. Did you know that? Yes, my Abuela died of heart failure. At least Tela had a full life and got to do some exciting things, like traveling."

"All Cubans," declares Tatiana, "have access to excellent health care. But there's only so much modern medicine can do against the whims and injustices of nature. Not even the American doctors, who have the latest medical advances and technology, could save her. Tela's collapse was inevitable. She shouldn't have traveled so far, true; the trip probably worsened her condition. But you know what, *prima*? I think that eventually, trip or no trip, her weak heart was doomed to fail her. Poor dear Telita. *La pobre.*"

~~~~

Bladimir asks about the movies Gina has seen. He begs her to describe her camera in detail. Too bad she didn't bring her quasi-holographic machine with her. "You'd never see a fancy thing like that in Cuba," says Bladi, "not even in the tourist stores, where you can buy almost anything with foreign money. Most Cuban people can't afford to shop at those *tiendas,* only tourists and high officials. My parents are high enough, and sometimes they buy nice foreign stuff. Problem is, they don't want us to have more than our neighbors, and turn into capitalist consumers. That's why I don't have a camera!"

He tells Gina that there are restaurants in Cuba where most Cubans can't eat, either, because "you need *fula*–dollars." Too many things are forbidden in his country, and people don't always know what's allowed and what isn't. But he shouldn't complain. His mother is a teacher, his father a respected agrobiologist; both are exemplary comrades. The family lives in a comfortable house (which Gina finds too crammed with old furniture, cluttered with knickknacks, poorly ventilated). "We usually have plenty of food," he says, "even meat once in a while. And shoes and clothes and some day I'm going to get a movie machine; not one as cool as yours, but at least I'll be able to start filming." He gets excited. "I'm working on a screenplay!"

They fantasize about making a big flick, the first co-production between Hollywood and Cuba. It would have to be a comedy starring La Gran Tela; the story of her visit to the North, starting with her last days in Cuba, right before the trip. Then the movie would show all that she did and saw in Pinos Verdes. Tela won't die, so the film can have a happy ending. Two sides: Bladimir's Florida and Gina's California, both from Estela's perspective. Together they have enough stories about the funny old lady to make at least one movie and two sequels, or a long-running sitcom, or a musical extravaganza: *Azúca!*

The cousins want closure. They need to celebrate their meeting with a pact of sorts, to make their newly found friendship and their kinship meaningful. On impulse, Gina takes off her gold chain, which bears a minuscule icon representing Cuba, and hands it to Bladi. "This is for you. So you remember me." He smiles, then pulls out from under his shirt a silver chain. She notes that, instead of the Island, it has the tiny likeness of a bird. "Thank you, *prima*," he says. "And this one is yours; it has a bambaé. You know about the bambaé?"

"A bluebird," she replies, proud to know the answer. "A girl who roams the skies eternally."

"Did Tela sing the song for you, too?"

"Yes. It has a nice melody, but tells a sad story."

"A story she invented, I think. She told it to me when she gave me this chain." He gently places it around Gina's neck. "Tela had it made for me as a birthday present when I turned fifteen. It must've cost her a lot! Our little secret, she said. No one else should know about it."

"And no one will, Bladi. Just you and me."

They confess their love for Estela, impulsively, and bond through their loss. Bladi misses her as though she'd been his grandma. Gina as though she'd been her mother.

They make plans.

"Some day things will be different, Gina."

"I hope so."

"We'll get to see each other as much as we want, no?"

"Yes, *primo.* We'll be a real family some day."

Bladi would love to accompany Gina on her trip home, maybe move to Los Angeles for good. "I'd miss my parents and sister, sure, but I think I'd be happier in the North." Unfortunately, leaving Cuba is out of the question. Soon he'll be called to serve in the military. He has managed to avoid the service because of his bad health, a heart ailment. But he's fine and fit now, the doctors tell him. And it's time for him to join the ranks. His family expects it of him.

No, he doesn't take much pride in being the son of exemplary comrades. And he doesn't want to be a soldier, or a UJC member. Yet there seems to be no other choice.

No. He's not willing to die for Socialism.

~~~~

Her home was closed up and sealed, as ordered by the government. But Bladi knew how to get in through the back window. They're not committing a crime, he reassures her. And if they get caught, he'll take the blame! As long as they don't make a mess or take anything, what's wrong with a brief tour? Gina deserves to see the place where her grandmother lived; she has the right to pay Tela's memory a visit.

The house looks small from the outside, but it's long and spacious inside, with three rooms (living room, bedroom, and kitchen) that lead one into the other; a thin blue veil hangs from each door frame. Walking from the living room (sparsely furnished, whitewashed walls) to the backyard, you sense a comforting order. The corridor ends in a vegetable garden, right outside the coal-stove kitchen. There are flowers beyond, in the back; and there used to be a pig in a muddy corral, and some chickens.

What would it be like to stay here, to sleep by myself in this house? Gina wonders. Would it be scary, spooky, a head trip? One thing is for sure: she wouldn't be alone. There are all those *santos* to keep her company. And, on scorching summer evenings, Estela and Nitín are seen outside, sitting on the veranda. They like to talk to the neighbors, watch people go by or listen to the radio. Estela loves the music programs; she sings along with all the great singers like Olga Guillot, Vicentico Valdés and Elena Burke. Her son cheers her on, praises her . . . *Canta, Telita!*

Abuela's altar covers an entire wall. You can't miss it as you go through the house; it's on the wall you first see as you enter the bedroom, on the right side, if you're facing the window. (Yes, there's a ceiba tree outside.) The altar has levels, like shelves. There are five or six statuettes per ledge, and several old prints.

San Lázaro and Santa Bárbara seem to be everywhere. Busy saints! He's the crippled man with the crutch, a decrepit Lazarus who protects the downtrodden. (As the sight of his misery assaults her, Gina wonders how such a frail person can help anybody.) Santa Bárbara looks quintessentially Catholic: imploring eyes and hands clasped in anguish. Gina read somewhere that this saint is an elusive *Virgen*, part Changó (a virile, powerful god) and part María. The androgyne of Christianity.

These are hungry saints. They like to be regaled with flowers and thin, fibrous strands of sugarcane. They like *mamoncillos* oozing with bittersweet sap, and slippery seeds of *anón*, their honeyed pulp. Abuela hasn't fed her *santos* lately, so you can't expect miracles from them. But when all their needs are met they can be generous. One day, long ago, these beings helped Estela bear the pain of losing her husband. And then, many years later, they granted her two wishes: seeing her son one last time, and meeting her grandchild.

~~~~

The entire family came along. Roberto managed to get a small government van and drove the whole way. They set out at midnight and traveled most of the night, avoiding the summer heat. Everyone except the driver slept. Apparently, Roberto took care of every detail. Not only did he find the Russian-made vehicle and temporary shelter (a barren cottage, as it turned out), he also borrowed a motorboat and got someone to pilot it. All these feats, Gina is led to believe, require a lot of planning and pull with the government. Obviously, Roberto is an esteemed and high-ranking official.

She wakes up to the sound of the waves, to the nascent sun that seems to be lighting up her eyes from within. The van is parked by a small cabin near the shore. She's told they will be staying there briefly, long enough to get some rest and carry out their mission. Then they'll set out for Havana shortly after nightfall. Gina has an early morning flight; she'll have to wait a few hours for it, but better to be early than late, states Delia.

~~~~

They haven't sailed very far, to elude seasickness, but nausea has already set in. They're all making an effort to control their discomfort, including Gina; although the lightness in her head is more from emotional than physical causes. Roberto, Delia, Tati and Bladi are standing, in silence, forming a circle around her, making the boat sway. Their silence lets in other sounds, bird songs, the breeze wafting over the water.

As Gina opens the box, all events become scenes from a nightmare: Estela's painful breathing, the hospital, her death. Gina had waited locked in her room, keeping vigil over Abuela's picture of Christ, over her make-believe rings, her candles, the book *Versos sencillos* opened to the page of a white rose . . . *for the cruel one who tears out my heart.* And she listened to her Daddy's stifled crying. He did what had to be done; he took care of business. Which meant having the doctor, the coroner, and the justice of the peace authorize the burning with their signatures. So that Estela could go from the ice tomb where her body was preserved, to the all-consuming fire. Ashes to ashes, as they say.

Then there was a package at the funeral home. Someone placed it in Benito's hands and he reacted as though the object were too heavy, as though it burned him. But the container didn't weigh that much, not really; it was made of cardboard, sealed all around with a cream-colored tape. A label on its lid displayed a number and the name of the deceased. Inside, there was sand, tiny stones, dusty rocks, gray earth. Abuela.

The bright aquamarine suddenly whitened by the boat's passing, the wake it leaves behind, the bird that follows them out to sea, back to shore. Estela can see it all with Gina's eyes, finally. She can swim in tranquil, crystal-blue waters. And there are no monstrous waves to nearly drown her, no tar on her feet. She walks on sand that glistens, white and fine like sugar. Yes, the island is still here; it wasn't swept away by a cyclone.

Gina will never forget this moment. She will remember herself detained in space and time over a handful of ashes, specks that stick to her pores, the old lady's body flowing through her fingers. And the stories will echo in her mind for as long as she lives. Anecdotes the family started to tell as if obeying the orders of a meticulous director. The composite portrait of Estela, a woman Gina loved but hardly knew.

The day she discovered the hidden treasure of letters, Gina undertook the task of making Abuela comprehensible. Señora Ruiz was real; she entered the adolescent's world as a living body, not a ghost or a fantasy. And yet, from Day One she seemed to have the texture of a dream.

How could Gina, a self-proclaimed American teenager, hope to know the Cuban woman's thoughts? Or hear the private words Tela spoke to herself? How could she attempt to describe the joys and the grief Estela had known? The most Gina could do was *translate* her. Which is precisely what she did one certain day, by transcribing the letters: missives laden with clues she couldn't read, wouldn't perceive; encoded secrets that some day she'd learn to decipher.

And so there were two Abuelas: one came to visit her granddaughter and died in California; her remains were sent back to Florida. The other one was the young woman's creation, a grandmother who speaks to us through Gina's perception of her. The Abuela whose words she rewrote to render her legible, accessible to an American teenager. Accessible to us.

The translated grandmother is watching her *nieta* from the depths of the Caribbean Sea. But the other Estela (a name that means "wake" in Spanish, as in the path left by a ship) says the voyage must begin. Is Gina ready? The time has come for her to really see her own face: that of a poor little rich girl trying to make sense of her visions, of a Pinos Verdes adolescent longing to feel and turn *Cuban.* Also the face of a woman who sings and talks and prays in a language her granddaughter understands. A woman who needs no translation.

Today she feels a new fear washing over her. Where did it come from? It's not the fear of getting killed (she's familiar with that one), but more like a weird anxiety, or like stage fright, a butterflies-in-your-stomach sort of thing. Yeah, hard to believe: fear of duplication. Dread of becoming a copy of herself, a character. Gina Domingo stuck in adolescence. The same chick behind a hundred different names, *duplicated*.

Nonsense! A dumb idea that some foreign lady put in her head. As if the Princess didn't have enough to worry about already! *Trapped In Your Image*, Scene One: She looks pretty as a picture, blowing out fifteen candles on her Black Forest cake. (No party, just a layer cake. Oh, and some *pastelitos*.) Two: Gina and Robby at the mall, holding hands. (Dad lets her go, yes, but only if she hangs out with nice, trustworthy girls from school.) Three: Girlfriend and Boyfriend kissing.

Does she feel sinful? Strangely enough, not a bit. (So much for her Catholic upbringing!) But she's a little apprehensive, and this other emotion is easier to describe: What would happen if Daddy found out that she's been "seeing" Robby, doing with him what you're supposed to do on dates? The whole shebang. The Real Thing. Benito Furioso wouldn't even give her a chance to explain. He'd beat the crap out of her, disfiguring her ravishing visage. And then he'd kill her perpetrator with his bare hands. Or he'd tie him to a satellite dish and electrocute him, leave his body there for days as proof that the crime was avenged, that the Domingos had restored their honor. Yes, Raging Bull Benito would save the family from disgrace. Oh my God!

The wealthy florist wouldn't understand; he doesn't know her. Daddy has never asked her how she feels about things. Does she love him? You bet. But she resents his obsession with work, his absences. He turns his back on life at home while Madame imposes her will; while she hides letters, guards secrets, and imprisons her daughter in a gilded cage: a universe of oblivion from which there seems to be no exit.

The Domingo flowers conquer hearts, but they haven't conquered Gina's. She doesn't care for Benito's award-winning masterpieces and bouquets because they mean nothing but money to him. Expensive presents for dead people: *dinerito*. She fantasizes, every so often, about being rich and famous (a movie director or a fashion designer; definitely not a writer because writing is too hard). She'll make lots of money just to have it, for the sake of being successful. Like father like daughter, maybe.

But what's the point? Yeah, she'll want to have a job, but not the kind that takes you away from your family. It'll be a low-key, low-profile gig that will allow her to travel, buy clothes, a VCR, a computer, and a video camera. She'd also like to drive a sporty car, sure, but not if she has to be a slave with hemorrhoids to get it. Not if it means turning into Mr. Sunday, alias Benitín, a stressed-out Cuban florist.

Does he love her? There have been plenty of hugs and kisses, sure. Fun trips to exclusive beach and mountain resorts, stays in nice hotels. He's bought her almost everything she's ever asked for. Recently, Daddy showed Gina his sentimental side, his nostalgia. He talked about the past: Nitín, Piedrecita. He let her see his tears and promised her: no more secrets, no more forgetting.

Still, he's someone she hasn't been able to reach, and someone who hasn't reached her. A person she fears just a little. A father she loves with all her heart.

~~~~

We see her as she wants to see herself: Gina on the quasi-holographic screen, strolling along a winding trail, bathing in a stream. Or Gina looking at the manicured grass, her mother's flowers, her father's satellite dish. She's in a haunted dungeon surrounded by ghosts. Spirits that hide behind her video camera, that dwell inside her head.

The Princess is piecing together fragments that make up her young life: computer files, video tapes depicting the world as she knows it, fading photographs that will soon be scanned and entered in cyberspace. Pictures forever available yet intangible. Images that mark, in all their technological innocence, the beginning of time.

Once she embarked on her journey, she had no choice but to imagine life without herself in it. She had no choice but to fill in the gaps piece by piece, having no one to help her. Because *mignonne* wasn't supposed to mention "that inferno." Because Maman couldn't even bear to utter the beautiful word that was the island's name. "You are too young to understand!" screams Madame like the perpetual replay of a crime. "*Ca suffit!*"

Yes, Gina agrees. Enough is enough. *Coño!* But she won't let the same old curiosity torment her. The horrors of urban reality won't get to her, either. She's stronger now, and has learned how to keep that bleak reality at bay. She doesn't need to grab her tummy, rock herself back and forth in order to forget the latest news flash: a multiple-casualty gang fight, a riot, a city burned to the ground, a building full of children that gets bombed.

Gina's hell. She, too, has one.

Her hell is full of voices, thoughts that creep in, driving her crazy. Her mind is being controlled by someone evil, a demon who knows more not because he's old but precisely because he's a demon. She hates him! She hates the tricks he plays on her, the grown-up words he makes her say, the dreams he makes her have. He's using Gina's eyes to see, her energy to live. He keeps pulling on invisible strings that are tied to her brain and her body, as though she were his puppet. And what she wants to do is yank the stupid chords and walk all over his wicked god-wannabe face. Fight him! Get him out of her mind! Out!

There is only one place where he won't go, a space he hasn't invaded. Gina can relax going there; she can cope by holding on to it: a huge window that overlooks the water, and a baby on the floor, a little girl who doesn't know about farewells, who doesn't know about death. See her? She's only a child watching the storm, touching the sand and the pink flowers. Playing.

~~~~

Deep in the YOU file, Ms. D wants to tell the truth about herself. She hopes to find the right words, explore as many meanings as each word allows, in order to define who Gina is. If she has learned anything from her diary and her *Bulletin* articles, it's the fact that describing other people is incredibly difficult. And that the easiest thing to do (also the most fun) is to write about yourself. It just so happens that Gina doesn't know how to depict her own mind, the person she's supposed to be. It just so happens that she's frozen in front of her machine.

What can she do to move ahead and complete her self-portrait? How does one move forward in life? *Adelante!*

Time for a movie. When you can't get inspired, when you've tried every trick in the bag and no life-size toons come to your rescue, it's time for a flick. But she's bored, so bored with her video collection. Should she go get a recent release? Anything would do just so she can veg out, even a category-four movie or an avant-garde classic. But that's not true! Only the first and second categories work for depression. And not even that today.

She turns on the VCR, inserts her tape of family clips: a visual tapestry she's been carefully weaving for over a year, a web of experiences that she'll never edit. Because if she expects her movie to be a tribute to her life, then life and movie both must be taken as they come, rough and choppy, unrehearsed.

Fast forward to Act Two, the best scene. In comes Señora Ruiz as though nothing has happened, looking healthy, alive. *Tela de Cuba* who greets and hugs *Gina de Amerika*, who brings a message from her saints to the girl's dreamed entities, who stays long enough on this strange planet for love to happen. Long enough on the screen for memory to thrive.

"Nuts," says Gina to her duplicated friend. "This is nuts, me talking to you as if you were really here. Like this is some weird future where people communicate only with quasi-holograms. Bizarre world, but here we are, Abuela, processing. The thing is, my problem is that . . . whenever I think about your death, I sink. Down the hole goes your *niña!* It's like I'm swimming and then, suddenly, I forget how to swim. And I can't touch bottom. There's no sand underneath me, just the depths of the sea. It's the pits, the bottomless pits! What am I supposed to do? Should I be praying for your spirit? Would that help you . . . help me? Our Father Who Art in Heaven, *Padre nuestro que estás en los cielos . . .* Amen.

"You told me once that it doesn't matter if we have a religion, because religions are made up of words, just like governments. And we don't need language to talk to the Buen Dios. But what do I use, Abuela? I don't have *santos* to mediate and speak for me. So how do I connect? How will I know if God is listening? Our Father, *Padre nuestro . . .* Bummer! I can't think straight, let alone pray through all this stupid crying."

Why is she still clinging to the male Creator? Why doesn't she try to imagine the other god, her friendly Carver of Dreams? That deity (She, *not* He) is gentle and kind, not someone you fear, not someone who punishes. That deity's voice—such a soothing voice—

comes to her, vividly, as she evokes a different source of divine power. Now she's no longer praying in the usual sense. She just feels that other form of energy: a spirit made of air and water, without a need for words or bloody sacrifices. Without a need for stale old prayers.

"Right before you closed your eyes, you kissed me. And then you whispered in my ear: *Life goes on.* How does your life go on, Telita? Step out of that screen where you're a star, my Cuban star, and gimme some answers! I know you have them. You're wise like the devil, who's supposed to know more from being old than from being the devil. But why can't angels be wise, too? Don't little devils have angel wings? If José Martí believed it, then it's a fact, no? I wonder what our poet would say about this pain I'm feeling. Is it 'sublime' like his? Like yours?

"I've tried to grow a white rose for those who tore out your heart, Abuela. *El corazón con que vivo.* But it died soon, didn't live long enough to see the sun. They deserve thorns and thistles, not petals, whoever 'they' are! They don't deserve my open hand, the simple verses you taught me, the gift of an honest friend."

~~~~

You call up several files, skim them, and create a new one named EL FIN. Which means The End for now, since reality goes on outside the text and there will be many more endings in your life. But this won't be an ordinary FIN. You want a grand finale, something romantic and memorable like . . .

A lingering caress. A kiss by the shore, beside the tenuous flames of a flickering fire, under the waning moonlight. Denuded hills, the lake, the first time . . . A threshold situation leading to love between the King and Queen of Homecoming.

But where does Abuela fit in? She doesn't. Because Tela de Cuba is your best pitch, a story you'll never sell, the movie that will never get filmed. Private catharsis when granddaughter finds grandmother but loses grandmother. Farewell tears and a promise: We'll always be together. *Para siempre!*

You close your eyes and place your hands on the keyboard. Then a siren is heard, and Estela's last view of the bay comes into focus: a spectacular sunset.

"Abuela! Where are you?"

"I am here, Gina."

"Where?"

"With my husband."

"Does he look the way you remembered him?"

"Yes, but better; he is stronger, happier."

"And what about you? What do you look like now?"

"I guess . . . just the way you see me."

"I had a nightmare, Abuela, a terrible dream about losing you."

"Don't worry, *mi niña.* You will never lose me."

"I know. A bad bug never dies."

"Yes. *Bicho malo nunca muere!* And besides, Ginita, if you're capable of dreaming about death, you're also capable of dreaming about life."

You open your eyes and notice that your fingers are typing. They write and you read. They write and you see Abuela standing next to Gina, watching her as she spreads Tela's remains over the place where an altar once stood, where vegetables and daisies once grew, where animals fed. In Florida.

~~~~

She packed one suitcase and filled her carry-on with souvenirs. She's determined to see the island now, before this summer ends. Before the big changes take place and the past, Estela's past, is gone forever.

Ms. D has accepted that life must go on (like the show) beyond these walls, outside the precious paradise that Daddy and Maman created for her. This bubble high up on a hill where the Princess won't live happily ever after. A tall tower of rose-colored cardboard, Gina's magical room, crushed by the rain and left in pieces.

Soon she'll get to see the ceiba and the guayacán trees, the sun rising over the silent blue hills. Soon she'll hear the song of the bambaé. Gina will dive into a stream in search of shiny stones and rescue them from their eternal silence. But there won't be anyone forcing her to do this, and so she will emerge from her quest unscathed. Alive.

No, she's not sitting in this empty bedroom, rocking herself because things have gotten rough and hard to understand. She doesn't see the red light flashing outside, on the street, or hear the voices of men who've come to take Estela. Men who will never bring her back.

God, it's so cold in her hideout! It has been freezing in here since the day Abuela left. Poor grandma. How sad she must've felt, waiting for a few words, her granddaughter's *palabras* that never arrived. Did she know, in some mysterious way, that sooner or later Gina would find the bundle of tiny frog heads and fat ballerinas? *Like a fairy tale in which you and I are the same age, two girls belonging in different eras . . .*

She has learned that Hell is for real, and it's losing a person you love. But she won't give in, won't feel pain because of someone she lost and remembers. Ms. D would rather be flying to Cuba, guarding this box full of letters and ashes. Inside, Tela slumbers away on a bed of flowers. At the break of dawn she will awaken. The two friends will glance at the horizon, breathe in the warm air, deeply. And through the lens of their dreams, Gina will finally see a brand new memory.